WESTERN

Rugged men looking for love...

Safe Haven Ranch
Louise M. Gouge

A Cowgirl's Homecoming
Julia Ruth

T0363174

MILLS & BOON

SAFE HAVEN RANCH
© 2024 by Louise M. Gouge
Philippine Copyright 2024
Australian Copyright 2024
New Zealand Copyright 2024

First Published 2024
First Australian Paperback Edition 2024
ISBN 978 1 038 90775 2

A COWGIRL'S HOMECOMING
© 2024 by Julia Bennet
Philippine Copyright 2024
Australian Copyright 2024
New Zealand Copyright 2024

First Published 2024
First Australian Paperback Edition 2024
ISBN 978 1 038 90775 2

MIX
Paper | Supporting
responsible forestry
FSC® C001695

Published by
Harlequin Mills & Boon
An imprint of Harlequin Enterprises (Australia) Pty Limited
(ABN 47 001 180 918), a subsidiary of HarperCollins
Publishers Australia Pty Limited
(ABN 36 009 913 517)
Level 19, 201 Elizabeth Street
SYDNEY NSW 2000 AUSTRALIA

Cover art used by arrangement with Harlequin Books S.A.. All rights reserved.

Printed and bound in Australia by McPherson's Printing Group

Safe Haven Ranch

Louise M. Gouge

MILLS & BOON

Award-winning author **Louise M. Gouge** writes historical and contemporary fiction romances. She received the prestigious Inspirational Readers' Choice Award in 2005 and was a finalist in 2011, 2015, 2016 and 2017; was a finalist in the 2012 Laurel Wreath contest; and was a 2023 Selah Award finalist. Louise earned a BA in creative writing from the University of Central Florida and a master's of liberal studies degree from Rollins College. She taught English and humanities at Valencia College for sixteen and a half years and has written twenty-eight novels, eighteen of which were published under Harlequin's Love Inspired imprint. Contact Louise at louisemgougeauthor.blogspot.com, Facebook.com/LouiseMGougeAuthor and Twitter @louisemgouge.

Visit the Author Profile page
at millsandboon.com.au for more titles.

Pure religion and undefiled before God
and the Father is this, To visit the fatherless
and widows in their affliction, and to keep himself
unspotted from the world.
—*James* 1:27

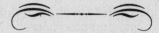

DEDICATION

My special thanks go to my wonderful agent,
Tamela Hancock Murray, and to my fabulous editor,
Shana Asaro, and her team, Rachel Burkot and
John Oberholtzer. You really made my book shine!
Thank you for all you do.

Also, thanks to my fellow author,
Debbie Lynne Costello, who provided research
into purebred dogs.

Finally, as with all of my stories, this book is
dedicated to my beloved husband, David,
my one and only love, who encouraged me
to write the stories of my heart and continued to
encourage me throughout my writing career.
David, I will always love you and miss you.

CHAPTER ONE

Outside Riverton, New Mexico
Late May

"You what?"

Olivia Ortiz stared at her elderly neighbor, barely sparing a glance at his too-handsome companion. "But, Albert, you promised to sell your land to me." She was standing in her own driveway, hands fisted at her waist in a defensive posture.

"I know, I know." Albert Winslow shrugged his bony shoulders and gave her an apologetic smile. "But wait 'til you hear what he has planned, and I think you'll like it. Will, how about you tell Miss Olivia what you have planned." As usual, the almost ninety-year-old gentleman repeated himself. He looked up at his much taller companion. "I think she'll like it."

"Um…" The younger man, who fit the very

definition of a tall, dark and handsome cowboy—with curly black hair thrown in for good measure—grinned, and his blue eyes sparkled in the sunlight, causing a silly hiccup in Olivia's chest. "Don't you think you should introduce us first?"

"Oh." Albert blinked and looked from him to Olivia and back again. "Sure thing. Miss Olivia, this is Will Mattson. Known this boy all his life. He's the grandson of my old friend Andy Mattson, Lord rest his soul. Will, this is Olivia Ortiz. She and her father own this property." He waved a hand around to include the fifteen acres that comprised her land, just over a quarter the size of his own fifty acres. Centered by matching pink adobe houses, the two properties were separated by a four-foot fieldstone fence, with a single flimsy, never-locked, much-used gate between them.

Will reached out a hand. "Pleased to meet you, ma'am." He gave her a wide smile, revealing perfect white teeth set off by his perfectly tanned complexion, which caused another hiccup near her heart.

What was wrong with her? She wasn't about to let herself fall for this man...or *any* man. No one could ever replace Sancho. Still, she briefly shook his hand as his name registered in her brain.

"Mattson? Are you...?" Annoyance replaced the shock that Albert's devastating news had delivered.

"Yes, ma'am." There went that cowboy "ma'am" thing again, punctuated by a boyish shuffling of his western boots on the dusty ground. "Can't escape it around here."

"Well, if you're a Mattson, why do you need this small property to add to the...what is it? Eight or ten thousand acres your family owns?" She didn't mean to sound so confrontational, but Albert had just crashed her desperately held dreams, so her social filters were crashing, too. "You plan to buy the whole county?"

"Unka Weeoo?" An adorable little brown-haired boy poked his head from behind the man's long legs. "Hokay?" His voice, barely above a whisper, wobbled, and his big blue eyes were round with fear.

How had Olivia failed to see the little guy? He must have been frightened by her outburst.

Will's expression became gentle, paternal. He scooped up the boy, who looked to be around four, and chucked him under the chin. "Sure thing, buddy. Everything's okay." He looked at Olivia. "This is Jemmy, my nephew."

"Hi, Jemmy." She swallowed a sudden lump in her throat. Her own son would be getting close to three, if only… She shook off the memory. "I have a daughter just about your age." Would six-year-old Emily be offended by being compared to a younger child? Olivia stopped short of asking the boy if he would like to meet Emily. That would seem like an invitation to these men to come inside.

Jemmy buried his face in Will's shoulder, then flung his arms around his uncle's neck.

"He's a little shy." Will gently massaged the boy's back.

What was the story there? Was Will babysitting? Olivia dismissed the questions. Her own question hadn't been answered. Why would a member of the wealthy Mattson family need Albert's property, set as it was in this little canyon beside the Rio Grande? It certainly wasn't enough land to run a herd of cattle, like on their other holdings. And she needed this land. It was her lifeline to restoring her very purpose in life, her only viable means of supporting herself and her daughter and giving them a future beyond what Sancho's life insurance provided.

While Dad's pensions kept them afloat for now, he often reminded her that he wouldn't always be there for her.

"Why don't you invite us in for coffee," Albert said, "so I can say hello to your father." He took a step toward the back door to Olivia's house.

"I, uh…" She brushed a strand of sweat-dampened hair from her forehead, then realized she'd probably streaked it with dirt. "I'm in the middle of planting these marigolds." She pointed to the line of prepared soil along the driveway. "The plants shouldn't lie out in the sun for long before going into the ground."

"Oh, come on, now." Albert took another step toward the house. "We won't be long, and I'd like to say hello to Lawrence."

She huffed out a harsh breath. When Albert got ahold of an idea, he didn't let go. Besides, this problem needed to be settled. *Now.* Maybe Dad could persuade Albert not to change his mind about the sale.

"Okay." *Not* okay. "Let's go in."

She led them through the long back room—a combination of library, reading room, office and model-train room—and into the living room.

"Have a seat." She waved a hand toward the

couch and chairs set in a semicircle around the white adobe fireplace in the corner. "Dad, we have company," she called out. To her unwanted guests, she added, "I'll make coffee."

She went to the kitchen and washed the dirt from her hands, then tossed out the remnants of this morning's brew and washed the pot.

Emily skipped into the kitchen. "Did Mr. Albert come over?" She grabbed a paper napkin from the table and reached up to brush Olivia's forehead, sending a small shower of dirt to the floor. Sometimes it seemed Emily mothered Olivia as much as Olivia mothered her.

"Thank you, sweet pea. Yes, Mr. Albert and his friends." *His* friends. Not hers. "One of them is a little boy. Why don't you go see if he wants to play?" As she put a new filter into the coffee maker and measured the grounds, she nodded to the covered plate on the table. "And take them some of those sweet rolls we made this morning."

Emily danced over to the sink and washed her hands, not completely drying them, then gathered small plates and napkins and put them on a tray with the sweet rolls. If Olivia hadn't been so upset, she would burst with pride. Her daughter was already the perfect little hostess, which should go a long way in impressing their next client, who would soon be renting their studio apartment. People who rented the studio wanted peace and quiet, and might consider the presence of a child a big turnoff, but Emily could charm a grizzly bear.

"What's up, kiddo?" Dad limped into the kitchen, leaning on his ever-present quad-cane and looking older than his sixty-two years.

"It's—it's…" Olivia's eyes burned with sudden tears. She blinked them back. "Albert wants to sell his land to the Mattson family instead of us."

"What?" His tone was more curious than outraged, unlike what she'd felt upon hearing the news.

"He wants to explain it to me. To us."

She had to remember that this land actually belonged to Dad, although he always referred to it as *ours* and let her do what she wanted to the property. Seven years ago, Mom had inherited it from her parents, and she and Dad had moved here from Seattle. By then, Olivia and Sancho had been married, so she didn't live here until—she breathed out a sigh—Sancho had died over three years ago, and she'd come here so her parents could help her raise Emily.

Then, last year, Mom died. Olivia swiped the back of her hand over the bothersome tears that ran down her cheeks at the memory. After such losses, would her grief ever subside?

"Huh." Dad started toward the living room. "I'll be interested in what he has to say."

In minutes, the coffeepot spat out its final drips. Olivia poured the fresh brew into an insulated carafe and set it on a tray, along with mugs, creamer and sugar.

In the living room, the men were already engaged in a lively conversation as they munched on the sweet rolls.

"Real tasty, as always." Albert took another bite.

"Yes, ma'am. Delicious." Will turned to Dad. "If you don't mind, Lawrence, I'd like to look at your model trains sometime." He accepted the steaming mug from Olivia. "Thanks, ma'am." He gave her a nod. "I think Jemmy will be real interested, too." With both hands occupied, he nudged the little boy with his elbow and smiled at him. "Won't you, buddy?"

Jemmy returned a round-eyed look, but didn't smile. They sure did look like a loving father and his son.

Olivia quickly quashed the thought. She

wouldn't do herself any favors by admiring anything about this man.

"Sure thing." Dad beamed. "I'm always up
for showing off my favorite hobby."

Olivia delivered the other mugs, then said in
a stage whisper to Emily, "You can get juice
boxes for you and Jemmy."

"Want to go with me?" Emily reached out a
hand to the little boy.

As before, he buried himself in his uncle's
protective embrace.

"It's okay, Jemmy." Again, Will's eyes exuded paternal kindness. "It's just in the other
room. You can see me through the doorway.
Wouldn't you like a juice box?"

Eyeing Emily with suspicion, Jemmy none-
theless scooted off the couch and, after a moment of hesitation, took her hand. She giggled
and led him from the room in her older-sis-
ter way, as she always did with younger kids.
Jemmy looked back at Will but didn't tug
against her grip.

As he watched them, Will released a quiet
sigh. "Thanks."

Olivia tried to subdue the empathy welling
up inside her. Was he raising this child?

"Now, let's get down to business," Albert

said, interrupting her thoughts. "Will, how about you tell Olivia and Lawrence about your plans. I think they're going to like them."

Olivia couldn't quite school her face into a polite expression, but Dad's interest was clear from his raised eyebrows, to his half smile, to his posture as he leaned toward their guest. But then, Dad was always friendly and interested in other people, even if they might not return the attitude.

Will shifted in his seat at the end of the couch. "Well, it's something I've been praying about for some time."

Oh, great. That makes it sound like God's already on your side.

"Albert's land, being tucked away in this little valley, would be the perfect location for my plans." He gave Olivia that white-toothed smile that probably charmed all the girls in Riverton and parts beyond. "I'd like to establish a boys' ranch for at-risk younger boys, away from the negative influences of their present lives. You know, kids who maybe come from abusive homes or have parents or older siblings who've chosen the wrong path. These boys need some foundation to their lives so they won't follow that same pattern. My aunt fosters four boys right now and wants to take on more, but her house and yard in town aren't big enough. I want to give her a home that is. And, of course, I'll live there, too."

Olivia felt as if a boulder had slammed against her chest, while her heart sank deeper with each word. Sancho had worked with troubled teens, and he'd been murdered for it. And this man wanted to buy the land that should be hers and bring a bunch of troublemakers to live on the next property, all too close to Emily. Added to that, a noisy herd of wild boys would destroy the peace and quiet she promised to her prospective clients. Who would come here for a quiet retreat from the world, only to be met with screaming, shouting kids?

"Isn't that a fine plan, Olivia?" Albert gave her a big smile.

Even Dad looked at her expectantly. Didn't he see the obvious problem? Time to address the foundational issue.

"I'm sure Mr. Mattson is sincere in his desire to help troubled children, but this isn't the place for it." She worked hard to keep the resentment from her voice. From Dad's frown, she could see she wasn't succeeding. "Albert, you are an old-school gentleman, and we both subscribe to old-fashioned values. When you agreed to sell your land to me, I took that as a firm commitment from you—a handshake, if you will, which to us is as unbreakable as a written contract."

Silence filled the living room, broken only by the sounds from the kitchen, where Emily chattered to Jemmy about the various flavors of juice in the refrigerator. What a wonderful big sister she would have made to little Daniel. But Sancho's death had traumatized Olivia, and she'd miscarried at six months.

Her husband, her son, her mother. How many more losses would the Lord send into her life? Must she also give up the dream that had begun to restore her mental and emotional health, and most of all, her faith? Add to that her financial needs, and she was determined to hold Albert to his word.

No, this deal must not go through. She had to do everything in her power to persuade Albert to keep his promise. But what power did she actually have?

As if showing her the way, her spine stiffened, and she sat up straighter.

"Albert, you know a gang of delinquent kids murdered my husband. I can't let the same kind of criminals take my livelihood, too, not to mention threaten Emily's safety."

A STINGING BUZZ streaked up Will's neck and raised the hair on his scalp. Wow. Just wow. Albert had told him Olivia Ortiz was a widow, but he hadn't said her husband had been murdered. And by gang members. No wonder she didn't like his plan. More like hated it, actually. What should he say now? Offer his condolences for her loss? Point out that his boys wouldn't be violent? And what was that about her livelihood?

Lord, I know You've brought me to this place. What should I say now?

"Man, I'm so sorry to hear about your husband." The words came out without further thought. "I can't imagine…"

He shut up before he stuck his foot in his mouth. When his sister died violently last year, he'd been devastated. Nothing anybody said had consoled him, and a few "friends" blamed her for sticking with that creep… *Sorry, Lord—* that abusive, narcissistic alcoholic she'd married despite the family's pleas. In spite of their own sad history, with Mom leaving when they were kids, Megan always thought she could fix things and people. Clearly, she hadn't succeeded with Ed. After he killed her, he barricaded himself in a motel room and was shot by a SWAT marksman who didn't realize Jemmy was also in the room. It had been six months since that shootout, and Jemmy still had nightmares.

"It's a rough world out there." Albert reached over and patted Olivia's hand. "But we can still do some good in our little corner, can't we? That's why I liked Will's idea so much."

Her wounded look moved Will, and she seemed on the verge of tears. The urge to comfort her came on strong, but he forced it back. Being too empathetic with some women could give the wrong impression, maybe even get him in trouble…again. Best to ignore her emotions and discuss only the facts of this matter. Of course, she'd looked pretty cute with that swipe of dirt on her forehead. She must have looked in a mirror and washed it off while she was in the kitchen.

Nope. Not going to think about her that way. That just leads to trouble.

"Ma'am, I'd be interested in hearing more about your plans. Albert tells me you've been hosting authors and artists in your studio apartment. How will you use his house?"

She cleared her throat and sniffed back the tears, settling a blank expression on her pretty face. *Stop that, you doofus. You can't think of her as pretty. It can only lead to trouble*—heart *trouble.*

"I plan to expand my business and make room for more artists who need a quiet place to express their art. A safe refuge from fans whose interruptions can destroy concentration, not to mention inspiration." Her expression softened as she warmed to her topic. "As Albert may have told you, these two properties were settled in the early 1900s by artistic women who were searching for that very thing. They supported each other and explored opportunities not available in the outside world during that era. I plan to carry on that tradition for this land." She laughed softly, a pleasing, musical sound. "Of course, things have improved for women since then, but artists still need peace and quiet when they're trying to write that next big novel or paint that glorious landscape. We're highly selective in our clientele, all of whom hear of us by word of mouth from their friends."

She sounded like a brochure for the place, but from what she'd said, she clearly didn't advertise.

"Tell them who's coming today, Olivia."

Lawrence's dark eyes flared with excitement. "None other than *New York Times* bestseller Nona—"

"Dad!" Olivia glared at him. "We never share who'll be staying here. Privacy. Obnoxious fans. Remember?"

"Oops." He laughed, clearly not embarrassed by her scolding. He turned to Will. "You get the idea, right?"

"Yes, sir." Indeed he did. More than that, he understood the need for privacy. All his life, people—especially women—had expectations of him because his name was Mattson. Despite Will being only ten years old when Mom left, Dad had expected him to be stoic, claiming a Mattson didn't give in to emotions. Then, after Will's last girlfriend had made clear she would expect a pampered, jet-set life as Mrs. Will Mattson, he'd decided to stop dating. Instead, he spent his energy and resources helping boys who had no agenda beyond wanting and needing love, a full stomach and a clean bed. Some of them needed a home where disreputable relatives couldn't find them and use them for selfish or even evil purposes. Boys like Jemmy. So far, Ed's relatives hadn't come up with any legal reason for claiming custody, but they'd made plenty of noise and threats.

So, understanding aside, he had to fight for the right to buy Albert's property. While he valued the man's promise to Olivia, he knew this area well, and not a single plot of land provided what this remote fifty-acre riverside valley did.

"Miss Olivia?" He gave her a gentle smile just short of pouring on the infamous Mattson charm. "I really need this land. A bunch of disadvantaged boys are counting on it. Won't you please release Albert from his promise to sell it to you?"

Confusion crossed her face. Then she lifted her chin and glared at him. "You mean you aren't going to call in your lawyers and claim a verbal contract doesn't count legally?"

He chuckled. "No, ma'am. I'm a lawyer myself—family law—but I don't believe in using the law to bully people." He glanced at Albert, who was closely watching the interaction. "I've found the best way to handle situations like this is through prayer and healthy arbitration, so everybody comes out of it believing the right thing's been done."

She blinked those dark brown eyes, and her jaw dropped. "Prayer?" She looked at her dad, then back at Will. "Do you say that so you can claim God is on your side?"

Will rocked back in his seat. "Uh, no, not at all. Just the opposite. I pray to learn God's will, even if it's not what I've asked for."

"Oh, I see. So—"

Olivia's frosty response was cut off by the sound of giggles in the kitchen, and not just from little Emily. It was a beautiful duet of lighthearted noise from two kids clearly having innocent fun. Will had never heard Jemmy giggle, and a lump formed in his throat. How had Emily, whom Jemmy had just met, broken through his nephew's paralyzing fears and caused such carefree laughter when his young cousins hadn't been able to?

"Unka Weeoo!" Jemmy dashed into the living room, his face bright with an excitement Will had never seen. He stopped and stared at the adults, apparently forgetting Will wasn't the only one in the room. His face clouded, and his thumb went into his mouth.

Will stood slowly. He'd learned not to make sudden moves around Jemmy. Instead, he walked to the boy and kneeled in front of him. "What is it, buddy? What did you see?"

Jemmy buried his face in Will's shoulder.

Emily skipped over to them. "Jemmy, Jemmy, come back. Mommy, it's the hummingbirds. They came back to the feeder." She took Jemmy's hand and tugged, but gently. "C'mon, Jemmy," she coaxed. "You'll miss it. And we need to make more sugar water for them."

Jemmy peeled himself slowly from Will's chest and let her lead him away, this time without a backward glance.

In that moment, Will knew one thing. He must make sure Jemmy had every opportunity to play with this precious little girl, no matter what it took.

CHAPTER TWO

"WHAT TIME DOES Nona's plane land? You don't want to be late." Their company had left, and Dad was helping Olivia clear the coffee table and carry the mugs and plates to the kitchen.

"Two o'clock." Olivia opened the dishwasher and began to load it. "I have plenty of time. Just need to finish planting the marigolds or we're going to lose them. If I'd known Albert and his friend were going to interrupt me, I wouldn't have taken them out of their starter pots."

"I can finish the planting." Contrary to his words, Dad plunked himself down at the kitchen table.

Olivia glanced his way, worry niggling into her thoughts. Over a year ago, he'd been crushed by Mom's death, and despite his love for her and Emily, sometimes he seemed to lose his interest in life. Maybe letting him plant the flowers would be good.

"Okay. Thanks. Just be sure to—" She stopped. It was okay if he planted them in a crooked row. Sancho always teased her about her insistence on perfection, whether decorating a cake or planting annuals along the front walkway of their Seattle home. "I think they'll need a little water."

"Sure thing." He shuffled the salt and pepper shakers like chess pieces, his usual habit when he had something on his mind.

"You want to talk?" She closed the dishwasher and went to the fridge to gather lunch fixings.

"That Will Mattson seems like a decent fellow." Dad didn't look her way. "Can't help but admire him for wanting to help kids and get them out of bad situations."

Her heart and mind still reeling from Albert's request, Olivia pulled out a chair across the table from him and sat. "So, does that mean you want Albert to sell *him* the land?"

"No." Dad shook his head and gave her a scolding look. "You don't have to take off in that direction." Then he chuckled. "Was just thinking he's about your age. Single. Christian. And—"

"And that's enough of that." She stood and

returned to the lunch prep, putting together sandwiches. Rather, slapping them together was more like it. When had Dad decided she was interested in forming a romantic relationship? Did she hassle him to respond to the widows at church who tried to get his attention? No way. She and Emily had a good life here with him. Why would they need to add anyone to their family? Especially not a rich, land-grabbing cowboy who was trying to destroy her dreams.

"So this rich guy plans to outbid you on the land deal?" Nona Albright sat in the passenger seat of Olivia's Explorer as they drove north from Santa Fe Regional Airport.

The moment Olivia had met the fifty-something author at baggage claim, they'd bonded over books, horses, purses and shoes. Nona broke the stereotype of the introverted writer. She'd managed to extract the story of Olivia's land dilemma within their first half hour.

"Well, not exactly." After a brief glance at her guest, Olivia kept her eyes on the winding four-lane highway toward home. "He just suggested we pray about it." Why was she defending the man who was out to steal her dream?

"Huh." Nona checked her appearance in the

sun-visor mirror. "If he's for real, that speaks highly of him. But some people use prayer as a tool to manipulate others."

"Like Arnett in your last novel."

Nona laughed. "Yes. I created that character from a real-life charmer I once knew."

"I can't wait to read your next book. When will it be released?"

Nona laughed again, a pleasant alto chuckle. "If I don't get it written, it won't release at all. My publisher had to push up my deadline. Hence my need for this getaway. My house is chaos central. So, when my older daughter offered to stay home with my teenage one, three dogs and more cats than I can count, I couldn't pass it up." She reached over and patted Olivia's hand. "I'm so glad you had an opening. Ina told me what a wonderful hostess you are and how beautiful and quiet your little ranch is."

Quiet for now. If Will Mattson got his way, it would turn into the Wild West. But she shouldn't drag Nona into her conflict. "I owe Ina big-time for giving me this idea. It's lots of fun to meet such talented people."

"And I look forward to meeting your dad and daughter. Lawrence and Emily, right?"

"Right." How thoughtful of her to remember their names, which Olivia might have mentioned a single time during their phone conversations as they arranged Nona's stay.

She turned off the highway and onto the first of several unmarked dirt roads leading to her ranch. A person had to know where they were going out here or they would end up lost—another reason she had to buy Albert's land. Only the small local communities knew about their two properties tucked away from civilization, and most of them valued their privacy as much as Olivia valued hers.

The final turn led to the road past Albert's property and then close to the fifteen-foot-high berm that protected the little valley from the Rio Grande's springtime flooding. A canopy of aspen and cottonwood trees arched over the rutted road, their abundant green leaves waving a welcome in the breeze. One final turn, and they were facing the gate to her property. Beyond the barbed wire and slatted fence sat her pink adobe house. She glanced at Nona, whose eyes were bright with appreciation.

"It's beautiful. Just what I imagined." Nona released her seat belt. "I'll get the gate." She was out of the car before Olivia could object. How nice that this client wouldn't require pampering.

They drove around the house to the door of the attached studio apartment, and Olivia helped Nona carry her suitcases and laptop inside. On her trip back to the car, she saw her guest staring across the fieldstone fence and followed her gaze.

To her surprise and annoyance, Will—with shirtsleeves rolled up to show off his tanned, muscular arms—was chopping wood beside Albert's long-neglected woodpile. Chopping wood in May, a month in which most people didn't even use their fireplaces. What was that all about?

"Oh, my." Nona glanced at Olivia. "Tell me that's not your rich land grabber." She laughed. "Or tell me he is, and introduce us."

"Um, yes, but—"

"Just kidding." Nona nudged Olivia's shoulder. "He's more than a little too young for me."

Olivia's answering smile felt more like a grimace. Was there a hint of matchmaking in Nona's sideways glance? Did the suspense writer have a hint of romance writer in her? *Please, no.*

Inside the apartment, Nona surveyed the large room's furnishings. "Oh, this is just great. Cute little kitchenette. Treadmill. Desk. And I adore your Southwestern decor." She brushed a hand over the orange, red, yellow and brown woolen throw draped over the back of the love seat. "I may have to change the setting for my book from eastern city to southwest ranch." Her laughter showed she was joking.

After a little more chitchat, Olivia excused herself. "I have to make the cornbread for supper. Is chili still okay?" They'd discussed food preferences over the phone, and Olivia had stocked up on Nona's favorites.

"Sounds good."

While she and Emily whipped up the cornbread, Olivia couldn't put aside thoughts of her dilemma. In truth, Will's suggestion that they should pray about the land situation had brought on some guilt.

Her prayer life had suffered after Sancho's cruel death, but after an inspiring sermon by her parents' pastor, who'd suffered his own losses, she'd started taking baby steps to restore her faith. Dad had reminded her that Emily needed to hear about Jesus, to *see* Jesus in her and in him before other voices caught her attention. Homeschooling her daughter with faith-based kindergarten materials helped. And now, she'd already registered for a homeschooling convention in July so she could purchase the best first-grade curriculum. She hoped those lessons would give Emily the spiritual instruction she needed.

As far as Emily seeing Jesus in her, well, she tried…until situations came up like the one today. How was she supposed to react kindly to someone who was trying to steal her dream of self-sufficiency? Until now, the Lord seemed to have paved the way for her to achieve that dream. Why would He throw this roadblock into her plans? More than a roadblock, it was a demolition. Didn't He care that she needed Albert's land so she could provide for Emily? Renting the studio to one client at a time didn't bring in enough income, and if Dad continued to decline, his pensions might need to go toward senior living arrangements sooner rather than later. She couldn't bear that thought, but she'd learned the hard way life often sent unexpected disappointments and tragedies.

She didn't realize her eyes had filled with tears until Emily hugged her waist.

"I love you, Mommy." The concern in her brown eyes melted Olivia's heart. Her daughter had such gentle, empathetic ways.

Olivia forced a light laugh to ease Emily's mind. "I love you, too. Let's get this cornbread in the oven." She scraped the last of the golden mixture into the cast-iron skillet, shoved it into the oven and set the timer.

"Mommy, I like Jemmy." Olivia started setting the table without being asked. "Is he coming to supper?"

"No, sweet pea. Our guest is Miss Nona."

"Speaking of whom…" Dad entered the kitchen, freshly cleaned up from planting the marigolds in a better line than Olivia had expected. "I'll be happy to tell her it's ready."

"Um…okay." Olivia knew he enjoyed reading Nona's thriller novels. "Don't go all fanboy on her."

"Humph." He feigned an indignant expression. "I may ask for an autograph in my books, but I'll keep it cool."

"Grampy, I like Jemmy," Emily said, grabbing his hand and repeating what she'd said to Olivia. Repetition meant this was important to her, so Olivia paid attention.

"You do?" Dad tweaked Emily's nose, which brought on the usual giggles.

"Yes, sir. Can I play with him again?"

Dad glanced at Olivia. "That's up to your mom, honey."

Olivia's heart sank. She was so careful about

which children she allowed into her daughter's life. Jemmy seemed needy but harmless, though letting Emily play with him meant contact with Will. Yet how could she refuse?

She couldn't. Which meant this situation was just getting worse and worse.

WILL CHECKED ON JEMMY, who was napping on Albert's couch, then returned to the kitchen to find something for supper. The nearly bare cupboard and fridge revealed Albert had been eating mostly eggs gathered from his dozen or so hens. Not the worst diet, but not the best, either. No wonder Albert's grandson wanted him to sell the land and move to Amarillo to live with his family.

The run-down look of the house was more cosmetic than structural, although it could use a new roof over the south bedrooms. The out-buildings could use some reinforcement and...

And Will wouldn't be making any of those improvements if Mrs. Ortiz had her way. For a moment in her living room, the lawyer in him had been tempted to ask who actually owned the place, who actually had the funds to buy Albert's property. Lawrence seemed to like Will's plans for a boys' ranch, but he'd let his daughter lead the conversation. After pondering his approach, Will knew he couldn't, in good conscience, come between father and daughter any more than he could ask Albert to break his word to his pretty next-door neighbor.

When he and Albert had left her house, he had to admit his usual optimism had taken a hit. So, he and Albert had brainstormed ideas to persuade her to change her mind. Nothing aboveboard and workable came up. In the meantime, Will could see Albert needed someone to move in and take care of him. Until such a person could be found, Will knew he had to stay. He'd already put his law practice into his cousin Sam's capable hands while he made his plans for the ranch, so he was free to do whatever it took to help Albert.

So, today he'd done some serious cleanup, both inside and out. He'd gotten a little out of shape, so it felt good to chop the wood and straighten the woodpile. Jemmy had taken seriously his job of stacking the cut logs. Never mind that Will had to restack them and remove a couple of splinters from the little guy's hand. Then they'd cleaned up the kitchen. No telling how long it had been since Albert had washed dishes.

And now, Will needed to figure out some supper for the old man, plus himself and Jemmy. The only item in the freezer was an unidentifiable, foil-wrapped block. Even if it was something edible, it was too late to thaw it. He'd have to go to town, but that might take too long. Jemmy would be hungry soon.

Only one solution to this problem. Even if it meant breaking one of his own rules about leaving the boy, especially when he was sleeping.

"Albert, would you watch Jemmy while I run an errand? If he wakes up, you can turn on cartoons." He nodded toward the television.

"Sure thing." Albert settled into a chair in the living room and picked up a book from the side table. "Take your time. We'll be fine. If something comes up, I have my cell phone right here." He held up the device.

"I won't be long."

The trip across the broad yards between the two houses took less than a minute. Will walked through the gate and around to the front door and knocked. When Mrs. Ortiz opened the door, his heart did an odd little flip. She sure was pretty in her jeans and peach T-shirt, even with suspicion filling her brown eyes.

"Yes?" She sounded guarded, of course.

He'd like to reassure her that he meant her no harm, but he had to stick to his mission.

"Mrs. Ortiz—"

"Olivia." She spoke her name as an order, which made him smile.

"Yes, ma'am. Olivia. I come to you with figurative hat in hand. Albert doesn't have much in the way of food in his house, and it's getting past suppertime. Do you…?"

"Oh, no." Alarm filled her face. "Yes, of course. I usually take something over for him every day, but I've been so busy." She huffed out a breath. "No excuses. Yes, of course." She glanced toward the kitchen. "We have plenty. Why don't you bring him over, and I'll give him dinner. And you, as well." She grimaced as though those last words tasted bad.

He chuckled. "You don't have to feed me, but I would appreciate a peanut-butter sandwich for Jemmy."

"Don't be silly. If you're helping Albert, I can feed you. Chili, cornbread, salad, sweet tea. Carrot cake for dessert. Dinner's in fifteen minutes." She shut the door before he could respond.

Carrot cake? Sounded good. He couldn't wait to try it. He chuckled all the way back to Albert's. Just as he'd thought, she had a kind heart. He'd seen it in the way she'd looked at Jemmy that morning. To know she often fed Albert only added to her appeal.

Appeal? What was he thinking? He couldn't let a pretty woman get under his skin and deter him from his plans. Especially not one who seemed insistent on standing in his way of making a home for his boys. He shouldn't worry, though. Miss Olivia had nothing in common with the women who usually tried to get his attention. In fact, if he wasn't so set on staying single, her brusque, standoffish manner might have hurt his manly pride just a tad. As it was, they had a mutual lack of interest in each other, which suited him just fine.

When he woke Jemmy and told him about their supper plans, his nephew grinned like Will had never seen before.

"I can play with Em'ly."

The brightness in his eyes almost made Will tear up. Somehow, he managed to answer.

"Yep. And eat supper, too."

"Olivia makes a mean chili." Albert seemed as eager as Jemmy. "And melt-in-your-mouth cornbread."

It sounded good to Will, but it wasn't until

they entered the other house and caught the enticing aromas that his mouth began to water and his belly rumbled with hunger.

YEARS AGO, OLIVIA had found her gift in extending hospitality. Nothing gave her more personal satisfaction than having company, giving them a comfortable bed and feeding them a delicious meal. Mom had set the example by frequently having guests. And Olivia and Sancho had often invited the elderly or church newcomers over for a meal after services. That was why Ina's idea about hosting artists had appealed to her enough to propel her into her present business.

And that was why feeding Albert had come naturally. It had been during one of his supper visits that they'd discussed her purchasing his land, and he'd said he would sell it to her. And now, that promise, as fragile as the old gentleman, was in danger of being canceled. She still didn't trust Will Mattson not to pull some lawyer trick to change Albert's mind, maybe even confuse the poor old man. No, that wasn't fair. Albert might be slowing down physically, but his mind was still sharp.

When he arrived with Will and Jemmy,

Dad, Nona and Emily were waiting in the living room. Emily skipped over to Jemmy and took his hand. His cute grin brought a smile to Olivia's lips. After she made introductions, they proceeded into the dining room. The kids sat at Emily's little table off to the side, and Olivia permitted herself a bittersweet moment as she pictured the son she'd lost sitting with them.

"My, oh, my, Olivia." Albert settled into his chair beside Nona. "I could smell your fine cooking halfway here. Bring it on."

Olivia laughed with the others as she carried the large earthenware serving bowl to the table, but her heart ached for her friend. She'd been so alarmed by what he'd said in his earlier visit that she failed to notice how frail he looked. In a moment of panic, she wondered if chili might upset his stomach, but he didn't appear at all worried.

Dad offered his usual beautiful prayer, thanking the Lord for His provision and for good friends to share it with. Then he stood and served out bowls of chili while Olivia passed the salad and cornbread. Everybody dug in and quickly offered high praise.

"'Scuse me, ma'am." After his first bite, Will

cast a look of concern toward the kids. "This is mighty tasty, but are they having this same chili?"

"No, of course not." Olivia tried not to sound defensive but failed. From the other end of the table, Dad gave a little shake of his head, so she modified her tone. "The cornbread's the same, but I always make a milder chili for Emily. If you prefer, I could take it away and make Jemmy a PB and J."

Hearing his name, Jemmy looked her way, and his eyes grew round. He turned his startled look to Will.

"It's okay, buddy. Do you like the chili?"

He answered with a nod, then hunched protectively over the bowl and took another bite.

"Sorry," Will whispered. "His dad used food as discipline, so sometimes he's scared his food will be taken away. We're working through that."

Olivia couldn't swallow the bite she'd just taken, so she washed it down with her iced tea. What kind of person could be so cruel to any child, much less his own? She glanced at the other end of the table, where Dad, Nona and Albert were deep into their own conversation.

"So, you're gonna finish the series up with this one?" Dad's interest in their guest hadn't reached fanboy level yet, to Olivia's relief, but he did seem extra friendly toward her.

Nona dabbed her lips with her napkin. "That's the plan." She smiled, and her amber eyes twinkled. "What do you think should happen to bring it all to a close?"

Dad chuckled. "Oh, no. I'm not going to tamper with genius. You just keep writing like you've been doing."

"So, you're a writer?" Will's expression exuded sincerity, but Olivia had her doubts. Who in the world hadn't heard of Nona Albright?

Nona, however, didn't seem offended by the question. "I am."

"And a brilliant one, too," Dad said. "I'll loan you one of her books. I have them all."

"And that's enough about me." Nona turned to Albert. "Tell me about you. How long have you lived here? And what can you tell me about the women who settled here in the early 1900s? I may need to write a book about them."

Albert beamed. "Ah. One of my favorite subjects. One of those women was my great-grandmother. I grew up right here." He took a bite of cornbread, but she was still looking at him expectantly. After he swallowed, he said, "I can show you her diaries, if you like."

"Oh, that would be wonderful," Nona said. "But tell me more about what it was like growing up here."

"All right." Albert chuckled. "When I was a boy, my folks started a birthday tradition for me. I was born on July fourth, so they started having a big party for me. Invited folks from the local communities. It grew into an annual Independence Day celebration." He looked at Olivia. "And that gives me an idea."

"Great." Olivia wasn't sure she trusted whatever he was going to say, although last year, she and Emily had loved his Fourth of July celebration. "Let me serve dessert, then you can tell us."

She and Nona cleared the table, and Olivia brought out her homemade carrot cake. After everybody was served and began to eat, Will hummed his appreciation.

"Wow, this is my first carrot cake ever, and it's now officially my new favorite dessert."

Olivia rolled her eyes. "Right." She focused on Albert. "Okay, what's your idea?"

"Oh, you're gonna like this. I've hosted that celebration for close to ninety years, give or take a few. But I'm just not sure I can do it again." His pale blue eyes took in both her and Will.

"I'm gonna need some help so I can go out with a bang."

"Sure. Glad to help." Will, seated across from Albert, leaned forward. "What can I do?"

"Well, I spent this afternoon considering some ideas for making things work for both you and Olivia in this land situation." He winked at Olivia, and her heart dropped. This couldn't be good. "I want the two of you to have a competition. I'll assign responsibilities to each of you, and whoever does the best job gets to make the final decision about who buys my place."

Nona's attention was riveted on the discussion. "How will you decide who does the best job? They both appear to be very capable people."

Albert frowned. "Hadn't thought that far."

"How about letting the folks who attend cast ballots?" Dad grinned at Olivia, who returned a frown. What was he thinking by contributing to this wild scheme?

"What a great idea." Nona gave Olivia a conspiratorial wink. "Let me know if I can help."

"Sounds good to me," Will said.

"What do you think, Olivia?" Albert's excitement was obvious from the way he bounced in his seat with boyish enthusiasm.

All she could do was offer a shaky smile as her heart sank even lower. Will would probably bring in a bunch of his relatives to vote for him. She didn't have a posse to help her out, so he would no doubt win this silly competition. And, of course, he would choose to buy the land, then once he moved in with those noisy boys, she might as well kiss her hospitality business goodbye.

CHAPTER THREE

"THIS CELEBRATION IS going to be fun." Nona
had insisted on helping Olivia clean up after
supper and had an instinct for where to put
items she cleared from the dining-room table.
"I'm glad I'll be here for it. And I really like
your cowboy. He sure is an old-fashioned gentleman."

Olivia cringed inwardly, but she didn't want
to alienate her guest by arguing about her nem-
esis. She glanced through the doorway into
the living room, where Dad chatted with Albert and Will, and the kids played with Emily's LEGO blocks on the rug in front of the
fireplace.

"Yes, he seems quite the hero. A knight in
shining armor." She wiped out the cast-iron
skillet with a paper towel and put it on the back
burner of the gas stove, where it would be ready
for tomorrow's breakfast bacon. "I can just see

him on the cover of a romance novel." She didn't care for most romance novels, so thinking of him that way put some distance between her rational brain and her silly, involuntary reactions to him.

As Nona brushed off the place mats over the sink, she laughed. "Hmm. There's an idea. I'm going to jot down a few observations about him. Maybe my next book after this one will be a romance."

Uh-oh. Best to change the subject. "So, where do you get your ideas?"

Again, Nona laughed. "That's the question people ask me most often. I grew up on Nancy Drew and in high school moved on to Agatha Christie, so I was always fascinated by suspense and mysteries, especially in real life. Just about anything can set me off on a creative tangent. For instance, as we drove here from the airport, I saw two intriguing things that set my creative juices flowing. Wrote them down as soon as I got unpacked."

"Wow. Though I shouldn't be too surprised. That's the way I am with recipes."

"Now, about this Independence Day, aka Albert's birthday celebration. What are we going to do?"

We? Nona's willingness to jump in and help surprised her.

"Good question. I assume I'll manage the food." Olivia had only attended the event one time—last year—when she'd finally tried to reclaim some sort of normal life after Sancho's death. "Maybe a cake-decorating competition? An old-fashioned cakewalk? Grilled hamburgers and all the fixings, for sure." She dried her hands on a tea towel and punched the start button on the dishwasher. "What do you think?"

"It helps to know your audience. Who usually comes? How many? Mainly children, or adults, too?"

Wow, Nona's creative mind sure was humming with ideas. "Families. All ages. Albert limits the invitation to the local communities to keep it under control. Local neighbors and friends from the San Juan area. Maybe a hundred to a hundred and fifty people."

"Fireworks?"

"No, those are not allowed. The area's had too many forest fires to risk it. When conditions are safe, he does let the kids have sparklers... under strict control."

"Ah. Very sensible."

Olivia sighed. "It's the only day of the year

when Albert's place gets noisy, so I hope you won't be bothered."

"That's over a month away, so I'm sure I'll be far enough along with my word count to take a day off." Nona turned her attention to the door and smiled.

And there stood Dad, his eyes on Nona. Again, she wondered, what was that all about?

"Say, Livy," Dad said. "If you're done in here, come on in the other room and let's talk. Albert has some more ideas."

Oh, great. More nails in my coffin. "Sure. Coming right away."

Once she settled in her favorite chair—and noticed Dad making a place for Nona beside him on the couch—she turned her attention to Albert and did her best to ignore Will. Did he realize the black curls across his broad, tanned forehead made him even more attractive? Did he arrange them that way on purpose? *Oh, stop that!*

"I'm coming up with more ideas." Albert's wide smile revealed his perfect dentures *and* his excitement. "Will was saying he'd manage the games, but I have a better idea. I think he should manage the food, and Olivia should manage the games. That way you're both doing something new, that you aren't already familiar with. What do you think?"

"Sounds good to me," Will said. "I'll bring over a side of beef and cook it on an open pit." He winked at Olivia, which sent an odd little tickle through her middle. "We Mattsons are known for our barbecue beef."

"Oh, well, then." Albert gave him a wily grin. "Olivia will provide the beef. I'll pay for it, of course. And you can manage the rest of the food."

"Oh, no." Will leaned back, rolled his eyes and laughed. "You sure do plan to make it hard on us, don't you? All right, then. I'm game. Olivia?"

She was already scrambling in her mind for the best barbecue recipe. Nothing came up. Her specialty was baking. For barbecue, she'd always bought bottles of Sancho's favorite sauce, and lately that seemed to suit Dad, too. But store-bought sauce did not line the path to victory. It would take some serious internet research to find the right way to prepare an entire side of beef.

"If I may jump in here." Nona's eyes were bright with interest. "What would you think if I set up a book-signing booth? I can have my daughter send me some boxes of my backlist, and I can sell them at a big discount. All the proceeds will go to your favorite charity."

"That's mighty generous, Miss Nona." Dad patted her hand. "I can help you."

"Great." She returned his smile. "And I'm going to send Ina a text to see if she wants to come and have a sketch booth. She used to do sketches for a living at a Florida theme park before her painting career took off."

"My, oh, my." Albert slapped the arm of his chair. "This just gets better and better."

Olivia gave him a strained smile. In the midst of all these fine plans for joining his birthday with a grand Independence Day celebration, everybody seemed to forget that she was in danger of losing not only her dream, but also her very means of supporting herself and her daughter.

As WILL DROVE his Chevy Silverado back toward Riverton, he shot a quick glance at the rearview mirror to check on Jemmy, who was strapped in his booster chair in the back seat. He'd never seen the little guy happy or laughing, so today had been a blessing beyond measure. From the first moment Emily took his hand, she'd treated him like he was her best friend. His Mattson cousins, of whom there were many, had also tried to befriend him, but their roughhousing and wrestling had frightened Jemmy, probably reminding him of Ed's abuse.

As for Olivia, while she obviously had no interest in befriending Will, she was kind and gentle with Jemmy. He could see a nurturing personality in her pretty brown eyes.

He chuckled as he recalled her alarm at Albert's suggestion about the competition. While she hadn't changed her mind about her so-called *right* to buy the property, she'd surrendered to the Independence Day plans, probably because of Nona's enthusiasm. And her father's. Lawrence sure was a generous, laid-back guy. He'd shown Jemmy his model train setup, and Jemmy stared at it with mild curiosity. But when Lawrence offered him an engineer's hat, he'd withdrawn again. Maybe next time.

And maybe next time, he could offer an olive branch to try to win Olivia's friendship, if not her agreement to release Albert from his promise.

A jackrabbit dashed across the road, and Will barely managed to stomp the brakes to keep from hitting it. "Whoa. That was close." *Better quit daydreaming.*

"Whoa!" Jemmy echoed. Another glance in the mirror revealed alarm on the boy's face.

"It's okay, buddy. Uncle Will's got this."

"Unka Weeoo go' dis."

Will swallowed the sudden lump in his throat. Jemmy's growing trust in him meant a lot, and he would do everything in his power not to disappoint the little guy. Or the four other little guys Aunt Lila Rose fostered, boys from seven to nine years old from dysfunctional families, each with special issues, the main one being the need for security. In addition to nurturing Will after Mom left, his aunt had been a foster mom for years after her own two children had grown up, which had inspired him to take the state-mandated courses to qualify as a foster parent himself. Together, they worked hard to let each boy know someone was watching out for them. It usually worked. Jemmy just needed more time with them.

After stopping at Walmart to pick up food and other items needed for survival at Albert's place, he drove to his aunt's wood-frame house in suburban Riverton. As always, the boys clamored for his attention, which caused Jemmy to withdraw to a corner of the couch and suck his thumb. Will didn't yet know how to help him get over this behavior, but he wouldn't force it.

He distributed the usual popcorn treats, mindful of Aunt Lila Rose's limitations on sweets at bedtime, and read to them a chapter from *The Lord of the Rings*. After reading time, he tucked each one into bed, listened to their chatter and their prayers, then returned to the living room, where his aunt was sitting with Jemmy.

"How long will you be at Albert's?" she asked. "Are you sure you don't want me to keep Jemmy?"

Alarm filled Jemmy's eyes, so Will squeezed his shoulder.

"No. I can't get by without my little buddy." He winked at his aunt, and she returned an understanding nod. "We'll probably stay until after the Fourth of July. I expect Albert to move to Amarillo after that. But I'll come by here every evening and read to the boys."

"That's good. They really look forward to your coming."

After a quick trip to his apartment to pack their bags, he and Jemmy drove back to Albert's. The rutted dirt roads weren't easy to navigate, especially in the dark, but he managed to find the almost hidden signposts along the way, thanks to his truck's elevation and high beams. Sometimes the light caught the startled look of coyotes or mule deer, or the rare peccary beside the road, which reminded him to take care as he drove. Too many lives had been lost in this area after wild Saturday-night parties. Two little brothers in Aunt Lila Rose's care had lost their parents that way only last Christmas. Will's constant prayer was that he could make a difference in their lives and steer them to a healthier lifestyle than their parents had indulged in.

Seeing a large, shadowy shape beside the road ahead, Will slowed the truck to a crawl. Just as he suspected, it was one of Olivia's horses. He should have mentioned to her earlier that her fence had a break in it close to the dividing line of the two properties. Did she know fences often developed breaks in the winter? Lawrence might know, but Will wasn't sure the older man was physically capable of checking to find weaknesses, much less repairing them.

Jemmy was sound asleep in his booster seat, so Will stopped, cut the engine, set the emergency brake and climbed out, then pulled a halter and lead rope from the truck bed. Every

Mattson worth his or her salt knew to keep tack and tools handy in case they came across a horse running loose or some other emergency.

"Here, boy."

The sorrel gelding tossed his flaxen mane playfully and turned away.

"Aw, now, don't do that." Will dug an apple out of a grocery bag and held it out in the light reflected from his headlights over the area. "Here you go." He held it out.

The horse tossed his head again, then gave in to the temptation and lipped the apple into his mouth. While he munched his treat and apple juice dripped to the ground, Will slipped the halter over his head and tied the lead rope to the back of the truck. He inched along the last hundred yards or so of the road to Olivia's property. Unlike the main Mattson ranch, no locked electric gate or intercom protected the entrance, so he had to climb out again to open the flimsy gate.

By the time he reached the front of the house, Jemmy had woken up. "Em'ly." He tugged against his seat belt.

"Whoa, buddy." Will unclicked the seat belt, lifted Jemmy out of the seat and carried him to the door.

After thirty seconds or so, Lawrence answered his knock. "Will, Jemmy. Welcome. Come on inside. What brings you here at this hour?"

"Dad?" Olivia appeared beside him, her dark hair tousled attractively around her face. Wow, she sure was pretty. "Will. What's going on?"

"Sorry to bug you folks, but I found your younger gelding on the road." He tilted his head back toward the truck, where the horse tugged against the lead.

Olivia gasped and charged out the door. "Dawson, what am I going to do with you?"

"Uh-oh." Lawrence clicked his tongue. "I never did get out to check the fences, even after Albert warned me that I should after the winter we had." He flicked on the outside lights, illuminating the front yard, then limped outside with the help of his cane.

They followed Olivia to the truck. All the while, Jemmy clutched Will's shirt but watched the proceedings with wide-eyed interest.

"I can check fencing tomorrow morning," Will said. "But for now, what can we do about this rascal?"

"We?" Olivia eyed him and gave him the first real smile she'd ever cast his way in the short time since they'd met. Wow. Sure did make her even prettier. "That's very Good Samaritan of you." She untied the lead from the truck but held on to it. "We can keep him here inside the house fence."

A whinny sounded some distance away, and Dawson answered in kind.

"Sounds like his friend missed him." In the shadowed pasture some thirty yards away, Will could make out the form of the other horse.

"That's Fred." Olivia took a step in that direction. "I'd better let them say hello, or Dawson will be fussy all night."

Will and Lawrence followed her, keeping far enough behind to avoid the frisky gelding's prancing hooves.

"Horsey," Jemmy whispered.

"That's right." Will squeeze-hugged him. "Horsey. Think you'd like to ride him?"

Jemmy buried his face in Will's shoulder, but not before Will could see a tiny grin. He chuckled. He'd make a Mattson cowboy out of this little dude yet, whatever it took.

While Dawson and Fred traded over-the-fence greetings, Olive unhitched the lead and handed it to Will.

"I don't know how to thank you. I'm not

worried about Fred or Buffy, our donkey, getting out. They always stick close to this side of the pasture." She brushed a hand down Dawson's neck. "Do you mind if I keep the halter on him until tomorrow?"

He shook his head. "Be my guest. And speaking of being a guest, I'd better get over to Albert's. I have the ice cream on ice in a cooler." He nodded toward the back of the truck. "But that only keeps it from melting for so long."

"Ice ceem," Jemmy whispered in his ear.

Olivia laughed. "Ice cream at bedtime. Hmm. Well, you'd better hurry." Her friendly smile disappeared, replaced by a cross frown. "I'll close the gate after you."

Was that a dismissal? *And don't let it hit you on the way out?*

"Yeah, sure. Thanks."

"No. Thank *you*. And don't worry about the fence. I can fix it tomorrow." Her tone was definitely dismissive this time.

Will glanced at Lawrence, who shrugged and apologized with a grimace.

"Yes, ma'am. I'm sure you can do that. But since I'm looking out for Albert now, it makes sense for me to check both properties and fix anything that needs fixing."

"Whatever." She waved a hand toward his truck. "We need to get to bed."

"Yeah, sure," he repeated. "Good night."

"Good night, and thanks again." Lawrence offered a hand, and Will shook it with his free one.

As he drove around the edge of their property toward Albert's entrance, he located the break again. It wouldn't take much time to fix, so he'd try to get to it first thing tomorrow… even though Olivia was obviously indifferent to his help. He couldn't get over her odd and rapid change of mood. He knew he hadn't done anything wrong. Not so much as a dip of his eyebrows into a frown.

Wait. Had he winked at her? Maybe. It was a Mattson habit he was barely conscious of doing, but maybe she didn't know that.

One thing was sure. That feisty lady was going to fight him all the way as they planned Albert's celebration, which didn't bode well for her changing her mind about the man's promise. Which also didn't bode well for him making a safe home for Aunt Lila Rose's boys far away from the dangers of their old lives.

Somehow, whatever it took, he couldn't allow that to happen.

OLIVIA CHECKED ON Emily to be sure she was still asleep. Her daughter loved Dawson and would have been upset to learn he'd gotten loose. The younger gelding was too frisky for Emily now, but once she learned to ride, he would be perfect for her. For now, reliable old Fred enjoyed Emily's riding lessons as much as she did. The two horses had formed their own little herd, along with Buffy. While Fred was the alpha, no one could convince the little donkey he wasn't in charge of everything that went on in the pasture. Too bad he hadn't kept Dawson from escaping.

Olivia looked for Dad to say good-night and found him working on his model train board. The tiny N-gauge engine puffed out little bursts of smoke as it chugged around the multilevel complex of tracks through the tiny town, mountains and forest. Since Mom's death, he'd spent more and more time with the trains. When he'd showed them to Jemmy, the boy had seemed interested and for a few seconds forgot to be shy with the grown-ups. She had noticed the gratitude in Will's blue eyes.

Blue eyes? Why did she always have to think of how blue they were? Probably because of the way their color was enhanced by upper and lower eyelashes as black as his hair. Even with her own eyelashes being black, she had to add mascara to have the same effect. How annoying that a man could have such an appealing feature without working for it.

"Going to bed?" Dad interrupted her silly musings.

"Yep. I might read a few more pages of Nona's last book." She nudged his arm. "Don't you dare tell her I haven't finished it."

He chuckled. "I won't if you won't tell her I'm still working on it, too."

"Deal."

"It's a real page-turner." He used tweezers to set a tiny N-gauge person on the tiny town's sidewalk. "But these days, reading makes me sleepy."

Olivia studied his profile. He was just past sixty, but he acted like a much older man. Almost like Albert. "Maybe you should try audio books. You could listen while you work on your trains."

"Huh. Good idea." He shot her a quick grin. "That was neighborly of Will to bring Dawson home. Good of him to move in with Albert to help him out. And you got to admire him for taking care of his orphaned nephew and studying to be a foster dad so he can help his aunt with the boys she fosters." He switched off the train's power and put away his tools. "You don't meet many young men who would do all that."

Will had qualified as a foster parent? That wasn't an easy process. He must have told Dad about it while she was out of the room. Yep, he sure was a knight in shining armor. But that didn't change the threat he posed to her dreams.

"Not bad-looking, either." Dad eyed her in a teasing way.

She walked toward the door, then turned back. "Tell you what. You don't try matchmaking for me, and I won't try matchmaking for you. Deal?"

He chuckled. "No deal." His cheerful tone made him sound more like his old self than he had since Mom died. But did he really intend to keep nagging her this way?

Argh! That was all she needed. Well, he and Nona and maybe even Albert could try to push her toward Mr. Will Mattson all they wanted, but they'd never seen her dig in her heels like she was about to do. That should set them all straight. Olivia Ortiz refused to be bullied.

Yes, it was admirable that Will planned to be a foster parent. Yes, it was good of him to move in with Albert to take care of him, old family friend that he was. But as she laid her head on her pillow, another possible motive for his actions came to mind. What if he planned to use his presence in the house as a form of squatter's rights? If so, what possible counter-offensive could she launch against a man who knew the law?

Simple. She had to win the competition for the right to buy Albert's land. Then she could boot that squatter back to whatever Mattson land he probably already owned.

CHAPTER FOUR

THE NEXT DAY, Olivia searched online for outdoor game rentals and came up with several fun ideas. A few phone calls later, she'd reserved a bouncy house, a cornhole board with beanbags and several other games suitable for younger children. Albert had told her some of the attendees would be teens, so she brainstormed with Dad. And Nona, of course. The author would be eating supper with them every evening and, with her warm personality, already seemed like a member of the family.

"Have you ever attended a Renaissance fair?" Nona included both Dad and Olivia in her questioning. "Or Scottish Highland games?"

"Yes. We went to Scottish games in Seattle." Olivia ignored the sting of the memory and reminded herself of the fun she and Sancho had had on that last outing before his death. They'd worn red-and-green plaid kilts, and even three-year-old Emily had enjoyed the day, especially when imitating the Highland dancers.

"What competitions did they have?"

"Axe throwing, caber tossing, archery, that sort of thing. Too dangerous without professional supervision." Another memory surfaced. "They had an open competition for stone carrying called the boulder fumble. Sancho—" she managed to say his name without choking up "—just had to try it. The stone weighed about two hundred pounds, and he did pretty well running over a hundred feet before he had to drop it. The winner was this huge guy who ran over sixteen hundred feet. I was just glad Sancho didn't drop that huge stone on his foot."

She finished with a laugh. Her dear hubby had been strong, but he'd also been a good sport about not winning. Oddly, the memory of Will chopping wood, sleeves rolled up to reveal his biceps, popped into her mind. With those strong arms, he'd probably do pretty well at the boulder fumble.

Stop that! Will might be strong and undeniably handsome, but he also wanted to take away her future. Her sense of competition—and *survival*—kicked in big-time whenever she remembered that stark fact.

"That sounds like a challenge our local young men would like," Dad said. "I'm sure we can come up with more ideas. Let's keep working on it."

The brightness in his eyes brought a lump to Olivia's throat. He hadn't taken much interest in life since Mom died. If for no other reason, she needed to include him in all of her plans for Albert's birthday bash. And, of course, Nona, who was also widowed. The two of them seemed drawn to each other, but Olivia didn't know whether or not to encourage this, for lack of a better word, *friendship.* If they got too involved, what would happen to Dad when Nona finished her book and returned to her family and home responsibilities, not to mention her glamorous life as a bestselling author?

THE PROBLEM WAS still on her mind the next day when she took Emily shopping in Riverton. Papacita's Friendly Mart, her favorite mom-and-pop grocery, specialized in ingredients for Mexican recipes, and she hoped to get the owner's advice on how to prepare a winning sauce for her barbecue beef.

Emily had outgrown the shopping cart, so

she walked beside Olivia as they wandered up and down the narrow aisles.

"Sweet pea, would you go get the milk?" At Dad's insistence, she had started letting out the leash a bit as her daughter got older, and the dairy section was just two aisles over in this small, safe store.

As always, Emily's face lit up when she was assigned an important responsibility. "Yes, ma'am." She trotted off and disappeared around the end of the soup section.

"What did I tell you?" The sound of a man's low, growling voice came from the next aisle. His question was followed by several curse words and the unmistakable sound of a hand meeting flesh. "You do as I tell you, boy, or you'll regret it. And quit yer crying, or I'll give you somethin' to cry about."

For the briefest moment, Olivia couldn't breathe or think. She'd just sent her baby in that direction. Mama-bear instincts took over, and she pushed her cart around the end of the display. Emily was nowhere in sight, but what she did see was a hulking, brown-haired man standing like an angry grizzly over a small boy of perhaps eight years.

"Now, put that under your shirt and tuck it

in." He spoke in a lowered voice as he thrust a flat can of sardines at the boy.

Shaking like a leaf in the wind, Olivia swiped her phone to change the screen from her shopping list to the video camera just in time to capture the man's actions, as well as the boy's terror as he obeyed. Just as quickly, she switched back to her shopping list, then focused on the shelf beside her as though searching for a particular item. If he hurt the boy again, she would have to intervene…somehow. *Lord, please help.*

The man strode toward her. "What are you doin'?" He reached out to grab her phone.

She managed to elude his grasp and dropped the phone into her jacket pocket. "I beg your pardon?"

"Gimme that!" He grabbed her arm and reached toward the pocket.

"Let me go! How dare you?" Jerking away from him, she used her loudest, sternest voice, as Sancho had taught her to do if she was ever confronted by a bully. "Papacita!"

Papacita, no small man himself, hustled up the aisle from the meat section in the back of the store. "Senora Olivia, what…?" He took in the scene and glared at the man. "Ah, it is you. I have told you, you are no longer welcome in my store. *Vete de aquí, vete de aquí!*" He waved one muscular arm toward the door. "And do not come back."

Releasing more curses, the man grabbed the little boy's arm and strode away, deliberately knocking several items off a shelf as he went.

"Are you all right, Senora Olivia?" Papacita touched her shoulder and studied her face.

She huffed out a sigh. "Yes, thank you. But you should see this." She showed him the video. "He's not only stealing from you, but he's teaching his son to do the same. Open your phone, and I can send it to you."

As he complied, Papacita snorted. "Not his son. Him and his wife take in foster kids to make a living. I pray for those little ones. I have never seen that one, so he must be new."

"Oh, dear. I'll pray for them, too. What's his name?"

"Grant Sizemore." Papacita chuckled without humor. "Local lore says his great-grandpapa Jeb Sizemore was a cattle rustler in these parts. Seems he passed his bad ways down to that one."

"Here, Mommy." Emily shuffled carefully around the end of the aisle clutching a gallon of milk in her arms.

"Thank you, sweet pea." Olivia took the jug and placed it in the cart, then gave Papacita a significant look.

He nodded, clearly understanding there was no need to mention the drama to her daughter.

"Hi, Mr. Papacita." Emily gave him a wide grin, revealing the space in her mouth where a tooth had come out last night.

"Ah, look at you." He winked. "Now you must drink all of that milk so a new tooth will grow in."

They all laughed, which helped soften the tightness in Olivia's chest, although the memory of the incident ate at her all the way home. What if she encountered Grant Sizemore again? Riverton was a diverse, spread-out community, and she didn't recall seeing him before. Maybe she wouldn't run in to him. *Please, Lord.*

What a contrast between that man and Will Mattson. Will's tenderness toward his little nephew had impressed her from the start. That was what all kids needed. How awful to think some people took in foster children for financial gain, then taught them to steal. What kind of start did that give kids who already had too many challenges to face in life? Should she report Sizemore to the authorities? Or leave it to Papacita, who'd promised to save the video she'd given him, along with the store's CCTV?

Papacita, whose name was Ramon Martinez, had also given her a barbecue recipe and a promise to reserve some prime beef cuts when the time came. "You may depend upon it, senora—it will be the best you can buy. I only sell Mattson beef in my store."

At the time, her mind had been on the incident with the unpleasant man, but now, as she recalled Papacita's comment about his beef source, she could only roll her eyes. Mattson beef. Of course. On her way to the grocery, she'd stopped by the party-supply store to put a deposit on the bouncy house and other games, not wanting to give her credit-card number over the phone. As she'd chatted with the perky young lady at the counter, she'd noticed her name tag. Julie Mattson. *Of course.* Would there be even a single business in this town where the Mattson name didn't come up?

And would that work against her drive to win Albert's competition so she could buy his house and ensure her and Emily's future?

AFTER WILL CHECKED the repairs in the fence breaks he'd made yesterday, with Jemmy's "help," he accepted Lawrence's invitation to see how his trains operated. He gazed around the multipurpose back room of Olivia's house. Partially filled bookshelves lined one wall, with two overstuffed chairs in front of them. At the other end of the room was a desk with a desktop computer and a table holding a printer and paper supplies. A rolling desk chair completed the picture of a functional but cozy home office.

In the center of the long room was the six-by-ten-foot train board. As promised, Lawrence had invited him to bring Jemmy over to see his N-gauge train. It was a welcome diversion and an opportunity to bring Jemmy out of himself. Aunt Lila Rose had advised a slow introduction to socialization, and this was a good step in that direction.

Despite knowing it was for the best, he was disappointed to see Olivia wasn't home. He couldn't let his natural attraction to her go any further. When Lawrence explained she was already making arrangements for Albert's birthday event, Will had a moment of annoyance. Then guilt. He was supposed to plan the food sales and baking competitions. But Aunt Lila Rose had informed him she would take charge of getting baked goods and planning the cake-walk. She would arrange the portable floor-ing, the music and the cakes to give away to the winners. The Old West game played at barn dances and church socials was a favorite of both Albert and Aunt Lila Rose.

Will's only task? Reserve a couple of food trucks, a job he'd completed within a half hour. Too bad Albert had decided Olivia would pro-vide the beef, but that would have been all too easy for Will. With Olivia not knowing many people in the area, would she be able to find help as easily as he had?

He shrugged off the thought. His boys needed Albert's property, and he wasn't letting go of it without a fight. A fair fight, of course.

"Let's make this official." Lawrence put on an engineer's hat and offered a child-size one to Jemmy. "Want to wear it this time?"

Most kids loved to pop on a hat, but as he had last time, Jemmy backed against Will's legs, drawing into himself as he usually did around other people. He hadn't been afraid of Lawrence the other day, so it stung Will's heart to see his renewed shyness around the older gentleman.

Lawrence took it in stride. "Emily should be back soon, Jemmy." He set a low stool beside the train board. "When she gets here, she can join us. Until then, if you want to, you can step up and help me figure out some stuff."

Rather than pressure Jemmy, Lawrence set about his task, humming as he worked. "Now, let me see. Should this little dog be at the train station or on the playground with the little boy?" Using tweezers, he held up a tiny figure in Will's direction. "What do you think?"

"Hmm." Will caught on to his game. He struck a thoughtful pose with arms crossed and fist under his chin. "If he's at the train station, he's probably waiting for someone. If he's at the playground, he probably wants to play with the boy." He glanced at Jemmy, who was following the conversation with a solemn expression. "But boys don't want to play with dogs, do they, Jemmy?"

Jemmy's eyes widened. "I want to." It was barely a whisper, but Will's heart soared.

"Well, then." Lawrence offered the tweezers to Jemmy. "You put him where he should be."

Jemmy looked up at Will as if asking permission.

"Step right up, buddy." Will winked at him.

With his help, Jemmy stepped up on the stool and took the tweezers from Lawrence. The tiny dog fell onto the train board. Jemmy gasped and recoiled. At least he didn't run away and hide.

"Oops!" Lawrence chuckled. "Slippery little rascal, isn't he?"

Will added a soft chuckle to assure Jemmy he hadn't made a fatal mistake. It had taken him five months to assure Jemmy that he wouldn't be punished for every little slip. But in new situations, the boy often relapsed.

"Try again." Lawrence used a jolly tone. "Let's get Spot over to his pal."

This time, Jemmy held on tight and placed the figure next to the child.

"Very good." Lawrence winked at him. "Now, let's get this train moving. Want to throw the switch?"

Now fully engaged in the activity, Jemmy nodded.

The distant sound of a car door closing diverted Will's attention. Beyond the living room and through the front door, he saw Olivia and Emily taking packages from her Explorer. Olivia's thick black hair blew in the breeze, and he forced down the involuntary admiration trying to get a foothold in his chest. Manners kicked in, and he hustled out of the house.

"Hi, Emily. Olivia. Can I help?"

Olivia eyed him suspiciously, then shrugged. "Sure. Thanks."

"Say, Emily, Jemmy and your granddad are playing with the trains. How about you go see what they're up to? I'll help your mom." He'd left Jemmy without thinking and sent up a silent prayer the boy wouldn't be alarmed when he realized it.

"May I, Mom?" Emily gave Olivia a cute, questioning smile.

After a moment, she nodded. "Sure."

While Emily dashed up the walkway to the house, Olivia picked up a box of canned food, which Will hurried to grasp.

"Let me."

She hesitated, and her perfect black eyebrows arched upward, as though she was surprised by his offer. Then she released the box into his hands. It had to be pretty heavy for a petite lady like her, but she hadn't acted like it. Sure couldn't call her a wimp. Maybe this was a warning to him not to underestimate her.

"Thanks." She grabbed a bag. "I saw you fixed the fence. Much appreciated." Not looking his way or waiting for a response, she brushed past him.

It took several trips to empty the vehicle, during which time she seemed determined not to look his way. Not a problem. He didn't want her to be interested in him. Still, he couldn't resist admiring her overall attractiveness, not to mention her energy.

Leaning far into the vehicle's cargo space, she tugged at a fifty-pound bag of oats. Will moved in and picked up the bag.

"Where do you want it?"

She paused before answering, then sighed. "Over there in the shed." She waved a hand toward the small structure inside the pasture.

He made quick work of putting the bag into the shed. Although the structure had no lock, it did appear to be waterproof, which was a good thing because saddles, bridles and blankets were also stored there. He had to hand it to Olivia. She at least had the right feed and equipment to take care of the two horses and the donkey. Could she ride?

And why did he even wonder? Maybe because he hadn't been riding since Jemmy had come to live with him, and he missed it.

The final item Will lifted from the Explorer bed was a forty-pound bag of scratch-grain chicken feed.

"You have chickens?" He glanced around the yard.

"Nope. This is for Albert's flock. He provides

all the eggs we can eat. He's very generous that way. The least I can do is buy him a bag of feed from time to time." She aimed a dazzling smile in the direction of Albert's yard, as if the old gentleman was standing there. "We really appreciate him."

Wow. She wasn't just pretty. When she smiled like that, she was beautiful.

Quit that! While he couldn't prevent his involuntary reactions to her beauty, her thoughtfulness and her obvious smarts, he could choose to ignore them. Best way to do that was to turn his attention to Jemmy and encourage his nephew's friendship with Emily. Besides, that smile hadn't been for him, it had been in honor of Albert's generosity toward her. Truth was, Olivia came close to turning a cold shoulder to him every time they were near each other, even when he was helping her, another reason for shutting down his attraction to her.

Who was he kidding? Olivia's lack of interest in *him* made her all the more attractive. And all the more trouble for his heart.

OLIVIA PUT AWAY her groceries before joining the others in the train room. Emily was being a "big sister" to little Jemmy, which made Olivia proud and concerned at the same time. How would her daughter react when Jemmy and Will moved back to town, as they would have to do once Albert sold his land to her?

Why was she thinking it was a done deal? The sale was still up in the air. Will was still staying at Albert's house. And if she didn't win the right to buy the land, Jemmy—and Will—would be permanent fixtures next door, along with who knew how many rowdier boys?

Giggles coming from Jemmy and the soft paternal grin on Will's face soothed her anxiety for a moment. As she'd noted earlier, this man's care for his orphaned nephew was impressive and stood in great contrast to Grant Sizemore's cruel treatment of his little foster child. While she hadn't seen Will in other situations, she could let herself admire him for that one trait.

"Look, Jemmy. Here comes the train again." Emily pointed to the tiny engine emerging from the train-board tunnel, pulling seven cars and emitting a puff of smoke and a soft *toot-toot* to announce its arrival at the miniature train station. "Toot, toot." Emily copied the sound.

"Toot, toot," Jemmy repeated, and they both giggled.

"Mommy, may Jemmy stay for lunch?" Emily's innocent, round-eyed expression was hard to resist.

Even the boy looked her way hopefully, then stared up at Will.

"I don't know, buddy. We shouldn't invite ourselves—" Will gave Olivia a guilty shrug. "Sorry."

She looked at the bag of chicken feed, which sat propped against the wall beside the back door, waiting for Will to carry it over to Albert's place. "No need to apologize. Emily invited him." She pointed to the bag. "While you take that over to Albert, I can fix PB and J for the kids. And carrot sticks, of course."

"Of course." He chuckled. "Say, buddy." He set a hand on Jemmy's shoulder. "You don't mind staying here while I go over to Mr. Albert's, do you?"

For about two seconds, panic crossed the boy's face. Then he looked at Emily, who took his hand.

"Let's go wash our hands," she said. "We can play with my LEGOs after lunch."

That seemed to settle the matter. Jemmy carefully stepped down from the stool and let Emily lead him from the room.

Will pressed a hand to his chest as though in pain and released a long sigh. "Wow. That little girl sure has a very special gift." He cleared his throat. "Thanks."

Her own emotions not entirely under control, Olivia barely managed a smile. "Well, you'd better take that feed over to Albert's."

He nodded and lifted the bag. "Yeah. Lawrence, thanks for showing Jemmy your train. I could tell he loved it. Did he miss me when I left the room?"

"Hmm." Dad wrinkled his forehead thoughtfully. "I think he was so fascinated by the trains that he didn't notice. Then Emily came in and they were both too interested in the operation to notice anything else."

Will glanced out the window and took a deep breath. "This has been good for him. I hope...but I don't want to intrude..."

"You bring him over anytime, Will." Dad clapped him on the shoulder. "It's no intrusion at all. I enjoy his company. And yours."

Oh, great. An open invitation to her adversary. Olivia groaned inwardly. Knowing Dad's hospitable ways, he'd probably find a way to invite all of Will's boys out from town to see the trains. If that happened, Olivia could kiss her privacy-seeking clientele goodbye.

CHAPTER FIVE

THE NEXT MORNING, Will made sure Chirpy was fed and locked safely in his special part of the coop before taking Jemmy outside to feed the rest of the chickens. Albert had told him the rooster could be pretty aggressive when protecting his hens, even to the point of pecking adults, so he might not hesitate to attack a little kid.

Will returned to the house and found Jemmy finishing up his blueberry and marshmallow cereal at the kitchen table, with Albert sitting across from him counting out his vitamins into daily pill organizers. Still not entirely trusting of the old man, Jemmy was okay being left in his company for a few minutes. When Will came in, the child lifted the bowl to drink the last of the purple milk, then got down from his chair and carried his bowl to the kitchen sink.

"Good job eating your breakfast." Will took the bowl and washed it. "Ready to feed those chickens?"

Jemmy nodded solemnly but said nothing. Aunt Lila Rose said it was important for him to verbalize his thoughts, something Will needed to encourage.

"What do we say?" He kept his tone light. If he spoke with even the slightest hint of disapproval, Jemmy flinched. At least he didn't cower, as he used to. But he did need to use his words, not just nod.

"Tank you?" He pointed to the newly washed bowl now sitting in the drain rack.

Will chuckled. "Sure. And you're welcome. But I meant about feeding the chickens. Want to do that with me?"

Doubt flickered across his little face, and he chewed his lip.

"Sure would appreciate you helping out, Jemmy," Albert said. He'd understood from the start how to tread lightly with the boy. "And those chickens get mighty hungry for grain after only having bugs to eat."

"Bugs!" Jemmy's face scrunched up with disgust. "Yuck."

Will and Albert chuckled, and when Jemmy

saw they weren't upset with his response, he laughed, too. One of these days, Will would figure out a way to explain that chickens actually liked bugs. For now, he would just go with the flow.

"Okay, let's feed them something better." In the utility room just off the kitchen, he used his pocketknife to cut open the bag Olivia had bought. "Okay, Jemmy, this is a two-man job. I need you to take the lid off that can." He pointed to the twenty-gallon metal trash can used for feed storage.

His eyes focused and his chest puffed out with the importance of his new responsibility, Jemmy stepped right up and removed the lid, then looked at Will for approval.

"Good job." Will lifted the bag and poured the scratch grain on top of the leftover cracked corn. He'd never had the job of choosing chicken feed before and hoped Olivia had made the right choice. If not, he'd get the proper kind when he went to town. He chuckled to himself. Until then, the chickens did have their bugs.

"Okay, now let's scoop some into this bowl." Will took a battered metal bowl from the shelf and helped Jemmy fill it. It was a bit heavy for the boy, and some slid over the side. "Oops,"

Will said quickly. "Don't worry. We can sweep that up later."

Once out in the sunshine, he drew in a deep breath, appreciating the freshness of the air. He'd grown up in Riverton, hardly a big city. But somehow, the air out here by the river always seemed fresher, more invigorating, much like the Mattson clan's Double Bar M Ranch a mile downriver from here. He looked forward to moving here permanently. *If* he moved here permanently.

As they approached the chicken yard, the hens made a beeline for the chicken-wire gate, clucking and climbing over each other in anticipation.

Jemmy leaned close to Will. "Do dey bite, Unka Weeoo?"

Uh-oh. He had no idea. Why had he assumed the hens wouldn't be as aggressive as the rooster?

"Tell you what. You open the gate and stand behind it, and I'll toss in a handful of feed."

Jemmy hesitated but obeyed. As he pulled the gate open, hens poured out into the yard so quickly, Will could only toss handfuls of grain in front of them. The hens scrambled to devour their share. Jemmy giggled, a sound Will had come to love.

"Here. You do it." He held out the bowl.

Jemmy scooped up a handful and tossed it, but it didn't go very far. A few hens turned their attention his way and hurried over. One of the smaller ones, pushed aside by the larger ones, looked up at Jemmy, turning her head back and forth as though looking for her share.

Against everything he'd ever done since coming to live with Will, Jemmy handed back the bowl and picked up the little hen to let her eat from his hand. Again, he giggled.

"It tickles." But he didn't drop the food or the chicken. "Ima call her Pecky." He looked to Will for approval.

Was it a good idea to let him name the hen? If she got bigger and didn't lay eggs, she would be bound for the stew pot. He sure couldn't say that to Jemmy.

"Pecky's a fine name."

"Hey, Jemmy." Emily skipped through the flimsy gate that divided the two properties. A few steps behind her came Olivia, a wicker basket looped over her arm. "Whatcha got?"

Still holding the little hen, Jemmy ran over to his new best friend. "This is Pecky."

"Hi, Pecky." Emily petted the chicken's head as it kept eating from Jemmy's hand.

"Good morning, Jemmy." Olivia smiled that gorgeous smile at the kids—but it disappeared as she looked Will's way. "Morning."

Wow. She really didn't like him. "Hey. How's it goin'?"

"Just fine. I came over to gather eggs for Albert." She patted the basket. "But if you're doing that, we can go home."

"You don't have to go." For some self-destructive reason, he didn't want her to leave. Maybe it wasn't self-destructive. Maybe he just wanted Emily to stay for Jemmy's sake. Yeah, that was it. "We're just feeding the chickens. I'm not sure Jemmy's ready for egg gathering." He added a grin, hoping for one in return.

Nope. No smile for him.

The kids were now headed toward the chicken yard, chatting away about Jemmy's little rescue critter. "Well, I'd better get back over there and distribute the rest of this." He glanced down at the metal bowl, which was still half-full of grain, and started walking. "Then maybe you could help me herd the chickens back into their yard."

Joining him, she said, "It's better if they're

outside when we gather the eggs. In fact, Albert lets them stay out most of the day. Toward evening, they always go back inside to roost." She looked toward the wooded area beyond the house. "Or if they sense danger from coyotes or snakes. Amazing creatures, these chickens."

"Huh. I didn't know that." He hadn't decided whether to keep them or not once he bought the property. How much more would he have to learn? Maybe it would be good for Jemmy and Aunt Lila Rose's boys to have the responsibility of taking care of the chickens.

"So, you didn't have chickens on your ranch?" Her almost friendly interest set off his gold-digger alarm.

"I didn't grow up on the Mattson ranch, if that's what you're referring to." He didn't intend to sound sharp. In truth, though, he was disappointed to think she was interested in his family spread, as though a man couldn't be a Mattson in these parts without being raised on the Double Bar M.

She blinked those dark brown eyes, then shrugged. "Oh." She joined the kids. "Hey, Jemmy, would you like to help us gather eggs?"

Without hesitation or a glance at Will, Jemmy nodded. Was that progress? Or danger? It was one thing for him to like playing with Emily. Another altogether for the boy to get attached to Olivia.

But Will had no way to stop it without moving back to town and forgetting his dream of owning this property and helping Aunt Lila Rose raise her foster boys. And he wasn't about to do either of those things.

"SOMETIMES THEY LIKE to hide their eggs." Olivia moved aside a handful of straw and found a brown egg nestled near the bottom of the wooden box.

She noted that Will stood outside the wooden structure watching as they went about their chore. And no wonder. Probably an inch or two over six feet tall, he'd have to hunch over quite a bit to come in here.

She touched Jemmy's shoulder. "Want to pick it up?"

"Uh-huh." The dear little boy barely hesitated before stepping over, picking up the egg and gently placing it in Olivia's basket. He seemed to understand that eggs required careful handling.

A few feet away, Emily had already dug out two gems, one pink and the other spotted. The kids giggled, as usual, as they continued their treasure hunt. At one point, Jemmy got chicken poo on his hand. Before he could wipe it on his jeans, Olivia managed to whip out a tissue and clean him up.

"One of the hazards of the job," she said with a laugh. "After we find all the eggs, we need to clean out their boxes and put in fresh straw." She again glanced at Will, who had watched them work without comment...or one of his flashy smiles.

Although he'd been all smiles at first, something had set him off. Oh, yeah. He'd grimaced when she'd asked about chickens on his family's ranch. It seemed he hadn't grown up there—so what? She'd be sure never to mention his family again, no matter how many Mattsons she encountered in Riverton. She had no doubt they'd all be helping him win the right to buy Albert's property. If he didn't own a piece of the big ranch, maybe that was one of his reasons for wanting this bit of land. As if he couldn't find another place just as usable for his boys' ranch.

With all the eggs gathered, except an unknown number beneath one hen nesting proudly on one end of the roost, Olivia glanced at her adversary. "Could you bring over the wheelbarrow and pitchfork so we can clean out this old straw?"

He blinked those blue eyes as if surprised. "Sure." He trotted off and soon returned with a wheelbarrow full of fresh straw and the pitchfork. "Want me to do that?" Without waiting for her to answer, he hunched down and entered the small space.

A space that seemed all the smaller because of his closeness. So close that she could catch the pleasant spicy scent of his cologne.

Oh, stop it.

"I'll wait outside while you do that." Olivia scooched around his large frame and toward the door. "Come along, Emily."

They stepped out and turned to watch Will show Jemmy how to clean out the boxes and put in new straw. The pitchfork was far too big for the boy, and he still clutched the little hen under one arm, but Will let him hold on as he worked. No doubt about it, he was a good father figure. And hardworking. Again, Olivia allowed herself to respect him for those traits. Nothing more.

Yet, when she'd stood close to his very masculine presence and caught a whiff of that pleasant cologne, she had to admit it took a lot of mental wrangling to keep from admiring him. Did he know how he affected women? Did he flash that toothpaste-commercial smile just for effect? Well, he could smile all he wanted. Here was one person who wouldn't fall for it. Not when she knew that underneath it all lurked a hard heart that would steal her dreams and future security without a second thought.

"I'LL TAKE THESE INSIDE." Olivia indicated her basket, which held a dozen or more eggs. After a beat, she added, "Emily, do you want to go with me or stay out here with Jemmy?"

"Stay with Jemmy." She petted the little chicken still in Jemmy's arms.

"Okay. I'll be right back." Olivia sashayed across the yard toward Albert's back door.

Will had to force his eyes back to the kids. Against his better judgment *again*, he'd enjoyed sharing chores with her. Her patience with Jemmy impressed him. Many adults ignored small kids, but she gave Jemmy as much attention as she did her own daughter.

"Say, buddy." He crouched down to eye level with Jemmy. "Don't you think Pecky would like to scratch around with the other chickens?"

He waved a hand at the hens still wandering around the yard and beyond.

Shaking his head, Jemmy hugged the little hen closer. "Dey bite her."

Both kids looked up at Will with soulful eyes. He blew out a long breath.

"But you'll have to leave her outside when we go in."

Again, he hugged the hen closer. "Can she stay in my woom?"

"Uh, well…" Will scratched his chin. "That might get kinda messy. Chickens are supposed to live outside and—"

To his shock, tears welled up in Jemmy's eyes. "I pwomise she won't make a mess."

"But…"

Then it hit him. Jemmy had never stood up for himself, much less another creature. Somehow he was identifying with this scrawny little chicken and was willing to risk Will's disapproval so he could take care of her. Will had no idea how Albert would respond to it, but he couldn't stomp all over this leap in Jemmy's emotional progress.

"You promise to clean up after her, like Miss Olivia did when she cleaned your hand?"

He nodded, and a wobbly grin appeared.

"Can you use your words?"

"I pwomise."

"Okay, then. We'll have to ask Mr. Albert if it's okay, but I don't think he'll mind." The old man had told them to make themselves at home. Hopefully, that included housing a chicken in Jemmy's bedroom. Will would have to devise some sort of pen to keep Pecky from roaming— and messing—all over the house.

Emily, who'd been watching with hopeful curiosity, clapped her hands. "She can lay her eggs on your pillow."

This brought a squealy giggle from Jemmy, and both kids hopped around happily.

Will's eyes burned just a bit. Because Dad didn't allow tears, he'd never been a crier, but since his sister's death, he often found his emotions close to the surface. He shook it off with a humorless laugh under his breath. He might not have grown up on the Double Bar M Ranch, but he'd spent a good amount of his childhood there with one of his older cousins, who'd been a father figure to him. The cowboys he knew could break a leg and never shed a tear. With that example of macho behavior and Dad's disapproval, he'd never dared to cry.

"I left half of the eggs with Albert." Olivia

returned with some still in her basket. "Of course, if you plan to do any baking, I can leave these."

"Baking?" He chuckled—then noticed she was serious. "Uh, not today. And Jemmy likes cereal, so we don't eat many eggs for breakfast."

"Yes, I noticed the box of junk you feed him. Sugar, chemicals, food coloring and marshmallows. Aren't you worried about his health? His teeth?"

Oh, great. Just what Aunt Lila Rose had told him. And he still hadn't made Jemmy's first dental appointment.

Olivia wasn't finished. "You should give him yogurt. Homemade granola. Even homemade pancakes. With pure maple syrup, of course."

"Right. I'll have to think about that." Annoyance threaded up his chest. "You got any of that homemade granola we could try?"

"Of course. I'll bring some over later."

"Fine."

"Good." She motioned to Emily, who quickly obeyed. "Come along, sweet pea. You still have your lessons to finish."

To Will's surprise, the little girl made no complaint, but merely said goodbye to Jemmy and skipped after her mother with her usual happy face. What child could so cheerfully leave a playmate to do homework? Was it the difference between girls and boys? Or was Will just remiss in one more thing? Was it time to start Jemmy's schooling? His one day in preschool had been a disaster, so maybe this homeschooling thing was the way to go.

So now he had two things to ask Olivia's advice on. How to feed Jemmy and how to educate him. If he asked anyone else, other than Aunt Lila Rose, they might question his competence to raise his nephew. After five months of taking care of Jemmy, he wouldn't let himself think about losing him. In fact, he'd fight tooth and nail to be the dad the boy needed. The dad Will never had.

CHAPTER SIX

OLIVIA PUT THE roast in the oven and set the timer. "Supper's cooking, Dad. We'll be back in a half hour. Maybe a little more."

"Sounds good." Dad set his Bible on the dining table and fetched a cup of coffee. "Take your walking stick and watch for snakes."

"Oh, you don't have to tell me twice." Olivia shuddered. Somehow she had to overcome her fear of snakes so she didn't pass it on to Emily. Those slithery creatures weren't the only dangerous species making their homes by the Rio Grande.

Out in the afternoon sunshine, she and Emily stopped by the pasture shed and fed the horses their daily oats. Then they walked beyond their property and climbed the fifteen-foot-high berm that bordered the river, from where Olivia studied the fast-flowing river.

"See how high the water is? In a few weeks, when it floods, it will come up even higher."

Emily's forehead scrunched up, as it did when she had a question. "Will it come this high?"

"No." She turned and waved a hand toward Fred, Dawson and Buffy as they grazed on the spring grass. "See how level our pasture is? That was caused by the floods that came this way for many centuries. The men who built the berm years ago knew just how high to build it so our land would be protected."

Emily nodded soberly, then gave Olivia her usual sunny smile. "Grampy said he'll take me fishing."

"Sounds like fun." Olivia wouldn't mention that state officials discouraged eating fish in this part of the river. And she wasn't sure it would be safe for Emily to be so close to the river even if she learned to swim. "Let's keep walking."

They continued along the top of the berm for several minutes before descending to the bend in the road that marked the south boundary of their property. Will and Jemmy came down the road from the other direction and appeared to be exploring, too. Oddly, her heart kicked up a bit, but she dismissed her reaction as merely surprise over encountering them. After all, she hadn't seen them since they'd cleaned out the chicken coop together two days ago.

"Jemmy!" Emily ran toward her friend, and they embraced, then danced around, as they usually did.

Olivia laughed out loud. "Oh, the pure joy of children."

"So true." Will chuckled as he came closer. "And good afternoon to you, Olivia. What brings you out this fine spring day?" His blue eyes sparkled, and he gave her his usual, white-toothed smile.

Her pulse quickened as her inner defenses went on sudden alert. She looked away to focus on the kids, who were walking hand in hand toward some cardboard boxes someone had dumped near the road. "Recess from home-schooling. Emily, wait. Don't touch those boxes." She hurried toward them.

"Hold up, buddy!" Will called out. "Might be a skunk hiding in there."

Olivia snorted. "A skunk?"

He shrugged and whispered to her, "Not as scary sounding as, say, a snake?"

Even so, his warning wasn't enough to stop the children. Before Olivia and Will could reach them, they were already moving the boxes aside.

"Emily!" Olivia's heart jumped to her throat.

"Mommy, look." Emily lifted a tiny, whimpering black-and-white creature and cuddled it to her chest. "A puppy." It began to lick her face.

"Puppy!" Jemmy squealed as he pulled another one from beneath the boxes.

"Wow." Will kneeled by his nephew, who struggled to hold on to the wiggly little dog. "Look at that. What a busy little guy."

"Oh, my." Olivia crouched by Emily and instinctively petted the adorable creature. "Are there any more?"

Will moved the boxes around. "Nope. Just the two." He examined the one Jemmy held. "Somebody just dumped these little guys." Jemmy's eyes widened, and his mouth dropped open. Will paused. "I mean, maybe somebody couldn't take care of them."

"Or forgot they were in the box when they threw it away," Emily said.

Count on her daughter to find a less dismal viewpoint. Olivia took a closer look at the puppy Emily held as it tried to latch on to her finger. "Their eyes are open, but I don't think they're weaned." She turned it over. "This one's a female."

"Wonder where the mother is." Will scanned

the landscape on the other side of the barbed-wire fence. "Can't see any signs of her."

"Too bad. We have so many coyotes out here. I'm glad they didn't find these little ones."

"Yeah." He leaned down to whisper in her ear. "What do you want to do?" His warm breath sent a pleasant shiver down her side.

She moved away. "Well, we sure can't leave them here."

"May I keep her?" Her daughter's soulful expression was mirrored by Jemmy's look at Will.

"Uh, um…" Olivia scrambled to think of a reason to say no. Nothing came to mind. In fact, her own heart longed to adopt this helpless creature. "At the very least," she whispered back to Will, "we have to take care of them for now."

"Unka Weeoo?" Jemmy's entire being begged the same question. "Can I keep him?"

Grimacing, Will looked at Olivia. "Got any ideas?"

"None at all. Oh, except that they have fleas." She couldn't bring herself to grab the whimpering animal from her daughter and put it back in the box. That would break Emily's heart… and her own. She'd have to find a way to get rid of the fleas later. Besides, these babies had no one else to help them.

She traded a look of resignation with Will. He nodded and gave her a half smile. In that brief moment of camaraderie, she recalled how she and Sancho had solved problems together. Two heads were definitely better than one in situations like this.

"Well, buddy." Will touched Jemmy's shoulder. "Looks like we've got some dogs to take care of. What do you think we should do first?"

"Feed them," Emily said.

"Fee' dem," Jemmy echoed.

"Well, there's that." Olivia laughed. "But I have no idea what to feed puppies."

"Tell you what." Will picked up Jemmy and his puppy. "I'll take them to my friend who's a vet. She'll have everything we need."

She? Irrational jealousy nipped at Olivia's mind. What on earth? "Sounds good."

"Let's go, then," Will said. "I'll drive. That is, if you don't mind."

"Not at all." She pulled out her cell phone and texted Dad to explain what they were doing. A few seconds later, he replied with several emojis—a dog, a grinning face, a celebratory balloon—all a clear approval of the puppy.

Dad sure did love his emojis. She sent back a heart and a thumbs-up.

They walked around her property's perimeter to Albert's driveway and up to the house, where Will's truck was parked. He put Jemmy in his car seat, along with the puppy he'd chosen. Olivia hustled over to her car, which was parked behind her house, retrieved Emily's car seat and buckled her in beside Jemmy.

"Hold on to this little girl," Olivia said.

"Her name is Bitsy," Emily announced. "Jemmy, name yours Sport."

"No!" His outburst surprised them all.

"That's okay, buddy." Will patted the puppy's head. "What do you want to call him?"

"Buddy."

Will grinned. "Sounds good to me. That okay with you, Miss Emily?"

"Yes, sir." Emily was too involved with her own pup to mind the contradiction.

"So." Olivia joined Will in front, settling herself in the passenger-side bucket seat. "Bitsy and Buddy. An overload of cuteness."

Will laughed. It was a throaty baritone sound that she enjoyed a little too much. Olivia had to remind herself not to get distracted by it. Instead, as they drove along the dirt roads, she basked in the music of the kids chatting and giggling in the back seat. In some ways, she could see Jemmy was as good for her daughter as Emily was for him.

"Here comes the bump," Will called over his shoulder as they neared the final turn before reaching the highway.

Before she could brace herself, the truck bounced into and out of a dip in the dirt road, briefly jarring her.

"Bump." Will glanced in the rearview mirror.

"Bump!" Jemmy shouted, then giggled.

"Bump." Emily giggled, too.

As they sped along the highway, Olivia stared out the side window and released a quiet, melancholy sigh. This was what her life was supposed to be. Family outings, Sancho driving. Emily and Daniel safely secured in the back seat...

"Quarter for your thoughts." Will shot her his infamous smile.

She shook off her downward-spiraling mood. "A quarter? Aren't you the big spender? What happened to a penny?"

"Inflation."

Now, she laughed out loud. "Right."

Against her better judgment, she had to put aside her memories of the past and choose to enjoy this day with Emily and Jemmy. And, begrudgingly, with Will, as they took on the puppy project for their kids.

SEEING OLIVIA RELAX a bit, Will allowed himself to enjoy the moment. With the puppies diverting their attention to a common cause, maybe they could even find a way to be friends.

It hadn't taken more than a beat for him to say yes to Jemmy keeping the puppy. His nephew had found yet another needy animal to care for, something Will would encourage. It might be the key to his coming all the way out of his shell.

Will's dad had never let him have any pets, but he'd loved playing with the dogs at the Double Bar M Ranch. He had to admire Olivia for letting Emily keep the other pup. Some women he knew were too fussy to deal with animals who needed a lot of attention, like dogs. Not his female ranch cousins, of course. But his last girlfriend wouldn't even tolerate a cat. Or a child. Olivia seemed to have opened her arms and her heart to his nephew. Not to Will, of course. He could see in her eyes she didn't trust him. Considering their conflict over Albert's property, he couldn't blame her too much.

Maybe after this nonsense about who got to buy the land was over and done with, he and Olivia could be friends. He'd win, of course, and move in to be her permanent neighbor, so being friendly was important, especially out here in the boondocks, where good people looked out for one another.

He drove up the highway toward town, past adobe houses and small touristy businesses that spotted the landscape. Olivia gazed out the passenger-side window, occasionally turning her attention to the road ahead. Her profile was a work of art... *Wait*. Where on earth had that thought come from? Hadn't he decided not to think about her but to concentrate on caring for Jemmy and Aunt Lila Rose's boys? On the other hand, when a beauty like Olivia crossed his path, how could he *not* think about her?

He couldn't believe the way she'd agreed to the trip to town, had just grabbed Emily's car seat and jumped into his truck with no hesitation. Most women, even Aunt Lila Rose, demanded time to fix their hair and makeup before going out in public. Not that Olivia needed to fix anything. She even seemed unaware of her own appearance. Didn't feel the need to tuck strands of that gorgeous black hair behind her ear in a flirtatious gesture, or look his way with coy glances from beneath those long black eyelashes. Instead, her focus was on the external world, on other people and their needs. Even her business of hosting artists came from her nurturing ways.

There he went, appreciating her many fine qualities again. Somehow, he had to cram all of these thoughts in a box to be tucked away. Or dropped in the Rio Grande to flow south and out of sight.

Ha! That's not likely to happen.

He pulled into the vet's parking lot, glad to see only a few cars. Maybe they could get right in and take care of these little critters, who must be starving, if their sad little whimpers were any indication.

"I can't believe it." Olivia stared out the windshield at the sign over the front entrance. "*Mattson* Veterinary Clinic. Is there anything your family doesn't own around here?" She shot him a sarcastic look as she grasped the door handle. "I thought you said this vet is your friend."

Instead of being annoyed by her comment about his family, Will laughed. "She is a friend.

She's also married to my first cousin twice removed. Or three times. I can't remember."

Olivia rolled her eyes as she opened the door.

No, she didn't flirt with him. Or give a hoot
about his family's long lineage. And given his
history with women who flirted with him because they assumed he was rich, that was a relief.

Sort of.

WHILE WILL SAW to Jemmy and Buddy, Olivia
helped Emily from the car. Her daughter held
tightly to Bitsy, who now slept in her arms. So
far, the fleas didn't seem to be on her. Maybe
they preferred to hide under Bitsy's fur. But
Emily would need a good bath before bed tonight.

Inside the clinic, Will was greeted by the receptionist, a perky, dark-haired young woman
who looked like she might be a Mattson, too.

"Olivia, this is my cousin, June." He winked
at the girl. "Her mom, Sue, the cousin by marriage I mentioned, is the vet, and June helps out.
June, meet my neighbor, Olivia Ortiz, and her
daughter, Emily."

"Howdy, Miss Olivia, Emily. Hey there,
Jemmy." June, who appeared to be around

nineteen or twenty, came around the counter and kneeled by Emily. "What do we have here?"

"This is Bitsy." Emily returned June's smile. "That's Buddy." She looked at Jemmy expectantly, but he moved closer to Will.

"Well, how do you do, Bitsy." June petted the puppy. "Would you let me take a look at this little cutie?"

Emily surrendered her new treasure. "She's hungry."

"She sure is." Letting the puppy latch on to her finger, June laughed, then looked at Will and whispered, "No mama?"

He shook his head.

"Well, we've got just the thing." June turned to Jemmy. "Hi, Jemmy. I'm guessing Buddy's hungry, too. Will you let me give him something to eat?"

Jemmy shook his head and clutched the puppy tighter.

"No problem." June addressed both Will and Olivia. "I'll be right back."

Within minutes, she'd found bottles and milk, and had settled both kids on the waiting room couch with their puppies. "We'll get them fed before Mom checks them out." She leaned toward Olivia as though they were old friends and whispered, "And we'll get rid of those fleas."

"Tell you what." Will sat next to Jemmy. "After you feed your little buddy, we'll let June and her mom give him a checkup while we go buy him some gear."

Olivia watched the brief confusion on the boy's face. "Geuw?" As usual, he couldn't quite manage the *r*.

"Sure. He'll need toys and stuff, maybe a bed of his own."

"An' a ball."

"Definitely a ball." Will tousled Jemmy's hair.

Emily had watched the interaction with interest. She looked at Olivia. "Bitsy needs gear, too."

"Definitely."

Will winked at Olivia. And gave her that infamous smile.

Ugh! Why had she echoed his word choice? Would he take that as some sort of camaraderie?

The kids reluctantly left their new charges in June's capable hands, and soon they were on their way to the local big-box store. As they drove into the lot, Jemmy whimpered.

"Oops. I forgot." Glancing in the rearview mirror, Will whispered to Olivia, "He doesn't like this place."

As he drove out of the parking lot, Olivia bit her lip to keep from commenting. His sensitivity toward his nephew's feelings was well and good, but it could easily turn into his raising a spoiled little boy who got his way all too easily.

Then again, who was she to criticize another parent? Hadn't she let Emily keep the puppy with hardly a thought? She'd have to watch herself. Besides, Will was doing a good job with his nephew. She could respect him for that.

Now, if he would only bow out of the competition for Albert's property, she might even find herself liking the man.

CHAPTER SEVEN

WILL DELIBERATELY DROVE past the pet store owned by one of his cousins to avoid annoying Olivia...again. Instead, he chose a larger chain pet store and was glad Jemmy didn't voice any objections, maybe because he could see the dog and cat pictures painted on the window.

Inside, they found the dog department, and with a little guidance, the kids chose toys and treats. They also chose puppy-size beds, indoor kennels, collars and other supplies. Jemmy and Emily both took this task very seriously. No giggling now, just careful study of the offered merchandise and a glance or two at their respective adult before final decisions were made.

Will's heart warmed as he watched his nephew. He'd done pretty well with Pecky, and this added responsibility should further boost his self-confidence. Whether the chicken and puppy got along was a problem they'd have to solve if and when it came up.

At the checkout, he pulled out his wallet. "I'll get this." She hadn't brought a purse, and it wouldn't hurt him to spend a few bucks for Jemmy's friend.

"You don't need to do that." Olivia held up her phone. "Apple Pay." She separated Emily's stuff and shoved it toward the clerk, not giving Will a chance to object.

Not that he would. Again, she was proving herself to be different from the other women he'd known. More independent. Not expecting him to pay for everything. Certainly not clingy. He had to respect that. And if he was being honest, he'd have to admit he was relieved, too.

Back in the truck, the kids chatted about their plans for their new pets. They sounded so serious he couldn't help but smile. When their chatter became silly, Olivia coughed, apparently trying to stifle a laugh. It was the first time he'd noticed her sense of humor.

"Bitsy's gonna jump this high," Emily said.

Will could imagine her holding up a hand.

"Buddy's gonna jump dis high."

Will glanced in the rearview mirror. Yep.

Jemmy's hand was higher than Emily's. Of course, his car seat was a different, higher design and gave him the advantage. And then there was the matter of training the pups *not* to jump, but they would cross that bridge when they came to it.

"Bitsy's gonna eat this much."

"Buddy's gonna eat this much."

After their giggling slowed down, Emily said, "Mommy, I'm hungry."

Will caught Olivia's eye and mouthed, *Ice cream?*

Her eyes brightened, enhancing her beauty. "Sounds good. Drive-through?"

"Right up ahead."

"Perfect."

Perfect indeed. She was turning out to be a pretty good partner in this adventure. He could see enjoying more of the same. No, he'd better shut down that thought right away.

At the order kiosk, they made their choices with little debate. When Emily asked for strawberry ice cream in a cone, Jemmy said he wanted the same. After picking up their order at the window, Will pulled into a parking spot, where he and Olivia put the provided plastic bibs on the kids before giving them their treat.

Even so, Jemmy ended up with ice cream all over his face and hands. Emily managed a little better.

"Got any wet wipes?" Olivia looked around the truck cabin.

"Ugh. Meant to get some for the truck, but forgot."

She shrugged. "You got the ice cream. I'll get the wipes."

Before he could object, she trotted to the convenience store next door and returned with the needed item. The wipes did the job on the kids but left smears on his gray leather seats. He couldn't help an involuntary grimace.

"Parenting sure can be messy." Olivia gave him a sympathetic smile.

"Right." He'd known that when he signed up to care for Jemmy. But a man had a hard time releasing his pride in his truck.

Back at Sue's vet clinic, the kids got excited before they were out of the car. Both were jumping around and giggling. Will was getting used to the music of that sound.

After he introduced Olivia to his cousin Sue, they let the kids hold their puppies on the waiting-room couch, then got down to business.

"These could be purebred border collies like

the ones they raise out at the ranch, but it's hard to tell at this age," Sue said. "With papers, purebreds go for about two grand apiece. Pretty expensive to be abandoned on a remote road. Did you find anything around them that might tell us where they came from?"

"Nope," Will said. "I doubt they're from the ranch. Rob keeps tabs on everything that happens out there, and he values his dogs too much to let them go missing. And nothing in the cardboard boxes gave us a clue. Could they possibly have chips?"

"No, they're way too young." Sue blew out a breath. "You need to wait until they're eight to twelve weeks old to do that. But it looks like they have a good home. For now. Just remember, if the mother's owner comes looking for them, you may have to give them up."

"Or offer a lower price." Olivia's jaw was set just as it had been when he met her last week and she found out Will wanted to buy Albert's land. This lady didn't like to be crossed by anyone threatening her or her loved ones. While that trait might work against him, he had to respect her for it. He would do anything to protect and care for Jemmy and Aunt Lila Rose's boys.

"I don't know if that would work," he said. "Breeders need to make a profit."

"Whatever. For now, let's just get them home." Olivia walked to the couch and reached out a hand to Emily. "I just remembered I have a roast in the oven. If my dad doesn't take it out when the timer goes off, we'll be eating a brick for supper." She helped her daughter cradle Bitsy. "It was nice to meet you, Sue. June."

"Likewise," the mother and daughter chorused.

June handed Will a plastic bag with the clinic's logo on it. "This is everything you need to feed them and work on the rest of those fleas."

"Thanks. Send me the bill."

"Send half to me." Olivia smirked at Will. Ouch. She really wasn't taking anything from him.

"Say, Jemmy." June kneeled beside him. "I sure would like to see you in my Sunday school class. We play games, have snacks and, best of all, learn all about Jesus."

Jemmy ducked his chin and moved back from her, but she kept smiling as she stood. "Emily, I'd love to see you in my class, too."

Emily returned the smile, then looked up at Olivia. "Mommy, can I go?"

Olivia sighed. "We'll see."

Sue and June followed them out to the truck, chatting with Will about family stuff. Olivia seemed to be trying not to eavesdrop, but he was glad she couldn't avoid hearing that he came from good people, that the Mattson name was respected in this town. Maybe that would motivate her to send a little respect his way, too.

OLIVIA SETTLED EMILY in the back seat of the truck before taking her place in the front. Beside Will. No way to avoid it. And no way to avoid the fact that he came from a nice family. June and Sue couldn't have been gentler with the puppies. Olivia would bring Bitsy back when it came time to spay her.

If someone came forward to claim the pups, well, she'd figure out how to help Emily overcome her disappointment. How would Will help Jemmy do the same? Not her problem.

But if that was so, why did she feel a pang of concern for the little boy?

"Need anything at the grocery store?" Will waved a hand toward the store coming up ahead on the right.

"No, I don't think so."

"You mind if we stop? I hate to waste a trip to town."

She shrugged. "Sure." She texted Dad to take the roast out of the oven.

He answered, Already done, and added a smiling emoji. Count on him to watch her back.

The store personnel didn't appear to object to two kids carrying puppies in the shopping carts their adults guided around the store. Olivia pushed her cart around the aisles and picked up several items she didn't need right away. But it would save her an extra trip later this week.

Once she and Emily rejoined Will and Jemmy at checkout, she couldn't ignore the sugar-laden cereals and junk food in their cart. Before she could stop herself, she snorted her disapproval.

"I suppose you have a Mattson relative who's a dentist who's going to save his teeth."

Confusion in his expression was quickly replaced by awareness. "Oh. Yeah. Well, we do get all the eggs we need from our hens, so I can make him scrambled eggs for breakfast." He grinned boyishly. "And look—I did get the orange juice with no sugar. And the no-nitrate bacon. And apples." He blinked those blue eyes, sending a jolt to her heart. "How'd I do, Mom?"

Smirking, she lifted the two boxes of cereal and a bag of chemical-flavored chips from the cart and set them on a shelf beside the checkout. "There. That's better."

"But Mom…" He reached for the chips.

Trying not to grin and failing, she smacked his hand. "No."

Now, he laughed out loud. "Yes, ma'am."

Somehow, Jemmy hadn't noticed their playful exchange, but Emily had. She grinned at both Olivia and Will. What was her daughter thinking? She really must stop this nonsense. Who in their right mind joked with the enemy, much less told them what they could or could not feed their child?

Heading home, Will drove past Albert's driveway and around to hers, then insisted on helping her take her groceries inside. Jemmy and Emily followed, puppies in hand.

"Well, what do we have here?" Dad bent down and pulled both kids into his arms. "What fine little doggies." He gently touched the pups and uttered silly words at them. Both children giggled and let him take their charges in hand.

Will stared at the scene, eyes wide, his jaw dropping.

"What?" Despite asking, Olivia understood right away. Today, Jemmy was taking to her dad without fear. "Progress," she whispered to Will.

His eyes rimmed red, he nodded. What a tender heart he had for his nephew.

And her own heart took another serious dip, like the big dip in the road to town. And just as jarring to her nerves.

"Oops." Dad stood and carried one wet puppy to the door. "They're sure not house-trained at this age. Kids, let's take them out to the porch and set down some newspapers. Then I'll get a rag to clean this up."

With Olivia and Will helping, the mess and her father were quickly cleaned up. Then Dad faced them. "So, who's going to keep them overnight?"

Just like they'd done all day, they exchanged a look, as if consulting each other came naturally.

"I assumed we'd let them stay with their new owners," Olivia said.

"Yeah." Will glanced toward the porch, where the kids now played with their furry new best friends. "We bought kennels for them to sleep in overnight."

Dad chuckled. "If you separate them, you won't be getting any sleep. They'll be howling all night missing each other. And their mama, of course."

Another shared look. If Olivia guessed correctly, her expression mirrored Will's. Eyebrows raised and jaws dropped as Dad's words sank in.

"Ho, boy." Will scrubbed a hand down his cheek, where a five-o'clock shadow had begun to appear. "Sure didn't think this through, did we?" His crooked grin sent a ping through her chest.

"Nope." She huffed out a humorless laugh that quickly morphed into a true giggle. "Any idea how to solve this?" She glanced at both men for input.

"Why not ask the children?" Nona entered the room from the back, as she'd done every afternoon since she'd arrived. Apparently, she'd heard enough of the dilemma to offer this bit of advice.

"Good idea." Dad grinned at her with a warm, familiar look that would have concerned Olivia if she didn't have a more pressing matter to deal with.

"Okay. Let's do it." Will walked to the door and called the kids in.

Emily danced into the room, cradling Bitsy in her arms. Jemmy slowly followed, clutching Buddy and looking at the adults warily. Poor little guy, so afraid of so many things. Olivia resisted the urge to sweep him up in a big hug and promise he had nothing to fear. But that would scare him more than anything. Besides, she had no right to make promises to a child who wasn't her own.

"So, kids." Will squatted down to eye level with them. "These little critters are just babies, so they need to stay together for a while longer or they might be scared and lonely. That means they'll have to stay here or over at Mr. Albert's house until they're a little older. What do you think we should do?" The tenderness in his eyes warmed Olivia's heart.

The kids looked at each other. Jemmy seemed about to cry, but Emily smiled. "Bitsy can sleep over with Jemmy and Buddy tonight. Then tomorrow night, they can stay with me."

When did her daughter become as wise as Solomon and as unselfish as The Giving Tree in the story Emily loved so much? Olivia couldn't speak for the lump in her throat.

From the soft look in his eyes, Will seemed as moved as she was.

"That's real sweet of you, Emily," he said. "Jemmy, what do you think? Can you take care of both puppies tonight and let Emily do it tomorrow night?"

Jemmy's face scrunched up, as though he was thinking it over. Then he nodded.

Will touched Jemmy's shoulder. "Use your words, buddy."

Jemmy blinked in his adorable way. "I can ta' cawe." As usual, his *r* came out as a *w*.

The relief swirling around the adults seemed almost physical, like a fresh breeze sweeping in from outdoors, uniting them all in the common cause of caring for these kids. But a nudge of concern teased at Olivia's mind. Once again, the solution had come from giving in to Jemmy's fears. Not that she thought Will should deny the boy security. But one of these days, he would have to tell him no for something or other...or end up with a child who demanded his own way all the time.

She would have to watch herself or she might be tempted to interfere, as she had in the grocery store. It was one thing to take sugary, chemical-laden cereals from Will's shopping cart—which she still couldn't believe she'd done. It was another thing entirely to intrude on his parenting.

But with their lives becoming so intertwined because of the kids and their puppies, and, of course, Albert's upcoming birthday bash, how would she be able to stop herself?

"IT'LL BE MIGHTY fine to have dogs around again," Albert said as he helped Will and Jemmy set up the puppies' wire kennel in Jemmy's bedroom. "It's been a few years since my last one."

"Yes, sir. I know what you mean." Will was glad the old gentleman stopped before telling them whatever had happened to that last one, most likely having died of old age. Jemmy didn't need to worry about death. He'd already seen too much of that in his few years. "Dogs can bring lots of fun to our lives, can't they?"

"And companionship." Albert nudged Jemmy's shoulder. "You gonna take good care of these little rascals?"

Picking Buddy up, Jemmy nodded soberly.

Will softly cleared his throat and gave him a questioning look.

"Yes, suw," Jemmy said.

Will smiled and winked at him. After being told to shut up for most of his short life, he was learning it was okay, expected even, for him to speak up at appropriate times.

The midsize kennel had plenty of room for the dog bed and space for them to move around. After giving them their bottles—a messy operation requiring several large terry towels to absorb all the slobbered liquid—Will covered the kennel floor with a disposable absorbent mat.

"That should make cleanup a little easier." He set Bitsy inside and reached out for Buddy.

Jemmy still clutched his puppy. "I can do it." As serious as a judge, he gently set his tired little friend inside the enclosure. Looking around, he picked up Pecky, who'd been watching the whole operation with interest. "Pecky, want to go in, too?" He started to put the little chicken inside the kennel, but she squawked and jumped out of his arms. She then strutted back to her boxed perch beside Jemmy's bed in what, to Will's view, seemed like a huff. He snorted out a laugh, and Albert joined him.

"A little jealousy going on there," Albert said.

Jemmy looked from his chicken to his puppy, then up at Will, his little face scrunched with worry.

"It's okay. They'll sort it out, buddy." He'd have to find a different nickname for Jemmy now that the dog had that moniker. Pal? Short Stuff? Did he dare call him *son*? No. Not yet.

Earlier, while the kids were still playing with the pups over at Olivia's, Will had gone out to the site where they'd been abandoned to clean up the cardboard for carrying to the dump. He also searched beyond the barbed-wire fence that lined the other side of the road but found no traces of the mother. Because they were so young and not yet weaned, she must be missing them. And, if she was purebred, as Sue had speculated, surely somebody would be looking for her valuable offspring.

With the animals now settled, Will turned his attention to supper. Olivia had sent over a generous portion of roast beef with all the trimmings and three slices of her amazing carrot cake. Since he'd met her almost a week ago, when she'd learned about Albert's paltry food supplies, she'd checked every day to be sure the old man had at least one nourishing meal, with Will and Jemmy reaping the benefits of her cooking as well. With her natural gift for hospitality, no wonder she wanted to expand her business.

While dishing out the meal, he glanced around the dine-in kitchen and through the door into the large living room. This house was a little bigger than Olivia's place, with five bedrooms, a den and three bathrooms. Most rooms were cluttered with furniture and boxes filled with generations of memorabilia.

Yesterday, Will had found Albert sitting at his desk staring at a pile of papers, seeming unable to figure out what to do with each page. Will had offered to help him, and the old man gratefully accepted. Now, they had files for the important documents, with the rest going through the shredder. Then Albert had asked for help with the disposal of the antique furniture his grandson didn't want. Will suggested Olivia might want some of the pieces. In fact, he could envision the way she'd use these rooms for her artist clients. They'd probably love some of the solid nineteenth-century tables, cabinets and sideboards.

Why was he thinking about it from her point of view? His lawyer training, he supposed. Trying to understand a situation from both sides. But it all came down to one unchangeable point: artists and writers could live and work anywhere, while his boys needed this particular property for safety and security. Somehow, he must win the right to buy it. But could he do that without losing his, for lack of a better word, *friendship* with Olivia? Or Jemmy's all-important friendship with sweet little Emily?

In the past several days since meeting each other, the kids had formed a bond as close as he and Megan had enjoyed while growing up in their dysfunctional home. A bond that had been broken when wild, dangerous Ed came roaring up on his motorcycle and swept Megan away to what was supposed to be an exciting life. It'd been exciting, all right, but not what his naive sister had imagined. He still didn't know how he would explain to Jemmy what a mess his parents' lives had been. Or when to do it. He'd have to do it before some busybody told the boy about the tragedy of their deaths.

He blew out a long breath. It never did any good to recall those days. If he did what scripture said and thought about things that were true and virtuous and worthy of praise, he'd have a better perspective on everything. Today's crazy and unexpected turn of events came to mind. From the discovery of the puppies, to the shopping trip, to the fun he and Jemmy had with Olivia and Emily, *those* were worthy of praise. As they'd driven back home, he'd almost felt like he had his own little family. But, of course, that could never happen, not with

Olivia being so stubborn and not even liking him. She would never back down, and when he bought the property, she might not let Emily play with Jemmy. He sighed again.

Lord, only You can give us a solution that works for all of us.

With the futures of Jemmy and Aunt Lila Rose's boys on the line, he was sure God would give them this perfect place to live. Wouldn't He?

CHAPTER EIGHT

"So, IT LOOKS like you and our hero had a fun day." The glint in Nona's eyes matched the teasing grin she sent Olivia across the supper table.

"Oh, yes." Olivia refused to rise to the bait. Nona hadn't stopped teasing her about Will. "Jemmy is quite the hero for the way he—and Emily, of course—insisted on rescuing those darling little puppies."

While Dad glanced back and forth between them, Nona chuckled. "Right. Such a heroic little boy." A hint of irony colored her voice.

"Jemmy's my best friend." Emily gave Olivia a worried look. "I never had a best friend."

Uh-oh. Her daughter had begun to pick up on unspoken cues hiding in the adults' tones. "Yes, he is, sweet pea. I'm so glad you like to play with him. And I know he'll take good care of Bitsy and Buddy tonight."

Redirection usually worked, as it did now, when Emily's sweet smile returned.

"Me too." She returned to her supper, daintily picking at the broccoli she didn't care for but knew she had to eat, helped by a drizzle of melted cheese. "And tomorrow night, I get to take care of them."

"Yes, you do." Even though Olivia knew she'd do most of the work, she found herself looking forward to this new adventure. "Nona, how's your book coming?" She'd finished reading Nona's last release yesterday evening and looked forward to the sequel.

"It's coming." She chuckled in her throaty alto way. "My characters just don't mind very well, so I'm finding the story going in a different direction."

While Olivia gaped, Dad nodded with interest and perhaps some understanding.

"What do you mean your characters don't mind very well?" Olivia said. "Don't you just write what you want them to do?"

"I wish." Nona rolled her eyes. "I always have a plan and a basic outline for my stories, but sometimes I find myself writing something entirely different because of the way my characters speak to me."

"That's the genius of creativity." Dad nodded sagely, as if he totally grasped the idea. Or maybe he wanted to impress Nona. Not that he needed to. The woman clearly liked him. A lot.

Olivia shook her head. She'd always thought writers and painters knew exactly how to ply their art. Maybe that was because she'd always planned her own life. But all her plans had been shattered by Sancho's and Daniel's deaths. And now, her business plans might be shattered as well because of the "character" who'd moved in next door.

How would her story turn out? And how could she get it back on track and write it the way she wanted to?

THE NEXT MORNING Emily hurried through breakfast and urged Olivia to do the same.

"Will Bitsy remember me?" she asked as they headed toward the back door.

"Once you pick her up, she'll be all over you." Olivia saw no need to discourage her by saying puppies usually liked anybody who gave them attention. They didn't become loyal companions until a little older.

Across the fence, she saw Will and Jemmy feeding the chickens, so she grabbed the egg basket by the back door. As they walked through the gate between the properties, Jemmy ran to meet them. As always, the kids gave each other a big hug, nearly falling over in their enthusiasm. And, as always, Olivia and Will laughed, both taking delight in the kids' joy. It was the only thing they agreed on.

While the kids chatted about the puppies, Will ambled over and gave Olivia one of his charming smiles, despite the weary sagging of his handsome features.

"Morning, Olivia. How are you today?"

"Better than you, it looks like." Oops. She shouldn't have been so blunt.

But to her relief, he laughed. "Yep. Those pups were pretty hungry a couple of times in the night. And, of course, they missed their mama and whimpered for quite a while."

Olivia's heart ached for the sad little pups. "And, *of course*, you didn't wake Jemmy to help."

He laughed again. "Nope. Not when he's just begun to sleep through the night without…"

"Ah." She'd been horrified when he'd told her about Jemmy's tragic first years and his recurring nightmares. "Well, it'll be our turn tonight. Dad and I already set up our kennel in Emily's room."

They watched the kids feed the chickens for a few quiet minutes. Will's face, haggard though it appeared, had a sweet glow about it as he focused on the scene.

"I see you let Chirpy out." Olivia noticed the rooster pecking away at the grain and occasionally one of the hens.

"Yeah, he seems to accept Jemmy's not a threat, which is good." He gazed down at her, and there went that smile again. He should pose for toothpaste ads.

Somehow, her dismissive thought about his looks didn't bring the satisfaction it usually did. After yesterday, when he'd performed every task admirably regarding the abandoned puppies, she was finding it difficult to dislike him. Which didn't help her cause. Just the fact that he wanted to destroy her dream should be enough to remind her he was the enemy. Well, *destroy* might be too strong. He simply had alternate plans for the land, but it was land that should be hers.

Oh, she really had to stop this line of thinking.

"Where are the puppies?"

"Asleep in the kennel. As Sue said, they're probably just a couple weeks old, too young to bring them outside."

"Good idea." Why did his instincts have to be so spot-on? And did that mean she'd have to ask his advice as this puppy project proceeded? Since the first day they met, every situation she encountered brought them together. Against her will, she couldn't make herself dislike him, as much as she tried.

"Need anything from town?" Will broke into her musing.

She thought for a moment. "Can't think of anything. Got everything we need yesterday. Do you have to go back?"

"Yeah, I need to go by my Aunt Lila Rose's and visit with her boys. Taking care of the puppies kept me from seeing them last evening. That's not good."

To her surprise, her eyes burned with sudden tears. How could she not respect this man who cared so much for needy boys? "I'm sure they missed you."

He shrugged and gave her a sheepish grin. "What they missed was hearing me read the next chapter of *The Fellowship of the Ring*. Since it's Saturday, I thought I'd catch them up."

"I'm sure they like you reading to them. We read to Emily, too. Right now it's *Black Beauty*. She really loves horses." She studied him for a moment. "But I'm sure those boys missed you being there, too. From what you've said, you're like a foster father to them. I'm sure you remember those fatherly bedtime hugs that gave you a sense of security."

To her surprise, he winced. "Yeah." What was that all about?

He took a step toward the kids. "Hey, Jemmy, we'd better go check on the puppies." To Olivia, he added, "Want to come?"

"Sure. Tell you what. You go ahead while Emily and I get the eggs. Then we'll come in."

"Sounds good."

As he and Jemmy walked toward the house, Olivia had to force her eyes away. If she'd ever wondered what a manly, knight-like stride might look like, Will provided the perfect example. But his reaction to her mention of a father's hug suggested he had a few chinks in his knightly armor. Instead of motivating her to hunt it down and use it to her advantage, that realization touched her heart and made her want to heal him. All against her own, and Emily's, best interests. She really must stop this sympathetic line of thinking when it came to Will Mattson. But how could she do that when they were in each other's company every day in ways she could not escape?

WILL STUDIED THE tattered stolen-dog poster on the hardware store's message board and could see the markings on the purebred female looked similar to the puppies' coloring. The poster added that she answers to "Lady" and her return would garner a sizable reward. Stolen about five months ago, she could've been bred and given birth during that time. But why would the thieves dump the puppies? As much as he wanted to ignore this poster to protect Jemmy and Emily from losing their new pets, he had to do the responsible thing. He snapped a picture of the poster, then pulled off one of the phone-number tags at the bottom to call later this evening.

Jemmy looked up at him with trusting eyes. "We get 'nother puppy?" He pointed to the picture.

"No, pal. At least not yet." Will gave him a side hug. "We've got enough to do taking care of Buddy, don't you think?"

Jemmy nodded and gave him a rare full-blown grin. "Buddy's lots of work." His expression turned unsure. "Not too much."

Will tousled his hair. "No, not too much." In fact, he could see how having this responsibility, along with Pecky, had already improved Jemmy's willingness to assert himself.

When Aunt Lila Rose and her boys came out to live with them, he'd have to share Buddy, but Will would cross that bridge when he came to it. Maybe that would be the time to get another dog.

He made the purchases his aunt had requested, then drove over to her house. As usual, the boys ran out and swarmed over him with hugs, each clamoring to tell him his latest news. Today, Jemmy marched up the walk and through the front door, and even returned Aunt Lila Rose's hug.

"That's progress," she whispered as Jemmy plunked himself down in the middle of the couch rather than retreating to the corner. "I'm so pleased."

"Yeah." Will hugged her. "He's really taking this puppy thing seriously." Last evening, after Jemmy was asleep, he'd called her and related the dog saga.

She chuckled in her maternal way. "First a chicken, now a puppy. You're going to be a busy man, Will."

"Yep. Speaking of busy, before I read to the boys, I need to run by the office and sign some paperwork for Sam. Nothing to do with our boys." His cousin was also busy, but had generously taken on Will's workload along with his own. "Can I leave Jemmy with you? Sort of a trial run at encouraging his emotional independence?"

She drew in a long breath, then exhaled. "I'll try, but you be sure to keep your phone on."

"Always do."

The plan worked until Will finished his business and was on his way back to her house. When she called, he answered with his hands-free system.

"Drive safely," she said, "but Jemmy needs you, so please don't make any unnecessary stops."

"Just a few blocks away. What's happening?"

She blew out a long sigh. "Well, you know how the boys like to play a little rough. You know I grew up with three brothers, so I understand and let them have their fun. They simply meant to include Jemmy in their wrestling, but he was terrified when Jeffie tumbled him to the floor and rolled him around."

"Did he get hurt?"

"No. In fact, the other boys were having so much fun, they didn't notice Jemmy retreating to his spot in the corner of the couch."

"Crying?"

"No." Her voice hitched. "Shaking like I've never seen before. And he won't let me touch him."

"Be right there." It took all of Will's self-control to keep to the speed limit, although he did blow through an intersection on a yellow light that he would've normally stopped for.

At the house, he tried to settle his anxiety before entering by taking a deep breath. Inside the entryway, he peeked around the wall into the living room. Jemmy was huddled in the corner of the couch, eyes wide. The four other boys gradually untangled themselves and greeted him.

"We're gonna read now." Nine-year-old Benji, the undisputed leader of this little gang, grabbed the book from a side table, then plopped down on the couch.

The other three took their usual places on chairs or the floor, and Will settled in his spot between Benji and Jemmy. He started to reach out to his nephew, but Jemmy lunged toward him and snuggled under his arm, thumb in his mouth.

Will again settled his rising emotions and cleared his throat. "Hey, guys. Ready to hear the story?"

While the other boys said yes, Jemmy just stared down at the book.

"All right." Will found the page where he'd left off two nights ago. "Let's see what Frodo's up to."

After reading the chapter, he took the boys to the backyard to shoot some hoops. When he'd first started coming over to help Aunt Lila Rose, he'd lowered the hoop to a reachable height for these guys. His cousins—his aunt's three kids—had grown up in this house and always held healthy competitions on the basketball court. Still a bit too small to hold the ball, Jemmy sat on the back stoop and watched, as usual. He'd settled down during the reading and seemed okay now. As Will dribbled the ball and let his more aggressive boys snag it from him, he had an idea.

After spending a few minutes listening to each boy talk about his week, Will promised to pick them up for Sunday school in the morning. Then he and Jemmy drove to the big-box store. Although his nephew didn't like the store, once Will told him his plan, he agreed to go inside.

Purchases made, they drove back to the ranch, as he'd started to call Albert's property. This was going to be fun, and he sent up a prayer Olivia would think so, too. Once she saw what a great place it was for bringing up needy boys, maybe she'd change her mind and give up her fight to buy it.

OLIVIA DIDN'T GET much Saturday baking done with two little puppies to tend to. Or, to be honest with herself, two little puppies to *play* with. Dad, and even Nona, suspended all other work and hobbies to do their share of spoiling the pups. And, of course, they were the center of Emily's attention. Everyone took a turn holding their bottles, enjoying the task while it lasted. Sue had advised giving them their milk in a bowl beginning next week.

Late in the afternoon, she glanced outside and across the fence to see Will and Jemmy busy with some project. Emily saw them, too, and dashed out the back door.

"Mommy, it's basketball!" she shouted over her shoulder.

"Emily, wait."

When had her daughter become so independent? She'd never before gone outside without asking permission, but now she seemed to think Jemmy and Will were just an extension of her family. Not good, but what could Olivia do? She followed Emily and soon discovered the cause for her excitement. Will was creating a little basketball court with a plastic child-size hoop and a small ball.

"That looks like fun." She should have done this for Emily long ago. Other than their walks along the river and their occasional horse rides, they didn't get much outdoor exercise.

"Yep." Will shoveled sand into the blue plastic base of the apparatus. "My aunt's boys play basketball, so I thought Jemmy should start learning."

"Good idea." Despite her approving words, she felt a jolt. He was settling in here like he already owned the place.

"Jemmy thought we should invite Emily over to shoot some hoops. What do you think?" He winked at Emily.

"I like it." Emily danced over to Jemmy and took his hand, then frowned. "Are you okay, Jemmy?"

The caution Olivia had seen in the little boy's eyes when they first met had returned. Sympathy welled up inside her. How she would love to embrace him and promise everything would be all right, but that would only frighten him.

Emily peered in the box, picked up the reddish brown mini ball and bounced it toward Jemmy. "Catch."

A small grin appeared as he grabbed at the ball but managed to kick it instead. Both kids giggled as they clumsily chased the small basketball across the yard.

Olivia traded a look with Will. "Did something happen?" she whispered.

He nodded. "The other boys were wrestling and got a little too rough with him. They wanted to include him, but it must have thrown him back to his...former life."

Olivia frowned. "Have you tried counseling? I mean, is there anybody in Riverton who deals with childhood trauma?"

He finished with the sand and pushed the plug into the base. "I have the name of a counselor in Santa Fe. Just been putting it off. Trying to give him a sense of security here first."

Olivia couldn't imagine how she would handle the situation. When Sancho was murdered, Emily had missed him, but she'd been too young to understand why her daddy wasn't there to tuck her in at night anymore. Olivia told her Daddy was in Heaven with Jesus, and eventually, she no longer asked about him. Even with her own heart grieving, Olivia thought it best to give her daughter that sense of security Will spoke of, something every child needed and deserved. As a result, Emily's happy disposition was a joy to everyone who met her.

"Want to play?" Will tossed her a second mini ball. "Let's show them how this game is played."

Catching it, she smirked. "Game on." She bounced the ball on the hard-packed surface Will had swept clean, and took aim at the hoop, which he'd set at about four feet.

Before she could release it, he slapped it out of her hands, then swirled around and easily tossed it into the basket. He raised his arms and shouted, "Score!"

Snatching up the ball, Olivia couldn't hold in a laugh. "Emily, Jemmy. Let's gang up on this big guy."

"Hey," Will protested. "Guys against girls."

"Humph. No way." She tossed the ball in a perfect arc, landing it in the little basket.

Emily and Jemmy joined the fun and soon they were tossing the ball in wild abandon, giggling whether they made baskets or not with the two balls. They didn't even seem to notice when Olivia and Will backed off to the side to watch.

"What a great idea." Olivia looked up at Will, as always a little intimidated by his height. "When you move back to town, I'll buy it from you for Emily."

He snorted out a laugh. "Pretty sure of yourself, aren't you? I've got big plans for this place, starting with winning our Independence Day competition." He winked and gave her that white-toothed grin.

Which tickled something deep inside her. A reaction to his attractiveness? She quickly shut that down.

"You wish." She sniffed with fake annoyance. Or maybe it wasn't fake. Why had she ever agreed to their competition? This guy exuded success in everything he did, whereas she had to scramble every time she tried to inch forward. And here he was, staying on what would soon be her property. As a lawyer, he'd probably be hard to evict once she bought it.

"Hey, I saw a poster in the hardware store." He pulled his phone from his pocket and thumbed through his photos. "This is it. Could be our pups' missing mom. She was stolen."

"Oh, dear." She studied the picture of the black-and-white dog. "Could be."

"Yep, could be." He shifted his stance and started to put his phone back in his pocket. "I'll call the number tonight after Jemmy's asleep."

Olivia watched the kids, who were bouncing around as much as the two balls they were trying to get into the hoop. "Why not call now?"

He thought for a few seconds. "Sure." He punched in the numbers. "Yeah, hi. I saw your stolen-dog poster." A pause. "Rob! Hey. Your name wasn't on the poster, and this isn't your usual number." He paused, then looked at Olivia to relay what the other person said. "Designated burner phone? Didn't want to announce that the dog belongs to a Mattson. That makes sense. Listen, we found a couple of puppies over here by Albert's place. I'm gonna text you a picture so you can see if they could be your female's pups. Get back to me, 'kay?" After hanging up, he thumbed a text into his phone and sent it.

"Let me guess. Another Mattson cousin."

"Yeah. Rob's the prime owner and manager of the Double Bar M." Will chuckled. "Everybody calls him Big Boss, which sounds pretty Old West, but it suits him. In addition to raising cattle, he raises and trains border collies for herding. This dog must be a new one because I've never seen her before."

"Little dogs herding big cattle? Wow. That must be something to see." Oops. Did that sound like a request to be invited out to the famous cattle ranch? She quickly added, "I saw border collies herding sheep at the Highland games in Seattle. Those dogs are amazing."

"Yep." He didn't seem to take offense. Maybe his guard was lowering in all matters Mattson. His phone beeped, and he opened the text. "Uh-oh. Rob thinks these pups might be Lady's."

"Uh-oh is right. The kids will be so disappointed if they have to give the pups back."

His phone beeped again. "Rob says he'll come out to see them tomorrow after church." He sighed. "Like Sue said, those dogs go for around two grand if they're purebred, so we might have to give them up. I'm not sure spending that much money is practical, at least not for me."

"Or me." Olivia's chest ached. Not only would Emily be disappointed, but she would be also. Little Bitsy and Buddy had already found a place in her heart. And she'd spent a bunch of money on the kennel and other supplies.

"Speaking of church, I've been meaning to invite you to mine." Will tucked his phone in his back pocket. "Riverton Community Church. I think you'll like Pastor Tim. He's—"

"Wait. You mean you go there, too? Why haven't I seen you?"

He stared at her for a minute. "I don't know. It's a pretty big church, and during the main service, I'm usually at the back wrangling my aunt's boys, so I can take them out if they get too fidgety. You know—come late, leave early."

"Good plan." She chuckled, glad for this change of subject. "And Dad is a front-row kind of guy, so we don't have much choice but to sit with him."

Will grunted. "Good for him. Hey, remember June invited Emily to her Sunday school class? Maybe if she went, Jemmy would feel safer there. What do you say?"

Why had she let her own insecurities keep her daughter from this important part of her spiritual education? "Sure. I'm open to any opportunity to help Jemmy. June seems like a sweet girl, and I want Emily to hear about Jesus from other people besides just Dad and me. So, yes, we'll meet you there."

His pleased grin shouldn't have made her heart flood with happiness, but it did. She was her own worst enemy. She was falling down an Alice-in-Wonderland rabbit hole and had no way to stop herself.

CHAPTER NINE

WILL ALMOST HAD himself convinced that he was spending extra time getting ready for church to honor the Lord.

It was partially true. He always shaved and combed his hair just so, even used mousse to keep that annoying cowlick curl from falling over his forehead, despite his Stetson always messing it up later. But when he chose the turquoise shirt, a turquoise-and-silver bolo tie and his new black jeans, he couldn't deny he wanted Olivia to see him at his best. In high school, Megan had always told him to wear turquoise because it made his eyes twinkle and would attract the girls.

Thoughts of his sister always brought a painful pang to his chest. She would like Olivia and—

No. He couldn't take this any further. He left on the jeans but exchanged the turquoise shirt and tie for a white shirt and black bolo, then added his plain black suit jacket before dressing Jemmy in his Sunday best shirt and a clip-on bow tie.

"Albert, are you sure you don't want to go with us?"

The old gentleman was resting in his recliner, coffee and remote in hand. "No thanks, Will. I'll just watch church here."

"You sure you can find it on Facebook?"

"Always have. Well, for as long as it's been on." He reached into his pocket and pulled out a small envelope. "Put this in the offering plate for me, will you?"

"Sure thing."

It took Will's four-door pickup and Aunt Lila Rose's van to safely transport all five boys to church. Mindful of the way one set of parents had died, Will was adamant about securing each boy in a seat belt, depending on his size. They parked next to the all-purpose building beside the one that held the sanctuary and herded four of the boys into their age-appropriate rooms. As usual, Jemmy clung to Will's hand like he'd never let go. Clutching her well-worn Bible, Aunt Lila Rose waved goodbye as she strolled toward her own class in the adult wing.

"Okay, pal, let's see if we can find cousin June." Will tried to emphasize the family connection as often as possible, hoping to give Jemmy a sense of belonging, an understanding that he had a bunch of people who loved and cared for him. Sweet June personified all of that.

He stood outside the pre-K room and peered in. Sunlight streamed in the large windows, casting a light on Olivia, who stood chatting with June. His pulse quickened, and he couldn't dismiss it as concern for Jemmy. Olivia's long black hair hung over one shoulder, and she wore a pretty yellow dress with blue flowers around the knee-length hem. Her only jewelry was a simple cross necklace and tiny pearl earrings. A hint of eye makeup she didn't usually wear brought out the sparkle of her brown eyes.

Wow. She was gorgeous.

"When you invited Emily to your class, I didn't realize you teach pre-K." Olivia glanced around the room, where a boy and two girls were playing with wooden puzzles. "Should I take Emily to another class?"

"If you think that's best." June spoke in her characteristic cheerful tone. "But I always need a helper. I'd love it if she stayed here, if just for this morning." She noticed Will standing in the door. "Hey there. Come on in." She squatted down to eye level with Jemmy. "Hi, Jemmy. Want to come in and hear some stories about Jesus?"

Not answering, he hugged closer to Will's leg and stuck his thumb in his mouth…until he saw Emily. "Em'ly." He broke away from Will and bounced over to her. The two kids hugged like they hadn't seen each other in a month instead of just yesterday.

June laughed. "Well, now I know where I stand." She looked up at Will. "He'll be fine, especially if Emily stays. Emily, do you want to stay and help me?"

"Yes, ma'am." Cute little Emily, a Mini-Me of her mother right down to the matching dress she wore, struck a maternal pose beside Jemmy.

Will chuckled, and even Olivia seemed pleased with the plan. She whispered something to her daughter and patted her on the shoulder. Emily led Jemmy to the kids' table, where they sat and began to work on a puzzle.

"Okay, you two." June smiled at Will and Olivia. "Let's get the kids registered, then off you go to find your own classes." She wrote their names and phone numbers on a form on her clipboard, then handed each of them a numbered card. "Here's your ID cards. Just tear them in half and write your child's name on one half and clip it to their tops. You keep the other half. Without that card, no one can take the kids from the room." She gave Will a significant look. Every Mattson relative knew about his custody situation and would circle the wagons if he needed their help. "Now, you two scoot. We'll be fine."

"Oh, I like this system." Olivia quickly complied, and Will followed suit.

"Just text me if you have any problems," Will said.

"Same," Olivia echoed.

They stepped out of the room into the spacious, light-filled hall. Olivia moved away from the doorway, leaned back against the wall and blew out a long breath.

"You okay?" Will also stepped beyond the doorway so Jemmy couldn't see him.

"More or less."

He chuckled. "Why? You're not worried about June?"

"Not at all. It's just that I'm not used to leaving Emily with anybody but Dad. I homeschool for a reason."

"Oh, yeah. I need to pick your brain about that. That may be the best route to go with Jemmy."

She stared up at him, and his pulse picked up again. Those brown eyes...

"I can pass Emily's kindergarten materials on to you. We homeschoolers do that a lot. That way you can see if it's right for Jemmy before you spend any money."

"I'd like that." With some difficulty, he broke eye contact and looked down the hall toward the lobby. "So, you haven't found a Sunday-school class yet?" Stupid question. If she had, she'd have already enrolled Emily in one for her own age.

"No." She chewed her lip. "Guess I'm as shy as Jemmy about trying new situations."

A familiar protective feeling stirred in his chest—a feeling often directed toward Jemmy, Aunt Lila Rose and her kids. A feeling he'd once directed toward Megan. But nothing he felt or did had kept his sister safe.

He shoved away the dismal memory and focused on the present...and Olivia. When had he begun to include this usually feisty woman in his circle of responsibility?

"If you want to, we can sit down there in the lobby." Will waved in that direction.

"You don't want to go to your class?"

He shrugged. "Ever since Jemmy's needed me twenty-four-seven, I've sort of gotten out of the Sunday school habit." That sounded pretty pathetic. He should go today and take Olivia with him. Instead, he informed her, "I'll just wait down there so I'll be close if he needs me." He chuckled. "Or, more accurately, if June needs me."

"Sounds like a plan." Olivia started walking toward the lobby. "Mind if I join you?"

"Not at all." No, he didn't mind in the least. Against everything that made sense in his life, he wanted to spend more time with this kind, beautiful woman who just happened to threaten the destruction of his dearest dream…and had maybe even wiggled her way into his heart without the slightest effort.

"WE USUALLY GO out for lunch on Sundays," Dad said to Will on the front lawn of the church. "Can we tempt you to join us?" With Nona beside him, he seemed happier than Olivia had seen him since Mom had died.

As for his invitation to Will and company,

she was less than pleased. Somehow, she'd found herself seated next to Will during the service. Even though he kept busy making sure his boys behaved, he managed to send her an occasional smile. After the first time, when her heart did a silly little flip-flop, she forced her attention back to the sermon.

Before Will could answer Dad, she piped up. "We should get back to the puppies. They're probably starving. We've been gone three hours."

"Oh. Right." Dad gave her a sheepish grin. "Well, this is why we drive separately. I'm taking Nona to lunch, and I'll see you all at home." He nodded to Will's aunt. "Nice to meet you, Mrs. Jenson."

"Nice to meet you, too, Lawrence. And Nona. Please, everybody calls me Lila Rose."

"Then that's what we'll do, ma'am." He seemed to include Nona in that *we*. "You all have a nice lunch."

As Dad and Nona walked away, Will and his aunt corralled their charges, who'd been chasing each other around on the grass.

"These boys are hungry as bears," Mrs. Jensen said. "We'd better do drive-through, Will."

"Yes, ma'am." He gave Olivia an apologetic

grimace, then smiled. "Tell you what. Since you're taking care of Buddy for us, I'll bring you some of that drive-through as soon as the boys are settled."

"Please say yes, Mommy." Emily gave her a hopeful smile.

Olivia brushed a hand over Emily's cheek. "Honey, that's a long time to wait for lunch. Aren't you already hungry? I am." She turned to Will. "Thanks, but we'll do our own drive-through."

"Can Jemmy come with us?" Emily reached out to the boy, who was hugging close to Will. "Jemmy, want to come with us?"

"Oh, I'm not sure—" Will stopped, probably because Jemmy had already taken Emily's hand. And he was smiling. "I—I don't know." Doubt, and maybe a hint of fear, crossed Will's face. Then decision. He squatted down to Jemmy's level. "Say, pal, would you be okay going with Emily and Miss Olivia while I take your brothers home?"

Jemmy's eyes widened briefly. Then he nodded. "I want to go with Em'ly."

Will looked up at Olivia. "Is that okay with you?"

She'd been so taken up with the emotion of

the moment, she hadn't considered what this meant. Would this darling little boy trust her? Or would he suddenly realize Will wasn't with them and become frightened? If that happened, how would she manage it? The kids smiled up at her, trust shining in their eyes and sealing her decision.

"I'll need his car seat."

"Right." Will jogged over to his truck and soon had the seat buckled into her Explorer.

"Come on, Jemmy." Emily climbed into her spot and secured herself in her car seat.

Without hesitation, he followed her and let Will buckle him in.

"Bye, pal. See you soon." Will tousled Jemmy's hair.

For one brief moment, doubt crossed the boy's face. Then he said, "Bye, pal. See you soon."

His eyes suspiciously moist, Will backed up and closed the door. "I'd better get going and help my aunt with her boys."

"Okay." Olivia hopped in the car and made her escape before her emotions took over. With the drive home taking twenty minutes and the long line they'd surely find at the drive-through, she worried about the puppies. "Let's get home and take care of those puppies. You two okay with PB and J?"

"Puppies and PB and J!" Emily squealed.

"Puppies and PB and J!" Jemmy echoed.

Then they both giggled with abandon and started one of their adorably silly conversations about their new pets.

Olivia had to blink hard to clear the tears from her eyes. This dear little boy had made amazing progress in the short week and a day she and Emily had known him. And all due to her daughter's gentle, loving ways. While Emily didn't understand what was at stake, Olivia couldn't think of denying either child their friendship.

Lord, help. I don't know how to keep from losing my right to buy Albert's property. Please don't let that happen. Please show me what to do.

This morning, Pastor Tim had expounded on Proverbs 3:5-6 in his sermon. But how could she "lean not on" her own understanding of the situation and choose to "trust in the Lord with all" her heart when her and her daughter's future depended on owning Albert's land? Hadn't He already directed her "path" to have this dream in the first place?

She couldn't solve her problems today, so she

set aside her worries and started singing "Jesus Loves Me," as she and Emily often did while out for a drive. The kids joined in with their sweet voices, which lifted her mood, at least for the moment.

They arrived home to find the puppies yipping and whining.

"Looks like we need to feed them first." Olivia settled each child on the floor with a puppy and a bottle while she cleaned up the kennel. Much giggling and silly chatter ensued, making music for her heart and further improving her day. If not for her fears about the future, she could enjoy the sweetness of these moments with the same carefree abandon as the kids.

WILL PARKED AT Albert's and took in the hamburger and fries he'd bought for the old man. "Did you eat yet?"

"No. Wasn't in the mood. That hamburger smells mighty good, though." He sat at the kitchen table and opened the bag. "Join me?"

"Thanks, but I need to check on Jemmy." Give or take a few brief times, they'd been constant companions for the past five months, so it felt strange not to have Jemmy with him.

He hustled across the two yards and knocked

on Olivia's back door. When she opened it to greet him, he felt a kick under his ribs. Wow, she looked cute. She'd changed out of her church dress and into jeans and an orange T-shirt, which she'd tied at the waist. Her hair was a bit mussed, and she smelled like peanut butter. For a moment, he couldn't speak.

"Hey." She blinked those dark brown eyes. "Come on in."

He did. "Sorry it took so long for me to get back. My aunt's boys needed some attention after lunch." He glanced beyond her. "How's Jemmy?"

"Fine." She smiled, and another kick hit him under the ribs.

"No problems?" Relief flooded his chest.

She laughed, that musical sound he'd like to hear more often. "Not a one. You give a kid a puppy and PB and J, and all is bliss."

He chuckled. "True that." He stared down at her, wishing he could dismiss this knot of reserve he felt toward her. "Well, I'd better check on him."

"Sure. He's napping in Emily's bed. With Buddy, of course."

"Napping? Yeah, I guess he's exhausted from his busy day."

They walked toward Emily's room and, sure enough, Jemmy was sound asleep, with one arm around his sleeping Buddy.

Will exhaled a long sigh. "Man, that's a beautiful sight," he whispered. "He looks like he doesn't have a care in the world."

"I know. Isn't that sweet?" she whispered back.

The maternal look in her eyes further stirred Will's emotions. Her genuine affection for a child not her own was truly incredible.

"Mommy, is Jemmy awake yet?" Emily bounced into the room with Bitsy tucked under one arm. "We want to take the puppies outside to play."

Her cheerful and not-so-quiet voice woke Jemmy, and he sat up in alarm. Eyes wide, he seemed to survey his surroundings before settling his stare. "Unka Weeoo." He scrambled from the bed, leaving Buddy behind, and headed toward Will. Then he stopped and turned around to retrieve his whimpering puppy.

"Come on, Jemmy. Let's go outside." Emily nudged him. "Mommy, we can go outside, can't we?"

Olivia looked up at Will, something he'd begun to like…a lot. "What do you think?"

"Can't hurt."

They trooped outdoors to the south side of the house, where the kids sat on the grass near the budding peach and apple trees to let their pets explore their surroundings. Not yet fully standing on their chubby little legs, the fuzz balls lumbered around, sniffing the grass, falling over and wrestling with each other. They also nipped at each other's ears, resulting in yips of complaint. Every movement was met with squeals and giggles from the kids.

As he watched, Will had an idea.

"Hey, Jemmy." He settled on the grass beside his nephew. "See how Bitsy and Buddy wrestle around with each other?"

Jemmy looked up at him, trust beaming from his eyes. "Yes, suw."

"That's what puppies do. And little boys, too. Like your brothers." Following Aunt Lila Rose's suggestion, he'd started calling all the boys "brothers" to give them a sense of family.

Jemmy stared down. "I don't like to w'estle. It huwts."

"They don't mean to hurt you, just like Buddy doesn't mean to hurt Bitsy."

The male puppy chose that moment to nip his sister, and she yipped in complaint. Will winced as he exchanged a look with Olivia. She shrugged and shook her head.

"No, Buddy." Jemmy snatched up his puppy. "Don't huwt her."

"It's okay." Emily picked up Bitsy. "She's okay. Like when we played basketball and you bumped me and I fell down. It didn't hurt."

Jemmy frowned and seemed to digest that idea. The puppies caught his attention again, and he jumped to his feet. "Come on, Buddy. Follow me."

Buddy wandered in a different direction, clearly not getting the message.

"Well, I'd better put supper in the slow cooker." Olivia reached for Emily's hand. "Let's go, sweet pea."

Will didn't want their time together to end. "Can I help? I'm a pretty good sous chef."

She side-eyed him and gave him a mischievous grin. "Are you inviting yourself to supper?"

Heat raced up his neck. "Didn't mean to. I just—" What excuse could he give? "Just wanted to let Jemmy play with Emily a little longer, if that's okay with you."

"Right." She laughed in her musical way. "Sure. Tell you what. You can help me show the puppies how to drink from a dish. That's next on the timeline Sue gave us."

"Hey, Will." Cousin Rob strode across the yard from Albert's place. "Are those the pups?"

"Hey, cuz." As Rob reached them, Will had to settle his heart. If he took the puppies, it would devastate Jemmy. "Yep. And this is my neighbor, Olivia Ortiz, and her daughter, Emily. You know Jemmy, of course. Olivia, this is Robert Allen Mattson the Fifth, owner of the Double Bar M Ranch, and otherwise known as Big Boss."

Rob shorted. "Some call me that. You can call me Rob." He grinned and touched the brim of his Stetson. "Nice to meet you, ma'am."

"I'm glad to meet you, Rob." Despite her polite words, she gave him a wary look.

"Don't mean to be rude, but I gotta get back to the ranch. You mind if I look over the pups?"

Will traded a look with Olivia, something that was becoming all too natural.

"Sure." She walked over to Emily. "Sweet pea, do you mind if I show Bitsy to Mr. Rob?"

Trust shining in her eyes, Emily smiled as she handed the puppy to her mother. Jemmy clutched Buddy and stared up at Will, fear written all over his face. Will tried to give him an encouraging smile, but it felt more like a grimace.

Rob gently took Bitsy in hand and examined her markings, then scratched behind her ears. "Sure does look like one of ours. And very much like the pups sired by our main breeding male. We bought Lady to introduce new blood to our kennel and to teach my kids some responsibility. Sadly, she went missing after just a few days." He glanced at Jemmy and sighed. "If Lady was pregnant when she was stolen, these are undoubtedly hers. The timing's just about right."

Olivia's shoulders slumped. "That's what I was afraid of."

The children's eyes were now wide and focused on the adults.

They all watched as Jemmy took a step toward the house, Buddy held tightly in his arms.

Rob let out a long sigh. "Tell you what. Let's do DNA testing to find out their parentage. We keep the DNA on all our animals, especially those with papers."

"Wow. You can do that? It sure would be helpful." Olivia kneeled down beside Emily. "Mr. Rob's going to take Bitsy for a little while…"

"Oh, no, ma'am." Rob handed Bitsy back

to Emily, kneeled down, then reached into his jacket pocket and brought out two small boxes. "We can do it here and now. Just won't get the results back for a while." He'd already labeled the boxes *male* and *female* with a Sharpie.

"Blood samples?" Will could imagine the complaints the pups would make if they had to be poked with needles. And the kids would probably get upset, too.

Rob shook his head. "Cheek swabs. Now, Emily, can you hold Bitsy for me?"

"Yes, sir." Her adorable, trusting smile brought a lump to Will's throat.

Rob tore open the box labeled *female* and pulled out a swab, making a big show of his actions. "Now, Bitsy, open wide." He held Bitsy's lower jaw and swabbed for several seconds before putting the swab into a small vial. "Good girl. That should do it. Thank you, Miss Emily." He ruffled the pup's head. "Okay, Jemmy, how about your little fella?" He motioned to him.

Eyes filling with tears, Jemmy walked slowly toward Will and offered his beloved pet to Rob.

"You can hold him," Will urged. "Come on now. Let Cousin Rob tickle his mouth."

Rob kneeled down again to repeat the procedure, only to have Buddy bite the swab in two and try to eat it. "Uh-oh." While everyone else laughed, Rob gripped Buddy's lower jaw and managed to extract the cotton-covered stick. "Whew. That was close. Wouldn't do for him to swallow it. Thank you, Jemmy."

Jemmy eyed him with a hint of confusion. Like most of the Mattson men in the area, Rob and Will resembled each other. Even with their age difference of around twelve years, maybe Jemmy could see he was family.

"So, do you want some help loading them into your truck?" Will tilted his head toward Albert's place, where Rob's truck was parked.

"Naw. You keep them for now." Rob ruffled Buddy's head. "Jemmy, you sure are taking good care of these little critters. Look how fat and furry they are. Keep up the good work."

Jemmy gave him a tiny smile, and his tears vanished. Progress!

"Okay, then." Rob stood. "I'll let you know as soon as I get the DNA results in maybe ten days, two weeks. Could be longer if the lab is busy." He tipped his hat to Olivia. "Nice to meet you, ma'am. The whole Mattson clan's been praying for this chump to find the right lady, and here you're right next door—"

"Whoa!" Will couldn't let him continue. "Let's not go there."

"Not hardly." Olivia glared at Rob. "The only things Will and I agree on are our kids and their puppies. If you want to pray for anything for Emily and me, pray that DNA won't match your dogs."

Rob gave her a sympathetic nod. "Yes, ma'am." He touched his hat brim again, then strode away.

"Sorry." Will gave her a sheepish grin. "Don't take him too seriously. As he said, the entire clan's been trying to marry me off for years."

She rolled her eyes and walked away toward the children.

This whole conversation made Will's heart sink. She obviously didn't like him, but he was afraid he was falling for her.

No. Couldn't be. As she said, the only things they had in common were the kids and their pups. With their dispute over who would win the right to buy Albert's property, that was hardly enough to build a relationship on. How could he continue to spend so much time with her and Emily for Jemmy's sake and yet protect his own heart at the same time?

Simple answer. He couldn't.

CHAPTER TEN

IN THE SMALL, three-stall horse shed, Olivia helped Emily give Fred a good brushing, removing the last of his winter coat.

"Okay, now the blanket." She watched Emily lift the woven saddle blanket from its hanger and try to toss it over Fred's fifteen hands height, maybe twenty inches above her three and a half feet. It slid to the ground on his other side, and they both laughed.

"Oops." Emily scurried around him, picked it up and tried again.

This time, Olivia settled it in place. "There. Now, my turn." She hefted the child-size saddle, tossed it over Fred's back and secured the cinch.

While she double-checked the halter and reins, Emily moved to Fred's head and chatted to him. The old gelding nuzzled her and leaned into her caresses, soaking up and returning her affection.

Impossibly cute in her jeans, T-shirt and Western boots, Emily had all the promise of a little rodeo queen. Not that Olivia had such ambitions for her daughter, but Emily always loved to see the queens at the rodeos they attended. If she showed an interest in competing, that might be the Lord's way of directing her path.

She led Fred out into the morning sunshine and breathed in the fresh country air. She loved this place. Loved that her grandparents had left such a beautiful legacy for the family. Why did Will have to go and ruin everything by wanting to clutter this peaceful place with rambunctious boys? On Sunday, his aunt's four foster sons had chased each other around the churchyard like a pack of playful puppies…although she had to admit they obeyed Lila Rose and Will without too much objection when it was time to go home. Maybe it was the promise of drive-through hamburgers that settled them down.

"Up you go." She lifted Emily into the saddle and adjusted the stirrups to the right length. "You remember your knee signals?"

"Yes, ma'am. Can I take the reins?" She giggled. "*May* I take the reins?"

"Maybe in a bit. Let's be sure you have your

balance." She led Fred around the perimeter of the grassy pasture. The dear old horse plodded along at an even pace, seemingly mindful of his precious load. When Olivia trotted for a few yards, Fred kept pace and slowed when she did.

As they came back around toward the shed, where Dawson and Buffy watched them with mild interest, Emily waved furiously and called out, "Jemmy! Come ride with me!"

Looking in that direction, Olivia felt her heart skip. Sure enough, there were Will and Jemmy, looking for all the world like genuine cowboys. Light blue jeans, matching blue plaid, open-collar shirts, Western boots and brown Stetson hats. Jemmy looked adorable. Will looked like a cowgirl's dream come true.

Ugh! Why couldn't she keep such thoughts at bay? She constantly needed to remind herself his looks were a charming facade that hid his plans to steal her livelihood.

"Since you didn't come over to collect eggs this morning, I brought you some." Will held up a small bowl. "I see you're busy. Want me to take them inside?"

"Thanks, but no. Just put them over there by the shed." She nodded in that direction, and he complied.

"Jemmy, want to ride with me?" Emily repeated her invitation. "You can sit in front of me."

He stared up at her, fear and indecision in his eyes. An ache that was becoming very familiar regarding this little boy surged up in Olivia's chest. What could she do to reassure him?

"What do you say, pal?" Will asked as he returned. "Want to ride?" He looked at Olivia. "You mind?"

"Not at all." Olivia bent down to Jemmy. "See how gentle Fred is? He loves little boys and girls. And Uncle Will can walk beside you while you ride."

Will shot her a warm look she felt clear down to her toes. Against everything that made sense in her life, she wouldn't trade this desire to help Jemmy for anything. Her involuntary reactions to his uncle were another matter entirely.

Finally convinced, Jemmy lifted his arms to Will, who gently set him up in front of Emily.

"'S'too high," Jemmy whined as he reached for Will.

"Aw, come on, Jemmy. It's fun." Emily pulled him back with a hug, causing his hat to slip down over his nose. "I won't let you fall."

He lifted the hat, indecision in his eyes, but said, "Okay."

As they walked around the pasture, Olivia on one side of Fred and Will on the other, she once again had that sense of family. Maybe Will and Jemmy weren't Sancho and Daniel, but they weren't bad substitutes. *The Lord giveth and the Lord taketh away. Blessed be the Name of the Lord.* Was it possible God was giving her and Emily a family for the one they'd lost?

What a wild, not to mention inconvenient, thought. Will came with too much baggage. Not just his vast Mattson clan, but his aunt's posse of little boys that he wanted to let loose on her quiet corner of the world. And Will intended to bring other boys out here as well. She couldn't be a part of that life. What about her plans? Her dreams? She wasn't ready to lose her independence and her very means of supporting herself and Emily.

Besides, she couldn't trust Will's charming ways. He was all cowboy manners and nice words, but she didn't doubt that was all part of his plan to win the competition she'd been so foolish to enter with him.

They came back around to the shed, and she reached up for Jemmy. "How did you like riding?"

"I like it." He gave her an adorable smile and fell into her arms.

Without thinking, she hugged him close, savoring the sweetness of his returned embrace. "I'm so glad." She set him down and turned to help Emily, only to see Will had claimed the honor.

Emily giggled and hugged his neck. "Thank you, Mr. Will."

"You're welcome, Miss Emily." He held her for a few seconds, his eyes suspiciously moist, then let her down. "We'll have to do this again, won't we?"

The emotion written on his face was real. His gentleness with Emily was real. And he was a good father to Jemmy. Despite everything she feared about him, she felt her list of objections begin to fade.

"Jemmy, want to play?" Emily took his hand. "Mommy and I are gonna stuff bags."

"Yay!" Jemmy bounced up and down. "Stuff bags."

"Stuff bags?" Will laughed. "Sure sounds like all kinds of fun." The smirk on his face contradicted his words.

"Humph." Olivia sniffed and lifted her chin with mock superiority. "Obviously, you've never filled grab bags. It can be very gratifying to put party treats in a red, white and blue bag."

"Ah. Now I see the method for your madness." Will copied her expression. "Am I right in guessing this is all about enticing people to vote for you on Independence Day?"

She blinked, attempting to look innocent. "Why, Mr. Mattson, are you accusing me of trying to sway the judges?"

"Not just accusing." Will crossed his arms and stared down his nose at her. "Indicting, deliberating and finding you guilty."

"Uh-oh. Lawyer speak." Olivia shuddered comically. "Now I'm really scared."

He chuckled. "You should be. I have a few secret weapons of my own."

"Such as?"

"You'll have to wait and see like everybody else."

Secret weapons. That was exactly what she was afraid of. He planned to pull some rabbits out of that Stetson hat, while she was still sliding down Alice's rabbit hole into a wonderland she wanted no part of.

WILL TRIED TO convince himself he was helping the enemy, but Jemmy was having too much fun for Will to think of Olivia in that way. They set up fifty or sixty flag-covered paper bags on her dining-room table to be filled with candy, small toys, puzzles, toothbrushes, travel-size toothpaste, combs, socks, crayons and coloring books that were all lying in shoeboxes on the sideboard.

"This is really cool stuff," Will said. "Just what the children in this area would appreciate. Where'd you get the idea?"

"I can't take credit for it." Olivia opened a bag of individually wrapped lollypops and poured them into a bowl. "Dad and Nona went to the party store and loaded up on all of this."

"Ah. You have helpers. Guess I'm gonna have to step up my game."

She shot him a withering look. "I'm sure you have plenty of people to help you."

Will shrugged. "Maybe so. Maybe not."

Her attempt at a rebutting snort ended on a chuckle.

He loved watching her laugh, even at his own expense. Loved their bantering. Loved spending time with her. She was quite a woman. And although she didn't want Aunt Lila Rose's boys to live next door, she couldn't hide her affection for kids—even ones who weren't her own, especially Jemmy.

Today, Jemmy didn't seem to have a care in the world. He'd had fun riding the horse and now followed Olivia and Emily around the table, reaching up on tiptoes to put the various items into the bags. As usual, he was as serious as a judge with this responsibility.

Thinking of judges reminded Will of his July appointment with Judge Mathis, who would have the final say about his adoption application. Will's Mattson name notwithstanding, a single man of twenty-eight who lived in an apartment might be seen by some people as a less-than-ideal adoptive father, even with Aunt Lila Rose supporting him. If Grant Sizemore had his way, he and Mabel would gain custody because Mabel was Ed's sister. If their application was favored over Will's, Jemmy's life would take a seriously bad turn. It didn't take much to figure out Grant and Mabel fostered children for the money, but if Will tried to prove it, they might accuse him of slander intended to undercut their own claims. Surely Judge Mathis would be able to discern what rotten foster parents they were.

Maybe Will had made a mistake to take this

route. Maybe he should have bought a house in town, but he'd been saving up for a long time to buy Albert's place outright. He couldn't afford to buy both properties. Maybe he should have asked Aunt Lila Rose to apply to be Jemmy's foster mom, but Jemmy still needed to learn how to trust the other boys before he'd feel safe living with them. No, the only solution was for Will to buy Albert's land and prove himself a responsible parent.

"Are you sure you kids aren't tired of PB and J?" Olivia had begun fixing lunch as though it was their everyday routine. "We could make tacos."

"PB and J," Emily and Jemmy chorused.

"How about you?" Olivia glanced at Will. "I can make those tacos for us."

"That's okay. PB and J works for me." How could it seem so natural to watch her prepping lunch for everyone? Just like he imagined a real family, something he'd never really experienced. "As long as we have carrot sticks."

She side-eyed him. "What? No chips? Sounds like I'm converting you to healthy eating."

He snorted out a laugh. "Could be." He wouldn't argue with her, not after the way she'd held on to Jemmy after she took him off the horse. She honestly cared about his nephew. Of course, he'd fallen in love with sweet little Emily, who was changing Jemmy's life more than anyone since his parents' deaths had traumatized him. How could Will not love her? And maybe, just maybe—although he'd known them less than two weeks—he was falling for Emily's mother, too.

That thought wouldn't leave him for the rest of the day and even stuck in his brain when he and Jemmy drove to Aunt Lila Rose's house. After greeting the boys, reading a chapter to them and tucking each one into bed with individual prayers, he settled a sleeping Jemmy on the couch and joined his aunt for coffee in the kitchen.

"You're falling for her, aren't you?" Aunt Lila Rose peered at him over her steaming cup, mischief in her blue eyes.

"Falling for who?" Will lowered his eyes, avoiding her intense gaze.

"Darlin', I've known you since before you were born. I can tell when you're avoiding the obvious. When you and Olivia came walking across the churchyard on Sunday, the way you looked at her gave you away."

"Aw, come on. I barely know her." He needed

to figure this out for himself without his aunt's two cents.

She chuckled. "It's not quantity of time, it's quality. Besides, you said you're over at her place almost every day. I'm beginning to wonder if you're actually taking care of Albert."

"As much as he'll let me." Will grunted. "At least I persuaded him to sign over power of attorney to his grandson. That way, if he...well, you know."

"Yes." She gave him a sad smile. "Joe Winslow's a fine man. I know he'll do what's right by Albert when the time comes." She leaned toward him. "And don't change the subject. What are you going to do about your relationship with Olivia?"

"It's not a relationship. It's..." He couldn't find the right word, which caused a stupid little ache in his chest. What on earth?

"Okay, then. I won't say any more." Her eyes took on a mischievous glint. "Tonight. No promises about tomorrow."

He shook his head. When Aunt Lila Rose latched on to an idea, she didn't let go.

He set a hand on hers. "Please keep praying that we can buy Albert's property. The more time I spend out there, the more I know it's the right place for you and your boys and Jemmy. I didn't want to get the boys' hopes up, so I didn't mention this to them, but this morning Jemmy got to ride Olivia's horse with Emily."

"Oh, how wonderful." Aunt Lila Rose beamed. "I haven't ridden for several years, but growing up on the ranch, it was my favorite pastime. It'll be fun to introduce the boys to horses." She wrinkled her forehead into a thoughtful expression. "I should probably talk to a realtor about selling this place."

Will released a long sigh. "Better hold off on that. Buying Albert's place isn't a done deal."

"Maybe not, but we'll give that competition our best shot." She grinned. "Wait 'til you see the cakes and cookies I plan to bring. We'll wow the attendees and ensure their votes."

Will cringed inwardly. To hear his aunt talk, this would be nothing more than a local fair where everybody had a good time amid friendly competition. But for him, as well as for all the boys he longed to bring up in safety and security, it was the making or breaking of a dream. He had to win. *Had* to.

But if, against his better judgment, he was starting to care for Olivia, how could he squash her dreams without destroying any chance he might have of developing a meaningful and possibly permanent relationship with her?

Simple answer: he couldn't.

THE LAST TIME Olivia wandered through a monument-supply business, it had been to choose Sancho's headstone. This time she didn't search through tears, but with a clear-eyed gaze as she chose uncut stones for her boulder fumble. While memories of Sancho still had the power to stir her emotions, today she was laser-focused on survival for herself and Emily.

The manager had directed her to the yard's back section, where rejected rocks of varying shapes and sizes had been laid out in orderly rows. Olivia decided on one that looked the right size for men and older boys to carry and a smaller one for any women who might want to join the fun. At the Highland games she'd attended, a whole team of female athletes had competed in this event, as well as many others.

"Are you done, Mommy?" Emily danced around among the stones, her impatience obvious. "Jemmy and I want to play basketball."

"Just about." Olivia motioned to the manager. "These two, please."

She paid for them and waited while he and

his helper hoisted them into a wheelbarrow and loaded them into her car. One more errand at the grocery store and they were on their way back, with Albert's house their first stop. She wasn't surprised to find Will and Jemmy outside with the puppies, who were getting big enough to scamper around the grassy lawn.

"Em'ly!" Jemmy hollered as he ran toward the car before it stopped.

Gasping, Olivia slammed on the brakes.

"Whoa, pal." Will scooped him up and walked over to the driver's side. "Hi, neighbor. What brings you to this side of the fence?"

"I need some muscle. Think you can haul those rocks out for me?" She hooked her thumb over her shoulder, then climbed out, with Emily scampering out on her own.

After setting Jemmy down, Will moved to the back of the car and opened the hatchback. "Whew. I don't know. Didn't have my spinach yet today."

She laughed. "Well, Popeye, maybe you can just shove them out onto the ground. We'll have my boulder fumble over here on the lawn—" she walked to the grassy part of the yard "—so we can just leave them here until the real athletes arrive."

"Oh, now you've done it. Can't let that go unchallenged." He reached into the back and maneuvered the largest stone to the edge, then hefted it. His bulging biceps strained the sleeves of his T-shirt, but no pain showed on his face. "Now, where did you say you wanted this?"

"Down. Just down." *Oh, my, he was strong.*

"You sure?" He just stood there grinning, almost challenging her.

"Well, then, how about over by the fence."

He strode in that direction, barely huffing with his load. Her own breathing hitched up a bit as she observed this display of strength.

"No, that won't do. Take it over by the old well." The well had been filled in, but its round stone wall remained. She would plant some pansies or petunias there once she owned this property.

Will walked that way.

"No, wait." This was fun. "Over by the house."

His stride barely slowed.

"No, that won't do, either." Olivia was running out of ideas. "Just bring it back over here." She motioned toward the grass.

He complied.

"Okay, you can drop it now, Popeye. But don't forget to eat your spinach."

He casually squatted to set down the stone rather than drop it, then retrieved the smaller one from the car and put it beside the big one. "Anything else?"

"Well, clearly, I didn't buy a big enough stone for the real athletes." To cover her silly breathlessness, she forced out a laugh. "Should have taken you along to find one you couldn't carry so easily. If all the men can do that, it won't be much of a competition."

"Yeah, but if the competitors have to run, it'll be harder. This one should work fine." He patted her shoulder, and a pleasant sensation streaked up her neck.

She made the mistake of looking up into those stunning blue eyes, and the nice feeling raced down to her heart. She huffed out another laugh. "If you say so."

She needed to get away from him before… "Emily, let's go fix lunch for Granddad and Miss Nona." The children had been occupied with the puppies, so they hadn't noticed this little "boulder fumble."

"Can Jemmy come?"

"No." She didn't mean to sound sharp, but somehow she had to rebuild her defenses against

Will's all-too-manly appeal. "I'm sure Mr. Will has plans, and so do we."

She made the mistake of looking back into those blue eyes. He winked.

Of course, he did.

"Okay, then. See you later." That devastating smile in place, he stepped back as though releasing her.

She drove around to her own driveway, determined to put Will Mattson out of her thoughts. But her mind kept returning to the sight of him casually carrying that heavy stone as though it was a bag of feathers. Not only did she admire his physical strength, but she also enjoyed his sense of humor. She could see spending more time with him and maybe not just because of the children. Would he enjoy the Santa Fe Opera? Or would the rodeo next week be more his speed? They could take the children to the rodeo and…

What was she thinking? She couldn't let Will get under her skin this way. But how could she stop it when she, like Alice, kept sliding farther down the rabbit hole?

WATCHING ACROSS THE PASTURES, Will followed Olivia's progress along the road to her house.

She sure was fun to joke around with, but it
had taken all the grit he could muster to act like
that stupid rock wasn't heavy. Right now, his
arms, his back, and even his legs ached. Man, he
needed to get back to the gym and resume his
strength training. He hadn't worked out, other
than chopping wood for Albert, since taking on
Jemmy's care. He wouldn't change that for the
world, but he also needed to take care of himself. Maybe tomorrow, he'd take Jemmy to the
gym and show him how it was done.

Or maybe he could ask Olivia to babysit
while he went to work out. Dropping Jemmy
off and picking him up would give Will more
time to spend with her and explore these feelings he couldn't dismiss. Or maybe he should
invite her and Emily the next time he went to
Santa Fe.

That was it. He'd invite them to the rodeo
in Santa Fe next week. She could probably use
a break from their competition as much as he
could.

That afternoon, while Jemmy napped, he
moved the woodpile to the back of the house
so it wouldn't be in the way of the festivities
in another three weeks. The activity gave him

some exercise and reinforced his resolve to get back to the gym.

"Hey, Popeye!" Olivia called to him over the stone fence separating the properties. "Didn't get enough strength training this morning?"

His heart kicked up. *Invite her now.* He sauntered over and leaned his elbows on a smooth spot on the rough stone top. "Hey, what are you up to this afternoon?" *Duh!* Stupid question. The watering can she held obviously meant she was tending the flowers growing along the house's back path.

She grinned as though she could read his mind. And it was a friendly smile, not reserved, like the ones she'd given him so often in the past. "Hey, I noticed Pecky's out in the yard with the other chickens. Is she okay?"

"Seems to be." Will grunted. "And a good thing, too. She laid her first egg the other day… in Jemmy's shoe. He didn't notice when he went to put it on and stepped on it."

"Oh, dear." Olivia winced. "What a mess."

"Yeah." He chuckled. "That's when he decided to try her again in the yard. With all the other baby chicks hatched, she's not the youngest anymore." He glanced toward the flock. "They're all getting along pretty well."

"I'm so glad. I can see how taking care of her was good for him, but now that he has Buddy, he still has an important responsibility."

"Right." He gave her his friendliest smile. "Say, I was just thinking. You and Emily want to go to the Rodeo de Santa Fe next week? I think the kids would really like it."

Her eyes widened and her jaw dropped. "I was just going to ask you the same."

"Great minds."

She laughed, that musical sound that he could listen to all day. "If not great, at least on the same track." She tilted her head toward Albert's house. "About some things."

"Right." He couldn't let this conversation turn antagonistic. "This would be Jemmy's first rodeo. He liked riding your horse, so this would be the next step in turning him into a gen-u-ine cowboy." He grinned.

She rolled her eyes, but returned one of her beautiful smiles. "Emily loves rodeos. I think she'd like to be a barrel racer."

"How do you feel about that?"

She shrugged. "I don't know. We'll have to see. An important part of homeschooling is teaching a child all the options out there and trusting the Lord to guide them to the career He wants for them."

"Sounds good. And I look forward to learning more about this homeschool thing." He was glad for this insight into her spiritual life. It wasn't always easy for him to trust the Lord with Jemmy's future. How much harder it must be for a widow to trust Him. "So. Rodeo?"

"Sounds good."

He chuckled at the way she echoed his words. So much to like about this lady. If it wasn't for their dispute over who got to buy Albert's place, he wouldn't hesitate to let himself fall for her.

Who was he kidding? He already stood on that precipice, and only one small bump, or rodeo, might send him over the edge.

CHAPTER ELEVEN

Popcorn and soda in hand, Olivia used her elbow to gently guide Emily to her seat beside Jemmy in the bleachers six feet above the rodeo arena. On Jemmy's other side, Will helped his nephew get settled. Over their kids' heads, he gave her his winning smile. Or maybe he was just as excited to be here as she and the kids were.

"Can you see okay?" He winked.

"Perfectly." She laughed at his silly question. They'd scored seats in the front row, right across the arena from the chutes.

As noisy attendees filled the stands, Jemmy stared around at the crowd, but he seemed more curious than alarmed. Although she hadn't known him very long, she could see this was progress.

Before the main rodeo began, little cowboys wearing helmets rode sheep around the arena for the mutton-busting competition. Olivia watched Jemmy as he stared wide-eyed at boys not much older than he was trying to hang on to the wooly beasts. Was he thinking he could do that, too? That would be a bold move for him.

Next came the rodeo queens riding at breakneck speed around the arena perimeter, some carrying flags and others waving to the crowd. Emily jumped out of her seat and waved furiously as they flew past. Miss Rodeo America, on her beautiful palomino, rode to the center of the arena carrying the American flag while a local high school girl sang "The Star-Spangled Banner." The announcer offered a prayer for the safety of all participants, and the rodeo began...with a bang.

When the first Brahma bull burst from the chute and tried to throw its rider, Olivia checked the kids for their reaction. Emily was fine. After all, this was not her first rodeo. She chuckled at the pun. Before she could share it with Will, she saw Jemmy hiding his face in Will's shoulder as the bull jumped and twisted violently, trying to throw its rider.

"It's okay, pal." Will pointed to the action. "Just watch."

After the cowboy managed to hang on for the requisite eight seconds, a horn sounded, and he jumped off and ran toward the fence, the bull right on his heels.

Jemmy cried out, and Emily grabbed his hand. "It's okay! Watch the clowns."

Dressed in baggy, mismatched clothes, the rodeo clowns diverted the bull's attention until the cowboy could climb the fence to safety.

"See." Emily giggled, and Jemmy joined in laughing at the clowns' silly but lifesaving antics.

After a moment, Jemmy appeared thoughtful. "Unka Weeoo, are you a weal cowboy? Why don't you wide the bulls?"

Will snorted out a laugh, then seemed to force the grin from his face. "Want some more popcorn, pal?"

This was too good to pass up. "Yes, Uncle Will." Olivia gave him a teasing smirk. "Why don't you ride the bulls?"

"Hey, whose side are you on?" He returned a playful scowl. Then to Jemmy, he explained, "Those guys are a special breed, pal. Not every cowboy is cut out to ride bulls. Just wait until you see the steer wranglers. That's more my speed."

From that moment, Jemmy settled down

to enjoy the various events, even the bucking broncos. With every event, Will looked her way as though checking to see that she was enjoying the rodeo as well. She returned a smile to assure him that she was.

"MOMMY, I WANT to be a barrel racer." Emily skipped along beside Olivia as they made their way through the crowded parking lot after the final event. "I want to carry the flag."

"That would be exciting, wouldn't it?" Olivia would explain later that the rodeo queens who raced around the perimeter of the arena, carrying flags that streamed above their heads, weren't always barrel racers, too.

Beside them, Will held Jemmy's hand as they walked. "How about you, Jemmy? What did you like the best?"

"The clowns." Jemmy looked up at Will for approval.

Olivia and Will traded one of their frequent looks and smiles.

"I like the clowns, too," Emily said. "They're silly."

Olivia took in Will's Western garb. As always, he sure did look like a cowboy. "Did you ever take part in a rodeo event?"

"Not formally. I did spend several summers at the Double Bar M and got pretty good at roping and reining. Those are parts of real-life cowboy work." He chuckled. "Even got to help gentle a couple of mustangs. That was like riding a bucking bronco."

"Ha. I can picture that." Olivia gave him a little smirk. "Why don't you enter the rodeo?" Not that she wanted him to, but it was fun to tease him. "Surely you're not too old to start."

"Ha, yourself." Will lifted Jemmy and swung him around on his back. "I would take you up on your invitation to ride Dawson."

"Just name the day." The thought of riding Fred beside him gave her a sweet longing.

"I'll do that." He glanced over his shoulder. "Hey, pal, how about riding a bucking bronco?" He jogged around in a small circle.

Jemmy flung his arms around Will's neck, his eyes wide with terror.

"Wait, Will. He's scared. Let him down." Olivia reached for the boy…just as he started to squeal with delight.

"Giddyap." He bounced in the loops of Will's arms, and they jogged the rest of the way to the truck, with Olivia and Emily chasing behind.

"Barbecue?" Will asked her as he buckled Jemmy into his car seat.

"Sounds good."

In fact, everything sounded good these days when it came to time spent with Will and Jemmy. Including the country songs they sang along to with the radio on the way home from their roadhouse supper.

As she tucked Emily into bed, her daughter gazed up at her with sweet innocence shining in her brown eyes. "Mommy, why can't we live with Jemmy and Mr. Will? That way we could both have the puppies all the time."

Tonight it was Jemmy's turn to keep them.

"Well, sweet pea, we're not really a family—"

"We are. We do everything together. It would be fun to be in the same house."

Olivia kissed her forehead. "Good night, dearest." She walked to the bedroom door, where Dad waited.

"Livy, I want to talk to you, if you're not too tired."

"Sure."

Walking without his cane, which he'd been doing since last week, Dad settled at the kitchen table. "I, uh, I'm not sure how to say this, but, well—"

"You're in love with Nona." Olivia's heart dipped, then shot upward. She grasped his hand across the table. "Oh, Dad, I'm so happy for you."

He chuckled. "Can't keep any secrets from you."

"Have you told her?"

Again, he laughed. "She told *me*. Said at our ages—well, she's still a spring chicken compared to me—we shouldn't waste any more time before shedding the loneliness we've both felt since our spouses died."

Olivia winced inwardly. How well she knew that same aching loneliness even a loving family couldn't soothe away. "Well, good for her. And good for you. What are your plans?"

"Still working on that. Once she finishes her book and we get past the Fourth of July—" he gave her a meaningful look "—we'll see what's what."

Olivia squeezed his hand. "I'll be praying for you." And praying for herself and Emily now that one more challenge to their future had arisen. If Dad married Nona and moved to Florida, how could she manage to run this place by herself? Or maybe Nona and her two daughters would want to live here. That would mean Olivia needed Albert's house more than ever.

THE NEXT DAY, Will took her up on the invitation to ride her horses. She and Emily found him at the shed getting ready to teach Jemmy how to saddle Dawson while the little guy sat on the nearby bale of hay. Both were dressed in jeans and Western shirts, with their Stetson hats completing the picture of two cowboys. Emily parked herself beside Jemmy.

"First the saddle blanket." He held it out and let the kids feel the heavy wool fabric. "This protects the horse's back from rubbing by the saddle." He nodded to Olivia. "Hey." His gorgeous smile sent a tickle through her heart.

"Hey, yourself. You sure you want to ride Dawson? He can be a little frisky." She wouldn't advise putting Jemmy on her younger gelding, but she'd wait to see what he planned.

"Just want to try him out. Fred's a little tame for me." He glanced at Jemmy. "Next, the saddle."

His muscular arms rippled as he easily hefted the adult-size saddle onto Dawson's back. Olivia took a deep breath and looked away from the all-too-appealing picture.

"Make sure it's set right so he'll be comfortable, then reach under his belly and grab the cinch." He followed through with the rest of the procedure, adjusting the bit in Dawson's mouth and checking the length of the reins. "Okay, Jemmy, I'm gonna take a little ride around the pasture. You stay right here with Emily and Miss Olivia." He looked at Olivia, eyebrows raised as though asking for her agreement.

She returned a nod. "We'll be right here."

After adjusting his hat, he led Dawson from the shed and mounted him. As expected, the gelding turned around, trying to return to his stall.

"Hey, now, boy. Wrong direction." Using his voice, knees and the reins, Will straightened Dawson's heading and tapped his heels into the horse's sides. Olivia could sense every command. This cowboy knew his stuff. With a toss of his head as his last resistance, the gelding took off in a canter across the small pasture.

Olivia could see the kids were enjoying the show, maybe remembering the fun they'd had at yesterday's rodeo. "Want to ride?"

"Yes!" Emily jumped up and headed toward Will, who was on the other side of the pasture, putting Dawson through his paces.

"Not so fast." Olivia grabbed her shirt. "I meant on Fred."

Emily slumped her shoulders comically. "Aw, Mom." Then she brightened. "Come on, Jemmy. Let's saddle good old Fred."

Soon they were mounted on the reliable older gelding and having the time of their lives as Olivia trotted them around the pasture. She hadn't felt this much freedom and unbounded joy since Sancho was still alive.

THE NEXT DAY, Olivia and Emily rode with Will and Jemmy to church, which was becoming an enjoyable habit. They left the kids in June's Sunday school class and attended Will's singles class. Several of the young women gave her the side-eye, but for the most part, everyone was friendly. She did catch two of the young men giving her a once-over, but apparently being with Will Mattson made her off-limits. It felt so strange to be among singles again. That was where she'd met Sancho. Yet, somehow, the memory didn't sting as much today.

After the lesson, they picked up the kids and headed toward the sanctuary. Once again, Olivia had that warm feeling that was becoming so comfortable. Maybe Will would take them all to lunch, since the puppies had begun to eat puppy mix and had plenty of water in their kennel. If not, she would invite him and Jemmy to share her leftover meat loaf. Whichever way it happened, she only knew she wanted to spend this Sunday with Will.

Was that good or bad? Safe or dangerous? She had no idea.

AFTER SUNDAY SCHOOL, Will ushered Olivia, Emily and Jemmy into a back pew beside Aunt Lila Rose and her boys. Greeting his aunt with a hug, he took in her weary expression. "You look like you could use a break. Why don't I take the boys this afternoon so you can have some 'me' time?"

She breathed out a long sigh. "That would be wonderful. My friends have been asking me to go for lunch with them for weeks now. It'll be nice to finally accept."

"Tell you what. You hitch a ride with one of them, I can use your van to cart the boys out to Albert's place and Olivia can drive my truck." He glanced at Olivia for the expected approval, only to see her face registering shock. A sinking feeling lodged in his chest. "Um, well, maybe—"

"Sure. Yes." She offered a smile that looked more like a grimace. "I'll be glad to drive."

During the service, he looked her way several times, but she seemed to avoid him. Had he made a terrible mistake expecting her to help with the boys? Had he ruined their budding friendship by making an assumption? Or was she just paying attention to Pastor Tim's sermon? Which was what he should have been doing.

Lord, please don't let me blow this. I've gotten used to Olivia being in my life, and want to be more than just friends with her. But I know You've given me a mission to help Aunt Lila Rose raise these boys. How can I figure out what to do?

As he prayed, the thought came to him. Maybe this afternoon he'd find out Olivia really couldn't deal with the boys the Lord had put in his care. If so, then after Albert's birthday bash, he'd have to pull back from spending so much time with her. And that would rip his heart right out of him.

But what if she discovered she actually enjoyed being with the boys? That would change everything. *Lord, You know what's best, but please change her heart toward these little guys.*

As usual, drive-through was the solution for

lunch. Will drove the van, and Olivia his truck. When he saw how well she handled the vehicle, he second-guessed his idea of distancing himself from her. What was not to like about this lady? Nothing.

Back home, or his soon-to-be home, he expected her and Emily to go over to her place. Instead, they both helped him carry the bags of burgers and fries into Albert's house and set everything out on the dining-room table. The old gentleman was glad for the company.

With everyone seated, Will offered a blessing. He breathed a sigh of relief when the boys put on their best manners. Well, except for the faces they made at each other across the table and their silly knock-knock jokes. At least they didn't throw french fries at each other.

"Knock, knock," Benji, the usual ringleader, challenged Jeffie.

"Who's there?"

"Auto."

"Auto who?"

"You auto know it's me by now."

The boys giggled, as did Emily. Even Olivia chuckled. Will could see a softening in her face as she looked at the boys. It was the same way she looked at her own daughter and Jemmy.

Surely she could see these boys weren't the hooligans she'd imagined them to be.

"Okay, I've got one, Benji." Olivia smiled at him. "Knock, knock."

Will didn't hear the rest of her joke for the thumping of his heart. All he knew was that she wasn't just tolerating his boys, she was engaging with them. That didn't mean she wanted to be fully involved in their upbringing, but it was a start.

Thank You, Lord.

OLIVIA JOINED THE fun as Will and his boys played tag football. She'd played on the volleyball team in high school, so she knew the value of team sports in developing character and sportsmanship. She and Emily had changed into jeans and T-shirts, but Emily preferred to play basketball with Jemmy rather than rough-and-tumble football.

She watched as Will made sure each boy had a chance to carry the ball over the imaginary goal line, reminding her of the way Sancho never let any of his boys feel left out. And, like Sancho, Will was made for this life. His generous, loving ways warmed her heart…against her better judgment. But now, she could see that judgment had been faulty, born of grief over Sancho's senseless murder by gang members. These boys weren't hardened to life yet, and Will was doing all he could to prevent that from happening.

The highlight of the afternoon came about when Will brought the six-week-old puppies out for the boys to meet and play with. The adorable fur balls soaked up the attention. Jemmy jumped into the middle of the fun, lecturing in his four-year-old way about how to take care of the pups. None of the other boys had ever had a pet, so this entire experience delighted them.

Olivia looked at Will, whose eyes were suspiciously red. She felt a little emotional herself seeing Jemmy come out of his shell this way. And all because his loving uncle took on the responsibility of raising a boy not his own. How could she not care for this man? But would it come at the cost of losing her own dreams?

THE FOURTH OF July arrived in all its New Mexico Land-of-Sunshine glory, with a bright sun above and a light breeze carrying the aroma of Papacita's smoked barbecue ribs and flank steak to every corner of the property, and probably beyond. Olivia studied the events layout with satisfaction. Yesterday, the equipment had arrived, and she and Will had directed their set-ups in the agreed-upon spots.

She looked up at the brilliant blue sky. "Lord, I've done my best. Please let me win this competition."

"Your will be done, Lord." Will came up beside her and nudged her shoulder. "Amen." Beside him, Jemmy held his hand, his eyes bright with excitement.

She looked up at Will's mischievous grin. "Humph. The Lord takes care of widows and orphans, so—"

"Exactly. That's why my aunt's orphaned boys need me to win."

"Right." She smirked. "And I'm so sorry you're going to be disappointed." Somehow her dismissive words didn't feel quite right. What *did* the Lord want from this competition? This day?

"And here they come." Will motioned toward the open front gate. "Let's go help Albert greet everybody."

Cars lined the roadway outside the fence, and families flocked in. Albert stood by the gate shaking adults' hands and handing out the gift bags to each child. Will had enlisted several of his teenage cousins to help with the various activities, which both eased Olivia's mind about everyone's safety and concerned her when it came to the voting. Could she disqualify them without seeming petty?

Also among the crowd were Will's aunt and her foster boys. The oldest boy, Benji, pulled a beach buggy loaded with Tupperware containers filled with cake and cookies. Unlike many of the other children, who'd scampered away from their parents toward the bouncy house and other games, Lila Rose's boys stayed close to her.

"Okay, you can go. Just remember to play nice." Lila Rose headed toward Olivia. "Good morning. Where do you want the cakes?"

"Hi. Welcome." Olivia pointed toward the portable flooring laid out next to the picnic tables and food trucks. "You can set up the cakewalk over there. There's chalk to mark the circle for folks to walk around. My old tape player will provide the music."

"Great. Come along, Benji."

"Howdy, Miss Olivia." The bright-eyed boy grinned at her. So polite, and apparently not at all cross that his foster brothers were already playing without him.

"Hey, there, Benji. How about I help your mom and you go play?"

He eyed Lila Rose. "Mom?"

She gave him a cheery smile. "Run along." She watched for a moment as he darted across the yard to join the fun. "Thanks, Olivia. He takes his responsibilities as the oldest very seriously, but he needs to play, too."

As she helped unload the beach buggy, Olivia digested this bit of information. How did this woman manage to teach her boys such manners? If they were this well-behaved all the time, maybe it wouldn't be so bad to have them living here.

What was she thinking? She had her own plans for this place. But she couldn't shake off the conviction Will's prayer had made her feel. *Yes, Lord, Your will be done.*

"Mommy!" Emily ran through the gate separating the properties, Dad, Nona and Ina right behind her.

Ina had arrived last evening and stayed with Nona in the studio apartment.

"I'll show you where we've set up your booth." Olivia led them to an open-air tent, where Nona's books and Ina's drawing supplies awaited them.

"Looks great," Ina said. "I'm glad you were able to get everything I asked for. Now, if I can just keep pace with everyone who wants a portrait."

"Mommy, where's Jemmy?" Emily tugged at Olivia's hand.

"Em'ly!" Jemmy ran to greet her. "Come play." He gripped her hand and pulled her toward the bouncy house, where June was managing the many children bouncing and squealing in the safely tethered structure.

"Look at them go." Dad chuckled. "When did that little guy become so brave?"

"Maybe it's because June's in charge." Olivia's heart warmed. "He's been in her Sunday school these past few weeks. And Will says Jemmy's decided Lila Rose's boys aren't too rough on him."

"I'm sure playing with Emily has helped, too." Nona watched Olivia's daughter with the fondness of a grandmother. "She's such a sweetheart."

"She sure is." Dad took Nona's hand. "Come on, darlin'. Let's get your books organized."

Her responding smile further warmed Olivia's heart. During these past days since Dad told her about his developing relationship with Nona, she'd grown closer to the author. Who could have imagined he would come back from the brink of giving up on life to discovering renewed energy after finding this dear lady to be his companion?

Several adults tossed beanbags toward—and sometimes *into*—the cornhole boards. Across the pasture in the archery range, others took aim at two straw targets painted with large bull's-eyes. In her own pasture, two young Mattson cowboys gave kids horseback rides on Fred. For the competitive events, Will had enlisted other relatives to judge the activities, so prizes could be awarded. Seeing him across the yard, she decided to confront him about their voting.

"It's nice of your relatives to come out and help. That'll give you some extra votes." She gave him a sassy grin, but behind her smile, a sense of unfairness lurked.

"Nope." He shrugged. "I told them not to vote."

She stared at him for a moment. "That's very sporting of you. Did you tell them what's at stake?"

"Nope," he repeated, then winked at her. "That's our little secret."

Whether it was his wink or his integrity about the voting or all the wonderful things she'd discovered about him, she knew in that moment she loved him. Alice had landed in Wonderland, and it wasn't as scary as she'd feared. If something more came of their relationship, he would be an amazing dad for Emily. What did it all mean for the future? Only the Lord knew. But she couldn't deny the love for him that continued to grow each day.

At midmorning, she corralled those who'd signed up for the boulder fumble on the lawn near the house. "Will, your name's not on the list."

Grinning, he shrugged. "Didn't want to show anybody up."

"Or be shown up."

"Hey, now." He winced comically. "Just being a good host."

A tall, brawny young man from San Juan carried the boulder with ease around the circular course, beating his competitors. A thirtyish woman from Riverton won the women's run. Even a few of the older children ran the course, carrying lighter stones to the cheers of the entire crowd.

At noon, the crowds lined up at the food trucks and bought fried chicken, turkey legs, french fries and ice cream. Olivia noticed the care everyone took not to litter, but to place their trash in the provided barrels. And their respect and deference toward Albert reminded her that she should get out of her own head more and try to befriend these same neighbors.

Throughout the day, guests paid a small fee to participate in the cakewalk, with the money going to charity. The music began, and participants walked around the circle, which was marked with numbers. The music abruptly ended, and Lila Rose drew a number from a bowl and called it. The person standing on that number then claimed one of the donated cakes. Would this be the favored event?

Enjoying the day as much as the guests, Olivia lost track of time. In the late afternoon, after Papacita declared the barbecued meat ready to serve, Albert gathered everybody, children included, and passed out ballots listing the various attractions. "Folks, I want you to mark your first and second choices for the events you like best. Everybody, children three and above included, can vote. Now, parents, you can help them mark their ballots, but don't try to influence what they vote for."

Once the rather chaotic voting was completed, he gathered the ballots in a pillowcase. "All right, folks, Jorge and I will go inside and count up these ballots to find out who—" he cleared his throat "—which event is the winner. You all line up and get your supper, and we'll announce the winner at the end of the evening." He and Jorge Lopez headed for the house.

Now Olivia's nerves kicked in. *Lord, please...* was all she could manage to pray. But when Will came up beside her and took her hand, she instinctively leaned into his shoulder, knowing somehow everything would be all right.

WILL DIDN'T KNOW exactly when it happened. He just knew he'd fallen in love with Olivia. Maybe it was her obvious affection for Jemmy and the way she'd joined in the fun with the other boys. Maybe her silly, harmless teasing. Maybe her disinterest in his Mattson name and its social position in the community and beyond. Maybe his undeniable attraction to her many strong traits and virtues. No matter why or when, he had fallen head over heels for this woman. They still had some issues to work through, but some of them would be resolved this evening when he won the right to buy Albert's land. He would propose right away and promise he'd help her keep her business going. His law practice and his share of the Mattson legacy would provide enough income for both of them, but he understood her desire to have some independence. Maybe she'd be okay with having just one client at a time, as she did now.

"Folks, I see some of you have started eating!" Albert called out, interrupting Will's thoughts. "But let's take a minute to thank the Lord for the food."

Everybody paused while he lifted his face upward. "Lord of all creation, thank You for food, fun and friends. Thank You for health, even for old codgers like me." He glanced at Will and winked. "And thank You that You've already chosen the winners of tonight's games and… other matters. But we know that in You, we are all winners. We pray in Jesus's holy name. Amen."

"Amen," chorused the crowd.

A breeze sent the mouthwatering aroma of

barbecued beef swirling around the yard, causing Will's stomach to rumble.

"Hungry?" He gazed down into Olivia's beautiful face, and his love intensified. It was all he could do not to tell her right away how much he loved her. How he wanted to protect her and Emily and to share life with them.

She returned a smile and, if he wasn't mistaken, he saw in her eyes a reflection of his love for her. Never had a lady looked at him with such genuine, selfless affection. Warmth and happiness spread through his chest such as he'd never experienced before.

"Sure." She sounded a little breathless, as though she was as caught up in the moment as he was. "Looks like Papacita and Lila Rose have the food line well in hand."

They located Jemmy and Emily and took their places at the end of the food line. Folks loaded up a sturdy brand of paper plates with ribs, hamburgers, hot dogs, potato salad, baked beans and all the trimmings. They found seating at the half-dozen rented picnic tables or sat on blankets laid out on the lawn. Albert had hired a small band to provide music for the evening, and they struck up their first set.

"Livy, Will. Over here." Lawrence beckoned to them from one of the tables.

Once they'd settled the children and all began to eat, Lawrence cleared his throat. "Livy, we've got some news for you."

Both he and Nona focused on Olivia, who grinned broadly.

"Go on."

Lawrence gripped Nona's hand. "This beautiful lady has agreed to be my wife."

"Oh, Dad, Nona. I'm so pleased." Olivia's eyes shone with happy tears. She jumped up and ran around the table to hug them both.

"Congratulations." Will reached across to shake Lawrence's hand. As always, the older man's grip was firm and confident.

"This afternoon I emailed my book to my editor," Nona said. "So, it's time for me to go home. I've asked Lawrence to go with me so he can meet my family."

For a moment, worry crossed Olivia's face as she returned to her seat. She quickly brightened. "That's great. I can't wait to meet them, too." The worried look returned. "Um, Emily and I are leaving in the morning for the homeschool convention in Albuquerque. The horses and the puppies…"

"No problem," Will said. "I'll still be here with Albert, so I can feed them and your hummingbirds."

Her happy expression returned. "Oh, thank you. That's such a relief. Hey, why not let Jemmy ride Fred again?" She laughed. "Turn him into a little cowboy, right?"

"Sure." He chuckled. "If he gets good at it and likes it, maybe one day he'll ride those bucking broncos."

With supper over, Lila Rose brought out her final creation, a huge sheet cake with ninety burning candles. "Time to sing 'Happy Birthday.'"

The crowd gathered around again and sang to their generous host. Some had brought cards and a few gifts, although Albert had told them not to. Even so, he graciously accepted a colorful patchwork quilt made by several of the ladies and a picture album of photos chronicling the history of his property. While helping Albert organize his clutter, Will had found numerous pictures from the past and had given them to a longtime neighbor, who put the album together.

With everybody's attention on Albert, Will took Olivia's hand and led her off to the side.

"I—I, uh…" For some odd reason, the right words stuck in his throat.

"Yes?" She looked up at him with sweet innocence and expectation.

Now, he didn't hesitate. Tugging her into his arms, he planted a kiss on those beautiful lips. To his relief, she rose up on her tiptoes and returned the kiss. Will thought his heart might burst with joy on the spot.

After a moment, he pulled back. "I love you, Olivia. I want to spend my life with you."

She blinked back tears. "I love you, too, Will." She laughed softly. "Tried not to, but couldn't resist."

"Ah, won over by the infamous Mattson charm." He smirked playfully. "If I ask you…" For some reason, he hesitated to say "to marry me." "…do you think you might agree to exploring our…uh…friendship further?"

More tears. "I might agree to that."

"Oh, darlin'. You're too good to be true." He kissed her forehead and swayed to the music that had started up again. He sang along with the old love song, "Can't Take My Eyes Off You." She followed his movement, feeling just right in his arms.

The song ended, and Albert again called for everybody's attention.

"Folks, we have a few prizes to hand out." He held up a handful of envelopes. "The prize for the men's boulder fumble is Reggie Garcia." He went on to name the other game winners and hand each one an envelope containing a gift card for the local big-box store. "Now, you all voted for the best part of our Independence Day celebration. And our second place winner is Miss Ina's portraits!"

Will's heart hitched up. He hadn't considered how pleased the guests would be over getting a personalized cartoon drawing by a famous artist. Now, would his win for providing the popular food trucks, especially the one selling ice cream, cause him to lose Olivia?

"And our grand prize winner is..."

The band provided a drum roll.

"The bouncy house!"

Will staggered back as though a boulder had slammed him in the chest.

CHAPTER TWELVE

THE INSTANT WILL stepped back from her, Olivia missed the physical contact with him. It took her a moment to realize she'd won their competition.

"Oh!" She clasped her hands to her chest. "I can't believe it." She looked up at Will. His shocked, devastated expression shouldn't have surprised her, but it did. Only now did she fully comprehend what this loss would mean to him and Jemmy…and Lila Rose's boys. "Will—"

He lifted a hand and turned away.

"Will…" she repeated, trying again.

"Just give me a minute." He walked several yards away.

"Olivia!" Nona hurried over to embrace her, with Dad right behind. "I'm so happy for you. Once you remodel Albert's house, I'm sure we can keep it filled with plenty of artists who'll love this place as much as I do."

"Congratulations, Livy." Dad's tone held much less enthusiasm than Nona's. "You must be pleased."

She shrugged. "I'm sure it was the kids who voted for the bouncy house." She glanced toward Will and whispered, "He's taking it pretty hard." How could their relationship go forward now? How would she have reacted if he had won?

Following Will to a shadowed area behind the house, she grabbed his hand. "Look, we have a lot to talk about. A lot to sort out."

"Yeah." He blew out a sigh so deep, she could feel it in her own chest. "Don't mean to be a bad sport about this, but..."

"You're not. You just had your plans, as worthwhile as they are, dashed to pieces." Why couldn't she just tell him right now she would let him buy the land? Somehow, the words stuck in her throat, maybe because it would be foolish to surrender her dream for momentary emotions.

"Listen, Will." She squeezed his hand, but he still wouldn't look at her. "I have to leave in the morning for my convention. When I get back, maybe we can sort everything out. If you want, I'll still get the kindergarten material we talked about for Jemmy. And—"

Now he faced her and gently grasped her arms, pulling her close for another kiss that made her knees go weak. He moved back and traced a finger down her cheek.

"I love you, Olivia. Nothing changes that." Even in the shadows, she could see his sad smile. "Like you said, we'll sort everything out when you get back. I'm staying with Albert until his grandson can get over here and help him move. Then I'll clear out so you can—"

"What part of waiting to sort this out don't you understand?" She grinned, hoping he could hear the humor in her voice.

He chuckled, but it sounded sad. He brushed a strand of her hair back from her face.

"Let's drop it for now." She nodded toward the crowd. "They're still enjoying the music."

"People sure aren't in a hurry to leave." He led her back into the lit yard. "Hey, look. Some of the guys are playing softball out in the field."

"Want to join them?"

"I could." He watched for a moment, then shook his head. "No, the kids are getting antsy, so I need to bring out our final surprise for them. Albert and I thought about having sparklers but decided against it because of the danger of sparking a wildfire. So, we bought glow sticks instead. Kids always like those."

He headed toward the house, and she followed. "Maybe we should have waited for the vote. The glow sticks would surely win."

He winced painfully.

"Too soon?"

"Ya think?"

"Sorry." She grasped his arm to stop him. "Will—"

"Shh." He brushed a hand over her cheek again. "Give me some time to adjust, okay?"

This time, she let him go. She had a few things to adjust to as well. Nona would soon be her stepmom, and her daughters the sisters she'd never had. The entire configuration of her family was about to change. At least maintaining her own business would help her keep some control over her and Emily's lives.

Who was she kidding? If she and Will decided to get married, they would have a Christian marriage, which meant both of them would surrender much of their personal control. And she couldn't think of anything better than being a wife to Will and a mom to Jemmy. Her marriage to Sancho had been a partnership, and he'd never bossed her around. Will would be like that. She'd seen it in everything he did and said. But, despite what he'd just said, she feared winning this stupid competition over who won the right to buy Albert's property might have destroyed her chance to find that out for sure.

THE HOMESCHOOL CONVENTION, set in the huge hospitality hall of a large hotel in Albuquerque, was the break she needed from the drama at home. She let Emily's interests guide which displays they visited and which videos they watched. Even if her daughter changed her mind as she grew older, this approach helped her develop discernment. The biggest problem Olivia had was keeping her mouth shut over some of Emily's choices. If she bought every book or teaching tool her daughter wanted, her budgeted money would be spent long before the week was over.

"Mommy, take a picture of the giraffe." Emily pointed to a tall cutout of the animal in a display for preschool books. "I want Jemmy to see it."

"Okay, sweet pea. Go stand by it." Olivia pulled out her phone and punched the camera icon. To get the whole giraffe in the picture, she stepped back several feet. Her heel caught on something, and she flailed her arms, trying to regain her balance, but found herself flat on her back on top of a flattened cardboard display. More stunned than hurt, she blinked as several people rushed to help. Heat flooded her face. How could she be so clumsy?

"Mommy!" Emily ran to her in tears.

"I'm okay, honey." Olivia tried to sit up.

"My dear," an older lady said. "You shouldn't move until the paramedics check you."

"I'm fine. Really."

Several others urged her to lie still, but she pushed up to a sitting position and pulled Emily into her arms.

"I'm okay. Just embarrassed. This display broke my fall." Offering a sheepish grin to the crowd, she stood. "Not so sure about the display, though." She assessed the cardboard. "Maybe a little gray tape will help. At least that's what my dad always says."

Several people in the crowd chuckled as they dispersed.

"Don't worry about it." The lady who owned the display patted Olivia's shoulder. "I've been using this one for years, so maybe the Lord's telling me it's time to replace it."

Despite the lady's dismissive words, Olivia and Emily helped her put it back together as best they could. "Thanks. This will do for the rest of the week," the woman said.

"Mommy, did you get the picture?"

"Let me check." Olivia glanced around. "Where's my phone?"

After searching for several minutes, they found the device several yards away...thoroughly shattered. She must have flung it away as she fell.

"Well, that's that." She shrugged. "Sorry about the picture, sweet pea."

More than that, she wouldn't be able to text Dad or Will. Not that Will would want to hear from her after losing his bid to buy Albert's property. He asked for time to recover, and she could respect that. And Dad was probably having the time of his life with Nona.

She'd never been obsessed with social media, but it still felt strange to be out of touch. Borrowing a thought from the lady who'd so quickly forgiven her for ruining her display, Olivia decided to look for the good in this situation. Maybe the Lord took away her phone so she could better concentrate on Emily and her needs. She still had her credit card to make purchases, and she could always buy a disposable camera at the hotel gift shop for those all-important photos.

"I'M NOT SAYING you should be overly concerned, Joe." Will tried to keep the worry out of his voice as he talked on the phone. "Just that your granddad hasn't quite recovered from his birthday bash. You'd have been amazed at how energetic he was all day, but it's caught up with him. He's been down and out these past two days."

"Oh, man," Joe said. "I'm sorry work kept us from coming to the party, but we're having one for him when he gets here. Maybe I should come get him now."

"I think that's a good idea." Will considered his next words. "I guess he hasn't had a chance to tell you about selling this place."

"No, but that's okay. I have a buyer who's ready to sign and pay on the spot. He's a developer who's buying it as is because he plans to tear the house down and build a tourist getaway. I'm waiting for Granddad to get here to finalize the sale, but the guy's really eager." Joe sighed. "I'd have already signed, but I wanted to respect Granddad's dignity rather than sell it out from under him."

It took a moment for Will to swallow his shock. With his power of attorney, Joe had every right to handle all of Albert's business dealings. "Um, so Albert hasn't told you he planned to sell to his neighbor, Olivia Ortiz? He promised her she could buy it."

"Oh." Joe was quiet for a bit. "Is she ready to sign? Does she have financing? I can bring the paperwork."

"Well, no. She's out of town, but—"

"Look, I'm sorry to put pressure on anybody, but I've got things going on with my business that I can't leave for more than a day. And I need the money from the sale upfront to pay off the loan for the addition we've built for Granddad. I need to take care of this now. If she can't sign and pay when I get there tomorrow, I'm gonna have to go with this other guy." He named the amount the other man had offered.

"I'll take it as is." The words came out before Will considered them. No matter how disappointed he was about their ridiculous competition, he couldn't let this place be sold out from under Olivia. "And I'll have a check ready for you." He had no idea what kind of financing she'd planned on, but he could use his own money and work it out with her later.

"That sure would uncomplicate things. So, we have a deal. See you tomorrow."

After disconnecting the call, Will felt a wave of satisfaction. He loved Olivia and wanted her to realize her dream. As disappointed as he was that he couldn't use this unique little ranch for raising Jemmy and Aunt Lila Rose's boys, he would do all he could to support her. What that meant for them when…*if* they got married, well, they'd have to figure it out when she got back.

He made sure Albert was settled in his recliner, TV remote in hand, then drove into town with Jemmy to arrange the cashier's check.

"Say, pal, you want to visit Benji and the boys?" Banking would be easier and faster if he did it alone. He glanced in the rearview mirror to see Jemmy's response.

"Benji and Jeffie and Mikey and Josh." His singsong recitation of their names showed his growing relationship with his foster brothers. He'd even endured a few bumps without complaint or fear as they played in the bounce house. "Em'ly's in A-bu-ku-kee."

Will chuckled. "That's right, pal. She'll be back on Saturday." And, if all went well at Will's adoption hearing the day after tomorrow, and if he and Olivia got married, they would be Jemmy's parents and Emily would be his sister.

THE NEXT MORNING, Albert was up early and feeling a little more like his spry old self.

"I hate to leave before Olivia and Lawrence get back, but I appreciate your taking care of the particulars on the sale." He took a bite of the scrambled eggs Will had prepared. "You sure you don't mind making trips back out here to tend the chickens?"

"Not at all." Will sat across from him. "Olivia's mentioned how much she likes having the fresh eggs, so I'm sure she'll want to keep them. And I have to feed the horses, too." And let Jemmy have another ride or two on Fred.

"I'm real pleased with the way you and Joe have taken care of this sale for Olivia." Albert eyed him for a moment. "In fact, you sure have been a good sport about all of this."

Will concentrated on his plate. He hadn't entirely worked through his feelings about losing out on buying this place, but surely the Lord had it all figured out. So much depended on what he and Olivia decided about their relationship. So much depended on the judge's granting him the right to adopt Jemmy, but that was no doubt a done deal.

Joe Winslow arrived from Amarillo around noon. Will checked for any problems in the purchase agreement and found none, so they signed on the spot, and he handed over the cashier's check.

"I'll take care of registering the paperwork," Will said. "We can take care of the rest through email." He'd have to wait for Olivia to return so he could register the deed in her name.

"Sounds like a plan."

With the sale in order, Will helped Joe load his pickup with Albert's stuff.

"I can't thank you enough for taking care of Granddad all this time." Joe reached out to Will. "It meant so much to him to stay long enough to throw that birthday party, but we never could have managed to come over here and help him with it."

Will shook his hand. "He's been an important part of this community for many years. He'll be missed."

"I was born here and lived here all my life,"

Albert said. "The neighbors were mighty kind to come out and celebrate with me, and I'll sure miss them. But my future's with my grandson and his family. I've got all my important papers and pictures, but you can help Olivia sort out the furniture and what all. What she doesn't want, you can donate to charity."

"Bye-bye, Mistuh Albewt." Jemmy hugged the old man who'd been like a grandfather to him these past two months.

Will had to hang onto his own emotions as they drove away. There would be a big hole in his own life now that Albert was gone.

After tending the chickens and packing up the puppies—who whined all the way to town because they didn't like being confined in the carrier—Will spent the afternoon at his apartment making sure he had all the information the judge might ask for tomorrow.

To HIS SHOCK, when he and Jemmy went to the courthouse, Grant and Mabel Sizemore sat in Judge Mathis's courtroom looking for all the world like decent people. Will had to swallow hard to keep from expressing his outrage. How did these two manage to fool everybody but him?

"Will, as you can see, Jemmy's aunt Mabel and her husband have joined us today." The graying, sixtyish judge peered at Will over her blue-rimmed reading glasses. "Like you, they are petitioning for custody of Jemmy."

Eyes wide, Jemmy stared up at Will and stuck his thumb in his mouth, a habit he'd given up weeks ago. Will gave him a reassuring hug. He'd brought him so they could celebrate after his adoption was confirmed, but the little guy didn't need to see this drama.

"While I appreciate your taking and passing the state-mandated courses to become a foster parent, as well as your prior claim to be granted guardianship of your nephew, I believe that a two-parent home is in Jemmy's best interest." The judge stared down at some papers. "Are you still living in an apartment?"

"Yes, ma'am." Will swallowed his rising panic. *Lord, help!* "But I just bought a house, and my girlfriend and I are making plans for the future. She's a widow with a daughter, and they've both bonded with Jemmy."

When he told Olivia he loved her, he should have proposed to her on the spot. Then he could honestly call her his fiancée. But he wouldn't lie to the judge. On the other hand, Olivia did agree to seeing where their relationship was going. Well, *might* see where it was going. Why hadn't he sealed the deal on the spot? Because he'd been too caught up in losing that ridiculous competition. And now he might lose Jemmy, too, because he hadn't put his love for Olivia above his disappointment over losing the right to buy Albert's place.

"Ah." Judge Mathis removed her glasses and leaned forward over her bench. "That does shed new light on the situation." She turned to Grant and Mabel. "I'm going to postpone my final decision until I can meet this woman and assess her qualifications. If nothing turns up to cast doubt on her, I will have to reconsider placing Jemmy with you."

"Now, Judge, don't you think we've already proved ourselves—" Grant bristled like a grizzly as he glared at Will.

"Now, honey." Mabel patted his hand. "You know Judge Mathis will make the right decision." She turned a too-sweet smile on Jemmy. "I can't wait to be your mommy, darling boy."

Jemmy pressed against Will's side as tears slid down his cheeks. Only when they got back to the apartment and Jemmy sat on the floor to play with the puppies did he smile again.

Heart pounding, Will knew he had to solve this problem immediately. He'd tried to call Olivia right after his first phone conversation with Joe Winslow, but she hadn't picked up and hadn't responded to his message. At the time he hadn't felt undue pressure to explain in the message that he'd bought Albert's property, but would turn it over to her once they sorted out their plans for the future. But this new situation meant he needed to sort everything out right away. He punched her number's autodial and waited. No answer. Could she be mad at him? What for? She won the competition. Now he was mad at her. Why couldn't she just answer her phone?

Because if she didn't help him get through this minefield with Jemmy's adoption, maybe they shouldn't get married after all. Annoyed, he left a brief message about buying the property and said he'd explain the rest when she got home. He ended the call.

Wait. What had he just done? She'd need a better explanation than that.

He started to punch her number again, but it buzzed with an incoming call. He swiped to answer without even checking to see who it was.

"Olivia! Finally—"

A deep male voice sounded in his ear. "Sorry to disappoint, Will." He laughed. "Girlfriend problems?"

"Rob." Will slumped back on the couch. "Sorry. And, no—no girlfriend problems." Or none he could talk about, anyway. "What's happening?"

"Good news, bad news. Which do you want first?"

Will released a long sigh. "Bad news, I guess." He looked across the room to where Jemmy was playing with the two puppies. Would he have to give up his beloved little Buddy?

"You know we always keep DNA on all of our dogs. We're still haven't found Lady, but the DNA says the pups are hers."

"Oh, man…"

"And now the good news. For you, at least. The father shows as all-American mutt, so we won't be able to sell them as purebred or even a mixed breed."

Will heard the words but couldn't sort them out. "So, that means?"

Rob chuckled. "It means whoever stole Lady didn't want mongrels, so they dumped the pups. Though, how they planned to sell any of her pups without papers is anybody's guess. Maybe they were going to forge them." He paused. "So, if you want to keep those two little rascals, it's fine with me."

After a moment, Will found his voice. "Thanks. That's the best news I've heard all day."

"Anything I can help you with?"

Will considered unloading on his cousin. Maybe he'd do that later if Grant and Mabel were granted custody of Jemmy and Will needed some backup to prove they weren't as reputable as they let on.

"No, thanks. You've already helped more than you know."

Now, if he could just reach Olivia with this bit of good news, maybe his life would get back on track.

ON THE WAY home from the convention, Olivia drove to the phone store to switch her broken one for an upgrade. She'd wanted to increase her storage, anyway, so she was glad she'd paid for replacement insurance that covered most of the new one's cost. After the chunk of change she spent on homeschool supplies, her budget was already strained. The grocery store was her next stop before heading home.

It seemed strange to drive past Albert's place and not see Will's truck parked there. She'd said her goodbyes to Albert before leaving, but she could sense his absence, too. Now, to make plans for remodeling his house. She and Nona had discussed several great ideas. It would just be a matter of financing.

Her own house also felt empty. Since Sancho's death, Dad had been her rock, but his life would soon change. For the better, of course, but where would that leave Olivia? Would she and Will find a way to combine their goals so both could follow the Lord's plans for their lives? Or would he be too disappointed about not buying a refuge for his boys? Surely, there were other places he could buy for his aunt.

She and Emily pulled their wheeled suitcases into the house, then brought in their groceries and bags of school supplies.

"Can I...*may* I read my new book?" Emily dug into her tote.

"Sure, sweet pea." She sat at the kitchen table to get acquainted with her new phone. Most of the buttons were the same, but she wanted to set it up with her own Wi-Fi and check for messages.

Once that was done, she checked her voice

mail. To her surprise, Will had left several messages. She punched the icon to hear the first one.

"Hey, Olivia. I hope you and Emily are having a good time." Pause. "Soon as you can, give me a call back." Pause. "Love you."

Despite his sweet signoff, she couldn't miss the tension in his tone. That call had been five days ago. The second message said much the same, with a hint of annoyance coming through his words. But the third message cut straight to her heart.

"I bought Albert's property because Joe said—"

He bought the property? After their agreement that she had that right? A sick feeling rose in her chest. She swiped the message to delete it and the two that followed. If only it would be that easy to delete Will Mattson from her life.

Suddenly exhausted from her hectic week, she crossed her arms on the table and rested her head on them. What had she been thinking to let him get close to her and Emily? What could she do now?

A knock on the back door shook her from her stupor. That would be Will, of course. He had some nerve to come over here to gloat. She stomped through the living room and library, and flung open the door.

"What do you want?" She glared at him, just as she had on that first day when Albert had brought him over for an introduction. And just as she'd feared back then, he had used his lifelong friendship with Albert to wrangle his way into her life and steal her dream away.

And then, he had the nerve to stand there looking all innocent and confused, the only appealing thing about him the puppy in his arms.

"I, uh, first of all, welcome home." He gave her that dazzling smile, which now looked like a victory grin.

"You have some nerve." To her annoyance, hot tears filled her eyes. "What do you want?" she repeated.

Only then did she notice Jemmy staring up at her wide-eyed, clutching Buddy.

Will shifted awkwardly. "What's going on, Olivia?"

"You have the nerve to buy Albert's property while I was away, and you want to know what's going on?" She took Bitsy from his grasp and backed up to close the door.

He planted one dusty cowboy boot on the threshold. "Olivia, I explained—"

"Did you or did you not buy and pay for Albert's property?"

"Yes, but—"

"Case closed. Please move your foot so this door can also be closed."

His wounded look almost persuaded her to—to what? He withdrew his boot, and she shut the door. Through the glass, she could see sweet little Jemmy's tearful expression before they turned to walk away. Her heart dropped to her stomach. She'd bought several pre-K materials for him and even planned to ask Will if she could have him sit in on Emily's lessons. Thank the Lord that she learned the truth about Will's deceptive ways before their relationship got too far.

What was she thinking? It had already gone too far. She had fallen for him. Had meant it when she agreed to explore their relationship further. Even began to dream about their future together. Why hadn't she listened to her own doubts about him? Instead, she'd fallen for his charming ways and dazzling smile. Oh, and who could forget those piercing blue eyes? Ugh!

Now the tears came. She hadn't sobbed this hard since Sancho's funeral. Bitsy wiggled in her arms, and she set her down. After a few moments of self-indulgent crying, she inhaled sharply and headed to the bathroom to wash her face before checking on Emily. To her surprise, she found her daughter had climbed into bed fully clothed and was sound asleep. And no wonder, after their busy week. That meant she probably hadn't heard Olivia's conversation with Will. *Thank You, Lord.*

Poor baby. She would be devastated when she learned she could no longer play with Jemmy. But after Will's betrayal, how could Olivia have any association with him or his nephew?

She managed to put away groceries and partially unpack their clothes before tending to Bitsy. The puppy could now eat from a dish, so Olivia set water and food in the kennel in Emily's room. Physically and emotionally exhausted, with no appetite for supper, she followed Emily's example and went to bed. But weariness didn't make falling asleep any easier… or stop her tears.

Bitsy's whimpering and whining came from Emily's room and only added to her sadness. Poor puppy was missing her brother. How long before she got used to being the only dog in the house? Probably a lot sooner than Olivia would get over Will's treachery. The thought renewed her tears, and she finally cried herself to sleep.

IN THE MORNING, Olivia dragged herself out of bed too late to get ready for church. She hadn't wanted to go, anyway, since she wouldn't be able to avoid Will there. She managed to sort through the school supplies and set those she'd bought for Jemmy by the back door. Will's truck wasn't parked by his new home. Had he gone to church, or just not moved in yet? With him gone, maybe she should collect the eggs...

Oh, how annoying. She hadn't bought eggs yesterday because she was so used to getting them from Albert. But she would never step foot on that property ever again, so she'd have to give Emily granola for breakfast, though it wasn't her daughter's favorite. She'd make a trip back to town tomorrow for eggs.

And she'd stop by the home-improvement store for supplies to nail the gate between the properties shut. That should drive home her resolve to never speak to Will Mattson again.

That plan failed to give her the peace and satisfaction she'd hoped for. In the back of her mind, she couldn't ignore the thought that she should have heard Will out. But nothing could change the fact that he'd bought the house Albert had promised to her, the house she'd won the right to buy through their competition.

Wasn't that reason enough to shut him out of her life forever? No matter how much it broke her heart…and Emily's?

CHAPTER THIRTEEN

"THE END." WILL finished the final chapter of *The Fellowship of the Rings* and closed the book. "All right, guys, what do you want to read next?"

"*The Two Towers*," Benji said.

"*The Black Stallion!*" Jeffie shouted.

Will chuckled. Jeffie usually followed Benji's every move, so voicing a different opinion was a healthy step in developing his own identity. "Okay, you guys talk about it, and we'll take a vote tomorrow."

Why did he say that? The last vote he was involved in didn't go well.

After praying with the boys and putting them to bed, he had coffee with Aunt Lila Rose in the kitchen. "Thanks for letting Jemmy sleep over. I need to get to the office early so I can start making it up to Sam for all the time I've taken off."

She reached across the table and patted his hand. "I'm just so sorry for the way things turned out. I like Olivia, and I'm still not convinced she isn't the right girl for you."

Will snorted. "Well, she's definitely convinced she's not." He'd never seen Olivia angry until yesterday. Annoyed, yes. Indignant about the puppies being abandoned, yes. But all-out anger over his supposed betrayal of her trust and her refusal to listen to his explanation revealed an intractable side of her he didn't know how to deal with. He only knew he still loved her and prayed he could find a way to reconcile with her.

At least Jemmy had settled down after their encounter with Olivia. He'd been upset over her angry words, plus not getting to see Emily, until Buddy's antics diverted him. He'd even agreed to the sleepover with his foster brothers. This was a huge growth step, and most of it was due to his friendship with Emily. Maybe after spending more time with the other boys, he would forget the adorable little dark-haired girl who'd brought him out of his shell. And maybe, given enough time, Will could forget that girl's dark-haired mother…somehow.

WITH EMILY BESIDE HER, Olivia guided the grocery cart around the aisles, finding more than just eggs to buy. She'd been so tired on Saturday, no wonder she forgot several staple items. She reached up to select a ten-pound bag of flour, then changed her mind and chose the five-pound bag. Dad had called last night from Florida to say he'd be there another week, so she would only be baking for herself and Emily. No more cooking for Albert. No more Jemmy gobbling up her cookies. No more enjoying Will's appreciative glances when he ate her carrot cake. And no additional hosting of clients beyond one or two at a time in the studio apartment. If Dad moved to Florida after he and Nona married, he would take his two pension incomes with him. Then how would she support Emily?

"Em'ly!" Jemmy came running up the aisle, arms wide.

Olivia's pulse kicked up. Where Jemmy was, Will couldn't be far behind. Instead, he was followed by Lila Rose's four foster sons and, several yards back at a much slower pace, the lady herself.

As Emily and Jemmy hugged, a lump formed

in Olivia's throat. Oh, how she had missed this little guy. When he gave her a hug, she had a hard time holding in her tears.

"Miss Olivia." Benji grabbed her hand in an awkward but cute attempt to shake it like grown-ups did. "Got any more knock-knock jokes?"

The other boys crowded around and looked up at her expectantly.

She managed to hide her tears with a laugh. When had she fallen in love with the lot of them?

"Well, let's see." She struck a thinking pose, then looked down at the cartons of eggs in her cart. "Okay. Here's one. Knock, knock."

"Who's there?" the boys, even Jemmy, chorused.

"Omelet."

"Omelet who?" they all answered.

"Omelet you finish."

Their blank looks gave her another laugh. "Omelet? I'm gonna let—"

"I don't think they know what an omelet is." Lila Rose chuckled in her maternal way. "Guess I'll have to fix them omelets one of these days."

"Ah." A warm rush of affection for this lady flooded Olivia's heart. When Lila Rose and her boys moved out to their new home, they would have plenty of eggs for omelets. "Okay, here's another one. Knock, knock."

Again, the boys said simultaneously, "Who's there?"

"Cereal."

"Cereal who?"

"Cereal pleasure to see you today." And she meant it with all her heart.

This brought the desired raucous laughter from all the kids, including Emily.

"All right, gang." Lila Rose motioned them to gather around her, and they quickly obeyed. "You all have your assignments. Run along."

The boys scattered, with Benji holding Jemmy's hand.

"Mommy, may I go, too?" Emily's big brown eyes held a soulful expression.

Hesitating only a moment, Olivia said, "Okay. Stay close to Benji and Jemmy."

She chewed her lip and took a step to follow them. While she'd let Emily fetch groceries at Papacita's store, this was the first time she'd be doing it in a bigger store.

"She'll be fine." Lila Rose chuckled again. "The employees here know our kids and look out for them. A bunch of them are related to us."

Two months ago, Olivia would have rolled her eyes. Now, she could only feel relief.

"I'm so glad we've run into each other, Olivia." Lila Rose's smile disappeared. "I know you and Will had a bit of a falling-out, but I'm asking you to pray for him. He may lose custody of Jemmy."

"What? Why?" She'd never want that. Despite his buying Albert's land while she was away, he was a wonderful father to Jemmy.

"Jemmy's father's sister has petitioned for custody, and because she and her husband own a home and are already foster parents, the judge thinks he should be placed in a two-parent home."

"Oh, that's heartbreaking." Olivia glanced in the direction the children had gone, wishing she could give Jemmy another hug.

"Yes, well, Grant and Mabel Sizemore have a lot of people fooled, but—"

"Grant Sizemore!" Olivia gasped. "I know who he is, and I can't believe any sane judge would place any child in his home."

Lila Rose stared at her for a moment. "How do you know him?"

"Just look at this." She located the video on

her new phone, thankful it had transferred from her old one.

"Oh, my word." Lila Rose gasped. "Please, you have to send that to Will."

Olivia hesitated. Would this just open a door she meant to keep shut? "Let me send it to you. You can forward it."

"Please." Tears shone in Lila Rose's eyes, and she grasped Olivia's hand. "I'm no good with these devices—"

"Mom, we got the spaghetti." Benji marched proudly up the aisle, followed by Jemmy and Emily.

"Good job." Lila Rose dabbed at her tears with a tissue as the other children rejoined them with their shopping treasures. She praised each one for getting exactly what she'd assigned.

Before she could think it through, Olivia tapped her phone screen to send the video to Will. She typed in: Ask Papacita for his CCTV of this.

There. That should do it. She wouldn't have to do anything more to save Jemmy from those horrible people.

But if that was so, why did she feel so melancholy when she hugged the boys goodbye, as though it was the last time she would see them, especially Jemmy? When she'd collected school materials for him at the convention, she'd envisioned the day when she would be Will's wife and Jemmy's mother. She'd mentally planned pre-K lessons for him and the lessons he could share with Emily. And now, that would never be.

Even today, as she watched these normal, healthy, rascally little boys help their foster mom with her shopping, her heart embraced them all. How could she begrudge them the wonderful home Will had bought for them? Was she being unreasonable? Or just disappointed that her own dreams would never be realized?

From the moment Albert had introduced Will—and his plans—to her, a tiny niggle of doubt about her own plans had tried to take hold in the back of her mind. She'd always shut down the thought because of her need to support Emily through her hospitality business. But what if having a father and brother were more important to her daughter? What if marrying Will and becoming a part of the vast Mattson clan would give her a supportive community she could always count on?

No. She could never marry a man who would betray their agreement. She would do all she could, even write a letter or speak to the judge in person about the Sizemores, to help Will officially adopt Jemmy. But she would never again trust him with her own future...or her heart.

FLANKED BY RAMON MARTINEZ, Will strode into the courtroom armed for bear. If Olivia's brief video wasn't enough to convince Judge Mathis that Jemmy belonged with him, Martinez's CCTV and his testimony about Sizemore's thefts should seal the deal.

To his surprise, more than a dozen Mattson relatives sat in the room smiling and nodding their support. How had they found out about his adoption dilemma? Ah, well. In this small town, everybody knew what the Mattsons were doing. He greeted them with nods.

Rob stood and shook Will's hand. "We've all been praying for you."

"Thanks." Will swallowed sudden emotion and made his way to one of the front tables, followed by Martinez. At the other table, Grant and Mabel stared down their noses at him. He couldn't wait to wipe those smug grins from their faces.

Yesterday, he'd been bowled over when Olivia's text arrived with the ten-second video showing Sizemore forcing the boy to steal canned goods. Her unexpected help gave him renewed hope for their relationship. But when he tried to text back his thanks, she'd already blocked him. Stubborn woman. What could he do to make her listen to his reason for buying the land? And that he'd bought it for her!

One problem at a time. Right away, he'd contacted Martinez, who was all too eager to help him. Now today he had to convince the judge. Tomorrow he would try again with Olivia. Maybe this posse of relatives could help him with that, too.

"Mr. Mattson." Judge Mathis peered at him over her reading glasses. "I see you didn't bring Jemmy with you. Will you have a problem obeying this court and turning him over to the Sizemores?"

Will stood. "Yes, ma'am, I will have a problem. And I'm sure you will as well when you see this new evidence." He held up his phone.

"And this new evidence." Martinez stood up beside him and held up the tablet he'd brought.

"What new evidence?" Sizemore sneered. "We've already passed inspections and interviews. We've been foster parents for five years. What more—"

"One moment, Mr. Sizemore." The judge beckoned to Will. "Let me see what you have."

He presented his phone. "Just tap—"

"I'm not a dinosaur, Mr. Mattson." She glared at him briefly before tapping the device. "Hmm. The video is a bit shaky, and the sound isn't clear, but…"

"Your Honor." Martinez stepped forward and offered his tablet. "This will give you a better view."

She played the video, then motioned to the bailiff and spoke softly. "I want you to take Mr. Sizemore into custody for child abuse and a Class C misdemeanor of inciting a child to steal."

"Yes, Your Honor." The uniformed bailiff marched over to the table. "Grant Sizemore, I'm arresting you on a charge of child abuse and theft." He recited the man's Miranda rights. "Do you understand?"

Sizemore's jaw dropped and his eyes widened. "But—but…" As the bailiff led him from the room, he glared at Will. "This isn't over. I'll get—"

"That's enough, Mr. Sizemore." Judge Mathis banged her gavel on the sounding block. Once Sizemore was out of the courtroom, with Mabel following him in tears, she continued. "Now, Mr. Mattson, we still have the issue of providing a home for Jemmy. I will give you one month to improve your living situation. If you move into that house you purchased, I will let you officially adopt Jemmy. Then if you marry your young lady and she passes her interview, she can also adopt him. Until then, he may live with you." She banged her gavel again. "You're dismissed."

The room erupted in cheers as uncles, aunts, cousins and various cousins-in-law rose to congratulate Will. Martinez clapped him on the shoulder. "I would be honored if you permitted me to cater your wedding reception. If you thought my barbecue was good, wait 'til you try the wedding feast I will prepare for you."

"Uh, that sounds nice." Will gave him a weak smile. This was not the time to tell his friends and family that Olivia wanted nothing more to do with him. In fact, there would likely never be a good time.

"DAD, YOU DON'T UNDERSTAND. He bought and paid for Albert's place while we were gone." Olivia held her phone away for a moment as she swallowed a sob. "What part of 'he cheated on our agreement' don't you understand?"

"Hold on. I think *cheated* is a pretty strong word." Dad sounded good, even over the phone. "Did he call and explain what he was doing?"

She sighed. "I dropped my phone and broke it on our second day in Albuquerque. Didn't get a new one until we got home. He'd left messages but didn't explain himself." She chewed her lip. "To tell the truth, I didn't give him a chance. Once he said he bought the land, I deleted his message. That was all I needed to know."

Silence on the other end.

"Dad? Are you still there?"

"Daughter, where's the good sense the Lord gave you?" He had the nerve to laugh. "You go right over there and ask him about it."

"But—"

"What are you afraid of?"

Good question. Was it fear of confirming his betrayal? Or embarrassed pride over not giving him a chance to explain?

"And now," Dad said, "in other news. Nona and I are working on our wedding plans. Her girls are on board with our marriage, and I want you to be part of everything, too. Her younger daughter, Jillian, will be a senior in high school in the fall. Her other daughter, Maeve, just completed her BA, but her plans are up in the air. So, we all have a lot to figure out." Dad chuckled. "Livy, you're gonna love these young ladies. They're a hoot, just like their mama."

As he continued to describe Olivia's sisters-to-be, a sinking feeling settled into her chest. She and Emily had been Dad's world since Mom died. Now, other people were taking center stage in his life. She was happy for him, truly happy. But where did that leave her and Emily? While she'd been in Albuquerque, dreams of her own possible future with Will had balanced her concerns about the coming changes. Those dreams vanished after she'd listened to only a part of one of his voice mails.

The night of Albert's party, they'd agreed to see where their relationship was going. They'd also put off sorting out their different plans for the land. Why had she assumed he would agree to her establishing her hospitality business? Of course, he would still want the place for his boys. She'd just been too busy at the convention to think too much about it. Or…had she just been avoiding the truth?

Now, things were becoming clearer. She wasn't mad at Will for buying the little ranch. She was mad at herself because she knew he'd been right all along. The boys needed Albert's home more than any possible guests she might have, and even more than she needed to expand her business. The Will Mattson she had come to know and love would never do anything to hurt her. He must have had a good reason for his actions. And if at their ages, Dad and Nona could be flexible about their future together, she needed to be flexible about hers.

So, if Will wanted a life with her and Emily, she wanted him and all the people who came with him in hers. Jemmy and Aunt Lila Rose and all her boys and the entire Mattson clan, whoever they were. As for those boys, she might have to buy a book of knock-knock jokes, but she'd figure that out later.

Now, how could she make it up to Will for refusing to hear him out?

Easy. She gathered the ingredients for her carrot cake and got to work making her peace offering.

WILL SIGNED THE stack of forms and legal documents his new paralegal, Lauren Parker, had put on his desk, then dug into one of his new cases, this one concerning an adoption. As he did for all his clients, he prayed for this couple, specifically that they would be able to adopt the infant left at the fire station where the husband served as a firefighter. While the mother hadn't seen fit to identify herself, at least she'd loved her infant daughter enough to put her in a safe place, where she would be found and adopted. And nothing gave Will more satisfaction than sealing the deal for such worthy couples.

Now, if only he could seal the deal with Jemmy's adoption. At least Judge Mathis had permitted Jemmy to stay in Will's custody until he worked out the problems regarding where they would live. He just had to figure out how to give his nephew two parents. Who could understand Jemmy better than he did? And Olivia had embraced the little guy with genuine love. She would make as perfect a mother to Jemmy as she was to sweet Emily. And Will had already started reading up on how to be a father to little girls. That was, until Olivia shut him out of their lives.

When he bought the place from Joe Winslow, he planned to sell the land to Olivia so she could establish her business. His loss meant he needed to find a house, maybe in town, for Jemmy and him. Aunt Lila Rose's three-bedroom home on a fairly small lot didn't have space for expansion, so moving in with her wasn't an option.

He'd gone into family law because of Aunt Lila Rose's work and his own family's dysfunction. He didn't want any child to go through what he and Megan had. Mom had left—he still didn't know what had happened to her—and Dad had withdrawn into his own little world, leaving the two of them to fend for themselves.

When Will was growing up, the only things that had made sense to him were Aunt Lila Rose's steady, loving guidance of her various foster kids and his time spent with his greatuncle Andy, who had taken him under his wing out at the Double Bar M Ranch. But Megan fell for a guy who, unlike Dad, seemed strong and decisive. Others could see Ed was a controlling narcissist, but Megan wouldn't hear it. Even before Ed beat her to death, then died in a hail of SWAT team gunfire, Will had determined he would do everything he could to protect Jemmy.

His work done for the day, he texted Aunt Lila Rose to say he was on the way. At her request, he stopped to buy some pizza makings, then helped her feed the gang their favorite supper. The boys, including Jemmy, had voted for *The Black Stallion* to be their next book, so he read the first chapter to them. They clung to every word as Alec Ramsay, a boy they could all relate to, went on his adventures with the magnificent stallion he'd befriended.

As always, he sat at the bedside of each boy and heard his prayers before tucking him in. Benji was the last.

"Mr. Will, when do we get to see Miss Olivia again?" He blinked sleepy eyes. "I've got some more knock-knock jokes for her."

Will shook his head. "I don't know, Benji. We grown-ups are pretty busy…"

"Is she mad at us?"

"No. Why would you ask that?"

Benji shrugged against his pillow. "When grown-ups get mad, they leave."

Will gripped his emotions so he could answer calmly. Like his own mother, Benji's single mom had abandoned him for reasons unknown. "Well, Miss Olivia isn't mad at you. She likes you a whole lot."

"When you see her, will you tell her we like her a whole lot, too?"

Will patted Benji's shoulder. "I'll do that."

As usual, Jemmy was asleep on the couch, so Will visited with Aunt Lila Rose in the kitchen.

"When will you see Olivia so you can give her Benji's message?"

Will gave her a mock-scolding frown. "You were eavesdropping."

"Guilty." She topped off his coffee. "Now, answer my question."

"I've already told you. She's blocked my texts and phone calls." At the memory, the day caught up with him, and he slumped in his chair. "I need to get Jemmy home."

"No, you don't." His aunt waggled a finger in his face. "What you need to do is go out to her house and tell her why you bought Albert's place." She sipped her coffee. "I'll keep Jemmy tonight so you can go out there first thing to-morrow morning."

"Aunt Lila Rose—"

"Don't Aunt Lila Rose me." She held up one hand like a stop sign. "Just do it."

Irritated and amused at the same time, he raised both hands in surrender. "Okay. Okay. But I'm taking Jemmy with me so she won't throw me in the river."

He'd also take the paperwork from the sale

and hand it over to Olivia as a peace offering, along with a promise to help her remodel the house to accommodate her future guests. If he really loved her—and he did—nothing would be too great a sacrifice to make her believe him. And after he got that settled with her, he would start looking for a bigger house in town, where he and Jemmy could live with Aunt Lila Rose and her boys. Maybe Judge Mathis would accept his aunt as the mother figure Jemmy so badly needed.

OLIVIA CAREFULLY TOOK the carrot cake she'd made for Will from the fridge, placed it in her Tupperware carrier and snapped on the lid. If he didn't show up at his new home soon, she would pack up Emily and head to town to find him.

Last night, she'd kept watch for him, to no avail. Anxious to settle things with him, she'd prayed he would forgive her for not listening to his entire message. Prayed maybe they could pick up where they'd left off the night of Albert's party. Prayed she hadn't ruined any chance to make a family with him.

"Mommy, Mr. Will's here. And Jemmy!"

Emily squealed with delight as she ran to open the front door.

While the kids hugged each other and ran off to play, Olivia could only stare at Will, her heart hammering in her chest.

"Hi." He gave her that devastating toothpaste-commercial smile and shuffled his feet like a schoolboy. "Got a minute?"

His shyness shocked her. When she could speak, it came out a whispered "Yes." She waved a hand toward the kitchen. "I made you a cake."

He blinked those gorgeous blue eyes, and for the first time since she'd known him, she saw a charming vulnerability. "You made me a cake?"

She snorted out a nervous laugh. "That's what I just said."

"Right. That's great. Thank you." He stepped over the threshold. "And, listen, I can't thank you enough for sending that video. The judge was about to give the Sizemores custody of Jemmy, but when she saw it, she was blown away. Had Grant arrested on the spot."

Olivia's eyes stung, and a lump formed in her throat. "I'm so glad. You're a wonderful father to Jemmy. It would have been a crime, literally, for that terrible man to get custody."

"You've got that right." He glanced down at the legal-size envelope in his hand, then held it out to her. "I brought you something."

"And that is?"

"Papers for you to sign so you can buy Albert's place."

"What?" She stepped back. "What are you talking about?"

"Olivia, I had to buy it or Joe was going to sell it to a developer. As is. Right away." His breathless rush of words hinted that he thought she wouldn't listen if he didn't hurry to say it.

Now, it was her turn to blink. "He was going to sell it? You mean he didn't ask Albert?"

"No. Once Albert gave him power of attorney, he was trying to do what was best for his granddad, which included building an additional room to his own house. He needed the money from the sale to pay for that, so he was ready to grab the first lucrative deal offered to him. He didn't know about our competition to buy the place."

It took a minute for her to digest this information. Finally, she said, "Well, that makes sense."

"I had enough savings to give him a check right away." Again, Will appeared vulnerable, almost apologetic. "I did it for you, Olivia." He held out the large envelope again. "The house and land are yours. And I'll help you with remodeling or whatever you need so it'll be just what you want for your guests."

Hot tears stung her eyes. Oh, how she had misjudged him, not only about his motives for buying the house, but also from the moment she'd met him. When her original negative opinion of him began to slip away as she got to know his true character, she should have known he would never do anything to hurt her. He truly was her knight in shining armor, rescuing her from losing out on Albert's land.

"So, do you want it or not?" He gave her a teasing grin.

"Yes." She snatched the envelope from him. "After all, we'll need a place for you and Jemmy and Aunt Lila Rose and her boys to live. I can't think of a better place than right next door. Can you?"

"No, but I—" He turned away and ran a hand down his jaw, then faced her again. "You'd give up your dream for my boys?" He choked out the words, and his eyes turned suspiciously red, his deep emotion endearing him to her even more. "What about your plans?"

"My plans have changed from definite to uncertain. When I got the idea for entertaining artists, I was looking for a way to support Emily and myself, but that included having Dad's help. Now that he and Nona are getting married, I don't know what the future holds. He owns this house, and Nona loves it, so they may want to live here. If not, I can always keep on renting out the studio." She gave Will a sheepish smile. "Besides, there's this cowboy who might be planning to propose to me. If he does, well, I might just accept. So, there's that. I mean, if he actually proposes."

Will dropped to one knee and lifted pleading hands. "Mrs. Olivia Ortiz, would you do me the honor of becoming my wife?"

She swallowed her tears. "Yes, Mr. Will Mattson. I would love to be your wife."

He patted his shirt pocket. "Uh-oh. No ring. Maybe we could shop for one today."

"Unka Weeoo, you okay?" Jemmy appeared in the doorway, his blue eyes round with worry.

Right behind him, Emily looked just as worried.

Will stood back up and pulled Olivia into his arms. "Jemmy, I couldn't be better." He gave

Olivia a quick kiss, then whispered in her ear, "We can improve on that later."

A pleasant shiver swept down her side. "Oh, you can be sure of that, Mr. Mattson." She turned to the children. "Who wants carrot cake?"

The now-grinning kids led the way to the kitchen table. Once Olivia had served everyone a generous piece of the cake, Will took a bite and closed his eyes as he savored it.

"Man, this is good. You're an amazing cook, Olivia." He eyed the kids. "Jemmy, I have asked Miss Olivia to be my wife. Do you know what that means?"

Nodding, the darling boy gave him a crooked grin. "She's my new mommy?"

"That's right." He turned to Emily. "What do you think?"

"You're gonna be my new daddy?"

"Would you like that?"

She answered by jumping down from her chair, running to Will's side of the table and throwing her arms around his neck. "Yes, yes, yes!" She planted a kiss on his cheek as he returned the hug.

Olivia tamped down the sudden ache in her chest. Emily's memories of Sancho had faded over the past three years, and she didn't want her daughter to ever forget what a good, heroic man her father had been. But the Lord had brought Will into their hearts and lives to fill the void Sancho's death had created. She offered a silent prayer of thanks and released the ache to make room for joy.

Emily returned to her place beside Jemmy. "That means you'll be my brother."

"And you'll be *my* brother."

Olivia tried not to laugh, but when Will laughed out loud, she let go, too.

"Silly Jemmy." Emily giggled. "I'm a girl. I'll be your sister."

Jemmy twisted his face in confusion, then grinned. "Okay." He giggled. "Sissy sister."

"Baby brother."

"I'm not a baby," Jemmy protested.

"I'm not a sissy." Emily smirked, then giggled, as did Jemmy.

Will chuckled. "I think teasing is going to be a big part of their growing up together."

"I don't know whether to be glad I was an only child," Olivia said, "or sorry I missed out on the fun."

"My sister and I were relentless in our teasing." A brief shadow crossed Will's eyes, but he gave his head a quick shake and seemed to dismiss whatever sorrow that memory brought up. "Okay, guys…and girls—" He winked at Olivia. "We have cake to finish eating and eggs to gather. Then I need to get to work. Sam's been carrying my share of the load for quite a while. Jemmy, Aunt Lila Rose's expecting you."

"Let him stay here with us, Will," Olivia said. "It's not too soon for me to start learning how to be a mom to a boy."

Will gave her that smile she loved so much. "I think you already have the hang of it. Just stock up on knock-knock jokes, and you'll be fine."

"Right. Got it." Her heart flooded with joy as she anticipated a future that had been so uncertain only an hour ago.

Thank You, Lord, for answered prayer.

CHAPTER FOURTEEN

"MAN, THIS IS a real problem." Will studied the list he'd made. "Fourteen male cousins I grew up with who live in the area and another nine scattered around the country and the world." He scratched his jaw. "How's a guy supposed to pick a best man without offending the rest of them?"

Seated next to him at her kitchen table, Olivia viewed his list. "Oh, my. Please do me a favor and make a chart of all these names and what branch of the family they come from. And maybe put a picture beside each name so I don't embarrass you or myself at the reception."

He pulled her closer and kissed her temple. "Not to worry, babe. We're used to it." He glanced at the legal pad in front of her. "You haven't written any bridesmaid names."

"I don't have a clue about who to ask." She sighed. "I'm the only child of two only children, so I don't have any cousins. After I married Sancho, we got busy with starting a family and working in his ministry, and I lost track of my college friends. After he died and I moved here, I just didn't have a chance to make close enough friends to ask such a personal favor of." She snickered. "When I hinted the idea to Lila Rose, she shut me down real quick." She nudged his arm and gave him a teasing smirk. "Maybe I should ask Judge Mathis. She seemed to like me."

"What's not to like?" Will tapped her nose. "Once we get back from our honeymoon, we'll get those adoption papers signed and make you Jemmy's mom officially." It had been a proud day when the judge declared him Jemmy's dad, and he wanted Olivia to experience the same joy soon.

"Until then, I still need a bridesmaid." She gazed out the window toward the dozen or so hummingbirds buzzing around the feeder. "*Somebody* has kept me too busy to make any new female friends around here."

Will didn't know whether to tease or console her. He opted to give her another side hug. He wasn't sure a double wedding was the best idea, but he'd do anything to make Olivia happy.

First, she'd wanted to elope, an idea Will liked a lot. Then Lawrence and Nona called to suggest they all get married together here at Riverton Community Church. As the only one who hadn't been married before, Will decided to go with the flow.

"Is Nona planning to have bridesmaids?"

"Yes," Olivia said. "Her daughters will share the honor. And Dad's asked Jim Wainwright to be his best man. Seems they got pretty close through their Sunday school class." She ran a hand over her blank page. "At least we know what Emily and Jemmy will be doing."

"Oh, yeah. Jemmy's excited about being our ring bearer. Emily?"

"She's excited about our matching dresses." She gazed up at him with those beautiful brown eyes. "And that's all I'm saying about it. You aren't allowed to see them until we walk down the aisle."

"I'm looking forward to it." Will planted another kiss on her temple. "You'll be the most beautiful Mattson bride in history."

"You sure about that?" She leaned against his shoulder. "That's a lot of history. All the way back to 1879."

"Ah, I can tell Lila Rose's been telling you about those thrilling days of yesteryear."

"Absolutely. You come from a long line of decent, hardworking cowboys. You should be proud of them."

He leaned back in his chair. "And still I can't figure out which one of their many descendants to be my best man."

"Here's an idea." She gave him that cute grin he loved so much. "What about Albert?"

Will stared at his bride-to-be. "Brilliant. Absolutely brilliant. We owe him big-time for introducing us." He paused. "You think he's up to it?"

She picked up his phone from the table and held it out to him. "Only one way to find out."

STANDING AT THE back of the church, Olivia clasped Nona's hand as they watched her daughters, Maeve and Jillian, walk down the aisle in their matching peach satin tea-length gowns. Nona had generously shared her bridesmaids with Olivia, making their double wedding a true family affair. Ahead of them, Emily, also in an adorable white dress, dropped orange rose petals along the carpet. Right behind her marched Jemmy, in his dress cowboy suit complete with jacket and bolo tie to match his new daddy and carrying a white satin pillow bearing four rings...all safely tied on with satin ribbons.

Olivia wore an ivory lace tea-length dress, and Nona had opted for ivory satin. They both wore short, gauzy veils, secured by satin bands and layered over their upswept coiffures.

"Ready?" Nona asked.

"Ready if you are." Olivia released Nona and clasped her bouquet of white roses with both hands.

The bridal march began, and the large congregation stood. The two brides walked side by side toward their respective grooms. Dad's friend and dear Albert stood to their right, completing the wedding party.

The ceremony passed in a blur for Olivia. For one brief moment as she recited her vows, she remembered doing this before. Then she gazed up at Will and knew God had sent him into her and Emily's lives. And what a blessing that Dad and Nona would still be part of their lives. Nona would continue to write her bestsellers, and Dad would manage the artists' retreat, only on a smaller scale than Olivia had planned. Will and Olivia had already remodeled Albert's former home to accommodate their own new family as well as Aunt Lila Rose and her boys. It would be a hectic household, but Olivia looked forward to the challenge.

At last Pastor Tim said, "I now pronounce you husband and wife, and husband and wife. Gentlemen, you may kiss your brides."

The sanctuary broke out in applause and plenty of cowboy-style yeehaws. Soon the two couples were cutting their twin wedding cakes, which would be served to their countless guests in the church reception hall. With Will having so many relatives, Olivia had suggested they post an open invitation. Papacita's lavish wedding buffet and the country band music filling the air meant everyone would have a good time.

"Congratulations, Will." Rob Mattson walked over, a glass of strawberry punch in his hand. "Miss Olivia, I don't know how my ugly cousin managed to win over a pretty lady like you, but welcome to the family. We're all glad you and your sweet daughter are joining us."

"Thank you, Rob." Olivia couldn't believe she'd ever felt disdain for this wonderful ranching family. And just maybe, she and Will would one day add their own children to its ranks.

"Now, how about you, Rob." Will nudged his cousin with his elbow. "When are you gonna get married? Those twins could use a mama, don't you think?"

Rob snorted. "It's not a mama they need, it's something to focus their energies on." He chuckled. "You're good with kids. Got any ideas for me?"

Will tsked. "Sorry, cuz. My expertise is younger kids, not teenagers." He glanced around the room and then gave Rob a sly look. "You know, my new paralegal is a single lady. How about I introduce you to her?"

Rob stared down at his wristwatch. "Would you look at the time? Gotta get back out to the ranch." He made a hasty retreat.

Olivia gave Will a sympathetic smile. "Guess we'll have to work on him. What's his story?"

Will sighed. "His wife, Joanie, died in an accident a few years ago. Took him a long time to recover—if one ever recovers from losing a spouse." He gazed down at Olivia, sending a pleasant jolt of love through her heart. "Sorry. You know more about that than I do."

She rose up on tiptoes and kissed his cheek. "But God can heal a broken heart if only we let Him."

"That's so true." He put his arm around her

waist and pulled her close. "Are you having a good time?"

"Yes, indeed. You?"

He pasted on a fake frown. "You sure those kids aren't making too much noise? I know you value your peace and quiet."

She watched the kids chase each other around under June's supervision. Although they were rowdy, they weren't destructive, just having their own kind of fun. Olivia didn't mind at all.

"Jemmy and Emily are having a great time. He's not so shy anymore." She chuckled. "Besides, peace and quiet are way overrated. There's nothing so sweet as the sound of kids laughing and having fun."

"I couldn't agree more." He squeezed her waist and gave her another kiss.

While she savored his sweet affection, peace and joy flooded her entire being. This was her new life, and she knew in her heart Sancho would approve.

★ ★ ★ ★ ★

A Cowgirl's Homecoming

Julia Ruth

MILLS & BOON

Julia Ruth is a *USA TODAY* bestselling author, married to her high school sweetheart and values her faith and family above all else. Julia and her husband have two teen girls and they enjoy their beach trips, where they can unwind and get back to basics. Since she grew up in a small rural community, Julia loves keeping her settings in fictitious towns that make her readers feel like they're home. You can find Julia on Instagram: juliaruthbooks.

Guide our feet into the way of peace.
—*Luke* 1:79

DEDICATION

I can't let this opportunity pass
without praising God for opening this door.

CHAPTER ONE

The ranch is in trouble.

JENN SPENCER COULDN'T get the text from her sister out of her head. For the past few months she'd been on the verge of coming home, but that terrifying statement gave her all the boost she needed. She hadn't spoken to her family in years, but now it was time to put the past behind them.

Jenn glanced around the old building she'd be renting during her time back home—both the salon on the ground level and the apartment above. Her new landlord was late, but that gave her a chance to check out her new space thanks to the back door code she'd been given in the rental agreement.

The place certainly needed a fresh start... maybe that was why she'd felt so drawn to this old building when she'd seen the listing online. There were cobwebs and dirty corners that needed cleaning up in her own life as well.

And that revelation was yet another reason she found herself back in Rosewood Valley. Northern California had always held a special place in her heart, but three years ago tragedy forced her out of town. Thoughts that couldn't plague her now...not if she wanted to move forward. While her late husband was always in her heart and on her mind, Cole would want her to mend those tattered relationships and live her life to the fullest.

She needed to meet with her landlord before she could venture to the farm and take that monumental first step. She honestly had no clue how she'd be received, but she needed to know how she could help save the place and restore broken bonds.

One baby step at a time.

Pushing aside the past and vowing to look toward a positive future, Jenn propped the back door open and made a few trips bringing in storage totes. She figured she had to begin somewhere if she was going to get her new life started...no matter how temporary. If things didn't work out, she'd have to face the consequences of her actions and possibly move from her hometown for good.

The nice spring breeze and the warm sunshine drifted in from the back alley, already boosting her mood. After about five trips, Jenn checked the time on her cell and wondered what was keeping her landlord.

Just as she lifted a stack of shampoo capes from the tote, a soft clicking sound echoed from the back door. Jenn turned her attention to the little brown pup that cautiously pranced through, with his little toe nails clacking on the chipped tile flooring and his nose to the ground as if following a scent.

"Oh, buddy. You can't be in here."

She took one step toward the light brown pup with his unkempt curly hair hanging down in his eyes. The poor thing cowered at her voice and scurried beneath the shampoo bowl against the back wall. Before she could figure out what to do with this unexpected visitor, the front door opened with the most annoying jingle. That bell would have to go.

Jenn straightened and shifted her attention toward the entrance as a tall, broad man stepped over the threshold. Like any true gentleman, he removed his cowboy hat upon entering. That simple gesture only revealed the handsome face beneath the shield of the brim. With his free hand he held on to an adorable little girl wearing a cute purple dress and matching cowgirl boots.

But the girl's hair had a serious wad of gum on one side. Jenn cringed as a memory of her childhood with her three sisters flashed through her mind. Another time, another mess of gum, more reminiscing she couldn't have prepared for.

"Good morning," she greeted, realizing this was her first interaction since she'd been back in town. "I'm not open yet, but give me a few days."

More like a month, but she had to get started so she could build back her savings. She'd just have to work with the dated decor for now and prioritize her needs and wants. Needs would be utilities and groceries. Wants…well, there were too many to list. Paint and flooring would be a good place to start. Maybe some air fresheners and a vase with some cheery spring flowers.

"I'm Luke. Your landlord," the man said. "Sorry I'm late, but we have a hair emergency."

She hadn't expected her landlord to be so…

attractive. Someone older, retired maybe, with thinning gray hair and a thick midsection had come to mind. Certainly not a thirty-something man that seemed to fit the mold of a proverbial Western cowboy.

"She said she wasn't open, Toot," the little girl whispered, staring up at her father.

Jenn chewed the inside of her cheek to keep from laughing. What did this little cutie just call her dad?

The man glanced at the girl, sighed, then turned his attention back to Jenn. "We have an emergency," he repeated. "She's getting birthday pictures taken later today and *somehow* there's gum stuck in her hair."

He gave her a side-eye, silently expressing his frustration at their current predicament. The muscle beneath his bearded jaw ticked.

"Oh, is that your puppy?"

The little girl broke free and started toward the back of the salon. A furry animal clearly trumped a gum fiasco.

"Honey, you can't just go after every animal you see," he stated. "You need to ask if you can pet her dog."

"That's not my dog," Jenn explained, shaking her head. "He wandered in right before you did."

Jenn had no clue how her morning had gone from wondering how to finally approach her family, meet her landlord and unload her boxes, to dealing with a stray dog and a wad of matted hair…not to mention the unexpected attraction to this stranger.

The girl poked her purple glasses up with her index finger then turned to Jenn.

"Can you get the gum out?" She picked up a thick chunk of hair beside her face and held it out for Jenn to see. "Toot bought me the cutest ribbon with purple flowers that matches my new cowgirl boots and I really want to be able to wear it for my pictures."

Clearly this sweet girl had a favorite color. Jenn's heart clenched as another memory flooded her mind. Her own matching bows and boots, the excitement of breaking in a new pair as she helped her father on the ranch. But the love for boots had faded these past three years and Jenn hadn't touched hers since she left Rosewood Valley.

They were forgotten…just like her dreams.

"Paisley, she's not open yet. We can find

someone else." The guy came to stand next to his daughter as he offered Jenn a warm smile. "I will come back to make sure you're all settled once I get her hair taken care of. She has an appointment with a photographer in an hour. I'm not normally this scattered but...kids."

He took Paisley's hand once again and started to turn, but those bright blue eyes gripped at Jenn's heart and she couldn't let them walk away. Maybe she couldn't solve her own problems with a simple haircut, but she could brighten this little girl's day.

"I'll meet you at that chair up there." Jenn pointed toward the front of the salon. "Let me find where my sheers and booster seat are and we'll get you picture-perfect in no time."

LUKE BENNETT ALWAYS counted his blessings when he could, and right now, the great gum debacle was getting fixed and he nearly wept with gratitude.

He knew nothing about raising a little girl, let alone a hair crisis. But his late brother had entrusted Luke enough to put him on the will. When Luke had agreed to be Paisley's guardian, he'd done so never imagining he'd actually have to step into that position.

As Jenn bustled around looking in one tote then another, Luke crossed to her and lowered his voice.

"If you don't have the time, I completely understand."

Her delicate hand stilled on one of the lids as her vibrant green eyes met his. The tips of her silky blond hair brushed against one shoulder and the pang of attraction startled him. She had a subtle, yet striking beauty. No makeup, her hair pulled up in a high ponytail...she looked just like her sisters. Yet there was something about this woman that intrigued him. Perhaps the underlying hint of pain he saw staring back at him or maybe the mystery involving her return, he wasn't sure. And no matter if he found her attractive or not, he didn't have the mental capacity to take on anything else in his life...not to mention he refused to risk his heart again.

Luke hadn't realized when he rented the building online that his new tenant would be Jenn Spencer—one of the girls the Four Sisters Ranch was named after. The very ranch he had his sights set on. He'd proposed something risky to Jenn's parents about acquiring their land, but he'd yet to get a reply. He wasn't backing down...not when he had too much on the line. Time was certainly of the essence for so many reasons.

"I remember being a little girl and getting excited for bows and boots," Jenn said.

A wide but sad smile flirted around her mouth, pulling him from his thoughts. Something haunted her. He could see the raw emotion in her eyes but couldn't get caught up in her troubles…not when he had a whole host of his own to combat.

"It's no problem as long as you all don't mind I'm not set up at all and this isn't normally how I work." She laughed. "I've only been here a half hour."

"Mind?" Luke shook his head. "You're saving the day if you can fix this. I have no clue what to do with a seven-year-old's hair, let alone one with a tangled mess."

"Well, we'll see what we're dealing with. Don't give me those accolades just yet." She dug farther into the tote and pulled out a black pouch. "Here we go. Now we're all set."

Jenn's focus shifted to the dog still hunkered under the sink. "Any idea who he belongs to? There's no collar and he just walked in from the back as I was bringing some things in."

Luke tapped his thigh with his hat and looked

to the pup who stared back with cautious eyes. He inched closer, not wanting to scare the poor thing. And a quick glance had him smiling.

"Your he is a she," Luke confirmed, then shrugged. "If you care."

Jenn laughed. "I hadn't even thought to look. I've always had male dogs growing up, so I just assumed."

"I've never seen her before. She looks like some type of a Spaniel mix. I can call a few people while you're fixing Paisley's hair."

She nodded. "I can't thank you enough," he added, relieved this nightmare might be fixed and they wouldn't have to cancel birthday pics.

Who knew being a single parent could be so difficult? Each day brought on a new adventure. Of course those "adventures" could be called disasters, but he preferred to try to stay somewhat positive. He still had a garbage disposal to work on because a doll head had gotten stuck in there. He didn't even want to know how that happened.

"No worries," she said. "And forgive me for asking, but what did Paisley call you?"

Luke laughed and shook his head. "Toot. It's a long story. I'm so used to it, I don't think about what other people wonder when they hear it."

"Sounds like a special relationship."

Jenn smiled once again before crossing the salon toward Paisley. *Special friendship* was a very mild way of putting things, considering he'd gone from long-distance uncle to permanent guardian in the proverbial blink of an eye.

Moving from Oregon to California and trying to start a new life, a new business, and put all of Paisley's needs first while dealing with the grief of losing his brother and sister-in-law had been the hardest time of his life. Not to mention the rental agreement on his brother's home was up in two months. They'd been preparing to build so they'd just been renting a small cottage, which was where he and Paisley lived.

He honestly didn't know how people got through such tragic events without their faith. He'd gotten on his knees in prayer so many times, begging God to give him the guidance to take on the role of father and make the best decisions for this new life he and Paisley shared.

Luke pulled out his cell and sent out several messages, trying to shift his focus from his own problems and worries to the misplaced pup. Hopefully he'd hear something soon. He highly doubted Jenn had the time or the space to keep a dog considering she was new to town.

"You know, I got gum in my sister's hair when I was little?" Jenn said.

Luke turned his attention toward the pair. Paisley sat perfectly still in the salon chair with a black cape around her shoulders as Jenn seemed to be examining the damage.

"You did?" Paisley asked, her eyes wide with curiosity. "Was she mad?"

"She was at first until our mom took her to get a new haircut and she loved the new style so much, she thanked me for the accident. Now, my mom—that's a different story. I had to do dishes every night for a month."

Paisley smiled and a warmth spread over Luke's heart. Smiles had been few and far between as of late, and no matter how short the happiness, he'd take it. That's all he wanted for his niece. Yet a sliver of guilt hit him as he listened to Jenn speak of her family. The way her father had insisted on keeping the potential sale of the family ranch a secret had Luke convinced that there had to be underlying friction with the homestead. He wasn't trying to rip the family apart, he just wanted a piece of their farm. He couldn't feel guilty for trying to provide the best life for Paisley.

A piece of land with a barn would be so ideal. He could renovate the large building for the livestock he tended to and he could build a nice, modest home for him and Paisley to start their lives. There was no secret in town that the Four Sisters Ranch had hit hardship. Wasn't this the best solution for everyone involved?

"I think if we cut just a little and make some layers around your face, we'll be good to go."

"Can I still wear my bow?" his niece asked, her eyes wide with worry.

"Absolutely." Jenn turned the chair away from the mirror. "I don't want you to see until I'm all done."

"Like a surprise?"

Jenn nodded. "This is definitely a surprise."

Luke kept his eye on the dog, who seemed to be perfectly content tucked in the corner. He'd been a veterinarian for five years now. While he specialized in larger farm animals, he'd learned early on that all God's creatures were essentially the same. They had true feelings, fears and instinct. This dog probably knew she was safe in here, but the pup still kept a watchful eye on them, just in case.

The girls chatted about hair and boots, and Luke realized how much Paisley needed female conversation. He made a mental note to add pampering into a monthly routine for Sweet P. Coming to a salon and having someone do her hair, plus girl talk, was exactly what Paisley needed in her life right now. Would this make up for all she'd lost? Absolutely not, but Luke planned on integrating positive moments every chance he could get.

Moving any female into his life on any level would be difficult. The scar left behind by his runaway fiancée still seemed too fresh, but he had to put that hurt in the very back of his mind because that chapter in his life paled in comparison to this current chapter.

He glanced back to the dog, who had finally fallen asleep. Likely someone in town was missing their family pet and hopefully they'd put a collar on her once she returned home.

"What do we think?"

Luke looked back just as Jenn spun the chair around for Paisley to see her reflection in the mirror. Jenn fluffed the blond hair around Paisley's shoulders and his niece's smile widened. His heart swelled with a happiness he'd been missing over the past few months.

"Do you like it?" Jenn asked.

"I look older." Paisley beamed. "I love it."

Jenn caught his eyes in the mirror. "Sorry about that," she said, cringing. "I wasn't going for older. I was going for gum-free."

Luke shook his head. "Gum-free was the goal," he agreed. "I think she looks beautiful."

"You have to say that," Paisley argued.

"Who says?" he countered.

Paisley pursed her little lips, thinking of a reply, when his cell vibrated in his pocket. He pulled it out and glanced at Jenn. Her striking eyes still held his and his heart beat a bit quicker. Good thing he had a call to pull his attention away from the beauty threatening to steal his focus.

"Hopefully this is someone about the dog," he explained before he turned to take the call from a number he didn't recognize.

"This is Luke."

"Mr. Bennett, this is Helen Myers from Beacon Law Firm. Is this a good time?"

He glanced to the girls, who had eyes on him, wondering if he had news about the pup. He shook his head and covered the cell.

"I need to take this," he whispered as he moved to the back of the salon.

He had no idea why a law firm would be calling him, and this wasn't even the firm that had handled his brother's will.

"I'm sorry, what did you say this was about?" Luke asked as he got to the open back door.

"I didn't, but my client Carol Stephens is seeking guardianship for Paisley Bennett and I need to set up a time to meet with you and your attorney. She would like to make this as seamless as possible for the child."

A pleasant breeze blew in from the open back door, random noises from the alley out back seemed to echo off the buildings, and Paisley and Jenn had started chatting once again. But all he heard was that someone wanted guardianship of his niece. *His* niece.

"I don't even know who this Carol is," he stated, then rattled off his lawyer's name. "You can call her if you need any further information, but the will was clear on who Paisley would be with. The name Carol wasn't even in the documents so I doubt she has a strong connection to my brother."

"She didn't think her name would be in the will, but that's a long story and one of the many reasons we need a meeting. Carol was Talia's best friend and cousin. She's the only family member Talia has left, but she's been overseas in the military. She's home now and is seeking custody."

Luke's hat dropped from his hand. He leaned against the doorjamb and attempted to calm his breathing. Getting worried or worked up wouldn't help things and he had no idea if this call was even legit.

But he did know that he was the only family member left on this side and Talia apparently was the only family member left on the other. Was that what this would all come down to? A ball of dread settled hard in his stomach.

"I'm not saying another word," he informed the woman. "If you need anything, you can call my lawyer, but Paisley is going nowhere."

With that sickening weight in his gut, he disconnected the call. Nobody could take his niece from him…could they?

CHAPTER TWO

"I NEED HELP."

Jenn clutched the dog in her arms and raced through the doors of the vet's office. The tiny waiting area with only three chairs was empty, but she'd seen a truck out front so she hoped someone was available. Fear consumed her as she glanced around for anyone to fix this problem.

"Hello?" she called.

"Jenn." Paisley jumped up from behind the receptionist desk and came around, her eyes wide. "What happened?"

Shaking, Jenn looked toward the doors that led to the back, hoping someone would come out. Any adult or provider who could take over this dire situation.

"I think she ate some of my hair color," she explained, swallowing the tears clogging her throat. "Is the vet here?"

"In the back. Come on."

Paisley led the way as she started calling out for Toot. Any other time she'd still find that name amusing, but right now her nerves were on edge and her heart beat much too fast.

Luke stepped into the narrow hallway from a side room, his eyes wide as he took in the sight. She'd had no idea he'd taken over Charles Major's clinic, but now wasn't the time for questions or trying to get to know her new landlord any better. She knew the old vet, as Charles had helped on her family's farm for years. But she wasn't going to get picky now.

"Jenn," Luke called.

He moved quickly, taking the dog from her. He led them into another room down the hallway. Luke lay the dog on the sterile metal table and turned his concerned eyes to her. Even in the midst of this chaos, an unexpected jolt of awareness hit her hard. She couldn't allow her thoughts to stray or become too distracted by a handsome stranger.

"What happened?" he asked in a voice much too calm in comparison to her own nerves.

She explained how she was in the front display windows using her vacuum for the dust and cobwebs when she heard commotion in the back and found the pup in the dispensary. Hair color covered the fur around her mouth and paws, tubes of color were all over the floor.

"Please tell me I didn't kill this poor dog!" she cried.

What a day for her first transition back into town. She hadn't even gotten the courage to go see the farm or her parents yet because she'd been procrastinating by cleaning and running over her speech in her head for when she finally landed on their doorstep.

What could she say to make up for all those years she'd stayed away? When she'd left Rosewood Valley after Cole suddenly passed, she'd been so angry and heartbroken. She'd said terrible things to her father, blamed him for Cole's death. She'd wanted her family out of her life… and now she needed to make amends.

"I'm not sure what's going on yet." Luke went into full work mode, his focus only on the dog now. "Let me do an assessment and run some tests. Why don't you go wait with Paisley in the lobby and I'll let you know something soon."

"I'll wait here."

He shot those piercing blue eyes over his

shoulder, but she held her ground and tipped her chin, silently daring him to make her leave.

In a flash, she recalled another time and place…another man. Cole used to get perturbed with her when she'd wanted to hang in the barns when animals were giving birth. He wanted space to work and didn't want her around if something bad happened. Always trying to shield and protect her from the messy bits of life.

Very likely that's why Luke wanted her gone now. But she wasn't going anywhere. Life was messy—there was no getting around that fact. She'd tried running from her past mess and now she had an even bigger one to clean up, so here she was back in her hometown and ready to tackle whatever she needed to set her life back on the right path.

Because she respected Luke and his position, she did step back to the corner to stay out of his way. Jenn marveled at the way he was so gentle yet efficient with the pup. Luke asked her a few questions as he worked and informed her he'd know more after the tests were run.

Just having his calm voice in her moment of panic really settled her nerves. As if his looks weren't enough of an attraction, now he had charm and comforting mannerisms…all qualities in her late husband that she both loved and missed.

She couldn't be attracted to her landlord. She didn't want that reminder of all she'd lost when her husband passed. A man with a child was everything she'd been hoping for, but that was another lifetime ago.

This phase in her life was all about a fresh start, repairing relationships with her family and saving her farm. Nothing more.

"GOOD NEWS." LUKE came back into the small exam room to find Jenn stroking the pup's tan fur. "Doesn't look like anything toxic in her bloodstream. I don't believe she ingested anything, but we will keep a close eye on her to make sure she's acting okay."

Jenn straightened and blew out a sigh. "That's a relief. I thought she was sleeping the whole time I was cleaning and I had no idea she'd gotten into anything. I'm not an irresponsible person—"

Luke gave her shoulder a reassuring squeeze. "It's okay. Accidents happen and I never thought you did anything on purpose."

A tender smile spread across her face. And as

beautiful as she was, it was the red-rimmed eyes that tugged at his heart. She obviously had a soft spot for animals. She'd grown up on a farm and hadn't ejected the stray pup from her shop, and he was sure there was likely some code or rule against animals in that type of business.

Why did he have to find her so adorable in a way that completely surprised him? He'd seen her sisters around the farm and in town and not one of them, while each pretty in their own way, had even remotely ruffled his interest. He didn't have time to start a relationship and there were too many reasons he shouldn't.

The main one being he'd just found himself in a custody dispute and he still wanted a piece of the Four Sisters' farmland. Was that why she'd come home? Did she know they were thinking of selling? What had Jenn heard?

He had no idea what brought her home, but he knew he still needed to keep quiet. None of this was his place to address. Whatever happened between him and Will and Sarah Spencer was between them. If they wanted to bring their girls in on the proposal, that was their business, but until he knew for sure what Jenn was aware of, Luke would remain true to his word.

Luke couldn't help but wonder why Jenn

hadn't taken the dog to her sister, Violet. Vi was the small-animal vet in town. Were the sisters not on speaking terms? Granted his office was closer to Jenn's salon, but still. Odd that she didn't go to family first.

There had to be a rift, but he shouldn't concern himself with anyone else's business. Not only did he have enough on his own plate, he'd been so burned before, the last thing he needed was to get swept away in someone else's woes.

"Can I take her home?" Jenn asked, breaking into his thoughts.

Luke stepped back. "Does that mean you're keeping her?"

Jenn reached up and tightened her ponytail as her eyes traveled back to the dog, who didn't seem to have a worry in the world.

"I can't just toss her out," she admitted. "I hope pets are allowed in the building you rented me."

Luke laughed. "Of all people, you think I'm going to say no to your pet?"

"She's not *my* pet," Jenn corrected, focusing back on him. "But I'll keep her until we can find a home."

Luke nodded. "Fair enough."

He went over instructions and what to watch

for once they left. He also let her know he'd be stopping by just to check in. Maybe he could have her come to the clinic, but he didn't mind stopping at the shop to see her—

No. To see the dog. He had to get his head on straight and focus on what was important. Paisley and buying a portion of the farm, in that order. Nothing else mattered.

"Toot."

Luke turned toward the door where Paisley stood in the opening holding up a dog treat in the shape of a sugar cookie. One bite had been taken and Paisley's nose wrinkled in disgust. They'd had her birthday pictures just a few hours ago and he'd come into the clinic to work on inventory. Thankfully they were here when Jenn came with her emergency.

"These cookies are terrible," she told him. "Where did you get them?"

Luke raked a hand over his jaw. "Those are dog treats, Sweet P. They are just made to look like human cookies."

The little girl's nose wrinkled. "Oops. Sorry. They were at the counter so I thought they were for people."

Jenn snickered and he glanced over his shoulder, pleased to see a smile as opposed to the sheer terror he'd seen on her face when she'd arrived.

"It's always something," he muttered, shaking his head. "So don't feel too bad about the pup. Paisley's eating dog treats."

He truly didn't know how he could keep an eye on her, run a clinic, try to fight for custody and get land secured for their future. He wasn't giving up, but he wouldn't mind catching a break.

"Is Jenn's dog okay?" Paisley asked. "Can she have the rest of my cookie?"

"I think the dog will be just fine," Luke told her. "And, yes, she'd probably like the rest of the cookie."

"That's a good name for her, don't you think?" Paisley asked, looking to Jenn for an answer.

Jenn tipped her head and grinned. "Cookie. I think that's a perfect name."

As Luke watched the two ladies fawn over the dog and the treat, he couldn't help but see a life he once thought he would have. A wife, a child, definitely pets. But four years ago his fiancée decided that wasn't her vision at all and left him standing at the altar like some fool. He'd learned his lesson and hunkered down into his work from then on out…until now when his focus shifted from himself to his niece.

"What else do you own in this town?"

Jenn's question pulled him from his thoughts. "Excuse me?"

"My building, you're a vet… Anything else you own I should be aware of? I feel like I'm going to go get a gallon of milk and you'll be my checkout clerk."

Her quick wit had him chuckling. "No. This is all I do. You're safe to get your milk."

The building she was in had belonged to his late brother who had just purchased with intentions of renting. His family saga and tragedies weren't necessary to get into right now. She'd no doubt find out enough if she listened around town.

The cell in his pocket vibrated and he excused himself.

Will Spencer, Jenn's father.

"I need to take this," he told her, feeling a bit awkward as he did.

Luke stepped into the hall, hoping the man was calling with an agreement to sell or at least a counteroffer. He needed that stability now more than ever. A solid plan for the future would go a long, long way in proving that he was the only option for guardianship of his niece.

CHAPTER THREE

"YOU ALWAYS DID love animals."

Startled, Jenn jerked around. Her heart leaped as she stared back at the most beautiful sight. Words caught in her throat and her eyes filled. She'd been so worried about coming home, but a piece of home had come to her.

"Erin."

The youngest Spencer sister stood in the doorway of the salon and all the years of absence seemed to settle right between them. Jenn had always been closest with Erin, though all the sisters had been the very best of friends growing up and working together as a solid unit on the farm.

What hit Jenn hard was seeing the same pitcher necklace around Erin's neck that Jenn wore. The piece every single Spencer woman owned and treasured held such a powerful spot in Jenn's heart. Even with the time and distance that separated her from her family, Jenn had never removed the precious necklace.

"I can't believe you're here," she said, unsure what else to say or even if she should close that gap between them—and not just the physical one.

Erin tucked a strand of her long blond hair behind her ear as she took a step inside and let the door close behind her. Jenn remained frozen, still insecure about how to respond here. She'd rehearsed in her mind a thousand times how she would react when she saw her family again, but right now, none of those variations mattered.

Maybe being caught off guard was the best-case scenario. Jenn didn't have time to think; she had to rely on her faith. She'd just assumed she'd see her family at the farm when she went later today.

"I wouldn't be anywhere else," Erin assured her. "I heard just yesterday that you were renting this building and I can't believe it."

"Why not?" Jenn asked with a slight shrug. "It's perfect to work and live, and the lease is only for six months."

Erin moved farther into the open space toward Jenn. "I guess I assumed you'd live at the farm."

"I'm not sure how welcome I'd be," she admitted.

Erin nodded in understanding, then chewed on her bottom lip. She'd always done that as a kid when she worried about something.

"How bad is it?" Jenn asked.

"As bad as it's ever been," Erin said. "But we're hopeful. Mom and Dad had to sell some cattle, but so far nothing else. I'm just concerned. They're getting older, the farm is still quite demanding, and with the drought last year, we lost so many crops and cattle." She sighed. "I'm just afraid... I can't even believe I'm saying this, but what if they sell the farm?"

"Did they say they were?" Jenn asked, refusing to even let that thought roll through her mind.

Another dose of guilt settled deep into her core. She should have been here all along and maybe she could have prevented this impending tragedy from taking place. The very thought of her parents having to make such a difficult decision to sell some of their livestock wasn't something Jenn had ever experienced before. She couldn't even imagine how tough things must be for her father to have made such a drastic call.

Guilt and anger consumed her for so many reasons. Jenn had let fear and emotions drive her away from the people she loved most. At a time she was hurting over the tragic loss of her husband, when she should have turned to her family, she'd pushed them away—going even further and placing blame right at their feet.

Over the past few years her mother had reached out, but Jenn had been so ashamed of how she'd left things. The thought of coming home to where her husband had died on the family farm, and also facing her family, didn't seem possible. The mere idea of stepping back had held her captive in her own mind with her own dark thoughts.

"I'm going to see Mom and Dad today." Jenn realized her reasoning seemed inadequate and late. "I'm scared, but I'm going."

"Scared is good because it shows you care." Erin hesitated, then tilted her head. "You do care or you wouldn't be back. Right? I hesitated on texting you but thought you should know how dire the situation is…and you're still part of the family."

"I never stopped caring about you guys," Jenn

whispered. "I stopped caring about myself and I'm glad you told me. It was past time for me to come home."

Erin took another step, and Jenn found herself moving as well. The second Erin opened her arms, Jenn fell into the loving embrace. She welcomed the familiar feeling and didn't bother holding back her tears. How long had she held all of this inside? The repairs Jenn needed to make with so many people might just start right here, right now, with something as simple as a hug.

Easing back, Erin smoothed Jenn's hair from her face. "No tears. You're home now. Don't leave me like that again. I need my big sister and I can't help you if you won't let me."

Jenn swiped her damp cheeks. "I thought coming back would be harder than this. I can't believe you're not angry."

"Oh, I'm angry," Erin admitted. "But I still love you and I need a haircut."

Jenn couldn't stop her watery laugh. "You don't even know if I'm a good beautician."

Erin gave her shoulders a reassuring squeeze. "You're my sister and that's all that matters."

The warmth that spread through her shouldn't be surprising. God didn't guide her this far, on this journey, to fail. Jenn had to hold tight to her faith because there would be hard days ahead—there was no getting around that.

"Do you think the rest of the family will be this receiving?" she asked.

Erin's lips pursed and the silence gave Jenn all the answer she needed. Erin had always been quickest to forgive. As the baby of the family, Erin thrived on being the peacemaker, which was what made her such a wonderful kindergarten teacher. Or did she teach a different grade now? There were so many basic details about her family Jenn didn't know. She didn't know because she hadn't asked or checked in...not even with Erin.

While each Spencer girl certainly had their own unique personalities, their sisterly bond had never wavered.

Until that fateful day.

Thank you, God, for letting Erin be my first family encounter.

Jenn took this meeting as another sign that coming home was the right decision for now. She had to take this first step or she would never know if there was a chance at redemption.

"Did you tell anyone I was coming to town?" Jenn asked.

Erin shook her head. "I was hoping you'd go to the ranch before Mom and Dad found out. You know word travels faster than wildfire in Rosewood Valley."

"Going back to the ranch…" Jenn curled her lips to stop the quivering that accompanied her emotions. "I haven't been back there since that day," she whispered. "I don't know if I'm more afraid of seeing the place where Cole passed or seeing Mom and Dad."

"You can't move forward without facing your past," Erin explained. "One day at a time. One step at a time. Right?"

Jenn pulled in a shaky breath, but before she could say a word, the clicking of paws drew her attention toward the back.

"Your dog is adorable," Erin stated. "What's his name?"

"Her, and it's Cookie." Jenn didn't dare move toward the poor thing. She still seemed skittish, but she was taking an interest in the water bowl Jenn had put out. "She wandered in the back door yesterday and made herself at home beneath the shampoo chair."

"Well, she seems to be yours now."

The last thing Jenn needed was another unchecked box on her priority list. And while Erin had been spot on about Jenn's love for animals, she wasn't exactly in a position to take on more responsibility.

"Want me to stay here while you go to the farm?" Erin offered. "I can clean up and watch your dog."

"She's not mine."

Erin smiled. "So is that a yes?"

"I won't turn down the offer."

"Just go with an open mind and don't think that years of absence and heartache will be repaired in one visit," Erin warned. "You know dad. He won't admit defeat with the farm on the brink of foreclosure so he likely won't be ready to welcome you with open arms so easily, either."

No, he wouldn't, and honestly, she couldn't blame him. He was a proud man and she'd hurt him. Now he was hurting with the only land he'd ever known, too. Somehow, she had to repair everything and lift their family back from despair.

"I shouldn't have been gone so long," Jenn murmured.

"You're here now and that's what matters."

Heavy silence settled between them while Jenn tried to gather her thoughts. There were simply too many and she could be overwhelmed, but she had to remain strong now more than ever.

"You could always take her with you to the farm," Erin suggested, nodding toward the pup. "Dad always needs good dogs."

Jenn crossed her arms and shifted her stance as she narrowed her stare toward her sister. "Is that your way of pushing me to go now?"

Erin shrugged. "It's been long enough."

No truer statement. Unfortunately, that panic still lived within her, and three years was an incredibly long time for her faith to be tested and for doubts to creep in. But she'd held strong. She might have turned her back on her family, but she'd never turned her back on God. She was human; she had a roller coaster of emotions like anyone else. Life was full of highs and lows and what mattered most was how you dealt with those valleys. Jenn hadn't handled her valleys very well, so she had to find a way to crawl back up and not let those lows keep her down.

"I don't even know what to say to fix this," Jenn admitted.

"Sometimes you don't need words. You know actions are always louder, but the damage won't be undone quickly. Give yourself, and Dad, some grace."

Her little sister still had that voice of reason. Maybe paying attention to everyone older had made her wise beyond her twenty-six years. Her hair had gotten longer, nearly touching her waistline now. Her eyes were still a striking shade of green and she had more of a shape than that tomboy figure Jenn recalled.

"My haircut can wait. Now go. I'll get to sweeping or something." Erin glanced around the salon and wrinkled her nose. "Or get some air fresheners."

Jenn couldn't help but laugh again as she reached for her sister and pulled her into another embrace.

"I needed this," she stated. "I needed you."

Finally, after all this time, she was about to see what she was truly made of.

"Easy, girl."

Luke eased his hand along the mare's neck and gave a soft stroke. He'd come out to Four Sisters Ranch after getting a call that one of the mares had taken ill. Thankfully Mary, the receptionist at his office, was able to watch Paisley for a bit while he ran out to check on the sick animal.

Mary was a godsend for sure. Her late husband, Charles Major, had been the vet prior to Luke so she knew not only the ins and outs of the office, but every person in the town and their history. There was no way Luke could have transitioned into a new town and new position without her. She didn't have grandchildren, so she graciously offered to watch Paisley.

His hands still shook from that phone call earlier from his attorney, though. Yesterday, Luke had called the lawyer that had handled his brother's will but had to leave a message. Finally she'd returned his call today and assured Luke that she would take care of anything that came up. But how could he not worry? A completely unknown source had threatened to take away the one family member he had left. The last tie to his late brother. The thought of Paisley not living with him had a heavy pit settling in his stomach.

"Sorry, I got held up."

Luke glanced over his shoulder as Will Spencer strode through the barn. The robust man always had on worn jeans, a plaid shirt and suspenders. His gruff voice and overbearing size could lead people to believe the man was mean or angry, but Luke had seen how Will was around his animals. The guy was simply a gentle giant, but a sadness always lurked in his green eyes.

Those same green eyes each of his girls shared, and that same sadness he'd seen in Jenn's. He might not know all the history there, but he'd heard it had been years since she'd stepped foot in Rosewood Valley.

"I haven't been here long," Luke stated, turning his attention back to the horse.

Just then the mare let out a deep, dry cough and Luke had a pretty good idea of the problem. He continued to run his hands over her neck, checking all of the swollen lymph nodes. The poor girl eased down and ultimately laid on her side. Poor thing must be exhausted.

Will came to stand just outside the stall. "Influenza?" he asked.

Luke nodded. "Seems like a textbook case." He glanced around to the different stalls, then to Will. "We'll need to separate this one from all the others. You know how contagious the flu can be, not to mention expensive if it takes hold of your other livestock."

Will's lips thinned as he propped his hands

on his hips. Worry lines etched in the fine lines around his mouth and eyes. The man looked worn down and exhausted. The cost of the farm was getting to him, and Luke wished the stubborn man would just agree to the partial sale of the place and do what was best for all parties involved.

"Fresh hay and fresh water on a regular rotation will also go a long way to recovery," Luke offered. "But anything you can do to keep them separated is going to be best. Maybe keep the others in the pasture as much as possible."

"The other barn is too small for all of them, so the pasture will have to do."

When Luke first arrived in town six months ago, it hadn't taken him long to realize everyone here worked hard. The tight-knit community wasn't one of wealth, but of love and support. He completely understood why his brother loved Rosewood Valley so much and why he wanted to raise his family here.

"I'll do everything I can to help stop the spread." Luke came to his feet and dusted his hands off on his jeans. "I have some vitamins I can supply and I'll be sure to check in every couple days to make sure the others are healthy.

Don't hesitate to call if she takes a turn for the worse. My line is always open."

"'Preciate that."

Luke pulled in a deep breath. "If you're ready to discuss selling, I can—"

"Not yet. We're just not ready." The farmer let out a sigh that spoke volumes for the thoughts no doubt swirling in his head. "Sarah and I are talking. I'd appreciate you keeping our conversations to yourself. My girls…they don't know what we're thinking. I don't want them to hear anything until Sarah and I know for sure. If we decide to go through with the sale, they will be devastated."

Tires crunching over the gravel drive pulled their attention to the open end of the barn. A small silver SUV rolled to a stop in the wide space between the barn and the two-story white farmhouse.

"Who in the world is that?" Will muttered.

The old guy looped his thumbs through his suspenders and started moving toward the visitor. But the moment Jenn stepped from the car, Will froze.

"That can't be," Will gasped.

Luke figured he'd be happy to see his daughter, but from the look on his face, this was anything but a celebratory homecoming. No, if anything this visit leaned more toward shocking and unexpected.

Jenn's eyes surveyed the area and came to land directly on him. That spear of attraction hit him hard once again. His headspace and his overloaded life right now didn't have room for dating, so he needed to push aside the fact Jenn was both adorable and maybe a bit vulnerable right now. He couldn't slay anyone else's dragons…not while he was fighting his own.

Luke figured he was all done with his work with the sick mare so he made his way from the barn and toward his truck. Whatever overdue reunion needed to take place did not involve him, especially since Will had requested his silence on the potential sale.

The fresh breeze kicked up around them, sending Jenn's blond hair dancing around her shoulders. He shouldn't find her this attractive or be so drawn to her, but facts were facts.

"I thought you didn't do anything else," she joked as he got closer.

"I'm the livestock vet," he explained. "I said you'd be safe getting milk."

A smile flirted around her mouth. But as she pushed her sunglasses on top of her head, he noted something other than amusement in her eyes. Fear? Worry?

"Good to know," she murmured. "I'm just here to see my parents."

"I was headed out. How's Cookie?" he asked.

"She seems perfectly fine, thankfully. I'm sure I'll be seeing you soon."

Luke simply nodded and headed toward his truck. They were bound together through the rental agreement for the next six months, so she'd be seeing quite a bit of him. He honestly didn't know at this point if that was a good or bad thing. He had a secret and he had baggage…but he also had a fascination that would be difficult to ignore.

CHAPTER FOUR

NOSTALGIA CURLED AROUND Jenn's heart and
squeezed. She hadn't counted on the rush of
emotions that would hit her the moment she
drove beneath that iron arch. Once a homey,
welcoming entrance, now a depressing reminder of all she'd left behind.

The white iron had chipped away in many
places and the welcome to Four Sisters Ranch
didn't seem as warm and cozy as it once had.
Paint had also peeled off various parts of the
white two-story farmhouse. The wraparound
porch didn't have the vibrant flowerpots at the
top of the steps. The balcony off her parents'
bedroom on the second floor seemed sad with
no rockers. The small barn in the back no longer stood, though the one out front did. The
large oak trees in the front yard remained tall
and strong. The old wooden bench rested beneath, and that familiar tire swing her father

had hung on her fourth birthday swayed in the spring breeze.

Some things remained exactly the same while some seemed like time and tragedy had taken their toll.

The scuff of boots on the dirt pulled her attention back toward the barn. Jenn squinted against the sun as Will Spencer stood in the wide-open doorway leading to the stalls. Even from this distance, she could see he'd put on a little weight, but he still wore those red suspenders and plaid shirt. He said nothing, simply stared back, very likely wondering why she was here or showed up with no warning.

Now that she'd arrived, she wanted to run away. But that's what had gotten her into this mess to begin with. The back screen door of the farmhouse clanged and Jenn turned to see her mother on the back stoop. Hair piled on top of her head in a silver bun, a yellow apron covered her simple white T-shirt and jeans. On a gasp, her mother's hand flew up to her mouth.

Sarah Spencer raced down the back steps and made a mad dash to close the distance.

"Jenn."

Just hearing her mother's voice sliced through the awkward tension and warmed Jenn's heart.

Her mother's arms came around her and Jenn closed her eyes, wanting just to live in this single moment right here. A viselike squeeze held her in place. She couldn't move, couldn't speak, as the tears slid down her cheeks.

Finally, after all this time, the fear that had held her captive for three years seemed to ease. For this one moment, Jenn had a surge of hope she so desperately needed. She wanted to believe that everything would be alright. She wanted to believe that she hadn't destroyed everything by her insensitive actions and yawning absence.

When her mom eased back, she gripped Jenn's face between her delicate hands. Just like Jenn thought, her mother had just come from the kitchen. Flour covered the front of her old yellow apron, which Rachel had sewn one Christmas.

"I can't believe you're here," her mother cried. "I've prayed for this for so long. I've dreamed of you walking in that back door."

She pulled her into another tight hug. Jenn glanced toward the barn where her father remained still, his weathered eyes locked on the scene before him. The fact he hadn't come over to see her absolutely crushed her. But what did she expect? Jenn had been the angriest toward him after Cole's death. She'd needed to place blame somewhere and her father had been a convenient target.

Would he ever forgive her? Had her words and harsh actions done irreparable damage?

"My baby is home," her mother cried, patting Jenn's back. "Please tell me you're staying. Tell me you're not just passing through."

Clearly her mom hadn't heard the news about Jenn renting the old salon. She pulled away and offered a soft smile, hoping this could be the start of building the bridge to come back home.

"I'm staying for now," she agreed. "I just… I'm not sure if this is the place for me yet."

"There's nowhere else you belong," her mother insisted. "This is your home."

Jenn's eyes darted toward her father, then down to the gravel beneath her sneakers.

"Will, don't just stand there," Sarah called to her husband.

Jenn didn't want to stand here and beg for anyone's attention or affection, especially her father's. Maybe he couldn't forgive her. Maybe she'd been gone too long, had pushed too hard to keep people away.

But she remembered Erin's warning that their issues couldn't be fixed in one visit. Years of heartache all settled right here between them, and only additional time would help them unpack all of the emotional baggage.

When her father turned and went back into the barn, her mother gasped again.

"Just give him some time," Sarah explained in that soft tone she'd always had. "Come inside and let's have some tea."

Jenn shook her head and swiped at her damp cheeks. "I don't think that's a good idea today, Mom."

But maybe tomorrow. She'd showed up. Her parents knew she was back, and that was enough for one day.

The worry in her mom's dark brown eyes couldn't be shielded. Her mother had always been so expressive with her feelings without saying a word. Sarah Spencer definitely wore her heart on her sleeve and made no apologies about being her true self.

"Don't leave town yet. Please."

Jenn took hold of her mother's hands and squeezed. "I'm staying for now."

She tossed a glance back toward the barn and realized this homecoming would go one of two ways: her father would never forgive her and she'd have to move on, or she could trust in

God's timing and believe she was brought home for a reason.

And God had never let her down yet, so she was ready to put in the work to repair her broken family.

"TOOT. THESE SPELLING words are hard."

Luke wiped his hands on the checkered towel hanging from the oven door and turned to Paisley. She'd only been home from school for a few minutes, but she always came straight into the kitchen and had a seat at the round table and started into her homework.

That must have been how her parents had raised her. Thankfully Paisley kept up with her studies. Even being in the first grade, especially being in the first grade, it was important to have a routine...or so he'd been told by his therapist.

Navigating his way through parenting had been and still was a fast lesson. Trying to learn all the rules and tricks in a short time was impossible. But he wasn't giving in or giving up. Paisley deserved everything he had to give. He just wished there was some magical handbook with all the answers. After his failed attempt at a wife and family, he never thought he'd see the day he was put into the role of a father.

"Let's see what we've got here," Luke stated as he crossed the kitchen to the eating area by the windows overlooking the small backyard. "I bet we can get this in no time."

"Why are words so hard?" she complained, handing over her paper. "I like math much better."

Luke chuckled as he took a seat next to her and glanced at the words. Homework was where their evening routine began. She came home and he started a snack for them to share. He always made sure to have his afternoons free unless there was an emergency that took him to the clinic or a farm.

"Can't we just ignore the words and eat the mac and cheese?" Her bright blue eyes rose to his. "I don't want to work today."

"Do you have other homework?" he asked.

"No. Just those dumb words."

"Then how about we do half the words, have our snack, then do the other half?"

She wrinkled her nose and shook her head. "I'd rather go to the salon and see Cookie and Jenn. She's nice and really pretty."

Yes. There was no denying her natural beauty. In fact, that woman had rolled through his mind more often than he was comfortable with.

Luke pulled in a deep breath and sighed. He hadn't seen Jenn in a few days, not since he left her at the farm. He couldn't help but wonder how her visit went with her parents. Had Will told her about the land sale proposition? She likely would've confronted Luke if he had. He knew enough to know she had been gone for years, that her husband had died, and now she was back. Other than that, her life was none of his business so long as she was a good renter and paid on time. He couldn't let himself care about any other dealings with the adorable Spencer sister.

He'd fallen hard and fast for a charming, sweet woman once before. He'd thought when he fell in love that they'd marry and start a family, but he'd been much too naive. Having someone wipe out his savings and leave him at the altar was quite the eye-opener.

Which was why vulnerable women were a thing of his past. He'd definitely learned his lesson and he had much more pressing matters at this stage in his life.

"We can't just stop in anytime we want," he explained, focusing on the here and now. "I'm sure we'll see the pup soon enough."

"Did you find the owner?"

"Not yet."

The timer on the stove went off and Luke set the spelling words down and went to drain the pasta. Thankfully he knew how to do basics, and simple meals seemed to make his niece happy. He hadn't ventured too far into experimenting with food. He got fancy the other evening and cut up hot dogs in the mac. With a heavy dose of ketchup, Paisley had deemed the dish a hit.

Once the pasta was drained, he added the powder pack of cheese. He was pretty sure that wasn't real cheese, but whatever. He wasn't trying to spruce up his culinary skills. He knew his strengths and being in the kitchen wasn't one of them.

"So how do you spell *house*?" he asked, stirring in the mixture.

"H-o-u-s-e."

"Perfect. See? You're already acing this test." Luke reached into the cabinet for a bowl. "How about *family*?"

Silence filled the room. He scooped her noodles while she thought, but when he turned back to face her, he noted her staring out the window with unshed tears in her eyes.

"Sweet P?"

She glanced his way as a lone tear slid down her cheek. "I don't like that word. Do I have to spell it?"

He placed the bowl down in front of her, then squatted next to her chair. He turned her to face him and took her delicate hands in his. His own heart broke for this situation life had thrust at them, but he had to embrace the fact they had each other and they could get through these tough days.

"Family looks a little different for us right now," he started, weighing his words carefully. "Family can come in a variety of ways and what makes a family are those people in your world that love you unconditionally. We have each other, right? It's okay to be sad and even be angry."

Her chin quivered and he wanted to turn her thoughts from that dark place that lived in her mind.

"Can you help me with something?" he asked, giving her hands a gentle squeeze. "Can you help focus on the good we still have? I struggle with that sometimes so I have an idea, but I can't do it without you."

Luke reached up and swiped the moisture from her cheeks with the pad of his thumb.

He wished he could snap his fingers and obliterate all of her pain or take it all on his own. He never wanted to see tears in her eyes again, but he also knew this was unfortunately part of their growth forward.

"I can help you," she whispered with a sniff. "I'm sorry. I just didn't have a good day at school."

"What can I help with?"

She shrugged and glanced away. "Nothing you can do unless you have a mom for me. There's a Mother's Day project due next week."

Mother's Day. That holiday hadn't even crossed his mind. But they were in spring and that day would be coming up soon enough—the first one since the passing of Talia and Scott.

"Then we will make the absolute best project and honor your mother," Luke replied. "Tell me what all you need and we'll make it happen. Now is the perfect time to show what an amazing woman your mom was."

A soft, albeit sad, smile spread across Paisley's face. "She was the best. That's what I want everyone to know."

Luke nodded and came to his feet. He eased down into the seat he'd vacated moments ago.

He didn't have a clue how to do a school project, so this would be another first. But he also knew there wasn't a thing he wouldn't do for Paisley. Maybe this project would be a way of healing even further and remembering all the good that Talia had brought into their lives.

"Then that's what we'll do," he confirmed. "Your mom will shine and you'll be able to feel her more than ever."

He hoped.

Luke had to make this sound like the greatest project, and it would be if he had any say.

"Now, what do you say you dive into your snack, we do some spelling, and then we dig through some pictures to get started?"

She inched forward and grabbed her fork. "Aren't you having some?"

He'd had enough mac 'n' cheese over these past few months to last his lifetime. He could go for a big juicy steak, mashed potatoes with gravy, some fresh-from-the-garden green beans. His mouth watered and his stomach grumbled at the thought of the best meal, but he wasn't confident in mastering all of that quite yet. Besides, there wasn't even room for a garden here at his late brother's rental house. But if Luke got that piece of Spencer land...

"I had a late lunch," he replied.

She took a few bites as he glanced over the word list once again. Before he could give her another, she set her fork down and turned her attention to him.

"Sorry I cried."

Luke smiled. "Don't be sorry for having feelings. I cry, too."

"Not as much as me." She sniffed a little and adjusted her glasses. "I have to keep it all in at school so I don't look like a baby."

"Cry here all you want, but you don't look like a baby. Do I look like a baby when I cry?"

She rolled her eyes and snorted. "You're a big man. You can't look like a baby."

"Well, you are a strong young lady," he retorted, tapping the end of her button nose. "You could never look like a baby, either."

Paisley slid out of her seat and came up beside him. Her little arms wrapped around his neck and Luke's heart tumbled in his chest. He might not know a thing about how to raise a child, let alone about a little girl, but he understood loyalty and love for family and that had to count for something. He'd do anything for Paisley and he had a feeling she'd do anything for him. They were a team now.

"I'm glad I have you," she murmured against his shoulder. "Even if you do make mac every day."

He chuckled and returned her hug. "Maybe we can try pizza or burgers next time."

She eased back, all smiles now. "Extra cheese on my pizza."

"Of course."

If only all of the hurts of the world could be erased with such a simple fix.

CHAPTER FIVE

"So how's everything going?"

Marie Horton's sweet voice filled the empty salon. Her dear friend from Sacramento had called to check in while Jenn was decorating the front windows. The cell lay on a station closest to the front and Jenn decided to take a break and have a seat in the salon chair while chatting on speaker. Jenn glanced around the place, pleased with the progress she'd made so far.

Baby steps in the new business and in life seemed to be the common thread holding her together.

"Some parts have been better than I expected and some haven't gone quite the way I'd hoped," she admitted.

Marie had been the one solid anchor in Jenn's life when she'd settled in a new town after leaving Rosewood Valley. As the preacher's wife, Marie had welcomed Jenn with loving, open arms and their connection quickly turned into a friendship. God knew just what Jenn had needed at that time and she'd forever be grateful to Marie for her compassion and listening ear.

She'd created a good life for herself in Sacramento. She'd got her cosmetology license, joined a Bible study group and made friends. Her work with the church and her experience growing up on a farm had even led to a successful series of farm-to-table church dinners she'd coordinated with Marie. That had been such a huge leap for their church and quite the fundraiser. Jenn couldn't help but feel like she'd made a difference during her time away from home.

"Have you seen your family yet?" Marie asked. "Or gone by the farm?"

"I've been to the farm and I've seen my youngest sister and my parents."

That had been three days ago. She hadn't heard from her father. Jenn had texted her other sisters, Rachel and Violet, after she'd gone to the farm, but neither had messaged her back. Her mother had texted a few times, asking Jenn to come for dinner, but Jenn didn't think now was the time to jump back into something so special and meaningful. She had to give everyone, including herself, time to acclimate to this change.

"Oh, wow. That's great progress," Marie replied. "Were those good meetings?"

Jenn crossed her legs and stared out the front window. She had a great view of the park across the street so she didn't want to obstruct that with her window decor. She'd gone for simplicity and hung vibrant flowers of various sizes and colors from the wooden ceiling and draped some thin white lights. Once she got her window clings with her salon name on the front glass, the entrance would be complete.

She wished everything was so easy to tidy up and make new. But none of this new life could be rushed. She had to cling to the patience her parents had instilled in her. Getting angry and frustrated is what got her into this mess in the first place. She'd learned so much since she left and she had to prove with her actions that she was a different person now.

"Chatting with Erin went well," Jenn replied. "My mom welcomed me with a hug I desperately needed and invited me to church this Sunday. I'm not sure I'm ready to face the entire town or the church just yet."

Nearly everyone in town went to the white

chapel on the hillside and she knew she couldn't hide from them forever, and she wasn't, but seeing them all at once in one place left her feeling a little insecure and unsure of herself. Not to mention, it was the same church she and Cole had been married in. So, no, she simply wasn't mentally prepared to step back inside those doors.

"Give yourself some time," Marie told her. "And how about seeing your father? How did that go?"

"We haven't spoken." Jenn swallowed the lump of remorse and guilt in her throat. "I saw him in the barn, but he didn't come to talk to me."

"And you didn't go to him?"

"I thought about it, but I don't want to push just yet. I know him and he needs to process the fact I'm back."

Silence filled the salon and Jenn glanced to her cell on the yellow chipped countertop that made up the front station.

"Are you making an excuse?" Marie asked after a yawning pause.

"Maybe," Jenn admitted. No need to lie or ignore the truth. "I'm still scared and I guess I just wanted him to take that first step. Literally."

She'd gone home, taking the biggest leap of faith in the past three years. Now she needed her father to be ready to talk.

"He will," Marie assured her. "Obviously I don't know him, but he's your father and I have no doubt he loves you. There's damage that can't be undone. But sometimes the strongest people and relationships come from the toughest times."

"I know and that's what I'm holding out hope for." Jenn sighed and turned in the salon chair to grab her phone. "I plan on going back tomorrow. I'm tired after working in the shop all day trying to get it ready to open."

"How's that going?"

"Once I eliminated the old musty smell and did a thorough cleaning, the place has shaped up nicely. I made some posts on social media and already have a few appointments scheduled for the end of the week. So, I'm hoping my state inspector passes me when she comes in, but I have everything up and running so there should be no problem."

Each positive step forward gave her a new level of hope. Jenn's goal was to add a little more each day and put one proverbial foot in front of the other to rebuild her life. She wanted to stay in Rosewood Valley, but the deciding factor would be how she was received. Not just by her family, though they were definitely a huge part of her journey, but also by the town. Did people still chatter about her running away and deserting her family? Did they trust her coming back with only the purest of intentions? Only time would tell.

"This is great news!" Marie exclaimed. "Good for you. Just keep moving forward and please know I'm here for anything you need. Day or night. I'm always a call or text away."

"I know you are and I appreciate you being in my corner."

"I'm not the only one in that corner. You've got a family that's there, too. Believe it or not."

Jenn smiled, loving how her friend could lift her spirits with her soothing words and calm tone. Just a quick call had Jenn optimistic for a future here in her hometown and encouraged that better days were ahead. She couldn't let herself believe anything else.

Once she disconnected the call, she came to her feet and slid her cell into the pocket of her jeans. She turned to find Cookie sleeping beneath the shampoo bowl again. Apparently that's where she felt the most comfortable, but she couldn't stay there. If the state inspector came in and saw a dog in the salon, Jenn would get fined and that was the last thing she needed. Once she opened, she'd have to keep the dog upstairs in her apartment and schedule a break somewhere in her day to take her out to the potty…which was across the street at the park. Not convenient, but that would have to do until the owner was found.

Jenn had a sinking feeling she was the owner.

Erin didn't have a bad idea about taking the pup to the farm. There would be plenty of space to run free and thrive. Jenn didn't think now was the time to show up with a drop-off, though.

Besides, she'd gotten used to her new roommate and didn't feel quite so lonely. Maybe God knew she needed a companion, one who couldn't judge and had unconditional love. The dog was lost and she couldn't ignore the parallel life they seemed to have. They were both just trying to find a place to fit in and be safe and loved.

"Ready to go upstairs?" she asked.

At the sound of her voice, the pup lifted her head and gave a quick wiggle of her tail. A small one, but still. Slowly the dog seemed to be showing signs of trust and happiness.

"Let's go, girl."

Jenn turned off the lights and led the way toward the back staircase leading up to her apartment. The old creaky steps and dated floral wallpaper leading to the second floor were just another reminder that none of this was her style. Of course taking wallpaper down was free, so she could put her restless efforts toward that endeavor. Maybe peeling and scraping would be a good outlet for her frustrations. The open loft apartment wasn't much better with the old, scarred hardwood floors and more random wallpaper. At least Jenn had her own furniture, which helped the place feel a little more homey.

If she did indeed end up staying in town, she'd definitely talk with Luke about eventually upgrading the place and maybe even see about buying the building from him. Of course those were long-term goals as her savings had taken a hit to come back and put down rent and deposits and get the start-ups for her salon. She didn't think Luke would mind if she decided to change out the decor of the apartment.

Her thoughts drifted back to the handsome

vet. She'd been so thankful he'd been around when Cookie got into that hair color. And that she'd seen him before she'd faced her mother. It had calmed her. But if she let herself think too much about him, she'd remember how her heart felt a little flutter the moment her eyes locked with his. She'd remember the way he seemed in a panic about his daughter with the gum and her birthday pictures. She'd remember his soothing voice when she'd been frightened about the dog.

She'd remember another man who'd made her heart flutter and the promise he'd made to her to love her forever. But their forever had been cut short.

Jenn massaged the back of her neck as she made her way to the bathroom. Maybe soaking in a nice hot bubble bath would relieve today's soreness and ease her mind a bit. Her fingers slid over the pitcher charm on her necklace. She'd never forgotten her mother's motto of pouring into yourself before you could pour into others. That saying had helped Jenn through life. And while sometimes she felt guilty for taking time for herself, she also knew she would be of no use to others if she didn't recharge every now and then.

Her phone vibrated, breaking into her thoughts. For a moment she considered ignoring it, but she should at least glance at the screen.

The moment her eyes landed on the sender, her heart clenched once again.

Her oldest sister, Rachel.

With a lump in her throat and her heart thumping at a rapid rate, Jenn grabbed her cell and opened the message.

We need to talk.

Jenn's thumbs hovered above the keys as she contemplated her reply. She wanted to see her sisters so badly. No matter the outcome or how they received her, Jenn had to take this step toward repairing each and every relationship. And even though Rachel had taken a few days to respond, Jenn eagerly typed out her reply.

I'm in the new salon across from the park on Sycamore St. I'll be here all day tomorrow if you want to stop by.

She hesitated before sending one more quick message.

I'd love to see you.

She held her breath, waiting and watching as the three dots danced on the screen, showing her sister was typing. Could this reconnection with Rachel be as easy as with Erin and her mother? Was that why Rachel had taken a few days to reply? Maybe she was just gathering her thoughts.

But what about Violet? Would she reply soon?

I'll be there in the morning after I help dad.

Jenn didn't know whether to be relieved that Rachel had agreed, or afraid of the unknown and what was to come. A heavy dose of both settled in her gut as she replied.

Can't wait to see you. Love you.

As she stared once again, hoping for a reply, Jenn realized that was the end of their conversation. No more words from her sister to give hope that their meeting would be a joyous one. Out of all the Spencer girls, Rachel was most like their father. She lived and breathed farm life and wanted nothing else in this world than to take over Four Sisters and raise her own family there.

Jenn had no idea what tomorrow would

bring, but at this point all she could do was relax in that promised bubble bath and say a prayer that everything would work out in God's time.

So MUCH FOR that relaxing bath.

Jenn piled her hair up on top of her head the next morning. She hadn't been able to soak or even wash her hair because there was no hot water. Last night, she'd made a cup of honey lemon tea, popped it in the microwave to get hot, and grabbed a book that hadn't really held her interest until she'd finally given up and went to bed.

Waking up in a surly mood was not how she wanted to go into meeting her sister.

Jenn had fired off a text to Luke, telling him hot water was of the utmost importance. Her own hygiene aside, she couldn't have her state inspector come and check things out before her opening if there wasn't sufficient water. She wasn't sure what happened, considering she had hot water while cleaning and mopping yesterday morning.

He'd texted back almost immediately and claimed he would stop by at some point today in between his appointments. She sincerely hoped this was a simple fix because she still needed that bubble bath. Any type of self-care and a little pampering was necessary. She didn't think such things were selfish, not when her mother had always told her girls that they had to take care of themselves before they could take care of others.

Jenn hooked the leash onto Cookie's collar and led her out the front door of the salon. The spring sun sent a surge of confidence through her. That boost of light and warmth lifted her spirit. She would go into this day and this meeting with Rachel full of optimism and with an open mind. She had to listen to what her sister needed to say. As difficult as this might be, Jenn had to let each family member share their side. They deserved nothing less, and if that meant being angry or saying harsh words, then so be it. Jenn would do anything to mend this family back into one solid unit.

As soon as Cookie did her business, she crossed the street and headed back toward her salon. But a familiar woman stared across the open distance.

Violet stood on the sidewalk just outside the shop door. Jenn didn't have time to be worried or react to the rapid beat of her heart and the gnawing nerves in her belly. She stepped off the street and shortened Cookie's leash so the pup would stick close to her side.

"I didn't expect to see you," Jenn stated, wincing at how that could be perceived as rude and unwelcoming. "I mean, I'm glad you're here. I just…when I didn't hear from you, I wasn't sure you wanted to see me."

"Of course I want to see you," Violet said. "You're still my sister, no matter what. I just had to process everything."

That familiar voice Jenn hadn't heard in years calmed the turmoil within. Violet had always been a little bit of the rebel. Jenn was glad to see her sister still loved changing up her hair color. Today offered a bright red, but her younger sister always looked gorgeous and could pull off any shade or style she wanted.

"I wasn't sure when you didn't respond to my text," Jenn offered.

"I didn't quite know what to say," Vi explained with a subtle shrug. "I still don't, but I couldn't let more time pass without coming."

Jenn nodded, completely understanding. She wasn't sure what to say, either, but the fact her sister had come here of her own accord set Jenn's mind on an even better path than before. So far two of her sisters had come to her, and her mother had literally welcomed her with open arms. This homecoming already had so many positives, which was what Jenn needed to focus on. She couldn't let her mind go into any type of negative space. Homing in on anything dark was certainly not the direction she needed to go. Light and love and all of that... that was what Jenn needed to thrive.

"How did you know where to find me?" Jenn asked.

"Well, Rosewood Valley is a small town with tons of chatter, but Rachel told me."

Of course they'd talked. Very likely there was a family group chat without Jenn. Hurtful, but understandable considering she'd been gone so long. Now they all knew she was back in town and they all were dealing with this news in their own way.

"Are you coming in?" Jenn asked.

Violet turned and glanced toward the salon, then back, her eyes drifting toward Cookie.

"Your dog is adorable."

Violet bent down and extended her hand, but Cookie wasn't having any part of the stranger.

Even though Vi was a vet, the dog had no clue of her sister's love for animals. And Jenn hadn't gone to her sister's clinic the other day because, well…she'd been afraid of how she'd be received. Not to mention Luke's office was closer to the salon.

"She's a stray," Jenn explained. "I'm still trying to find the owner."

Cookie scooted closer to Jenn's leg and Violet smiled as she came back to her full height.

"Looks like you're the new owner. Dogs are smart with good instincts and she knows she's safe with you."

Yeah, Jenn was fully aware she'd become the chosen one, but there had to be someone wanting their pet back. In a town this small, someone could come forward at any time.

"So, you coming in?"

Vi's attention came back to Jenn. She realized she was holding her breath, wondering what her sister would say once they pushed past the small talk. The nerves in her belly curled but Jenn had to let her sister take the lead here. Whatever made Violet comfortable, Jenn would follow.

After a moment, Violet nodded and stepped forward. She pulled one of the double wooden doors open and gestured for Jenn and Cookie to follow.

"Your window displays look nice," Violet commented.

Jenn smiled as she stepped inside. "Thanks. I just finished them. Still waiting on my salon decal for the front glass, but that should be ready this afternoon."

She bent down and unhooked Cookie. The dog immediately went to the back, beneath the shampoo bowl. Poor girl was still scared, but at least she wasn't skittish with Jenn anymore.

"So, I assume you didn't stop by to discuss my windows or the dog." Jenn turned to face her sister once again. "Did you want to dive right into the past or keep our conversation casual for now?"

Violet shrugged as she glanced around the shop. She moved to one of the two stations against the wall, turned the chair around, then sank into it. With one foot propped on the footrest, she kept her other on the floor and slowly pivoted the seat back and forth. A stall tactic.

Considering Jenn had been absent from this town and Violet's life for the past three years, taking another few minutes to collect the right words seemed appropriate.

Jenn didn't have those magical words that would erase the fear and anger. She didn't have the ability to make her family understand her actions, but she hoped in time, and with her coming back, they would listen to her side. But she was fully aware she'd have to extend the same courtesy and listen to them as well. No, not just listen, but understand and live in their point of view for a time. The only way to bridge their differences and hurts was to cross to the other side of the scenario and put herself in their place.

"I'm not sure what to say," Violet finally said, bringing her chair to a stop. "I've rolled this conversation over and over in my mind for so long and now that you're here, no words are coming to me."

Jenn nodded. "Well, I can start by saying I'm sorry." The most difficult words to say, yet usually the most important. "I needed to get away, but I could have gone about things a better way and not stayed gone so long."

"You're right. You could have handled things better." Violet rested her elbows on the black leather arms of the chair and laced her fingers together. "When you lost Cole, we all knew you were hurting. But shutting everyone out and placing the blame directly on Dad was wrong."

That heavy, dark moment in her life came rushing back. The harsh words, the tears, the unbearable heartbreak. Cole had been a hard worker, helping tend the family farm, and he could never say no to her father. That fateful day Will Spencer had asked him to go out into the fields when he wasn't well had been the worst of her life. Her beloved husband had never come back.

Channeling those feelings was the only way to help her now.

"I can admit I was wrong," Jenn agreed. "I'm here now because I want you all to know how much I care. I know I haven't shown it recently, but you all are my life. There wasn't a day that went by that I didn't want to reach out, but I just didn't know how."

"You're back because the farm is in trouble."

Jenn nodded. "That's the part that gave me the final push I needed."

"Would you have ever come back if everything was just as it was before?" Violet asked.

Jenn made her way to the other station next to her sister and took a seat. She had to be completely transparent here if she had any intention of moving forward in a positive direction.

"I like to think I would have," she admitted. "I had made a new life, but nothing ever felt permanent. I got my cosmetologist license and was working for a wonderful lady. I had a Bible study I attended once a week at a local coffee shop and I have a good friend from the church I'd been attending. She's been urging me to reach out and come home. Then when Erin texted me, I knew that was a sign that the time had come, and I couldn't run anymore."

"And what were you running from exactly?" Vi asked, tilting her head to the side. "From the family that loved you and mourned Cole's loss as well? Or were you running from your own guilt over how you treated our father?"

Now pain fueled her sister's words. Jenn expected this and her sister deserved to let all of those pent-up emotions and words out so they could deal with everything.

Violet opened her mouth and lifted her hand to say something just as the front door opened and the bell chimed. She'd still not taken that annoying thing down.

When Jenn turned to see who the new visitor was, her breath caught in her throat as she stared back at her oldest sister, Rachel. Looked like she'd get her entire family reunion wrapped up right here. Nothing like jumping straight into it.

CHAPTER SIX

JENN CAME TO her feet, unsure if she should cross and attempt to hug her sister or remain still and see how Rachel responded. These next few moments were crucial in their repairing process.

The oldest of the Spencer sisters hadn't changed much in the past three years. She still embraced that whole cowgirl lifestyle. With her signature side braid, button-up shirt, faded jeans and her well-worn dusty boots, Rachel had no doubt come straight from the farm.

Rachel's eyes darted to Violet then landed firmly back on Jenn. No smile, no arms wide-open for an embrace. That open wound in Jenn's heart seemed to crack even wider, but she couldn't focus on the pain. She had to focus on the hope that she could mend these broken fences.

"Should I go?" Vi asked.

"No need," Rachel said, her gaze still locked on Jenn. "We're all in this together."

Maybe that was a good sign? Jenn didn't know whether that meant they were all one big family or they were all in the same mess but on opposite sides.

"I'm glad you stopped by," Jenn told her sister. "You look really good, Rach."

"Thanks."

The dry reply had a new wave of discomfort and awkward awareness pumping through her. At least she'd discovered her biggest hurdles—her father and Rachel. Erin and her mother were going to be Jenn's support system and apparently Violet wanted to be in the neutral zone. Jenn didn't want any of them to be on different ends of the playing field. She wanted them all on the same side, together, as one united family...just like they used to be.

Jenn figured she might as well just start things off and break through this unwanted tension.

"I'm sorry," she said simply, then realized the words might sound empty and meaningless. "I know that can't be a blanket statement that covers all that has happened between us, but I am truly sorry for not reaching out over all this time. I know words probably don't mean anything to you right now but—"

"They don't."

Rachel's curt reply had Jenn cringing. Violet's echoing gasp was proof that this situation had gone too far for too long. Rachel had deep wounds…wounds that Jenn had caused. And as much as Jenn wanted to pull out her own defense on her reasons why, she didn't want to stand here and make excuses for the years' long gap of her absence.

"I understand you're angry," Jenn started again. She crossed her arms over her chest and realized that stance might look confrontational, so she dropped her arms to her side once again. "I also know I can't fix everything from the past with a few words or a quick visit. I'm here for as long as it takes."

"And then what?" Rachel asked. "You'll leave again?"

Jenn shrugged, still holding on to the honest approach. "I'm not sure what the future will bring. I'd like to stay. I'd like to try to find my way back to my family. If I'm not welcome here, then I'm not sure I could remain in a town where I would run into everyone but not be accepted. So only time will tell."

Her sister stared, lips thinned, as if trying to think of a reply or gather her thoughts.

The front door chimed once again and Jenn glanced around Rachel just as Luke stepped through. He took in the sight of the three women and stilled.

"Apologies." He held up a hand and offered a smile. "I didn't mean to interrupt. I can come back later."

"Come on in," Violet told him as she stood. "I need to get back to the clinic and I think Rachel has to get back to the farm."

"Actually, I don't—"

Violet smacked her sister's arm. "Dad needs help, remember?"

Rachel blew out a sigh but had manners enough to paste on a smile a she addressed Luke. "I've been here long enough."

Long enough? More like ten minutes.

But maybe that time frame was already more than she'd counted on. Jenn's nerves ramped up even higher. She and Rachel had settled nothing, if anything, Jenn knew full well where she stood with her oldest sibling. Ground zero. She'd have an uphill battle to fight, but Jenn wasn't letting that deter her from making the climb. Life was full of valleys and mountains, and standing in the valley now, she had nowhere else to go but up.

"I'm glad you two came by," Jenn told her sisters as they made their way toward the door.

Luke eased aside and held the door open. "Hope I didn't run you guys off."

"Not at all," Violet assured him. "I have appointments in a little bit anyway. Just wanted to see my sister."

"Maybe we can get together at the farm," Jenn called, hopeful.

They both glanced her way, but only Violet replied.

"Yeah. Maybe."

Once they were both gone, Jenn's heart sank just a little more. Definitely not the homecoming she'd been hoping for. Actually, she wasn't sure if things could have gone worse. Only moments ago she'd been full of hope and a little excitement, but that had diminished fast and left her with the harsh reality that the hurdles she had to jump were higher than she'd expected.

Their meeting was brief and painful, so Jenn still didn't have any more direction than she did before Rachel arrived.

Luke closed the door behind the women and turned to her. A shroud of concern covered his handsome face. Those piercing eyes held her in place with a level of care and worry she hadn't seen from him before. She didn't necessarily like having her private life on display for anyone, let alone Luke, but with this small town there was no way to hide everything. She had no doubt he'd already heard rumors about her and her family.

"I'm sorry," he started with a sigh. "I didn't mean to interrupt."

Jenn tipped her head and attempted a smile she didn't feel. "Don't be sorry. I'm not sure you were interrupting. Maybe more like saving me."

Luke took a step toward her and she realized for the first time he didn't have Paisley. They seemed to be a strong duo and other than the brief encounter at the farm, she'd only seen them together. Likely she was in school, but being here alone with Luke seemed odd. She found him too appealing and much too distracting.

"I won't pretend I know what's going on," he said, "but I can listen if you need to talk."

Shocked by his generosity, Jenn smiled. "I appreciate that, but nobody wants to get mixed up in my family's drama. Drama that I caused, by the way. I take full blame, but this is such a

delicate situation and I'm afraid I'm not handling it very well."

Luke slid his hands into his pockets as he took
another step closer. That striking gaze continued to hold her in place and she wondered what
thoughts, or even judgment, rolled through his
mind. He seemed to genuinely care and want to
help, but she wasn't so sure there was anything
anyone could do at this point. Everything from
here on out solely rested on her shoulders. A
heavy load to bear, but unavoidable.

"You're communicating with your family,
so I'd say that's a step in the right direction."

Luke's calming words eased some of that
heavy weight off her shoulders. Just having
someone from the outside and detached from
the situation give any type of advice seemed to
calm some of her nerves. Or perhaps that shift
in emotions stemmed from her unwanted pull
to her new landlord. Regardless, she appreciated the fact he took the time to comfort her.

"I assume you're here to check out the water
heater and not listen to my problems."

Luke shrugged, clearly in no hurry to move
along his visit. She couldn't help but compare
that subtle fact about Luke to Cole. Her late
husband was all work all the time. Rushing

from one project to the next. Luke had a laid-back attitude that calmed Jenn in a way she didn't even know she needed.

"No reason I can't do both," he informed her.

Another rapid wave of warmth spread through her. She wasn't looking for attraction or anything else. Family first. That had to be her motto now until her relationships were all restored.

"That's sweet, but just getting hot water by tomorrow is all I can ask for," she joked as she turned toward the back of the salon. "My inspector is coming at noon to give the okay for me to open, which I need because I've already scheduled several appointments for Friday."

His footsteps echoed behind her as she led the way to the utility room. She glanced at the sleeping dog, thankful she'd calmed down after the visitors. At least one of them had calm nerves.

"Looks like Cookie is liking her new home," Luke commented. "I've still not heard of anyone looking for their lost dog. Violet would be a good one to ask, too."

Jenn cringed. "I didn't even think to ask her to check around. I was just so shocked to see her show up unannounced, I guess nothing else crossed my mind."

Violet had followed her dreams of becoming a vet. Jenn had kept up with her sisters via social media and knew her sister's love of animals had turned into the perfect career. Jenn also hadn't thought how Violet and Luke would very likely know each other, considering they were both in the same line of work. Even though Luke focused on farm and livestock, while Violet did smaller animals, they had to run into each other or even call on each other every now and then.

Jenn couldn't help but wonder if Luke knew more about their family situation than she'd initially thought. In a town as small as Rosewood Valley, there weren't many secrets...especially when a prodigal daughter returned to the fold. She didn't like the idea of being the center of the gossip mill, but that was out of her control and she couldn't worry about what anyone other than her family thought of her.

When they reached the small utility room, Jenn stepped aside to let Luke assess the situation. If he knew about her family's history and drama, he was gentlemanly enough to not say a word. Did he know their farm was in trouble? No, she highly doubted her proud father would ever say anything to anyone about struggling. Her father would go down on a sinking ship before asking for a life jacket.

Luke stood with his hands on his hips and stared at the water heater.

"I have no clue about these things, so I'm hoping you do," she stated, breaking through the silence. "And I'm hoping this isn't too costly of a fix."

Jenn watched as he glanced around and muttered under his breath. She crossed her arms and tried not to compare Luke and Cole once again, but the memory slammed into her with no warning. Cole had always been a hands-on guy and one that always knew how to fix things. Busted pipes in their little rental on the edge of town had been no problem. They'd laughed in the midst of the chaos of shooting water, a flooded bathroom and soaked clothing. Cole had made everything in her life an adventure right up until his final day.

"Jenn."

Blinking, she pulled herself from her thoughts and directed her attention back to Luke. He faced her now, the crease between his brows growing deeper at his apparent concern.

"Sorry," she said, dropping her arms to her side. "You caught me daydreaming."

"I said we're going to have to replace this. I can go buy one today, but I might not be able to install it until later tonight. I'm due at the Millers' farm in an hour and it's a county over."

"I wonder who else could install it," she murmured, trying to think of anyone she used to know who did repairs or maintenance. "I can ask around. I don't want to stress you or cause a long day. I'm sure you're busy with Paisley this evening."

Luke slid his thumbs through his belt loops and widened his stance. "She can come with me. I'm sure she'd love to see Cookie if it's not too late since it's a school night. Shouldn't take but a couple hours to install so long as there's no complications."

"Well, if it gets too late, I can always take Paisley back to your house and get her in bed," Jenn offered. "If that's okay with you. But I also don't mind calling around to see who else can install. I'm sure the hardware store has a list of contractors."

Luke shook his head. "No need to pay someone when I know how."

"I didn't even think you might have help already with Paisley," she amended, embarrassed that she'd just assumed. "I just didn't want you to go out of your way if she needed you."

"I don't have evening help," he replied. "If I get called out on an emergency, she just has to go with me. It's only happened a couple of times since I've been in town."

Jenn paused and thought for a second. "How long have you been in town?"

"About six months."

Jenn realized she didn't know much about him at all other than he was a single father, livestock vet and now a fairly new resident. She shouldn't ask more questions. Luke's personal life certainly wasn't any of her concern, but she couldn't help the curiosity that got the best of her.

"Where did you move from?" she asked.

"Small town in Oregon where I grew up."

"So you're used to small towns. You must feel right at home here in Rosewood Valley."

Another casual shrug as his gaze darted away for the briefest of seconds before returning back to her.

"I've visited plenty over the years, but it's still quite an adjustment," he told her. "Paisley loves it here and this is home to her, so this is where I'll be. She's all that matters."

Confused, Jenn blinked and tucked her hair behind her ears. "Paisley has always lived here? But you just got here?"

Luke stared for a moment before he offered a slight smile. "Yeah. I guess I just thought you would've heard my backstory by now. You know, being a small town and all."

"It's not like I talk to many people," she muttered.

Luke blew out a sigh. "I'm Paisley's uncle and now permanent guardian. The rest is probably a story for another time."

The hesitancy and tenderness in his tone told Jenn that whatever Luke had been through, or was still going through, had hurt him on a deeper level. If he wanted to disclose more, he would. But men were stubborn creatures. Her father, her late husband, both hardheaded and full of pride. As much as she wanted to know more about Luke, she also had enough issues without digging into anyone else's. Besides, if he wanted to open that door wider to let her in, he would.

"We all have those painful parts of our past we don't want rising to the surface." She figured they already had that much in common. "You'll hear quite a bit about me, no doubt, considering you do work with my dad and other ranches and farms. I'm sure the gossip mill is all abuzz with the prodigal daughter coming home."

His brows drew in slightly as he tipped his head back. The wave of worry emanating off him calmed something within her and she had no clue how he managed to do that with little to no effort.

"I'm not one for gossip," he replied in that firm yet soft tone. "I try my best to stick to my own business and try not to get caught up in others'."

"That's good to know."

"I should get going."

Luke started toward the doorway and Jenn eased aside to let him through, but he stopped just in front of her. She had to draw her eyes up to look at him and another wave of awareness sent warmth through her belly.

"For what it's worth—" Luke began "—and just from the little I know about your family, they are amazing people and I'm sure everything will work out."

Something about his reassuring words soothed her once again. She didn't know how a virtual stranger and outsider knew exactly what to say, but he managed to give her a sense of peace for the time being. No, he'd actually been bringing her peace since she met him. That fast, hard pull toward him should worry her, but there wasn't one worry in her mind where Luke was concerned.

"I pray that's the case," she replied. "I just want it to be easy and I know that's not going to be how this will work."

"Nothing in life is easy, but it's our actions and reactions that can change any course."

Yeah, and she'd derailed three years ago, so her actions would have to be drastically different than before. And her reactions couldn't go into that default mode of anger. She'd had time and therapy to help process what happened, and to understand that her father hadn't caused Cole's death.

"If you're going to cry, can you give me a heads-up?" He bent down slightly to meet her gaze. "I'm not the best at handling tears and I tend to get awkward."

Jenn couldn't help but laugh at his crooked grin framed by his dark, cropped beard and she knew she'd given him the exact reaction he wanted. How did this man who didn't even know her somehow figure out how to make her smile when her heart was breaking? Not to mention when he was dealing with his own turmoil.

"I'll save the tears for private," she promised. "I'm just frustrated and worried more than anything. I wish I could see into the future and know everything will be okay."

That intense stare of his held her in place. She wondered what he was thinking, found herself caring more than she wanted to admit. Not only was he an extremely handsome man, he also seemed to have a giving, compassionate heart. How could he not capture her attention? How could she not return that same type of grace and empathy?

"We're not guaranteed easy, are we?" he asked. "But I am a firm believer that things work out the way they should."

"I used to feel that way," she admitted. "I don't know anymore."

He opened his mouth to say something else, then closed it. With a brief nod, he eased past her and started toward the front of the salon. Jenn followed behind, wondering if he found her to be a negative person. She didn't mean to be, but she also couldn't help how she felt or her true feelings.

"I'll let you know what time I'll be back later," he told her as he reached for the front door. "Hopefully I won't be too long at the Millers'."

"I'm not going anywhere," she assured him.

Once he was gone, Jenn turned just as Cookie came out from beneath the shampoo bowl. She stared at Jenn like she was looking for some guidance or waiting for her to do something. Right now, she wasn't sure what to do or where to go. Every part of her wanted to head back to the farm and see her dad. She'd give anything to help him in the barns again. To work alongside him like she'd done as a young girl. Her parents had taught her to be well-rounded and independent.

So much changed on that fateful day. But Jenn figured the only thing she could do was try again. She'd have to keep going back, keep proving that she wanted to mend their relationship. Not only did she need to fix what she'd broken, she had to make sure the farm and her childhood home were saved. She couldn't even fathom how worried her parents must be, but

Jenn had to find out exactly what was going on before she could figure out a solution.

The drought had taken its toll on the crops last year and her mother's canned goods for the farmer's market would've been affected. Not to mention all the baked goods she sold to the local bakery and most of that was done from ingredients from their crops as well. Selling some of their livestock had to have been one of the most difficult decisions her father had ever made… and she hadn't been here to help or support them during that stressful period.

Cookie sat in front of her and pawed at her leg. Jenn suddenly had an epiphany. Maybe she could incorporate a little of her experience from her time away and bring that into Rosewood Valley. It certainly wouldn't hurt to discuss the idea with her mother or sisters.

The farm-to-table events she'd set up at her church just months ago had been a big hit and a great moneymaker for their youth programs.

What if they could do the same at the farm? Would the people of the town embrace such a new, fresh idea for this area? Would her family think she was crazy for proposing this scheme? First they'd have to trust her again and they'd have to work as a team to pull everything off.

She shot off a text to her sisters that she'd like to talk with them if they had the time to stop by her shop.

Maybe, just maybe, she could salvage her relationships and the farm with one master plan.

CHAPTER SEVEN

"THEY'RE ALL GOOD to go."

Luke squatted down to his bag and reorganized his supplies. After all the vaccines he'd given this week, he needed to double-check his inventory back at the clinic and make sure he was well stocked. He'd gotten sidetracked the other day with Jenn and Cookie. Plus, still being the new vet in town, he had a reputation to uphold. Not only that, Luke didn't want to disappoint any of Charles's old clients. Taking over this clinic had been a blessing and perfect timing for the events of Luke's life.

"I appreciate you taking the time to come all the way out here," Allen Miller stated, rocking back on his booted heels. "It's not just anyone who would have kept on all the farms in this county."

"I love my job." Luke came to his feet and hoisted his medical bag at his side. "I'm happy to have the work and the opportunity. I should be thanking you all for giving a new vet a try."

"You had big shoes to fill. You've done really well. I know some were concerned with you being younger, but you've proven your worth."

Luke didn't know he'd been the topic of conversation or that his age had been in question, but he was glad to know he had the approval of so many farmers in the area. Without them, he wouldn't be employed or be able to care for Paisley.

And now he could add more attorney fees on top of everything else if he had to head to court for a custody dispute. He'd put every dollar he had to keep his niece where she belonged. While he was told the process would likely move slow, his attorney had been texting him and keeping him updated every step of the way. Even when there was nothing to report, she reassured him not to worry and she had everything under control. She had more confidence than he did that any judge would see Paisley was best with Luke, especially considering that was how Paisley's parents wanted her raised. While they might be gone, the intent of their will was as plain as black and white.

Hopefully the case wouldn't even make it to

court and Paisley would never have to know anything happened. Of course if there was family who wanted to see her, Luke would meet with them in person and supervise. He had to be protective of Paisley regarding everyone he brought into her life. He'd never had a more important job.

"I'm glad you're all pleased." Luke's boots scuffed over the sprinkling of hay on the concrete barn floor as he made his way toward the wide-open door. "Don't hesitate to call if any of your swine have reactions to their vaccines, but they should be fine."

"Will do." The farmer nodded. "Be safe traveling back. Supposed to storm soon."

The sun had disappeared behind the dark gray clouds and his first thought was how Paisley would love putting on her rain boots and dancing in puddles so long as there was no thunder and lightning. Maybe he could get the water heater installed and get Paisley to the puddles before bedtime.

Luke waved bye to Allen and climbed into the truck. Just as he sat his supply bag on the passenger seat, his cell vibrated in his pocket. He fished the device out and stared at the screen. His lawyer. He didn't know if he should be scared or excited, considering the past few exchanges had merely been a text. He hoped with each interaction that he'd find out Talia's cousin was dropping her custody battle. Wouldn't that be the best-case scenario?

He swiped the screen and put the phone on speaker as he put the truck into gear.

"Autumn," he answered, circling the drive to head out. "Please tell me you have good news and we can put this all behind us."

"I'm afraid that's not the case. Beacon Law Firm claims their client wants to move forward and, I'm sorry, but you're not going to like this next part."

He gripped the wheel and held his breath. "What is it?"

"Carol is requesting to meet Paisley in person as well."

A ball of fear coiled tight in his gut as he pulled down the tree-lined drive leading toward the county road. He attempted to relax his breathing, something he'd learned from his therapist, and tried to get control of his emotions before he spoke. He had to stay in control here, of his words and his actions.

"Do I have to let her see Paisley?" Luke asked. "I don't even know this woman so I'm not sure that's the best move. I'm not just going to subject my niece to a stranger who will try to sway her to come live with her."

"I understand your position and no, we do not have to make the two meet. For now," Autumn quickly added. "If the judge orders a meeting, then we won't have a choice, but we can definitely put this off and I think that's for the best as well."

A wave of relief slid through him. One hurdle dodged. But how many more did he have to go? That whole fear of the unknown had him clinging to his faith and selfishly praying a little harder than before.

"Could I maybe talk with Carol on my own?" he asked. "I understand her wanting to see her family, but at the same time, she would have to understand the situation. Paisley knows me, we're in the only home she's ever known, and this is what Scott and Talia wanted."

"I would advise you not to reach out to her," Autumn warned. "That's not a great move and, like you said, we don't know her. She could twist your words, and we don't want anything going against you. You have to look like the solid foundation for Paisley. You moving to her hometown is a great step. You already had that in place so it doesn't look like you're making moves just to impress a judge. How's the land coming for the home and the new clinic?"

Luke sighed as he made another turn to get onto the highway to take him back to Rosewood Valley.

"Slower than I'd hoped," he replied.

And by *slower*, he meant at a standstill. But he had hope. The Spencers hadn't come out and told him no, so that meant there was a chance. He had a surge of guilt, though. As he got to know Jenn a bit more and listen to her touch on her fears and worries, he'd been keeping this secret that he wanted her family's land to provide a more stable environment for Paisley. They needed a fresh start, something that could be just for them. Having a home and clinic in one place just made sense.

Still, his growing attraction for his new tenant, coupled with the fact she trusted him and had started confiding in him, did not sit well with his conscience.

"Keep working on that." Autumn's stern voice echoed through his truck. "We want to show not only stability but progress, and that you're putting all of Paisley's needs first just like her parents intended."

Paisley had been blessed with the very best parents. Luke worried time and again that he wasn't near their level, but he'd try harder and harder each day to show Paisley how much he loved her.

"I'm not doing all of this to impress some judge I don't even know," Luke grumbled, more than frustrated. "I'm doing this because it's the right thing to do and because I love Paisley like my own."

"I know this, but nobody else does. I'm well aware you have your niece's best interest at heart. I also know you are taking your duties seriously in carrying out the wishes of your brother. I promise, I'm in your corner here and doing everything possible to make sure Paisley stays right where she belongs."

Any other outcome terrified him. He'd never been this scared of anything in his entire life, not even when he'd been left at the altar with nothing but unopened wedding gifts and a broken heart.

Sylvia had done a number on him and it had taken quite some time for him to realize that they weren't meant to be and that she'd done him a favor by leaving.

But he couldn't let his mind travel to that unsettling place of his past or the unpredictable future. He had to hold on to his faith and be optimistic. He had to keep going with his life like he and Paisley would be a team forever. He'd gotten used to his little wing-woman and there was nobody else he wanted in his life right now.

"So what are the next steps?" he asked.

"Well, I'm going to go back and tell them that we are not bringing Paisley to the first meeting. You will have to fly to Washington when the magistrate sets the date. The system is pretty backlogged, so I don't imagine this will be fast or soon."

Wonderful. Just what he wanted, for this whole ordeal to drag out. One more thing to stress about. Relying on faith had gotten him through so much in life. Vet school, his breakup with his fiancée, the loss of his brother and sister-in-law, this move. He knew God guided every step of the way and had a plan, but Luke truly wished he knew Paisley would stay with him. That's all he wanted. Maybe he wasn't the best father figure—he had no clue what he was doing—but he and Paisley were finding their footing together. They were growing as their own family unit and they shared that deep bond from the loss of two very important people.

"I guess you didn't deliver terrible news, considering," he told her. "I appreciate all the work you're doing. Sorry if I'm cranky at times."

"Like I said, it's understandable. Nobody wants their world rocked like this and not to come to Carol's defense, but I think she just wants a piece of her family, too."

That was what terrified Luke. If the judge saw this woman—a married veteran with a stable life—would that trump everything in the will?

"I'll let you know as soon as I hear anything," Autumn added. "Don't lose hope. We've got this."

Luke thanked her and disconnected the call. As he continued down the highway in silence, he tried to push aside all the thoughts clouding his mind, but he couldn't. All his failures and reasons why he wouldn't make a good guardian ran through his head.

Would the judge see that he'd never had a committed relationship? Would he come across as unstable because he was still single and had just moved?

More than ever, he needed to acquire that land from the Spencers. Setting roots had to count for something, right? He had to prove he was the right choice, aside from the obvious will. Luke needed to make sure a solid plan was in place before any meeting with the judge or before this case progressed any further.

All he could do was press Will a bit more. But making the elderly man understand this was the best option for everyone, and a solid step to save his farm, was the only way to go into this. Luke couldn't push too far or too hard or all of this could be lost and he'd be starting over.

Paisley couldn't go live with anyone else. He refused to even think of his life without her.

"COME ON, COOKIE."

Jenn stood outside of her car holding the back door open and snapping her fingers at the pup. She smacked her legs, whistled and tried to co-erce the dog from the back seat. But Cookie merely backed up with her butt against the op-posite door. Jenn wasn't sure what other tips or tricks or mind games to play to get the dog comfortable enough to get out of the car.

The sky grew darker and a rumble of thun-der sounded in the distance. She really wanted to get into the barn or even the house before the rain cut loose.

"Jenn."

Her father's voice boomed from behind her. That familiar, stern tone had her straightening as the ball of tension grew in her belly. She hadn't heard his voice in three years, let alone heard her name pass through his lips. She wanted to cry over that sweet sound. She wanted to run into his arms and get one of those strong bear hugs he was always so good at.

But time and tragedy had changed everything and robbed her of the life she'd always envisioned.

Slowly, Jenn turned and shoved her hair from her face. Her father stood several feet away, his thumbs hooked in those signature red suspenders. He stared across the gravel drive from beneath the wide brim of his worn brown hat.

"Hi, Dad."

"Your mother went into church to set up for a dinner. Should be back around five."

Jenn laced her fingers in front of her, not sure what to do and never believing in a million years she'd ever feel uncomfortable around the man who'd raised her and loved her unconditionally. But he was talking to her, so she wasn't going to back away.

"I'm here to see you, actually."

"That so?" His hands dropped to his sides, but he remained still.

Jenn dipped her chin. She recognized his stubborn side and she also realized that his pride and heart had taken a hard hit because of her.

"Yes," she confirmed. "I have a pet now and thought she could use the yard to run around but she won't get out of the car."

"A pet? Does that mean you're staying in town?"

Will Spencer started taking a few steps toward her and she noted the slower pace than what he'd once had. Farming wasn't an easy life and he'd been doing this for decades. She wondered what else had changed about her father since she'd last been here. How was his health? Was there anything else within the family she should worry about? Or was the farm the most pressing issue now?

"I'm renting a building in town from Luke," she explained. "The one on Sycamore."

Her father's steps halted as a crease formed between his thick, silver brows.

"Luke? My vet?"

Jenn nodded.

Another flash of hesitation moved over his face, but Jenn had no idea why the mention of

Luke's name gave her dad pause. Was there an issue between the two men? Luke never mentioned a thing and he knew full well who her father was. Surely there wasn't any tension. She couldn't imagine either man at odds with the other. And wouldn't her sisters have said something?

A nudge on the back of her thigh pulled Jenn's attention back to the car. Cookie stood right behind her now as if trying to see if there was actually a threat outside the safety of the vehicle.

"What's your dog's name?" her father asked.

"Cookie." Jenn shrugged and focused back on her father. "It's a long story. She's not actually mine. She was a stray that ended up at the shop and I can't find the owner."

"Then you're the owner."

Jenn sighed. "That's what Violet said."

His eyes narrowed slightly, enhancing the crow's-feet around the corners. Yeah, he'd definitely aged over the past three years. Jenn couldn't help but wonder how her actions had affected his health.

"You saw your sister?" he asked.

Jenn nodded. "I've seen everyone now."

"Rachel?"

Once again, she nodded.

"So, you really are here to see me?" he asked.

Jenn reached back, needing to find solace in her new furry friend. Cookie turned into her hand, clearly wanting the comfort as well. Maybe they were the best team as they waded through this uncertain period together.

"I think it's past time," she replied. "Don't you?"

He continued to stare at her, and nothing but the low thunder overhead filled the silence. A slight breeze kicked up and Jenn tucked her hair behind her ears. She could grab a clip from her purse, but she didn't want to break this moment.

Her father continued to simply stand there, saying nothing. Everything about him from his weathered hands to those signature suspenders only reminded her how much she'd missed him. Missed working in the barns or in the field, missed spending quiet time or getting sound advice. So much had changed on that fateful day when she'd lost her world and placed the blame directly at her father's feet.

The fact that he hadn't turned his back on her like last time seemed promising…at least that's how she was interpreting the situation. Jenn couldn't help but wonder if her mother said something after Jenn had left the other day. Had they discussed Jenn being back in town? Had her parents talked about how her father hadn't spoken one word? While her mother might be calm, soft-spoken and at times passive, there was no way she would have just bit her tongue over the way Will Spencer had treated his daughter that day.

And this was precisely why she'd brought Cookie. Having a buffer and something else to break this inevitable tension had been a must.

Jenn turned and reached into the car, carefully hoisting the dog up in her arms. Maybe she'd realize this was the best place to visit. A nice wide-open area to run and be free for a bit. Jenn would keep an eye on her so she didn't venture too far into the fields and get in with the cattle, but she didn't believe Cookie would, timid as she'd been acting. Maybe she didn't like storms.

"Are you leaving her here?" her dad asked.

"I figure it was good for her to be out of the apartment, so we both came for a visit."

She set the dog down, but she remained right by her side. Jenn hadn't even considered that Cookie might be afraid of the storm rolling in as they'd left home. Jenn didn't want her terrified, so maybe they should at least get into the barns.

"You needed the support of a dog to visit me?"

Will Spencer had always been a keen man with a sharp mind. Time might have aged his face but nothing had touched his ability to know her inside and out. No other man in this world knew her like her father. No matter the differences or the wedge between them, nothing could erase their bond. She had to cling to that bond now and trust their solid foundation would see them through.

"After my last visit, I wasn't sure how I'd be received."

Once again, her father's thumbs slid into his suspenders as he ran his hands up and down in that memorable way. The man seemed to do his best thinking while wearing out those red straps.

A fat drop hit her arm and Jenn glanced to the darkening sky as the clouds rolled in with a bit more intensity.

"Spring storms are unpredictable," her father muttered as another drop hit her. "You staying or going?"

Jenn pulled her attention back to him. "I guess that depends on you."

"You're still my daughter."

He turned and started toward the back of the house, and Jenn figured that was the only invitation she was going to get to follow along. She snapped her fingers at Cookie and fell into step behind her dad. Thankfully the dog did as well and by the time they hit the back porch, the skies opened and sheets of rain pelted right where they had been.

She never thought she would have to wait for an offer to go inside the house she grew up in. And maybe she could walk right in, but Jenn wanted to be respectful. She'd left, not had any contact due to shame and embarrassment, so she couldn't expect to just pretend nothing happened. She needed to face her past before she could confront the issue with the farm and how to help.

Honestly, Jenn didn't know what area to address first—the blame for Cole's death or the long absence. One thing was certain, this storm raging outside was nothing compared to the turmoil rolling through her family.

"Get on in the house," he grumbled. "I need to go finish working on the stalls."

Jenn knew an excuse when she heard one, and years ago she would've called him out on it. Now…well, he was at least talking to her, so she'd give him his space. Besides, no storm would keep Will Spencer from a task. If anything required repairs, he'd always had the mentality that everything needed doing right that minute.

"Do you need help?" she offered, always remembering her manners and because she genuinely cared. "It's getting nasty out there."

"I've got it."

Without another word, he headed back out into the storm, leaving her on the covered porch with her pup. He rushed toward the barn and out of sight. He hadn't asked her to leave, but he also didn't want to accept her offering of help. He needed time to himself and she respected that.

Baby steps, right? Hope wasn't lost, she'd just have to be patient.

CHAPTER EIGHT

THE PLACE SMELLED the same. Like yeast and love.

Jenn had always found the kitchen of her childhood home to be like a big, cozy hug. Her mother loved to bake and always had something amazing in the oven or on the counter ready for any unexpected guest who might stop by. She'd instilled that trait into each of her girls and still to this day, Jenn loved to get creative in the kitchen. Her mother's biscuit recipe was hands down Jenn's favorite. She'd made them a few times for church events over the past three years. Each time they'd been a huge hit and Jenn thought of her mother with every compliment from the parishioners.

Cookie remained right beside her as Jenn took in her familiar surroundings. The long island in the center of the kitchen still seemed to be the hub of the room. A basket of fruit sat in the middle, along with a pile of mail, a folded dish towel, a forgotten cup of coffee that made her smile. Clearly her father still had that afternoon cup like always. The temps could be thirty degrees or ninety. The man insisted on an afternoon jolt of caffeine.

On the counter next to the sink sat a plate with a glass dome lid. No surprise a platter of cookies was ready for any guest or family that stopped by. Her mother had always been the gracious hostess.

Obviously some things never changed, which soothed her soul and relaxed her a bit more. Jenn didn't know what she expected when she stepped back into her old home. She honestly hadn't given the space much thought since she'd been focused on the people and not the things. But seeing the same floral wallpaper, the same framed sign with her mother's favorite scripture above the breakfast table, and the yellow apron hanging by the pantry, eased even more of those jumbled nerves inside Jenn. Maybe she needed this familiarity to help with her transition. And perhaps being alone for this next step was for the best. This way she could take her time and walk through, like reacquainting herself with an old friend.

Rain pelted the windows and she moved through the house, taking advantage of her privacy. She tried to practice potential conversations she'd have once her father came in. Would he want to listen to her first or get his own thoughts off his chest? She'd let him take the lead and go from there. She had no way of knowing how things would go or how this day would end, but she held tight to the fact she'd jumped a few hurdles just to be here and she had to keep up this positive momentum.

Jenn started to pass through the dining room, but paused at the table and chairs. This wasn't the same set that had been in her family for generations. Where had they gone? Jenn had always thought those pieces would go to her once she built a house with her husband. Or at least, she'd assumed as much since she'd been the first one to get married.

That gut reaction of recognizing her loss hit her once again. Coming back home stirred up too many memories, but thanks to a long string of counseling over the years, she had learned to not only cope with her grief but live with it. She and Cole had been ready to build their dream house back on the family land when the accident happened. They'd started off in a small rental in town, then to save money, they'd moved into the loft apartment over one of the barns on the farm until they could save enough to break ground.

Jenn hadn't ventured to that part of the property yet, and she honestly didn't know if she'd be ready for that monumental step anytime soon.

Moving beyond the new furniture and into the living room, she smiled when she saw her father's old recliner. She couldn't believe that thing was still standing. She'd been a little girl when he'd bought that big ugly leather thing. Her mother had tried to protest that it was too large and an eyesore for their small living room, but then she'd realized that Will Spencer worked hard in the fields and barns and just wanted one thing in this house. He never cared about decor or anything else and never asked for anything of his own. He'd just wanted a comfortable chair to relax in at the end of a hard day's work.

Jenn turned toward the fireplace and spotted the row of various frames and photographs. Pictures had always been so important to her mother. The woman was always snapping every event to lock in the precious memories. As her eyes traveled over the different pictures, Jenn was pleased to see that several were from her childhood. She'd never been omitted from the family, even though she'd removed herself for a short time. Her mother's love never wavered.

And for that, Jenn knew she'd carry this guilt forever. Now she just had to learn how to live with it and overcome, to be a stronger daughter, sister, friend and Christian.

Swallowing the lump in her throat and straightening her shoulders, Jenn pulled in a deep breath. As difficult as this part of her journey was, she had to push the past and the negative thoughts to the back of her mind. When she turned again, she laughed at the sight of Cookie, who had taken up residence in the corner of the worn, plaid sofa.

"We're not moving in," she told the pup. "Don't get too comfortable."

The dog curled tighter into a ball and nestled deeper into her position. Jenn had no idea what made this animal so comfortable around the Spencer clan. Maybe she knew good people. Jenn had always heard dogs were keen to personalities.

The screen door opened and slammed shut. Jenn assumed her father had returned from the stalls, so she turned to head toward the back of the house once more. Maybe they could talk a little more in depth now…she hoped.

"That man is going to be the death of me."

Jenn chewed the inside of her cheek to keep from laughing at her mother's muttering filtering in from the kitchen. Sarah had grumbled that same statement beneath her breath Jenn's entire life. As frustrated as she'd get with her husband, Sarah Spencer loved Will with her whole heart. Those two had an unbreakable bond. Jenn looked up to them and wanted a love like theirs. She'd *had* a love like theirs, so the question now was, would she ever find that again? Were people blessed enough to fall twice?

Jenn truly wanted to believe that she deserved a second chance and that one day, she would recognize when the right person came along. Somebody worthy of her opening her heart once again. But the risk of it being shattered scared her, and that was a fact she couldn't deny. But did she want to live the rest of her life in fear?

"Jenn," her mother called just as Jenn stepped from the dining room into the kitchen.

"Hey, Mom."

Her mother rested her purse on the center island and opened her arms just like she'd done the other day. "Oh, honey. You don't know how happy I am to see you in here."

Just as Jenn stepped forward to accept her mother's love, her mom dropped her arms and shook her head.

"No, wait. I'm all wet," her mom complained. "It is crazy out there and your father is insistent on repairing those broken stalls. I don't know why he won't just come in."

"Because I stopped by and he's still processing," Jenn stated simply. "And I don't care if you're wet, Mom."

Jenn closed the distance between them and embraced her mother, inhaling that familiar lavender perfume. Her petite mom always gave the strongest hugs. Jenn held on a bit longer than she used to, but she had time to make up for.

"Has he seen you or talked to you?" her mom asked as she eased back.

Jenn nodded. "I was trying to get Cookie from the car when he came up to me."

"Cookie?"

"My dog. Well, she's not *my* dog, but mine until I find the owner."

Her mom glanced around. "Did your dog stay out in the storm?"

Jenn released her mother and laughed. "Oh, no. She made herself at home on your couch."

A wide smile spread across Sarah's face. "Good for her. I hope you both make yourselves at home here."

Jenn started to reply, but her phone vibrated. She pulled it out and glanced at the screen.

I'm here with the new heater. P came with me.

"Oh, shoot." Jenn noted the time and groaned. "I don't know how I lost track of time."

"What's wrong, honey?"

"Just a minor setback at the salon," she explained. "My landlord is there now to fix it, I hope. Can I get a rain check on my visit?"

"Darling, don't you dare insult me by asking if you're allowed to come back. This is your home."

Her home. No matter what had taken place in the past or what the future held, nothing would change the fact that all her core memories and her family belonged here. Having her mother state that so adamantly smoothed out another wrinkle on Jenn's path.

She nodded. "I promise to be back. Not sure how full my schedule is tomorrow, but soon."

Jenn called for Cookie, who took her time coming in from the front of the house. Her little paws clicked on the hardwood as she came to stand obediently next to Jenn.

"Are you sure you want to go out in this storm?" her mother asked.

"I'll be fine," she assured her.

Her mother gave her one last hug, just as tight as the first.

"I love you, Jenn. Be careful."

"Love you, Mama."

That transition back into her mother's love and affection seemed too easy. She knew her mom had unconditional love and knew she was forgiven, but Jenn also recognized that she'd have to address the past to fully heal all wounds—hers and those of the people she loved.

"BUT WHEN WILL they be here?"

Paisley swiveled around in one of the two salon chairs and asked the same question she'd asked since they arrived twenty minutes ago.

"Honey, I already told you she's on her way."

Luke smiled gently. "It's rainy and she was visiting her parents."

Paisley brought the chair to a stop and adjusted her glasses as she stared out the front window. Luke knew what had to be rolling through his niece's mind. Apprehension and alarm. But he couldn't dwell on the bad weather and the accident that had robbed them of his brother and sister-in-law. He had to put on a brave front; he had to show Paisley that not every worry resulted in a disaster or tragedy.

"Everything is fine," he assured her. "How about you come help me in the back while we wait?"

That way they'd be away from windows and Paisley didn't have to see anything going on outside. He was slowly learning that distraction was sometimes the best option for a child. Anything to keep her mind on moving forward and overcoming the pain.

"I don't know anything about tools or fixing things," she told him, still staring toward the main street.

Luke crossed the salon and spun her chair so she faced him. He braced his hands on the armrests and smiled again.

"Well, I didn't know anything about hair

bows or little girls, but I'm learning. Maybe we can teach each other as we go."

Her lips quirked into a half smile. "You haven't done *too* bad with me, I guess. You did get those purple boots I love."

If only life's problems could be fixed with purple boots...

"So, what do you say?" he asked. "You up for handing me some tools when I need them?"

She nodded and Luke took a step back to allow her space to hop down from the chair. She marched toward the back, in those purple boots she so loved, and he noted her hair seemed to be falling from the style he'd tried this morning before school. He never knew there were so many videos to watch about doing hair. He felt ridiculous saving so many to his phone, but he knew Paisley loved all things girly and her mother had been a master at making her look adorable. Maybe Jenn could show him a few things because hands on might be a better way for him to learn.

Granted Jenn was busy trying to get things open and her new business started, so he'd casually mention it if she had the time. Paisley would probably love if he learned how to step up his game. And perhaps selfishly he just wanted so spend more time with the one woman who had captured his attention since his failed engagement. The timing wasn't great for him to even entertain a relationship, but God had a plan and maybe part of His plan was Jenn. Only time and his heart would tell.

"Okay, first we have to get this big thing out." He patted the side of the water heater. "You're going to help me unhook it and then I'll have Jenn help me get it out the door while you and Cookie play. Sound like a plan?"

Paisley gave two thumbs-up. "I'm ready."

Luke opened his tool bag and pointed to various objects, educating Paisley on what each one was and its purpose. After that quick Contractor 101 course on an eight-year-old level, he got to work shutting off the water. Just as he was figuring out the best way to get the old contraption out from such a tight space, the back door opened and a flurry of activity ensued.

Cookie came rushing in with a clatter, her wet paws trying to find traction on the old wood floors. She shook her whole body, sending water flying around them. Paisley's squeal of delight as she raced toward the dog had Luke chuckling. Then Jenn stepped through the door and she apparently didn't find anything amusing if her scowl was any indication. Her hair hung in ropelike strands around her shoulders and her shoes squeaked as she took another step inside.

"Still raining, I see."

The joke just slipped out, but she apparently had a sense of humor because a smile flirted around her mouth as her gaze cut to his.

"Just a mere sprinkle," she replied with a soft smile. "I'm sorry I lost track of time, but I really need to dry off before I can help."

"Not a problem." He pointed toward Paisley, who was petting and holding a very wet dog. "I've put my best girl on the assistant job for now, so take your time."

Jenn turned to Paisley. "Honey, there are towels in the cabinet by the shampoo sink. Would you want to get some and dry off Cookie for me?"

She glanced at Luke. "I'm supposed to help Toot."

"Go on ahead," he told her. "Then you can come back and help me. I promise there will still be work to do. Cookie is dripping everywhere."

She nodded and patted her thigh, calling for Cookie to follow her toward the front of the shop.

"I really am sorry," Jenn repeated, lowering her voice and scrunching up her nose like she'd done something wrong. "Have you been waiting long?"

"Not at all and there's no need to apologize. I already drained the water from the tank and just need your help getting it out. No rush on my end."

She offered him another one of her sweet smiles before heading up the back stairs to the loft apartment. Luke released a sigh and tried not to think about how gorgeous she'd looked with her hair in disarray and her minimal makeup smeared from the rain...

And he shouldn't be thinking anything about how cute she was—makeup or no makeup. Yet he couldn't help where his thoughts went—he was human.

"Get it together," he muttered to himself, turning back to the task he should actually be worried about.

While he scolded himself, he couldn't discount that their innocent meeting might just be Divine intervention. He really wished he knew because that gaping wound from Sylvia had taken a long time to heal. Only someone truly special could slide into his heart once again.

Taking a risk at this time in his life terrified him, but he couldn't ignore his feelings so he'd have to take all of this day by day. He just didn't know how strong he was to open up again, especially after the damage to his heart with the loss of not only his only sibling, but his sister-in-law.

There were so many factors working against these unexpected feelings he had toward Jenn, he really wasn't sure how everything would pan out.

Once Jenn discovered that he wanted her family's land, she likely wouldn't be friendly toward him and would probably find him deceitful, so his worries of opening his heart again might be a moot point. But he'd promised Will and Sarah that he'd keep this under wraps and he'd always been a man of his word. He still felt like he was lying every time he talked to Jenn, knowing this secret lived inside him.

Had she come back home because the farm was in trouble? Or had she come back for another reason? Did she have some grand plan to save her family homestead? Luke never wanted to see anyone fail and he hoped the Four Sisters thrived…he just wanted a portion of their space so he could start building a solid life.

He had to move forward with his plan. It was the home he wanted for Paisley. The country location was perfect because Scott and Talia were planning on building in the country, so Luke knew he could continue to fulfill their wishes. And it would show the courts he was the right fit, the *only* fit for his niece. Proving stability and a solid family homelife was the only way he could fight this ridiculous custody battle that never should've become an issue to begin with.

While he didn't have to have this exact piece of property, it made the most sense for several reasons. The Spencers were in a bit of a bind and any large income could make or break them in keeping the rest of their land and their home. Plus, having an already established barn that he could use, and having an office on-site, would be better than the setup he had now.

He'd already started this process and hoped to be making momentum. It wasn't like there was a ton of real estate available that would fit his and Paisley's needs.

His niece's laughter filtered through from the salon. She'd been asking for a dog for some time now. Apparently Scott and Talia had promised her one with the land they were going to build on, but Luke wasn't in a position to take on anything else at this point. Cookie came into their lives, sort of, at exactly the right time. She could get her dog fix to hold her over until the time came for them to choose the right one…just as soon as they found a place to live first. The lease was coming to an end, but Luke knew the landlord would work with him, considering the special circumstances.

Luke managed to get the water heater unhooked and pulled away from the wall. Now all he had to do was wrestle this thing outside and get the new one in. Doing this in the middle of a storm wasn't the smartest, but if her inspection was tomorrow, they had no other choice. He'd at least wrapped the new water heater box with a large tarp, so it was safe from the elements. Once the lightning stopped, they could get everything swapped out. He just hoped it didn't last into the night. Paisley had to be at school by eight and he liked to get her in bed before nine.

It wasn't too long ago that schedules meant nothing to him if it didn't involve his job. Now everything he did centered around one little girl…and he was perfectly fine with that. A year ago he'd never believe he'd be in a new town starting a new life in a parent role. He never would have dreamed his brother and precious sister-in-law would be gone, leaving their child an orphan. Life literally changed in a split second.

"Okay, how can I help?"

Luke blinked and glanced around the water heater to see a refreshed Jenn. She'd pulled her hair up into some knot on top of her head, scrubbed her face clean of the makeup mess, and had pulled on an oversize T-shirt and a pair of sweatpants. Definitely different from any woman he was used to…and much too lovely for his sanity.

"Why are you looking at me like that?" Her brows drew inward as she stared back. "Please don't tell me there's another issue."

He blinked and scolded himself. He wasn't some teen with a silly crush. He was a grown man with responsibilities, and that didn't include flirting with his tenant.

"No, no. I was just lost in thought." He patted the old heater. "This needs to get outside and I'll need your help getting the new one in, but we might have to wait for the storm to pass."

Jenn pursed her lips and glanced around the

corner wall toward the front of the salon. "I hate for you to take up your whole evening and I know Paisley has school in the morning. How about I call and reschedule my inspection?"

"Absolutely not. I know what it's like being self-employed. Each day not working is a hard blow. We'll get this taken care of, but I'm not sure Paisley will want to go back home in this weather."

Jenn tipped her head. "Is she afraid of storms?"

Luke swallowed. "Yeah. Um…my brother and his wife were killed in an accident on a stormy night. She was actually worried when you weren't here yet."

Jenn's mouth dropped as her hand went to her chest. "Oh, that sweet girl. I had no idea, Luke. I'm sorry. I seem to be saying that quite a bit to you lately."

"And you have no reason to," he replied. "So maybe she could go upstairs with Cookie? If she gets tired she can crash on your couch or something."

"If it starts getting too late, you guys go on home. I assume she'll feel safe with you driving her rather than me?"

"I'm really not sure on that one. This is the first big storm she's been outside of the house in since the passing of her parents. I'm pretty much taking this evening minute by minute."

"Gotcha."

"Actually, each day is minute by minute," he countered with a sigh. "Some days I feel like I'm nailing this parenting thing, and others... well, she eats dog treats as you saw."

Jenn scoffed. "Stop that right now. Do not question yourself. I'm obviously not a parent, but you were put into a delicate situation that not just anyone would step into. Give yourself some grace."

"That's what Pastor Dane spoke about last Sunday," Luke told her. "Grace. It hit me, and I'm trying, but there are times where this new life is difficult."

Jenn reached out and gave his arm a reassuring squeeze. "Paisley loves you and trusts you. She feels safe and happy in your care. You're all the family she has right now, so that's already an unbreakable bond."

Luke nodded, knowing every point she made was valid. He had also been telling himself the same things. Only now, someone else threatened to sever that bond. He couldn't let that happen. He'd fight with all the love inside him to keep Paisley right where she belonged.

"Which church do you go to?" she asked.

When he told her, Jenn's brows rose as she dropped her arm. "No way. That's the church I grew up in."

"Your parents still go there," Luke tacked on. "I've seen your sisters there, too."

"So you know my whole family?"

Luke had to tread carefully here, but he also had to be honest. "I haven't spoken much to your sisters. Well, Vi just a few times because of our similar fields, and Rachel a couple times at the farm. I don't really know your other sister."

"Erin."

Luke nodded, not sure what else to say here. Maybe circling back to the work would be best because he didn't want to venture too far into her family life.

"Hopefully this storm passes soon so we can get that new heater in and Paisley can get to bed on time."

Jenn tapped her finger against her chin, clearly in thought. Her short, painted pink nails captured his attention and he found himself wondering what was rolling through her mind.

"Since we can't do much with the storm, we could all just go upstairs," Jenn suggested. "Paisley and I can bake some cookies or something to distract her and keep her busy. Plus we can eat cookies, so…a win-win in my book."

Luke couldn't help but smile as so many thoughts raced through his mind. Her main concern right now was Paisley, not her pressing issue to get her business open. And she didn't mind opening up her home—or loft—to them so they could be comfortable.

If he wasn't careful, he'd start falling for this woman. Could he trust his heart? After what he'd experienced with his fiancée and then the loss he'd just gone through, was he still too vulnerable and not ready for anything more than a good friend?

"If you're sure," he replied.

Her stunning smile spread wider. "I wouldn't have offered if I wasn't."

CHAPTER NINE

"Now crack two eggs."

Paisley looked at the egg in Jenn's hand, then darted her gaze back up. The little girl sat up on the island with her legs crossed, looking too adorable and giving flashes of a life Jenn could have had. But this wasn't her daughter, Luke wasn't her husband and this familial setting wasn't hers to own. She was merely helping a friend, nothing more.

"What if I mess it up?" Paisley asked, wrinkling her nose.

Jenn scoffed. "Everyone messes up one time or another. That's how we all learn. I trust that you're going to make the best cookies we've ever had."

Paisley pushed her glasses up her nose and grabbed an egg. With her teeth worrying her bottom lip, she tapped the shell on the edge of the bowl.

"My mom always did it like this," she murmured. "Why isn't mine breaking?"

"Tap a little harder."

Paisley smacked the egg against the side of the bowl once more and the entire thing spilled onto the counter, with some of the shell dropping over the edge and into the bowl.

"Ugh. I knew I couldn't do this right."

Jenn grabbed the roll of paper towels and pulled off several. "Nothing wrong here," Jenn insisted as she wiped off Paisley's sticky hands. "There are more eggs and I'll get this cleaned up. Confidence is key in everything. Remember that. Next time, you'll get it. And if not, you'll get it after that. Why? Because you're going to have confidence in yourself. Right?"

Paisley gave a slight shrug as Jenn shifted to clean the counter. Luke moved from the window facing the street to cross the open loft apartment. He came to stand beside the island and slid his hands into the pockets of his jeans. He said nothing, but his gaze met Jenn's and that soft smile that flirted around his mouth had her heart doing a little dance.

None of this was real. This wasn't some second chance she'd been given. She barely knew the man, honestly. Just because she found him attractive and adored his niece didn't mean they could strike up a relationship.

She hadn't come back to town in the hopes of that coveted second chance. She wasn't sure they even existed for everyone, but she certainly had more pressing matters to focus her mind on. Getting sidetracked by Luke's handsome features and his giving heart wouldn't help her mend fences with her family or figure out just how dire their situation was with the family land.

Making these cookies gave her another idea for the farm to table. She wanted to incorporate some of her mother's amazing desserts like rhubarb pie or warm apple turnovers. She'd add that to her growing list of recipes she'd started. Once she had all her thoughts and a well-laid out plan, she'd approach her family. She was still waiting to see if her sisters would respond to her text.

Jenn turned back to Paisley and handed her another egg. "Now, let's try this again. You've got it."

The sweet girl tapped and tapped, finally cracking the egg and carefully plopping it into the bowl with the dry ingredients. Only one small piece of the shell fell in.

"Now we get that little piece out and move on," Jenn told her. "Well done. I drop shell all the time, so you're practically a pro."

Paisley beamed as she glanced to Luke, then to Jenn. "I had confidence just like you said."

"See? We knew you could do it, you just had to believe it yourself."

Paisley sighed. "I wish I would've had that advice for my last spelling test," she muttered.

"You did perfectly fine on that," Luke chimed in. He placed a hand on Paisley's shoulder for reassurance. "Some of those were difficult and you only missed two."

"But I didn't get the bonus points right," she told him. "I just want you proud of me."

Luke wrapped his arms around her. "Honey, I couldn't be more proud of you. I don't expect perfect. I just expect you to try and now that you have Jenn's advice, there's nothing you can't do."

Jenn's heart clenched at the tender exchange, but a piece of her hurt knowing Paisley only wanted to do everything right for Luke. That in and of itself spoke volumes about their bond and their love. And while Jenn didn't know them well, she knew enough to know that Paisley could do no wrong in Luke's eyes.

Luke released her and tapped his fingertip to the end of her nose. "Now, let's get going on these cookies I was promised."

She giggled, which Jenn assumed was the exact response he'd been going for.

In no time, they had chocolate chip cookie dough on the pan and in the oven. Jenn grabbed some disinfectant and cleaned the area of the egg spills while Paisley washed her hands. The aroma of cookies soon filled the open space, pushing Jenn's childhood memories to the forefront of her mind. Nearly all of her recollections revolved around the kitchen and her mother and sisters. So many stories and laughter and life lessons were shared during those times. And perhaps a little life lesson had been shared here as well with Paisley.

"How about a movie while we wait?" Jenn suggested.

Paisley nodded. "But not a baby movie because I just had a birthday and I'm older now."

"Of course," Jenn insisted. "I never once thought you a baby. I only let big girls help in the kitchen."

Luke gestured toward the sofa. "Have a seat, kiddo. And if you get sleepy, you can fall asleep.

I'll get you home and tucked in as soon as I'm done downstairs. Okay?"

Jenn still felt guilty for having him stay, but he'd insisted, and considering this was his building, she couldn't really argue.

Once the movie was playing on the television, Paisley cuddled deeper into the old sofa with a pile of pillows and a blanket from Jenn's bed, which was at the other end of the loft.

Luke went back to the window as Jenn pulled the pan of hot cookies from the oven and placed it on the stovetop.

"Rain letting up any?" she asked, reaching to turn the oven off.

"Looks like it. Would you want to help me get that new one inside or do you want to wait until it's not raining at all?"

"I won't melt," she told him with a smile.

Luke came to stand in front of the sofa, looking down at Paisley and blocking the view of the movie.

"Jenn and I are going down to work on the water heater," he told her. "Do not touch the pan of cookies. It's still hot. If you need anything at all, we're right downstairs. Okay?"

"Can I get a cookie before you go?" she asked.

"Coming right up." Jenn was already on it,

scooping two onto a plate and grabbing a small glass of milk. "I'd let them cool a bit, but here they are."

She delivered the snack to the sofa where Cookie seemed to be waiting for her own.

"None for you," Jenn told the pup.

"Make sure the dog doesn't get any," Luke stated firmly. "Dogs cannot have chocolate."

Paisley held her plate and cup. "I'm not sharing cookies. These are all for me."

"You worked hard on those," Jenn replied. "You deserve it."

"But no more," Luke added. "School tomorrow. We don't need you hyped up on sugar before bed."

"Can I take one for my teacher tomorrow?"

"Of course," Luke told her. "Now be good and remember we're just downstairs."

Jenn led the way to the first floor and propped the back door open at the base of the steps that led outside. An old broken cinder block clearly had been the makeshift doorstop, so she sat it in place. Just a fine mist of rain fell now, and a very distant rumble of thunder was all that was left from the spring storm.

"Thank you."

She turned at Luke's statement, finding him on the bottom step.

"For what?" she asked.

He rested his hand on the end of the rail. "For making Paisley feel confident. She's been struggling lately."

"Because she wants to prove something to you."

"Yeah, I know." He let out a sigh and shook his head. "I don't know why. I've never told her I expect anything from her. We're just going day by day, you know?"

"I never thought for a second you were pressing her for anything."

Jenn took a step toward him just as he came down off the step. That worried look all over his face had Jenn wishing they knew each other better. The guy looked like he could use a friendly hug, but would that be weird or awkward?

"May I say something as an outsider looking in?" she asked, trying for a non-touching approach.

"Please. I'm struggling as well."

"It's not so much that the two of you are struggling, it's that you still haven't found your footing. You have to push aside that doubt and focus on each other. Nothing else matters. Nothing else *can* matter."

Luke continued to hold her gaze as he pulled in a deep breath. She hoped she hadn't overstepped and she hoped he understood she had his best interest at heart.

"You and Paisley have come to mean a lot to me," she added, hoping again she wasn't going too far. "I just have to be honest and tell you what I see because you both love each other and, in the end, that's all you need."

"You're right," he replied. "Nothing matters but Paisley, which is why I'll do everything I can to keep her."

Jenn blinked. "Keep her?"

Luke raked a hand through his hair and sighed. "Apparently my sister-in-law has a cousin that is asking for guardianship. I just found out about all of this and it's stressful."

How worrying for him. Jenn figured he wouldn't have opened up to her about something so important and personal and unguarded if he didn't trust her. That fact humbled her and in some odd way, helped her in her own journey. She felt as if she'd just stepped deeper into a new level of coming home and watering those roots she'd had planted for so long.

Yes, she knew plenty of people in this town, but making new friends was part of the fresh start she needed.

"First of all, thank you for opening up and trusting me," she started. "I want you to know I'm here for you and I'm always a safe place. I can't imagine the stress you're under."

Jenn had so many questions swirling around in her head, and she needed to pinpoint the right ones and try to help.

"Where was this cousin when they first passed away?" Jenn asked. "I mean, why is she just now coming forward? Sorry, I have so many questions that are absolutely none of my business."

"No, it's fine," he said. "I had the same questions and this actually feels good to talk about. I haven't spoken to anyone except my attorney. Carol was Talia's cousin and away overseas in the military until recently. I guess when she came back, she realized what had happened and wants custody of her cousin's child. But Paisley doesn't know this woman, so I haven't said a word to her."

"No, I don't blame you. This is certainly quite a bit to take in."

Luke nodded, resting his shoulder against

the doorframe of the back door. "She's married with a stable life so I have that working against me."

Jenn's brows drew in. "Is this a happy marriage? Is she still active in the military and going to be gone again? Don't sell yourself short, here. Weren't you the one in your brother's will who he wanted as custodian? That has to speak volumes to any judge."

"That's what I'm praying for."

Jenn stared back into those mesmerizing eyes and wished more than anything she could make his worry and pain disappear.

"Now I should be the one apologizing," he stated. "You have enough going on and I just unloaded my issues."

His bold words startled her and she shook her head as she crossed her arms. "Hey, that's what friends are for, right?"

Friends. That's what they were and she wanted to lay that out there. Maybe he was interested, maybe she was, but no matter what else happened or didn't happen, she knew this was a man who could be trusted. And she valued their short time together already.

When he said nothing, she did start to worry she'd gone too far.

"At least, I like to think we're friends," she amended, dropping her arms to her sides.

"Absolutely," he confirmed. "But none of my friends have ever made me cookies so you might just get elevated to best friend status."

Best friend. Her last best friend had been Cole…but surprisingly the idea of letting Luke into that role didn't terrify her.

CHAPTER TEN

"GOOD MORNING."

Jenn greeted her next client on this gorgeous sunshiny morning. The water heater was put in without any more issues, she'd passed her inspection and she'd already gotten her first official day under her belt as a salon owner.

"Morning," Mary Major replied as she shut the door behind her. "What a beautiful spring day."

Jenn clutched the purple shampoo cape and nodded. "That it is."

"I'm so glad you opened this place back up." Mary hung her purse on the row of hooks near Jenn's station. "My last stylist never could get the cut just right."

Jenn remembered Mary from living here before. The woman had strong opinions, knew every single person in Rosewood Valley and never hesitated to give her unsolicited advice.

But she'd also run the local large livestock veterinary clinic with her late husband like a champ. Mary knew her stuff and there wasn't a thing she wouldn't do for anyone in town.

The woman eased into the salon chair and faced the mirror. "I have a confession," she stated. "While I do need a haircut, I really couldn't resist seeing you again. I can't believe you're back after all this time."

Jenn smiled, though inside she winced. She had a feeling that was why her book had suddenly gotten full. Word had spread that not only was she back, she was ready for business and social time. Some townsfolk probably did legitimately care about her and how she was doing, while others were just being nosy and ready to spread gossip. Well, she would hold her head high and focus on herself and being the best businesswoman possible. She couldn't control what others thought or what they said, but she could protect her heart and that was what she'd have to do.

"It was time for me to come home," Jenn said. Might as well just be truthful. "I need to do some repairing and I needed employment, so this was the perfect setup for me."

"And renting from Luke. You got a great landlord."

Jenn slid the cape over Mary and fastened the closure. "He's been so helpful in this transition back home. I don't know what I would've done without him."

"He's one of the good ones," Mary agreed. "I worried who would fill the shoes of my Charles, but Luke has done an exceptional job. Not to mention having to take custody of his darling niece. Such a tragedy the way that poor girl lost her parents."

Jenn didn't bother replying. Though the entire situation was indeed a tragedy, Jenn had a feeling that Mary just wanted to talk. That had been an early lesson in standing behind the chair. Know the clients and get a feel for their day. Mary loved chatting and even if Jenn chimed in every now and then, Mary wouldn't slow down.

"The Lord has His hand on all of this, though," she went on. "My Charles hadn't been gone but a month when Luke came to town. Having him take over the clinic was certainly a blessing, and the old farmers really seem to love him."

Of course they did. Jenn couldn't imagine

anything about Luke that someone could find fault in. After the way he'd opened up to her the other evening, she had a better understanding of what all he was dealing with. New town, new position in his career and personal life, and now a custody dispute. That definitely had to remain in Jenn's head. No way would she repeat any of what Luke had shared, especially to the town's busybody.

"And Paisley is such a doll," Mary crooned. "I love when she comes into the office. I always give her little chores because she is like a sponge. She just absorbs all the information and wants to work and feel useful. It's tough with Mother's Day coming up."

Jenn had completely forgotten about Mother's Day. She made a mental note to do something special for her mom, but she truly had no idea what.

"Apparently there's a Mother's Day breakfast at school on Monday," Mary added. "Paisley was at the office the other day and asked if I'd go with her. Poor thing. This has to be so traumatic for such a young one."

At thirty-one years old, Jenn couldn't imagine losing her mother at this age, let alone as a young child.

"That's sweet of you to step in," Jenn told her. "I'm sure that day will be difficult."

Jenn wondered why Luke wouldn't just keep her home on that day, but she also assumed that Luke wasn't one to run away from feelings or hard times. He'd want to face them head-on and not dodge the issue. Unlike her, who ran at the hardest moment in her life and pushed aside everyone she loved for as long as possible.

"So tell me about your absence," Mary chirped. "What did you do all of those years you were gone?"

The change in subject left Jenn a bit winded. "Well, I got my cosmetology license and worked in the same salon for two years."

Jenn rested her hands on the back of the chair, already thankful she'd blocked out more time for Mary's appointment. This wouldn't be a quick trim.

"I had a great church family and friends," Jenn went on. "And even started a farm-to-table program at the church for fundraising for their youth program." Could something so simple and fun work here?

"Well, it sounds like you had quite the life there." Mary beamed. "What made you come home to stay and not just visit?"

She didn't want to get into the text Erin had sent, proclaiming the struggles with the farm. That had to stay within the family. Jenn had no idea what people in town knew, but her father had always been a prideful man and there was no way Jenn would discuss it.

"Rosewood Valley has always been home," she replied simply. "It's nice to be back and see how some things are exactly how I remember and some things have changed."

"Well, I'm glad you're home and I'm sure your family is happy to see you again." The woman's expression softened. "You all went through so much when Cole passed. So tragic."

Yes, it was, but Jenn didn't want to focus on the pain or the loss. When she thought of Cole, she tried to remember their good times and the love they shared.

"You know, that's something you and Luke have in common," Mary tacked on with a smile. "He's experienced a devastating loss, too. Not to mention he's single and one of the most genuine people I've ever met."

Oh, no. No, no, no. There would be no matchmaking. The only matchmaker Jenn trusted was the good Lord Himself.

Jenn laughed, trying to act like she thought

Mary was joking, though she knew the woman was quite serious.

"Good thing I'm not looking for a boyfriend." Jenn slid her hands through Mary's hair and shifted the conversation. "So how are we cutting today?"

Mary smirked, but thankfully moved on and explained how she'd like her new style. Jenn tried to focus, but all she could think was how much she'd been drawn to Luke lately. Not just Luke, but his darling niece. But was she drawn to him because of the picture in her mind of the life she'd always wanted or was there more?

Could she have that second chance she'd only read about?

Thankfully Mary was easily distracted by whatever topic Jenn threw at her, and once Mary had the perfect cut and was on her way to lunch with friends, Jenn started cleaning up her mess.

The door chimed and Jenn gripped the handle of her broom as she met her sister's gaze. Rachel stopped, as if unsure if she should enter or not.

"You're always welcome," Jenn told her. "Are you here to talk or for a cut?"

Rachel grabbed her signature braid and shrugged. "I probably could use a cut, but I don't have time today. I ran to the feedstore for Dad and saw your text about having something to tell us."

Jenn nodded and propped her broom on the wall beside her station. "I do. You're the first one to take me up on that."

Rachel blinked. "Seriously?"

"I'm just as surprised as you are." Jenn laughed, hoping to break the tension. "I'm glad you're here."

Rachel shut the door but didn't move any farther into the space. That was fine. At least she'd come by.

"I'll be quick," Jenn started. "And I don't need an answer or anything right now. It's an idea that I'd like the family to think about."

Rachel crossed her arms and stared across the distance.

Jenn couldn't believe she had her oldest sister's undivided attention, and she wasn't about to waste this moment. "I'm sure you know I'm back because Erin texted me. I mean, it was past time for me to come home, but that text about the farm being in trouble was all the nudge I needed."

Jenn took a step forward, but before she could continue, Rachel chimed in. "I sold my house about a year ago to help offset some costs."

Jenn jerked back. "What?" she whispered. "Rachel, you loved your house."

"I love Four Sisters Ranch more and now I can live in the loft above one of the barns on the property. It all worked out, but even with my house funds, we just had to sell too much livestock so our production is low."

Jenn's heart ached for her sister. She'd had no idea just how dire the circumstances had gotten. Her idea might just make a difference.

"I started a program back in Sacramento." Jenn smoothed her hair behind her shoulders. "It was a farm-to-table event we hosted once a month to raise funds for our youth program at church. I would make mom's biscuits for church dinners and those were a hit, then I did some jellies. One thing led to another, and an idea blossomed to try a full meal and charge per plate. It was such a success, and I don't think we have anything like that here in Rosewood Valley."

Rachel blinked a few times but remained silent. That sliver of hope narrowed.

"You hate the idea," Jenn murmured.

Rachel held her hands up. "I'm just processing it. Rosewood Valley doesn't have anything like that. The concept sounds interesting, but we have to dig into the logistics before we jump in headfirst."

Jenn nodded as joy rushed through her. But Rachel dropped her hands as she continued.

"Are you staying to help?" her sister asked.

Jenn pulled in a deep breath. "I suppose that's a legitimate concern for you and the rest of the family, but yes. I have intentions of staying. There's nothing I want more than to help and prove how sorry I am."

Rachel gave a quick nod and moved back toward the door. "Well, time will tell and so will actions. I certainly hope you're here for good. We all need to heal."

She turned and opened the door but threw one last glance over her shoulder.

"Great idea by the way. I'm curious to see what the family thinks."

Then she was gone. Well, that made two of them. But once she had the details laid out in front of the whole family, Jenn was confident they'd embrace it and be one step closer to getting their farm back to the glory it once was.

"Sweetheart, we have a slight issue."

Paisley slid her purple boots on and stared up at Luke as he curled his fingers around his first cup of coffee on Monday morning.

"Mary is sick and cannot do the breakfast today," he explained, hating to have to tell Paisley. This day was already difficult enough, and now the fill-in mother figure couldn't attend.

His niece's face fell as she looked down to the floor. He wished he could snap his fingers and be done with this day and the Mother's Day holiday coming up this weekend. Unfortunately, facing battles was the only way to get stronger. He wondered if he was being too harsh for a child, but that was the only way he knew how to cope.

"You can stay home," he offered. "Nobody would think anything of it. I don't have appointments until eleven, so I can take you to breakfast in town first."

Paisley brought her gaze back to him. "Can you call Jenn?"

He jerked. "Jenn?"

"I bet she'd come with me. Will you call her?"

A whole array of feelings spread through him. Sure, he could call her, but would she feel put on the spot? Would she feel obligated? Not to mention how last-minute this was.

"Please, Toot?" Paisley wrinkled her nose. "Or do you think she'd say no?"

Luke had every ounce of confidence that if Jenn was free, she'd be there.

"You go on and brush your teeth and I'll see what I can do," he assured her.

Once she scrambled from the room and down the hallway, Luke set his mug on the coffee table. He pulled his cell from his pocket and thought about texting, but a call would be faster. He only hoped she was a morning person and he didn't wake her.

He tapped her name and waited for her to pick up.

"Good morning," she answered on the second ring. "Is everything okay?"

Of course she would answer sweetly and ask about his needs.

"Not really," he replied. "But before I ask the biggest favor from my new best friend, I want to preface this by saying you don't have to say yes if you are busy or not comfortable."

"Well, now you've got my attention."

Luke kept his eye on the hallway as he lowered his voice. "Paisley has a Mother's Day breakfast at school this morning and Mary was going to go with her, but she's sick. Is there any way—"

"I'd love to."

Luke chuckled and shook his head as relief spread through him. "I had a feeling that's what you'd say, but it's last-minute and I'm not sure of your schedule."

"I'm always off on Sunday and Monday. The timing is perfect. Should I pick her up? I don't even know where you live."

Paisley came back down the hallway, her eyes locked on his as she silently asked for the answer. Luke nodded, then laughed as she gave a fist pump in the air.

Luke gave Jenn the details and said they'd meet her at the school. He wasn't so sure how this amazing woman had dropped into his life in such a fast yet effective way, but he'd have to say something to Will. Luke didn't like keeping this secret. Not to mention, he really needed to peg the man down for some type of answer. He had to get things moving in a more stable direction. His rental agreement here was almost up, the custody issue had put yet another strain on the timeline and Luke really wanted to start a solid life with Paisley. He wanted a forever place to call theirs with a yard she could run around in, a dog chasing her, maybe a tire swing. A family life that she deserved and had been robbed of.

Paisley came bouncing back in with her backpack. "I'm ready to go!"

"Do you need to take the project in?" he asked.

"Not until Wednesday and I want to add more glitter to it if we can tonight."

Of course. Because there wasn't enough glitter on the posterboard covered in pictures of Talia. This girl definitely wanted her mother to shine so he'd live with glitter particles all over the kitchen floor.

"Did Jenn sound happy, too?" Paisley asked as they headed toward the garage.

Luke couldn't get Jenn's elated tone out of his head. She had been thrilled and her excitement warmed his heart in areas that hadn't been touched in so long.

Paisley climbed into his truck and reached for her seat belt, but stopped short as she faced him. "Don't tell Mary, but I'm kinda glad that Jenn gets to be there today."

Luke tapped the tip of her nose. "It's our little secret."

Because secretly, he was glad Jenn was going, too, and now he'd have to figure out what to do with his growing attraction and strong feelings for the sweetest woman he'd been deceiving. When Sylvia had hurt him, he'd vowed to never blindside or deceive anyone like that. Yet here he was, holding in a secret. He had no clue what Will and Sarah Spencer would ultimately decide, so until then, he had to keep this burden to himself.

CHAPTER ELEVEN

"JENN SPENCER. I heard you were back in town."

With a cringe, Jenn turned to face a familiar voice. She'd barely taken two steps inside her old elementary school and met up with a smiling Paisley when she was called out. She hadn't taken into account seeing other people and facing her past. All she'd known was that when Luke called with panic in his tone, she couldn't say no.

"Good morning, Carla," Jenn greeted with a forced smile.

"I had no idea you'd be here today," Carla stated glancing at Paisley. "And who is this?"

"I'm Paisley," the girl said. "Jenn is my best friend."

Jenn's heart swelled and she didn't think it possible to be so affected by being here and having this sweet child at her side, hand in hand.

"Oh, you're Luke's niece." Carla's eyes widened as they shifted back to Jenn. "Are you and Luke…"

"Friends," Jenn confirmed. "It was great seeing you again."

She held on to Paisley's hand as she turned and headed toward the cafeteria. The crowd seemed to move quickly through the old hallway and Jenn focused on the students' adorable artwork lining the walls from each class instead of her rapid heartbeat.

She didn't even think people would assume she and Luke were an item. She hadn't had time to think at all, actually. She'd only known Paisley needed someone and Jenn didn't have plans for the day.

"That lady seemed nosy," Paisley whispered as they found a table.

Jenn couldn't help the slight snort that escaped her. "People like to talk, especially when they don't know the full story. They just want all the information."

"But you didn't lie." Paisley took a seat on the bench and looked up at Jenn. "You and Toot are friends. I'm glad he found you. Or maybe you found him. I don't know what happened first, but I'm glad it did."

Yeah, Jenn couldn't deny she was pretty

pleased, too. She always believed people came into lives at precisely the right time. She wasn't sure who found whom, but she had a feeling she'd found another piece of a solid foundation in her life. A building block seemed to just slide into place where Luke was concerned. Part of her felt like he'd been part of her life for much longer than just a couple weeks. The support he'd instantly offered spoke volumes of the type of solid friendship he provided.

"Jenn?"

At the familiar voice, Jenn turned to see Erin coming toward them.

"What are you doing here?" her sister asked, her bright green eyes wide with confusion and glee.

Jenn stood back up and smiled, pleased to see a familiar, friendly face.

"Paisley asked if I'd join her this morning. This is Luke's niece."

"I know Miss Paisley." Erin beamed down at Paisley. "I'm so glad you brought my sister."

Paisley's eyes widened as she looked between Jenn and Erin. "Wait a minute," she said, holding her little hands up as she turned around on the seat. "You didn't tell me you were related to Miss Spencer."

Jenn laughed. "I didn't think about it."

"Is she your teacher?" Jenn asked.

"No," Erin replied. "I'm second grade now. I moved up from kindergarten a couple years ago. Paisley is in first grade, but I'll have her next year and can't wait." She winked at the child. "I hear what a smart student she is and how she's always helpful around class. I definitely need good helpers."

Erin had made a career move. Just another reminder of how some things had changed and she'd missed out and had no clue. Not only did Jenn want to work on repairing her family, she wanted to get to know them all over again.

"I can't believe Toot's best friend and Miss Spencer are sisters." Paisley's focus continued to shift between the two, then she narrowed her eyes. "You guys even have the same necklace. That's cool."

Instinctively, Jenn's hand went to the pitcher charm hanging from the chain.

"Our mother bought all of us one of these," Erin explained. "There are four of us sisters."

Paisley adjusted her glasses as her eyes got even wider. "Four sisters? I don't have any. That would be amazing. Are you all, like, best friends?"

Jenn met her sister's gaze as they both continued to smile, but the tension seemed to settle between them. Yes, they were the closest of the four, but they'd still not resolved the past few years.

"We better get ready to start," Erin stated in her teacher tone. "We can talk later."

Jenn didn't know if she was relieved that the topic was dropped or crushed that her sister hadn't said how close they were. But this was not the time or the place to get into the past.

Jenn eased back down next to Paisley as the principal introduced herself and started with a few remarks about mothers and the importance of women as role models. Paisley reached over and took Jenn's hand in hers and every bit of Jenn's resolve threatened to crumble. She could not break down in tears here. She was here to support Paisley and to have fun, not to reflect on what she needed to rebuild with her own family.

The principal continued to talk, recognizing the strong teachers who were often mother figures within the school. Happiness welled up within Jenn at the praise regarding her sister. She'd always been a natural nurturer.

When the cafeteria workers brought around

the breakfast, Paisley wrinkled her nose and leaned toward Jenn.

"You want my pears?" she whispered.

"I was going to ask you the same," Jenn murmured in reply. "I don't like them, either."

Paisley's bright eyes came up to meet Jenn's. "So what do we do with them?"

Jenn glanced to the rest of the tray with a fresh blueberry muffin, a bowl of what looked like strawberry yogurt and the fresh pear slices. She pursed her lips and focused on Paisley, who waited on an answer.

"I say we eat what we like and politely lay our napkin over the tray when we're done. Then nobody will know what we left."

Paisley's delicate mouth split into a grin that offered a view of the recently lost tooth.

"I knew you'd have the answer," she said. "And I knew you'd be nice about it. You're the nicest person I know, except Toot. You guys are kinda the same."

"The same?"

Paisley nodded and reached for her blueberry muffin. "Yeah. Always trying to make sure other people are happy. That's why I like you so much. You and Toot make me happier than I've been."

Those words from the most precious little girl had Jenn's heart taking a tumble. Paisley unwrapped her muffin like her statement hadn't just made a monumental impact on Jenn's life. Knowing that something as simple as a life lesson that stemmed from a dislike of pears had Jenn smiling. She was so glad she came, that she could help make Paisley's life a little brighter.

Paisley held her muffin in one hand and reached for Jenn's hand with the other. "Thanks for coming today."

Jenn swallowed the lump of emotion and nodded. This darling girl holding her hand was all that mattered in this moment. "I wouldn't want to be anywhere else."

LUKE HAD JUST finished up at another local ranch. Springtime brought all the babies on the farms and new life always gave him a burst of happiness. He glanced to the passenger seat and wondered if his attempt at a thank-you gift was too much or ridiculous. He felt he owed Jenn something for jumping in at the very last minute to assist with Paisley. That selfless act couldn't go unnoticed.

Since he had time to spare between his last appointment and when he had to get his niece from school, he felt this was the perfect time to swing by the shop...even if he did feel silly with his gift.

Luke pulled into an open spot about two shops down from the building he now owned. There was no discreet way to get his thank-you gift inside without being obvious. Perhaps he should've parked around back.

No. There was nothing wrong with bringing a present to a friend, especially one who had done something so sweet. And perhaps this generosity also stemmed from that level of guilt over the farm. Luke had called to set up a meeting with Will Spencer but hadn't heard back. Luke not only wanted to move forward with the possibility of purchasing some land, but he also wanted to fill Jenn in on the situation. If Will and Sarah wanted to be the ones to tell their daughter, that was perfectly fine with Luke, but the woman deserved to know. For all the joy and smiles she'd brought into his life and Paisley's she shouldn't be kept in the dark.

Luke moved down the sidewalk, clutching the gift at his side, with his shoulders back like this was perfectly normal. He didn't see anyone around, but in a small town, someone was always looking.

As he stepped into the nook leading to the double doors of the salon, he spotted the closed sign. He knew she was closed today, but would she have the shop locked? He hadn't thought of that. Of course he had a key, but he respected her privacy and days off.

He gripped the antique brass knob and smiled when the fixture turned beneath his palm. The moment he stepped in, the strong scent of chemicals or whatever she used for her clients filled the space. He figured that was better than the stuffy air the old building had before she came along.

Luke closed the door behind him and glanced around. He wondered if she was upstairs or in the back. Now he felt silly because he should've called first or at least texted.

"Jenn?"

No answer. He reached into his pocket for his cell when a noise from the back caught his attention. Cookie came out and didn't get too close to him, but she did give him a glance before turning and going back to where she'd come from. Clearly just making sure there wasn't a threat. The dog might be leery, but she was smart and protective of Jenn.

Luke looked back to his phone to make the call when he heard the sniffle.

"Jenn?"

Another sniffle.

"Just a minute."

Her voice drifted out from the room she called the dispensary. Confused at the sadness in her tone, he wondered if she was back there crying. Should he turn around and leave? Of all the times to drop in unannounced.

"I have something for you," he stated, moving toward one of the stations. "It's no big deal. I can just leave them out here and—"

Jenn came from the back room and dabbed at her red-rimmed eyes with a tissue. His heart clenched at the sight and he dropped the bundle of tulips on the stylist chair and closed the distance between them in about two strides.

"What is it? Are you hurt? Is it your family?"

Without thinking, he gripped her arms as a level of fear mixed with concern seemed to take over.

"No, no. My family is fine," she assured him with another slight sniff. "It's just been an emotional morning. You happened to come in at the wrong time."

"Or maybe I came at the right time," he

countered with a gentle squeeze. "What can I do to help?"

Watery eyes came up to meet his and an overwhelming sense of that need to protect and shield her from harm consumed him. He hadn't been kidding when he'd told her he didn't do well with tears. But right now, the urge to console her overrode any awkwardness.

"Nothing you can do." She dabbed the tip of her red nose. "Just going to the school and seeing so many people I used to know, having Paisley hold my hand like she was thrilled I was a stand-in, and seeing all of those happy moms and daughters…it hit me all at once. And Paisley and I…we—we had a moment over pears." Luke had no clue what that meant, but clearly that was the icing on the cake for her emotions. More tears spilled and she brought her hands up over her face in some attempt to hide her vulnerability.

Luke slid his hands up and down her arms to offer some sort of solace. He'd never once thought of how she'd feel or how her past might come into account when he called her this morning.

"I'm sorry," he offered. "When I called earlier it was out of desperation for Paisley. If I'd known anything would trigger such strong emotions, I never would have pulled you in."

"Oh, I loved going with her."

Jenn dropped her hands then attempted one of her signature smiles, but he knew a forced gesture when he saw one.

"I'm glad I could be there for such a special day, so she didn't have to go alone," Jenn added. "No matter what my issues are, I would do it again to see that smile on Paisley's face."

The kindness that lived in this woman never ceased to amaze him. Luke realized he was still holding on to her and slowly eased back. God had His hand on every situation, there wasn't a doubt in Luke's mind. He just wished he knew how to handle everything going on within his own life so he didn't cause Jenn more heartache down the road.

"Selfishly I'm glad you were there for her, too," he admitted. "Paisley really admires you."

Jenn's grin widened, more genuine this time. "I adore that darling girl and I was wondering something."

Luke rested his hands on his hips, completely resisting the urge to envelop her in a comforting hug. He'd give anything to take away this pain she struggled with.

"I know Paisley has gone to work with you, but do you think she'd like going to my family's farm to see some of the horses?" Jenn asked. "I haven't ridden in so long and that always calmed me. I thought she might like something like that if we can't get our schedules together."

"She'd love that," Luke replied. "With this fast move here, and dealing with my brother's insurance, and now the custody case, I'm afraid I haven't scheduled time for the fun things."

"You're moving?" she asked.

Luke nodded. "The house my brother lived in was a rental until he and Talia could build. There's only a short time left and I'm running out of options."

Actually the only option he had was still up in the air. Too many emotions settled deep into his gut, but he couldn't exactly let them all out now.

She dabbed once more at her eyes and fisted her tissue. "Do you have anything in the works?"

And there went that familiar, unwanted, heavy dose of guilt. He wanted to open up completely to her, but he'd made a promise to her father. Luke had always been a man of his word and valued honesty and integrity. He'd staked his reputation for his career on those exact qualities.

Now he was faced with doing the right thing, but for whom? The right thing for Will? For Jenn? For himself?

"I have something I hope will work out," he admitted. "I just don't know yet and I promised the owner I wouldn't say a word."

"Well, I pray everything falls into place for you and Paisley," she told him. "I'm sorry I was so upset when you got here. Had I known you were coming, I would have composed myself sooner."

"Don't apologize for being human and having authentic feelings."

He certainly couldn't take her apology, not with this deceit hovering inside him.

Jenn pulled in a deep breath and sighed. "So, what did you need before you had to console me?"

"I wanted to say thanks for this morning." He moved toward the chair where he'd dropped the bouquet. "I thought these would look nice in here and that you deserved something for your kind gesture to Paisley."

Jenn's eyes widened at the sight of the flowers. Then moisture gathered once more and she had that soft yet sad smile. Right now, he wasn't sure if this was a good or bad thing he'd done.

"I wasn't sure what type of flower you liked, but tulips seem to be the flower of the season," he tacked on, more because he wanted to fill the awkward silence.

"Tulips are my favorite flower," she whispered. "My late husband always brought them for me in the spring. This is just... Wow. A really nice memory and touching gesture all rolled into one."

A spear of relief hit him. He'd chosen the right gift and made her smile with a pleasant memory at the same time. He hadn't realized he'd been holding his breath for her reaction, but he made a mental note that tulips were another key to unlocking deeper layers to this amazing woman.

"You didn't have to bring me anything," she told him, bringing the buds to her face for a quick sniff. "But I won't turn down fresh flowers."

"I did and you deserve them," he replied. "And to answer your question, Paisley would love to see the horses. Are you and your family on better terms now? Have you had a chance to sit down with them?"

Jenn pursed her lips. "Not really. Mom will always welcome me and Dad is talking to me, but nothing has been resolved. I have apologized to each of them, but you know, that's just a small step on this journey. I have to keep proving to them that I'm here for whatever they need. I know there are some issues with my family that brought me back home, but I can't get into that and I just hope they let me help. I need them to understand I want to make things okay again, if that's even possible."

He knew of the ordeal she couldn't speak of, but he had to pretend he didn't. He had to remain an outsider when it came to the business of the farm. Whatever else they wanted to do with the land was up to them. He prayed Will would sell just that front portion with the barn for Luke to have his practice and his future home. He just had to make Will see that selling that fraction of property would be best for all parties. They would essentially be helping each other out.

"I'm sure your family will see how much you care," he replied. "I don't know everything that happened, but you're back and trying. That counts for something, and like you said, you can keep showing them how much you love them by being there over and over. They'll see that you are serious."

Jenn dipped her head as a corner of her mouth kicked up. "You ever think about becoming a therapist? You know, if the animal gig doesn't work out."

Luke shook his head. "Oh, no. I'm definitely not the one to be dishing out advice. I'm simply telling you what I see from my point of view."

"It's nice to be able to talk about this to some-one," she admitted. "Especially an outsider. You probably have a better view than me since I've been stuck in this cycle for the past three years."

Don't pry, don't pry, don't pry. This isn't your place and you can't fix her problems.

"Can I ask what made you leave to begin with?"

So much for that quick self pep talk.

Jenn glanced to the flowers and he wondered if he'd overstepped his bounds. She deserved her privacy and to keep her pain to herself. Maybe bringing those bad memories to the surface wasn't the best way to handle this situation.

"Forget I asked," he amended with a wave of his hand. "It's not my business."

"No, you're fine."

She clutched the flowers and moved to the

chair at the shampoo bowl. She sank down and pulled in a deep breath. Luke had a feeling she wanted to talk, so he waited while she gathered her thoughts. He crossed to the stylist chair and spun it around before he took a seat as well. Jenn ran a fingertip over the yellow ribbon on the stems as Cookie sauntered back in and made herself comfortable at Jenn's feet.

"My husband passed away on the farm," she began. "We had only been married a short time, a few months, actually. We lived in a loft above one of the barns and had plans to build on the property. I even still had wedding gifts in boxes that hadn't been opened. I wanted to save the good stuff for our new place."

A sad smile formed on her lips as she stared down at the multicolored buds. Luke wished he could erase her pain and sadness. But he'd learned over these past several months that talking and getting those emotions out in the open only aided in healing. He wasn't sure if Jenn had spoken to anyone over all this time or how her process was going. He did know grief had no time limit.

"Cole and Dad worked flawlessly together," she went on, now bringing her attention to Luke. "They were both workaholics and one day my dad asked Cole to get some cattle in from the pasture. Cole had been up all night sick and I told Dad to have Rachel do it, but Cole insisted. He was gone longer than we all thought he should've been. When Dad rode out to see what was going on, he found Cole on the ground with his horse beside him. We thought Cole had fallen and hit his head or something, but it turned out he'd had a heart attack."

Jenn paused as she chewed on her bottom lip for just a moment before continuing.

"He didn't make it to the hospital," she finished.

There was nothing like that crushing blow. That single moment in time when someone made that devastating statement that your loved one was no longer living. Nothing could prepare a person for that life-altering time. It was something everyone experienced at some point or another in their lives, but it was also something that not many people shared. Having Jenn open up to him turned something inside his heart…that same heart that had taken a beating more and more over these past couple of years seemed to be healing. And not just healing, but *feeling* once again.

Luke had no clue what to say or how to

console her. Maybe only listening was all she needed. Still, he should say something so she didn't feel alone, so she knew he cared…and he certainly cared more than he should. Much more than a friend. These growing feelings and his attraction were becoming impossible to ignore. He suddenly found himself wanting to uncover every layer until he knew everything about Jenn Spencer.

"There's no words I can say to make your pain go away," he started. "I appreciate you trusting me with your feelings and just like you told me the other night, you're safe with me. I'm always here to listen or give advice if you need any."

She offered a soft smile that melted his heart.

"I haven't even told you why I left," she added. "You might not find me so nice."

"There's nothing you could say that would change my opinion of you."

Jenn crossed her legs and shook her head. "Don't form your opinions just yet. I said some pretty harsh things to my family, specifically to my father, before I left. I let anger and pain drive my actions and my words. I became selfish and ran from my heartache instead of staying with the people who love me the most. I'm not proud of how I handled myself, but I'm back now to make amends. My family is struggling a bit, so they're more vulnerable than before. I'll always carry that guilt, but all I can do now is try. That's actually one of the reasons I came back was to help them with this hardship. They're proud, so I won't go into details, but I have to be here now for them."

Jenn had a heart of gold and a giving nature. He truly didn't believe there was a selfish bone in her body and he knew her well enough to understand how she would always feel guilty for leaving, but coming back and facing that past spoke volumes on her character.

And him keeping this secret from her spoke volumes on his, especially since she didn't want to divulge her family's issues. He already knew enough, but he couldn't say a word. And now he had confirmation on why she was back—because the farm was in trouble. He'd suspected as much, but her confirming it took his guilt to a new level.

"You're brave for tackling your flaws head-on," he told her. "Not many people would do that, so don't beat yourself up too much. Just understand your family is hurting, too, and you guys can help each other heal."

Her brows drew in as she tilted her head. "You sure you aren't a therapist?" She laughed.

"Trust me, I'm much better handling animals than people."

"Oh, I'm not so sure about that," she countered as she came to her feet, clutching the flowers. "You've listened to me go on and on about my problems and you've given solid advice that makes me feel like I'm not such a bad person."

Luke also rose and hooked his thumbs through his belt loops. He'd have to leave soon to get Paisley from school, but he wasn't quite ready to go. Not only did he value adult time, but he also valued this time with Jenn.

His cell vibrated in his pocket, but he'd let it go to voice mail and check it in a moment. He didn't want to break this connection.

"Nobody could ever think you're a bad person," he assured her.

That megawatt smile widened and he was so glad they'd gone from tears to happiness. He wanted to continue to do that for her—to be the one to make her smile and see the sunshine in life again.

"I'm really glad you ended up as my landlord." She took a step toward him and placed a hand on his arm. "And I'm grateful for the listening ear and flowers. You really made my day."

He wanted to ask her on a date. A real date with dinner, maybe take her hand to lead her down the street under the moonlight. But he couldn't do a single thing for a variety of reasons. The private conversations with her father and the fact she might not be ready for such a large step. After hearing so much about her late husband... Clearly they'd had a special love and bond. Was she ready for someone else to come into her life and try to start a relationship? Was he ready himself?

Maybe they'd met at this point in their lives so they could help each other heal. He wondered if that was the case, but until he knew for sure and had some direction from above, he'd have to bide his time.

Luke could wait because someone like Jenn would be worth everything.

CHAPTER TWELVE

LUKE DROVE BENEATH the arch to Four Sisters Ranch as his heart beat a little faster. He gripped the wheel and prayed this meeting would go according to God's will. Luke had to hold tight to the faith that everything would work out exactly the way it should for the best interest of not only his future, but also Paisley's.

He'd left Jenn's salon and checked his phone to find the missed call had been from Will and the guy wanted to meet to discuss the sale. Luke had picked up Paisley from school and taken her back to his office where Mary thankfully offered to watch her for a bit.

This meeting would be a pivotal point, no matter the outcome.

The gravel crunched beneath his truck tires as he pulled up near the horse barn and killed his engine. The afternoon sun shone down on the property and the bright warmth instantly gave him hope for today. After coming away from Jenn and feeling even closer, he had to believe his life was going in the right direction.

Luke stepped from his truck, pocketed his cell and headed into the open bay of the barn. He might as well go ahead and check on the livestock while he was here and make sure the influenza hadn't taken hold of any other animal. Even if the Spencers decided not to sell, Luke would still tend to their needs and care for their stock just like before.

Will stepped from the small office in the rear of the barn and adjusted his worn hat.

"Thanks for coming," the old rancher greeted. "Want to come on back?"

"Absolutely."

With each step he took toward that tiny office, Luke's nerves skyrocketed and his heart quickened. He'd waited for this moment for months and had to respect whatever decision Will delivered. But that didn't mean Luke couldn't plead his case before Will started talking.

"I appreciate you meeting with me," Luke stated as he stepped into the narrow space.

A small desk, two chairs and a narrow floor-to-ceiling shelving unit on the wall were all that made up the simple area. Life on farms were simple for the most part. It was all the grunt work that made everything run smoothly and that people didn't often see or appreciate.

"I'd like to say something first, if you don't mind," Luke requested.

Will eased his large frame down into the squeaky old leather chair and nodded. "Go ahead."

This was it. His last chance to plead his case.

"I know this situation isn't ideal or even comfortable for you and your family," Luke began. "I respect whatever decision you and your wife have come to, but I also have to reiterate the fact that selling a portion of your land to me is a smart move. It's no secret that I'm in a bind and need a place to go for my home practice. But I know you're in a bind, too, and deeding off a section of your land is better than potentially losing it all later. I value family, as I know you do, so please know that everything I'm doing is to provide for mine and for yours."

Luke remained literally on the edge of his seat as he finished his speech. He hadn't even thought about what he wanted to say, he just went with the words on his heart. Will Spencer had never been an easy man to read. The stoic, stern look on his face provided no indication as to his thoughts or how he'd reply.

"You are right this is difficult for the family," Will began. "Sarah and I have discussed this in great detail and weighed all of our options. We are willing to sell you a portion of the land with the front barn. We feel this is the best move so we can still retain the bulk of the land, plus the home that my grandfather built."

Luke didn't know what to say because this reply actually stunned him. He had wondered once it came down to a decision that Will would actually be able to let go of any part of his property, but Luke wasn't about to second-guess this decision. He wondered how the rest of the family had taken this.

"I can't thank you enough," Luke stated. "I promise to care for my part just like you have."

"I know you will, son, and that's why I'm comfortable with this transaction. Now, as far as the price, we discussed a range and Sarah and I are pretty firm on what we need to get our farm back up and running and to get some of our cattle back. It won't be perfect, but we're trying to be fair and still take care of our own."

Luke nodded. "I understand."

When Will shared the price, it was a bit more

than Luke wanted to spend, but he'd make it work. He wasn't about to turn down an opportunity like this, not when he'd prayed for so long. Finally, a door had opened.

Now, if he could erase that custody dispute, he and Paisley would be just fine.

One life hurdle at a time.

"How did your girls take this news?" Luke asked.

He'd just seen Jenn and she hadn't said one word. Did she even know? Now that a verbal deal was done, there would be no reason to keep this from her any longer.

Will let out a deep sigh and rocked back in the creaky chair. "We haven't told them yet. We know they might be upset at first, but they'll see this was best in the long run. We plan on having a family meeting soon."

And then Jenn would know. He didn't want to keep this from her any longer. He wanted to have a blank slate to start fresh. She deserved nothing but honesty, especially after she'd poured her heart out to him. Would she feel betrayed? Like he'd deceived her or tried to get close to her on purpose?

"Will, I have a favor." Luke shifted in his seat, more than uncomfortable with this situation. "Jenn and I have become pretty good friends and I feel like I'm lying to her by keeping this secret."

The old guy rocked forward in his seat and grunted. "Is that so? Jenn's renting from you, isn't she?"

Luke nodded, suddenly feeling like he was trying to impress his crush's dad.

"She's a strong woman," Luke went on. "I know she'd understand the situation, but keeping this from her doesn't seem right."

Will's green eyes stared across the antique desk. That same emerald color he'd seen in all the sisters could be piercing or mesmerizing, depending on the situation.

"Sarah and I will tell the girls when we feel the time is right." Will came to his feet, a silent indicator this meeting was about to come to an end. "I'd appreciate you keeping all of this to yourself for the time being. Things are…shaky within the family right now, so the timing isn't the best. I've put off making a concrete decision about this farm long enough and with that late frost a few weeks ago, we lost some of the produce we could've used to sell at the markets, and I don't want to have to sell off any more heads of cattle."

While Luke didn't like that the family had fallen on hard times, he was taking this blessing and using this chance to make everything right and good. Will and Sarah would bounce back from this. They were strong people with decades of farming experience, not to mention they were a solid family unit. They had a support system.

They had Jenn.

"I can't keep lying to her," Luke stated, rising to his feet as he held Will's intense stare. "I'd never tell you how to handle your own family, but I'd appreciate you talking to her soon. I want her to continue to trust me and not think I've been deceiving her."

"My Jenn won't think that," he confirmed. "She's got a big heart and loves with everything in her. Although her emotions do get the best of her at times and she leads with that instead of common sense. She's a bit like me, I guess. We can be hardheaded, but definitely know a good person, and she knows you're genuine."

The sad undertone of such a robust man caught Luke off guard. He'd never heard Will speak in such a remorseful way. Clearly this man harbored the same pain Jenn did. Luke prayed they'd come to peace soon.

Coming into this meeting, Luke said he'd trust and respect whatever decision Will made and that included figuring out what was best for his family. If he wasn't ready to disclose the sale, then Luke just had to be patient. And he hoped Jenn understood his actions when the time came.

JENN FINISHED SWEEPING the floor after her last client of the day had left. Her favorite soft classical music filtered through the shop and she hummed along to the familiar melody. She turned to dump the dustpan and caught sight of the classy white tulips on the table in the waiting area between two pink velvet chairs she'd found online. Little by little this place was becoming her own and settling in felt good.

Between the steady work, her pup that she might as well just embrace as her own, and the connection with Luke and Paisley, she nearly had the perfect fresh start. She'd only been in town a few weeks but did wish her family progress would move faster.

She'd been working on a spreadsheet regarding the farm-to-table idea. She'd also been researching recipes and trying to figure what would go best for the crops her family typically could have on hand during various seasons. She wanted something solid to take to them when she met up with the entire crew and was pretty confident she had a well-thought-out plan. She wondered how much time they'd need to process her return or if they'd ultimately open their arms once again, but hopefully with this plan to help breathe new life into the barn and help boost their finances, they'd see just how serious she was about sticking around and proving herself.

Jenn tapped her foot on the trash can pedal near her workstation and dumped the contents of the dustpan. In the midst of working at night on her spreadsheet, she'd completely forgotten her dispensary was running low on a few items. She needed to place an online order for more hair color and retail merchandise. She hadn't realized how fast those products would fly off the shelves, but she was thrilled her hometown had embraced her little shop.

The front door opened with a soft, pleasant chime, since she'd finally replaced that horrid bell, and Jenn shifted her attention to the entrance.

"I have a surprise!"

Paisley came skipping in with a small purple

gift bag in her hand and an adorably wide smile on her face. Could there be a sweeter child? Considering all she'd been through, Luke had to be doing something extremely right.

"A surprise?" Jenn asked, propping her broom on the wall. "I love surprises."

"Well, it's not really for you." Paisley came to a stop and wrinkled her nose. "It's for Cookie."

"Oh, that is so nice," Jenn told her, then glanced up when the door opened once more and Luke sauntered in. "I was wondering how she got here."

That crooked grin he offered certainly did not help the fact she was trying to ignore her attraction. She hadn't felt a pull toward anyone since Cole passed and coming home with all of her emotional baggage wasn't the best time to try to see if she was ready for anything.

What if she took that leap of faith with Luke? What if she wasn't ready and she ended up hurting him? Or perhaps he wasn't even interested in her in that way.

He had brought her flowers, though. Yes, he'd said as a thank-you, but flowers implied more in her opinion. Still, guys had a different mindset, and she wished she didn't put so much thought into this, but she couldn't help herself. This whole scenario was unfamiliar to her. She'd dated Cole through high school and then they'd gotten married. The courtship had been flawless, like God had designed them for each other. Jenn didn't have experience in dating or how to even go about asking someone out.

Goodness. Was she already at that stage? Did she want to take that leap? Just the idea of getting close with another man sent her heart racing. She'd never even held another man's hand. Mercy, she didn't know if she could do this.

"Jenn?"

Paisley's tender voice pulled Jenn from her worrisome thoughts.

"You okay?" Luke asked.

Shaking her head, Jenn laughed. "Sorry. You caught me daydreaming. So, should I go get Cookie for this surprise? I'm sure she's upstairs sleeping on my couch."

"Go get her." Paisley bounced up and down. "I want to give this to her and Toot brought some of my birthday pictures for you if you want one."

"If I want one?" Jenn asked, placing a hand on her chest. "Of course I want a birthday picture of my very best friend."

Paisley smiled wider and Jenn gasped. "Wait

a minute," she murmured, leaning down. Jenn took her chin between her finger and thumb and tipped her head. "Did you lose another tooth?"

"Yep. And the Tooth Fairy brought me a note that said she'd been so busy, she ran out of money but she'd get me tonight."

Jenn pursed her lips as her gaze caught Luke's. He merely shrugged as he held a small envelope.

"Well, I'm sure she'll return and leave even extra since you had to wait."

Jenn shot a wink to Luke and he merely chuckled as he shook his head.

"Can I go get Cookie?" Paisley asked.

Jenn straightened. "Absolutely."

Paisley ran toward the back of the shop and raced up the back steps. The floors creaked overhead and the sound of giggling filtered through the old building.

Jenn crossed her arms over her chest as she met Luke's piercing blue gaze. "No cash, huh?"

"I almost texted you, but I feel like you've bailed me out enough."

"I would've brought over something in a heartbeat. Now you just have to give more."

Luke narrowed those beautiful eyes. "I think you should pitch in after that promise you made."

"How much does a tooth go for these days?" She reached into her pocket and pulled out a twenty. "This cover it?"

Luke's brows rose as he held up a hand. "Um…that's a bit much for this fairy. I can't be dropping bills like that. Do you know how many teeth kids have?"

The horror and shock on his face had Jenn laughing once again. He seemed to do that for her. Make her smile for no reason, give her a bright spot in her day, and make her fall straight into believing that second chances truly did exist.

"I have some ones, if that will help," she offered as she slid the twenty back into her pocket.

"You're not paying," he said. "I've got it covered now. When they lose teeth late at night, there's a slight panic that kicks in."

"Well, now you know to keep something on hand. Was this her first tooth?"

"Second, but the first one she lost at school so I had a little time to prepare before bed."

Jenn couldn't imagine the fun of such simple things like playing Tooth Fairy. There were so many tasks like that that she wondered if she'd ever get to experience. She was still young, but not as young as she'd been when she and Cole had planned their family together.

The pounding of footsteps on the stairs and paws on the hardwood pulled Jenn's attention to the back of the salon. Cookie raced in with Paisley and the two looked like the perfect team.

"Do you like it?" Paisley beamed. "We got her a new collar. It's purple to match my boots."

Jenn looked closer at Cookie and noticed the purple sparkly collar peering beneath the fur. "Oh, that's so cute. You guys did not have to get her anything."

"P insisted," Luke explained. "We were picking up some supplies over at the feedstore and she found this."

"Well, I think it's perfect," Jenn gushed.

"Can we take her for a walk in the park?" Paisley asked. "I got my chores done at home and I don't have any homework."

"Honey, she might have plans this evening," Luke murmured.

"Actually, I'm free," Jenn told them. "But first I want to see those gorgeous birthday pictures."

"You haven't even seen them." Paisley took

the envelope from Luke and pulled out the pictures. "How do you know they're gorgeous?"

Jenn shrugged. "I know what you look like and you're gorgeous, so I know your pictures will be, too."

"I didn't know what you'd want so I had Toot get you four."

Paisley handed over the images and Jenn's heart clenched at the sweetest face staring back. One picture she was sitting on an old wooden fence in a field. The wind blew her hair away from her face. The next she had her head thrown back laughing as she clutched several daisies. One picture she seemed to be in motion on a tire swing beneath an old oak tree. She knew that tree was in the field beside the church on the hill on the edge of town. She'd been on that tire swing many times herself.

But it was the last image that truly captured her heart. Luke and Paisley hand-in-hand, walking away from the camera with the sunset in the back, but the two were looking at each other. The perfect moment locked in time of the family they were creating together.

"Are you crying?" Paisley asked. "Do you hate them?"

"What?" Jenn blinked and realized a tear had

escaped. "No, no. I love them. I'm just so happy that you wanted to give these to me. May I keep all of them?"

"Of course," Luke told her. "Do you have a leash for Cookie?"

"Hanging by the back door."

While Jenn propped the photos on her workstation, Luke grabbed the leash. The moment he came back, Cookie started doing circles and prancing toward the front door. Jenn swiped her keys from the top drawer of her station and gestured.

"Let's go," she told them.

Luke held on to the leash with one hand and took Paisley's in the other as they neared the crosswalk on the corner. Jenn locked up and met up with them, then they strolled over to the park entrance together. This place had always been so special to her. Her family would come here for walks or pictures. Their Sunday school picnics were always in the center of the park with the gazebo, the old stone bridge arching over the creek, and a small pond with a fountain nearby. Proms, weddings, really any special occasion, called for a trip to the Rosewood Valley park.

As they entered the wrought iron gates leading through the main entrance, Paisley stopped and turned to Luke.

"Can I hold the leash?" she asked. "I promise to be careful."

Luke hesitated and glanced to Jenn.

"I'm fine with it," she told him. "Cookie has never pulled me before. She's too obedient to try to get away."

"Please, Toot?"

Luke handed over the leash. "Stay with us, though. If there's an issue, I want to be able to step in."

"She'll do just fine," Jenn murmured.

Paisley started just a bit ahead of them, skipping alongside the pup. Her lopsided ponytails bounced against her shoulders and Jenn made another mental note to show Luke some easy styles. She just hadn't had time.

"I worry too much sometimes and others I don't think I worry enough because my mind is preoccupied with everything else going on."

Luke's words tugged at her heart. "She knows you're trying. That's all you can do. And the fact you're worried only proves how much you care. Give yourself some grace."

"You've said that before."

"That's because you need reminding."

They curved with the paved path and Jenn caught the eye of a group of women doing yoga beneath the tall maple trees. One woman in particular seemed to be zeroing in on Jenn.

Carla. But of course. No doubt she'd take this sighting and run with it. Jenn didn't care if people wanted to gossip about her and her life now. She was happy and working on starting over. She couldn't prevent others from talking and she simply had to focus on her own life.

The park seemed busier than usual, but that's what happened once the weather started turning from winter to spring. Every warm day a cause for celebration.

And she wasn't naive or oblivious to what this looked like. A little girl and a dog walking ahead of a single man and single woman. This was an image that had been in her head for so long, and now here she was right in the middle of her own dream...but this wasn't how she'd designed her life to be. This wasn't her family, though she was growing more and more used to this duo with each passing day. The touching gift from Paisley for Cookie had pulled Jenn into their little world a bit more.

But she needed to make things right with her own family before trying to push ahead and see

if there was more between her and Luke beyond a friendship. She had to discuss her idea
for helping the farm and find out if they were
ready to forgive her.

For this moment, though, Jenn intended to
enjoy her evening walk with a man she might
just be falling for.

CHAPTER THIRTEEN

THIS WHOLE DOMESTIC scenario was certainly not lost on Luke. Years ago this was exactly how he'd envisioned his life, but his fiancée hadn't shared the same outlook. Looking back at the heartache he'd endured after she left, he could see now that God's hand had been on that situation and she hadn't been the one for him.

And everything he felt for Jenn seemed different in every single way. She brought a sense of hope and light, she wasn't afraid to expose her heart and be vulnerable, and she adored Paisley. He honestly didn't know what else he could ask for, other than a chance at happiness with her on a deeper level.

She'd come back to Rosewood Valley to heal her family so he had to believe she wanted a fresh start.

The subtle ringtone from her cell pulled her from her thoughts.

"Oh." Jenn paused and reached into her pocket. Luke waited while she read the text, but also kept his eye on Paisley and Cookie.

Jenn let out a little gasp that jerked his attention back to her.

"Something wrong?" he asked.

"No, I'm just surprised and now a little nervous," she admitted, sliding the cell back into the pocket of her red cardigan. "My mom is calling a family meeting and that was a group text with all of us on there. It's tomorrow at four."

Those expressive green eyes came up to his and his heart kicked up. Not only because of the level of worry on her face, but because he wondered what that meeting would bring. Were Will and Sarah going to finally disclose the sale? No matter what the meeting was about, this was another step Jenn needed to complete in order to continue on her journey toward healing.

They started walking once again and he had no doubt thoughts were racing through her mind.

"Nothing to worry about," he assured her. "Your mother obviously wants to mend things."

"She's always been one to take action. She doesn't like conflict. When we were younger, and my sisters and I would argue, she'd make us stop talking and hug for two whole minutes. She set a timer and those seconds felt like forever."

Jenn's soft laugh flittered on the wind and seemed to wrap around him like the sweetest embrace he'd ever had. Her hand accidentally brushed his as they walked side by side along the path. Luke didn't allow himself the time to think or talk himself out of his actions. He reached for her hand like it was the most natural gesture in the world.

And when her fingers slid through his and she gave a gentle squeeze, Luke released that breath he'd been holding. Maybe they were on the same page here…he just prayed they remained that way once she uncovered the truth.

A scream cut through the tender moment, and Luke jerked his focus to Paisley. Cookie darted off toward a ball that bounced by, Paisley held the leash, but got pulled down to the sidewalk before ultimately letting go.

Both he and Jenn took off running, her for the dog and him for Paisley. He crouched next to her and raked his gaze up and down, looking for any injuries. A tear in the knee of her jeans revealed a scraped knee, but she sat up cradling her arm with tears streaming down her face.

"It hurts," she cried. "Where's Cookie? She saw a ball and pulled me. I couldn't keep up."

"She's right here." Jenn came back holding on to the leash as she squatted down as well. "What's hurt, honey?"

"My arm." Paisley sniffed as more tears fell. "I can't move it."

Luke knew just by the way she was holding herself that the arm was likely broken. A wave of nausea overcame him at the thought of her hurting in any way. While he'd been daydreaming and holding hands with Jenn, his niece had gotten hurt.

He scooped her up into his arms and came to his feet.

"I'll meet you at your truck," Jenn told him. "I'm putting Cookie in and we'll take Paisley to the ER."

"No need for you to come," he told her as they rushed back to the main entrance. "I can handle this."

"But you don't have to alone."

He couldn't think right now, didn't know how to fix this right this second as Paisley sobbed against his chest. He should've been paying attention. He shouldn't have let his selfish thoughts cloud his parental judgment.

"I want her there," Paisley murmured.

Then it was settled. He just had to get himself together and be strong for her. He couldn't get swept up in his own guilt and remorse right now. His little girl needed him and he was almost positive this was her first broken bone, so no doubt she was scared in addition to the pain.

Once they were on their way to the hospital, Luke might have run a few yellow lights that teetered on being red. He'd risk the ticket at this point. Jenn, with her calming voice of reason, offered soothing words to a still crying Paisley. Just having Jenn here helped his nerves as well, but none of this would have happened had he been watching his niece.

"The doctors will fix you right up and when we get done, I'll get you some ice cream if Luke doesn't care," Jenn stated. "Whatever kind you want."

"Chocolate chip," she sniffed as she leaned against Jenn.

"Two scoops of chocolate chip, it is."

He pulled into the ER entrance and raced around to help Paisley out. Once again, he carried her and tried to control his movements so he didn't jerk her around too much.

A flurry of activity seemed to happen at once. Thankfully the waiting area wasn't busy and a nurse ushered them back to a room. X-rays confirmed the break and Paisley cried even harder while Jenn cradled her and rocked her in one of the hard plastic chairs. Luke gave insurance info and couldn't bring himself to take a seat. His nerves were still on edge and figured Jenn was doing the best job of consoling Paisley at this point. He was glad she'd come and offered to be by their side. She certainly didn't have to, but again, her selflessness spoke volumes for her character.

In no time, they were back on the road with a newly wrapped arm with a purple cast…because what else would she choose?

And apparently they were stopping for ice cream. He'd do anything to make her smile and take her mind off the pain and the worry of the upcoming weeks trying to maneuver with one arm.

He owed both of them an apology—Paisley for losing track of his responsibility and Jenn for taking her hand and just assuming that's what she'd want. He hadn't asked and they hadn't had time to discuss that turning point in their relationship. He needed to tell her how he felt before she learned of the sale. He didn't want her believing the worst in him and when the time came, he needed her to understand his actions. If they had a firm foundation before that time, he thought they might just have a chance.

But between the sale and then the custody hearing, there was a possibility he could lose it all and lose any future with a woman he'd come to truly care for...just like before.

Now that the pain meds had kicked in and the ice cream helped dry up the tears, Paisley had asked to go back to Jenn's apartment so she could make sure Cookie was okay. Paisley sat in the corner of Jenn's sofa and Cookie rested at her side as P toyed with one floppy ear, lulling the pup back to sleep.

"Well, this was quite an eventful day." Jenn sighed as she rested on one of her barstools.

Luke leaned against the island and faced Jenn. He'd never gotten that worried look from his eyes or the creases between his brows to diminish since the accident. She reached for his hand and curled her fingers around his.

"She's okay," Jenn assured him. "Kids break

bones all the time and they bounce right back. She's already excited about who all can sign her cast at school. She really is one special girl to always look on the bright side of things."

"She wouldn't have to do any of that had I been paying attention," he muttered.

"Then if you're at fault, I am, too," she countered. "I had no idea Cookie would take off after a ball. She's never done anything like that with me or I would not have let Paisley hold the leash. I'll take the blame."

He jerked and shook his head. "Absolutely not. She's my responsibility." Luke leaned in and lowered his voice. "How is this going to look to the courts?" he asked. "I still don't have a permanent living arrangement lined up, I also let her break her arm."

"Hold up. You didn't *let* her do anything. Accidents happen, right?"

Luke quirked a brow. "Is that why you've come to realize since being gone? That Cole's death was an accident?"

Jenn stared back, shocked that he'd made that correlation, but his tone wasn't malicious or judgmental. His question came across as totally legit.

"I'm sorry." He blew out a sigh and flattened his palms on the stained countertop as he dropped his head between his shoulders. "I shouldn't have said that or compared the two situations. Clearly they're not the same and I didn't mean to be insensitive."

"You're not insensitive and maybe the situations aren't the same, but that doesn't mean we aren't experiencing parallel moments."

Luke raked a hand through his hair and moved around her to take a seat on the other stool. Jenn turned to face him, finding herself closer than she thought she'd be. His broad shoulders and stubbled jaw screamed rugged and tough, but this man was a big softy and had a giving heart.

"I can't ignore what's happening here."

Luke's low words after a long pause of silence had her breath catching in her throat. She waited for him to elaborate because this was one area she definitely wanted him to take the lead on.

"I'm attracted to you," he told her, glancing over her shoulder to check on Paisley before shifting that cobalt gaze back to her. "I've tried to tell myself this is a bad idea, but the more I say that, the more I want to spend time with you and learn everything."

Jenn's heartbeat quickened and she honestly couldn't believe this was happening. She never thought she'd find love again and honestly hadn't been looking for it.

If God was giving her a second chance with her family and with a man He chose, who was she to second-guess?

"I think I'm ready to move on," she told him. "This is hard and scary and I have so many emotions, but I feel the same. I want to know everything about you and Paisley. You both just make me happier and I've smiled more in the past few weeks than in the past three years."

A grin lifted the corners of his mouth. "I haven't seen Paisley this happy since her parents passed."

A burst of hope consumed her, warming her throughout. She didn't believe in coincidences. She believed in God's timing and she'd had to restore her faith since Cole's passing. Coming home had been the riskiest move, but she was starting to see why her journey had led her back at this precise moment.

"I should be honest as well and tell you that I might just find you attractive, too."

Luke's wide smile framed by that dark, close beard had her stomach in knots. She'd finally put her thoughts out in the open, and knowing Luke reciprocated her feelings sent a burst of warmth and hope through her. She'd wondered if she'd ever get such a reaction from anyone ever again.

Luke reached for her hand and laced their fingers together. The gesture still seemed right and comfortable. Nothing forced or awkward. Luke put her at ease with so many aspects of her life and she couldn't wait to see where they went from here now that they'd opened up. Would he ask her on an actual date soon? She hadn't been on a real date in so long, but the nerves in her belly weren't from fear or apprehension, but rather excitement at the new chance she'd been given.

"I should probably get Paisley home and settled in for bed."

But he didn't move. He continued to stroke the back of her hand with the pad of his thumb and hold her gaze with those beautiful blue eyes. She could lose track of time with this man and she knew without a doubt she was falling for him. The idea of falling in love again used to seem foreign, even scary, but she felt safe with Luke. He had a stellar reputation, an unwavering faith like hers, and had gone through heartache only to come out stronger on the other side. They already had so much in common.

"Please let me know if she needs anything," Jenn told him. "I hate this for her and for you, but we'll get through this."

Luke came to his feet, tugging her along with him as he continued to hold her hand.

"I like the sound of the 'we' part," he stated, and if possible his grin widened. "And thanks for being there for us tonight. This was really my first emergency and I didn't handle it well."

"You did just fine," she assured him. "And don't worry about anything with the courts. She's safe, she's where your brother wanted her, and she's one of the happiest little girls. You're doing a great job."

Luke's arms came around her and Jenn wasn't sure who needed this comforting embrace more. Perhaps leaning on each other was what forged their bond so quickly and perfectly.

"Why do you always know the right things to say?" he asked.

Jenn chuckled as she leaned her head against his chest. "I'm a beautician. We're also therapists, because our clients tell us everything and need advice."

Luke eased back and laid his hands on her shoulders. "You should charge more."

"Only if my landlord raises my rent," she joked.

"I have a feeling he won't do that."

When he stepped away, Jenn didn't like the loss of contact. She knew he had responsibilities, and that was one of the reasons she was so drawn to him. But at the same time, she wanted him to stay. She wanted to curl up on the sofa and watch a movie, pop popcorn and snuggle with a blanket.

"We don't have to go yet, do we?" Paisley pouted as she continued to pet the sleeping dog.

"Afraid so," Luke told her. "The doctor wrote you off school tomorrow, but you still have a bedtime and I have to work. So you can come with me or hang at the office with Mary."

"You can stay here if you want," Jenn suggested to the little girl. "I don't have a full day, but I'll be downstairs."

She looked to Luke and shrugged. "I mean, if you're okay with that. I just thought Paisley might be more comfortable."

"Can I?" Paisley asked, staring up at Luke with her wide eyes.

"I'm fine with that. But we need to get you

home and in bed." He faced Jenn once more. "I'll need to head out about ten in the morning so I'll bring her by around then. That work?"

"Absolutely. I just have that family meeting at four."

"I'll be back by three at the latest."

Jenn shot Paisley a wink and the little girl giggled. Not only was she falling for the man, she was falling for the most precious child. Now she just needed to sew up the unraveled hems with her family and this new chapter in her life would be on the perfect path.

CHAPTER FOURTEEN

Luke maneuvered his truck away from his last stop of the day and headed down Sycamore Street toward Jenn's shop. While yesterday had been an awful day with the broken arm, he couldn't help but look to the silver lining. And that lining surrounded Jenn in all her beauty, both inside and out. She seemed to be that missing piece in his life, like she'd been designed to fit flawlessly into the void he'd had for so long.

The way she'd handled Paisley had been nothing short of nurturing and motherly. Not that anyone could ever replace Talia, but Paisley needed a female role model in her life. Someone she could trust and look up to as a good example. Jenn had all the qualities Luke had ever wanted, and some he didn't even realize he was looking for.

He'd just pulled into a parking spot in front of

the salon when his cell vibrated on the console. Luke put the truck in Park before answering.

"This is Luke."

"Hey, Luke."

Autumn's voice penetrated the space and instantly put him on alert.

"The initial date has been moved and closer than I'd thought. I'm hoping you can meet in Washington in three days."

"Three days?" he repeated. "So soon?"

"I know, it's much sooner than we'd anticipated, but the judge had an opening and we might as well not put off the inevitable."

Luke pinched the bridge of his nose and closed his eyes. The hum of his engine and the traffic around him filled the silent space. His thoughts were all cramming against each other in his head and he honestly didn't know what to say.

"I know you're worried," Autumn added. "But I'm right there with you and we have your brother's will on our side. I truly believe this will go in your favor."

"What if it doesn't?"

That niggle of doubt pounded in his mind and on his heart. How would he tell Paisley? At seven years old, her world had already crumbled once. She'd just found her new normal and was getting somewhat back on track. So if this judge, who knew no parties involved, decided that a married couple with a stable life was the better option, there wouldn't be a thing Luke could do to stop that ruling.

"We're not going to think like that," Autumn firmly stated. "I'll email you all of the documents you will need to bring, along with the address to the courthouse. This will be in the judge's office, so not an actual courtroom."

"I don't have to bring Paisley, do I?" he questioned.

"No. This will just be adults. But there might not be a decision made that day, so prepare yourself. And there could also come a time when the judge does want to meet Paisley and maybe get her opinion or see how she interacts with Carol."

"She doesn't even know the woman, to my knowledge."

"Just another advantage in your favor," Autumn reminded him. "There are far more boxes checked for you than Carol."

Luke blew out a sigh as he stared into the wide window of the salon. Jenn passed by every now and then, broom in her hand. He didn't believe this woman had come into his and Paisley's lives at this exact moment only for Paisley to be ripped from his care.

"Just send me all the information and I'll be there," he assured her. "And thanks."

"We'll get through this."

Luke disconnected the call and all he could think was that if he had to tell Paisley she wouldn't be living with him, wouldn't see Jenn, wouldn't see Cookie or her friends at school…

The whole life she'd had here would cease to exist, and Luke refused to believe anyone would be that heartless to remove a child from a stable life.

But her arm was broken, the sale wasn't even under contract for the new land, the rental lease would be up soon. He could play this mind game all day with himself, but in the end, he knew he had no control here. And maybe that's what irked him the most. For so long he'd lived alone, doing his own thing, controlling his own outcome…or so he'd thought.

Losing his brother and raising Paisley were all serious indicators that he controlled absolutely nothing. God had the ultimate say and Luke just needed to be still and listen. But that was the hard part. He was human and flawed and just wanted answers.

Right now, though, he had to get Paisley and give Jenn the break she needed to go to her family's meeting—which was just another area that gave him worry. He had to trust that everything would work out just the way it was supposed to.

JENN TOOK A deep breath before knocking on the back door. She felt silly knocking, but she still wasn't sure if she should just walk right in.

"Why did you knock?"

She turned to see Rachel at the base of the back porch steps. She only had one braid over her shoulder and she clutched her well-worn brown hat in her hands.

Jenn hadn't spoken or even texted with Rachel since the other day at the salon. She wondered if her sister had given any more thought to the farm-to-table idea.

"I didn't know what to do, really," Jenn admitted.

"You know Mom won't want you knocking." Rachel mounted the steps and came to stand directly in front of Jenn. "And this is a family meeting. Family just walks on in."

Rachel held the door open and gestured Jenn inside.

"Let's see what Mom has in store for us," Rachel murmured. "I hope we don't have to hug for two minutes."

Jenn chewed the inside of her cheek to keep from laughing. This was the one and only time in her life, she wished for just that. She could use a good two-minute hug, especially now that she and Rachel seemed to have turned some type of corner.

But the moment she stepped inside and eyed all the contents on the long island and her mother's smiling face, she knew this was no regular meeting.

"Surprise!" Her mother beamed. "We're canning beets."

Jenn knew this familiar assembly line setup. They'd canned her entire life, though typically more in the summer and fall. Spring was a rarity, but apparently this was the only way her mother knew to get all of them in one place for a good amount of time.

This was about to get interesting.

"Your father will be in shortly," Sarah told them. "He's still working on those stalls in the barn."

Erin and Violet stepped in from the living room. Erin with her wide smile and Violet with her vibrant hair. Her sisters appearing just like she remembered here in the family home had Jenn's heart swelling. And if emotions were overwhelming to her, she couldn't imagine how her mother felt.

"What about the hugs?" Rachel asked. "Wouldn't that be quicker than canning?"

Their mother went to the hooks on the wall next to the pantry and plucked off a variety of aprons. She handed one to each girl, then slid her favorite yellow one over her head.

"I'm all for hugs," she told them. "But I also need to get these beets canned and we're done dancing around Jenn being back. There's too much that needs to be said and not over a text or a phone call."

"I couldn't agree more," Jenn chimed in.

"I'm sorry I didn't stop by after your last text," Violet chimed in. "I've been swamped at the clinic."

Erin winced. "And I've been so busy at the school. I'm sorry."

Jenn shrugged. "No worries, really."

Erin nodded, then gestured at the canning supplies. "Before we dive into this, can we address the rumors in town about Jenn and a certain vet dating?"

Jenn jerked as all eyes immediately turned to her.

"Who's saying that?" she countered, not denying the statement, though they hadn't gone on a date. Yet.

"I heard it, too, but didn't want to bring it up," Violet added.

"Girls, no gossip." Their mother had that stern tone, just like when they'd been kids. "We're not here to discuss Jenn and who she might or might not be dating."

Jenn hadn't even thought of the impact her relationship with Luke would have on the family.

"Would it bother anyone if I did date Luke?" she asked, glancing around the room.

Silence filled the space until her mother piped up. "It's been three years, honey. You don't need to ask us how we feel. It matters how you feel."

"But I want to know," she insisted, her eyes moving to her sisters. "There seems to be so much up in the air right now and tension between us. I guess we can start there."

"Mom is right." Erin nodded. "If this is something you're ready for, then I definitely support you. I'm thrilled, actually. No matter how things are between all of us, you still deserve to find love and happiness."

Of course Erin would be in her corner, and their mother. Jenn expected nothing less. But she turned her attention to Violet and Rachel as she held her breath. The girls stared back at her, but instead of seeing bitterness or resentment in their eyes, they had a new look. Something akin to compassion.

"It's not up to us," Vi told her. "And Luke is a great guy who took on a huge responsibility when his brother passed away. That act alone says a great deal about his character. Not to mention, he's got a stellar reputation with farmers. I've never heard one negative word about him."

Jenn would imagine finding anything negative with Luke would be quite difficult.

When Jenn met Rachel's gaze, her oldest sister simply shrugged. "You'll have no complaints from me. He's been nothing but amazing here on the farm. He's had to bring Paisley a few times."

"Oh, that dear girl of his loves our tire swing," her mother added. "I looked out my window one day and the image of her there took me back to when you all were little. It was nice having those memories come to life."

Jenn could instantly see Paisley in that swing hanging from the old oak in the front yard. Her hair probably lopsided, her purple boots on, not a care in the world. Innocence could be so precious, and Jenn loved that Paisley had felt at home here.

"Let's talk and work." Her mother moved to the island and pointed. "Come on, girls. These beets won't can themselves."

Jenn smiled as she went to the end of the island where there was a box of lids for the jars. The jars were all lined along the countertop, spread out on either side of the sink. Beets sat in large pots ready to be boiled and chopped.

"I'll cut," Violet volunteered. "Rach, you're too aggressive with the knife, so why don't you help Jenn?"

Rachel rolled her eyes as she pulled her apron over her head and flopped her braid out. "I had one mishap when we were teens."

"And we don't want another," Erin added.

"Oh, I love the sound of my girls bickering in the kitchen." Sarah clasped her hands together and smiled. "I won't even make you hug. I'm just happy you're all here. It's been too long and that's why I called this meeting. We need to stop dancing around the subject of Jenn being back and all this anger and pain that has filled us for the past three years."

Jenn knew that was her cue to pick up the conversation and either apologize again or begin her defense. Probably best to do both.

"That's why I'm back." Jenn pulled in a deep breath and flattened her palms against the island. "I stayed gone too long, I'm well aware of how that impacted you guys. Unfortunately, I can't turn back time or change my actions. All I can do is apologize and show you all that I'm here to stay if you'll welcome me back. I don't expect us to be perfect overnight, but I pray that we can find our way back to each other."

"I think the person you should be apologizing to is Dad," Rachel stated.

Jenn glanced at her sister and started to reply when the back screen door creaked, pulling all of their attention to the man in question.

"I don't need an apology." Her father remained in the doorway as he hooked his thumbs in his suspenders and kept his focus on Jenn. "All I've ever wanted was for you to come home so I could tell you how sorry I am. I never meant any harm to Cole. Working hard is all I know and he thrived on that same work ethic."

Jenn nodded. "You two were perfect together. I can see now that nothing that happened that day was your fault. That realization came from a great deal of therapy and prayer. I hurt so bad back then and I wanted someone to blame his death on. You never should have been the target."

Saying those words out loud for the first time to her father immediately lifted that heavy weight she'd dragged around with her for so long.

Her mother shifted and came up beside her. "Will, tell her everything. It's time."

Jenn blinked toward her mom and then back to her father. "Everything? What is she talking about?"

Her father sighed and shook his head. "It's about Cole's death."

Jenn's heart clenched as her mom took hold of her hand. What were they keeping from her that her parents both had those prominent lines between their brows. The worry on their faces did nothing to help her nerves.

"We learned after you'd gone that he had an underlying heart condition he'd been born with." Her dad took a step toward her. "There was nothing anyone could have done. There was no way of knowing he had this problem. Nothing he did on the farm that day caused his death. His heart attack was just a product of his illness. The coroner's report was mailed here with your name on it, so we kept it for a while. Then when we didn't hear from, we opened it and learned the truth."

Jenn tried to wrap her mind around what she'd just heard. None of this made sense. How did she not know about this? And why hadn't anyone told her before now? If she'd known, that could have changed everything. Why hadn't she tried to reach out sooner? Or why hadn't they?

She swallowed the emotions clogging her throat and tried to focus.

"We knew you were upset," her mother told her in that soft, caring tone. "We wanted to give you the space and time to heal. I always knew in my heart you'd come back, but it had to be on your terms and not because of anything else."

"I don't even know what to say," Jenn muttered.

"Maybe there's nothing left to say," her father told her. "Maybe the fact that you're home, that we're all ready to mend this broken family is all that we need."

The stinging in her eyes and throat had Jenn swallowing hard, but she knew that battling tears away wasn't the answer. She was human, surrounded by people who loved her, and they all just wanted to move forward in a more positive direction.

"I thought…" Jenn closed her eyes as a tear slid down her cheek and tried to speak again. "I thought I'd ruined everything with my harsh words that I didn't mean. I wanted to return so many times, but then I let fear take hold of me. The longer I stayed away, the easier it was to ignore the problem."

Rachel inched closer to her side and slid her fingers through Jenn's free hand.

"I'm still angry you ran away," she admitted. "Angry we were all hurting and none of us other than Mom reached out. But I see the pain you're in and I don't want that. I want us to all be one unit again. Now more than ever."

Jenn turned to look at her beautiful sister who also had tears in her eyes.

"That's all I've ever wanted. And I know there are problems with the farm, so I want to help."

Her mom squeezed her hand tighter before releasing. She moved back around the island and started busying herself with the beginning process of canning the beets.

"That's another thing we all need to discuss," Sarah told them as she pulled out just the right utensils and laid them on the counter. "The farm."

Jenn released her sister's hand and dabbed at her damp cheeks. Will Spencer came on into the kitchen to stand next to his wife. Jenn caught Rachel's worried look before turning to face her parents.

"Should we have a seat for this?" Erin asked.

"Not unless you want to," their father replied. "We've been thinking of ways to generate more income here on the property. Nothing has come to us and as you know we had to sell a few head of cattle to offset some unexpected expenses."

"We can't sell the house," Violet inserted. "Just make sure things don't come to that. We'll find a way to get more money."

"I've been working on something since I got back and wanted to wait until we were all together to discuss."

Jenn glanced down the island to the pot of beets. The last time she'd done anything with beets was with Marie for a farm-to-table dinner at their church.

She had all eyes on her now. Maybe this was grasping at straws and nothing would come from her plan, but perhaps this would spark something that might take hold and grow roots. She had to try and she had to show what she'd been working on.

"At the church I attended, we were raising money to build up the youth program," she started. "I did some canning and would give out samples at the women's retreats or as gifts for wedding showers. Anyway, when we were thinking of fundraisers, someone mentioned having dinners and then my friend Marie said I should use some of my jams or veggies because they were so good and fresh. Long story short, we ended up doing a farm-to-table gathering. The first one was such a huge hit, we did more. They kept growing and Marie just told me the other day that they have more planned and that my idea has brought in more money than they'd originally prayed for and now a few of the youth are planning a couple of mission trips."

Jenn pulled her cell from her pocket and tapped a few things to pull up her notes and some saved images.

"So what if we did something like that here?" She placed her cell on the island for her family to see as she scrolled through her pictures. "We could turn that front barn into something special and open it up to farm-to-table events. I've laid out here what seasons we could do different events, all depending on the crops we have at that time. It would take work from each of us, but I really think we can bring something fresh to Rosewood Valley."

Jenn glanced around, wondering what her family's reaction would be. Her mom leaned in a little closer and zoomed in on the image of a barn decorated with rustic yet elegant place settings, lighting that draped from the rafters, and potted plants that gave the space a cozy feel.

"We could do up to forty guests at a time, setting ticket prices based on the meal," Jenn noted. "Some could be a little fancier and some more laid back. That way we can reach a broad scope of people and their tastes."

"I like it." Rachel nodded with a smile. "We know fresh foods and we know farming. Our front barn would be perfect since we don't house any livestock there. It might take a little to invest into getting it ready, but overall, I think it's a solid plan. People could reserve it for large groups like for proms or weddings. Family reunions or we could even offer couples' nights out."

Jenn returned her sister's grin and a surge of optimism flooded her. So her sister really did liked the idea and not only that, but she was also now backing up the plan.

"That's not a bad idea and I really think it's something we could make work." Her mother straightened and turned her attention back to Jenn. "But that front barn won't be available."

"Why not?" Violet asked, taking a seat on one of the barstools. "You're not tearing it down, are you?"

Their mother's eyes shifted to their father and he let out a sigh.

"We're not tearing it down," he confirmed. "But we are selling it."

Jenn blinked, confused at that statement. "You're selling the barn? How is that even possible? It's on our property."

He nodded in agreement. "We're selling that piece of the land with it as well."

"What?" Erin exclaimed.

"No," Rachel said at the same time.

Jenn didn't take her attention off her dad. She wanted to know why he'd come to this conclusion and if it was too late to stop the sale. Hadn't she just presented a great plan? Did they need to do something so drastic like break up their land?

"Have you signed papers?" she asked.

"Not yet. We have a verbal agreement."

Jenn shrugged. "Then call it off. There are other ways to fix this without selling off pieces."

"Maybe so, but this is going to be a good move for all parties involved," her dad added. "Your mother and I have thought long and hard about this. We've been praying for a couple months now on this decision and feel this is the right path for us."

Jenn shouldn't get worked up or agitated without hearing all of the information, but she couldn't deny the sharp edge of annoyance that speared her.

"And who has talked you into selling?" she asked. "Because I don't think you would have thought of this on your own."

His eyes met hers. She didn't like that look. She'd seen it before when he didn't want to reveal a truth to her. She'd seen it the day he'd come to tell her that Cole was unconscious in the field.

"Dad?"

"Luke Bennett is purchasing the land."

Jenn felt her lungs constrict, and she struggled to take a breath. The dream of a second chance she'd been hoping for suddenly vanished.

CHAPTER FIFTEEN

LUKE CHECKED HIS cell once again. He'd asked Jenn earlier to see if she could keep Paisley while he was out of town for a couple days for the custody dispute and she'd happily agreed. But he hadn't heard anything from her since the family meeting. The fact that there hadn't been one single bit of communication from her end had a sickening pit forming in his gut.

He stepped onto the front porch with a mason jar of sweet tea in one hand and his phone in the other. Paisley had gone to her room to color a picture for Jenn to hang on her refrigerator in her apartment. Paisley had said Jenn needed more color in that place, and Luke loved that his niece was so fond of someone this special.

But had he messed things up by going with her father's wishes? His loyalties had been torn and no matter what he'd done, he would have betrayed someone he cared about.

Luke padded barefoot over to the porch swing as a new set of worries rolled around in his mind. If she had indeed found out, was she talking her parents out of the deal? And not just her, but what did the other sisters think? Will and Sarah valued family just as much as he did so their opinions would certainly hold weight. What if the girls convinced their parents that the sale was a mistake? Then where would he be?

He'd be at the mercy of a judge and have to admit that Paisley had a broken arm and soon they wouldn't have a house.

Luke set the tea on the porch railing and raked a hand over the back of his neck. Until he heard from Jenn, he wouldn't be able to relax. He'd told Paisley she'd be staying with Jenn for a couple days and his niece had squealed with excitement. But if Jenn changed her mind because of the family meeting, he'd have to ask Mary. He didn't have many options.

Tires crunching over gravel yanked his attention from his troublesome thoughts. Seeing Jenn's car pull up the long drive had Luke coming to his feet. She'd never been here before, but the town was small and clearly she had no trouble getting his address.

He took a sip of his tea before setting the jar back on the rail, but he remained on the porch as she came to a stop just behind his truck.

Her eyes met his through the windshield and he saw the truth all over her face.

She knew.

There was no way around this confrontation and he'd known this whole time the talk was inevitable. Had known at some point they'd have to face this reality. He just wished there had been a better way…but that hadn't been his call.

Jenn broke eye contact as she exited her car. With slow, careful steps, she came around and made her way up the stone path toward the porch. Luke leaned against the white post and crossed his arms over his chest. He tried to force a casualness he certainly did not feel.

Those vibrant green eyes met his as she remained at the bottom of the steps and rested her hand on the rail.

"Did you use me?"

Her accusation caught him off guard. "What?"

"For the land," she tossed back. "Did you use me to get closer to my father? Maybe to see what I knew about how dire things were? Or perhaps to try to get me in your corner?"

Luke willed himself to have patience here. She was hurting and had just discovered this business deal. He'd had months to process the possibility and very little time to come to terms with the fact the deal would go through…unless Will and Sarah changed their minds after speaking with their girls.

"I had already talked to your father well before you came to town," he defended. "I've never used anyone for anything, let alone a woman I've come to care about."

"You lied to me."

Luke shook his head. "I never lied. I made a promise to your father that I wouldn't say a word until he and your mother decided what to do."

"You listened to me talk about my family problems," Jenn went on, the hurt lacing her voice couldn't be ignored. "You knew who I was the moment we met, but I had no idea there was already some plan in place to steal part of my family's property."

Luke straightened. "I've never once tried to steal anything. I respect your parents and I saw there was a need and I was in a bind myself. I thought this was the most logical solution."

Jenn crossed her arms and widened her stance

as her chin tipped up and she leveled him with her stare.

"I don't like being deceived," she volleyed back. "I opened my heart to you and all this time you were trying to take a piece of my family's livelihood. You knew I came back to help them and still kept this to yourself. I know what my dad told you, but I thought we had something special. I thought we trusted each other and could lean on each other."

"We do and we can," he countered. "I've opened up more to you than anyone. Nothing has changed between us. Or nothing has to change. Don't let this ruin what we've built."

All could not be lost, not when he was so close to having the most amazing woman in his life. She'd admitted she had feelings for him. She couldn't just turn that switch off...could she?

She eyed him fiercely. "But what we built wasn't on a truthful foundation."

The front door opened and closed, and Luke tensed as Paisley came out to stand beside him.

"Jenn. I didn't know you were coming." Her little voice had so much happiness and excitement. "I just finished something for you."

Luke glanced down to see Paisley holding up

a picture she'd colored of a house. In front of it stood a dog and three people. His heart ached at the sight and he didn't have to guess who those people were. Paisley wanted a family like she'd had. She wanted that happiness and stability... and he thought he'd found all of that for her... and himself.

"You drew that all by yourself?" Jenn asked, starting up the steps. "That is so beautiful, Paisley. You are a true artist."

"I need to work on my dogs," Paisley stated. "I don't think this looks like Cookie."

Jenn glanced to the paper and nodded. "I think it's exactly like Cookie. I can't wait to put this in my apartment. I do need more artwork if you'd like to make anything else."

"Really? Maybe when I come stay with you, I can bring all my stuff and you can tell me where you want new things."

Jenn's smile faltered for the briefest of moments, but enough that Luke caught it. Her eyes darted to his, then back to Paisley's. "I would love that. Maybe you can show me how to draw a house like this. I was never good at art."

"This is going to be the best sleepover ever," Paisley exclaimed. "Would it be okay if we made a blanket fort and watched a movie, too? Me and Mommy always did that."

Luke's heart clenched. Just another piece she'd been missing from her life that he hadn't known. He'd give absolutely anything to erase that pain she held inside. Unfortunately, that wasn't how life worked and all he could do was his absolute best and pray that was enough.

"Of course we can," Jenn replied. "My sisters and I used to do that all the time. I'm an expert builder. We're going to have so much fun."

That compassionate, loving nature of Jenn's had Luke swallowing a lump of guilt. Even though he'd hurt her, she still found it in her heart to love on his niece like nothing had happened. He honestly didn't expect her to just deny Paisley or turn her away, but Jenn continued to prove over and over just how special she was. He couldn't lose her and he had every intention of fighting for everything he wanted.

Jenn, Paisley, the land. He wanted it all and he didn't think that selfish to acknowledge. He had to get a solid foundation to secure his future. There wasn't a doubt in his mind that he was on the right track. He just needed to hold tight to his faith that everything would work out the way it was meant to.

"Honey, can you go inside for a minute so Jenn and I can talk?" Luke said.

Paisley glanced to him, then to Jenn, then back to him. "Is something wrong?"

"Not at all." There he went lying again, but he had to shield his niece. "Just boring adult conversation."

"Okay, then. See you in a couple days, Jenn." She skipped back inside, not a care in the world.

The moment the door closed behind her, Luke shoved his hands in his pockets and glanced to Jenn, who now stood just one step below him. Close enough to touch. And he wanted nothing more than to reach out and comfort her, but considering he was the one who'd caused her pain, he kept to himself.

"There's nothing I can do to change what happened," he started. "I never once intended to hurt you or deceive you. I'm sure that's what this looks like from your angle, but you know me, Jenn. You know that's not my character."

Jenn held his gaze for a moment before glancing away toward the setting sun. He studied her profile, not at all surprised how her natural beauty still captivated him. This woman had a strong personality, a loving heart, and those qualities made her passionate about those she cared for. Those were also the same qualities that had him falling for her in such a short time. He valued everything she brought into his life and hadn't even realized what he'd been missing until those traits were thrust in his face.

"I don't know what to believe anymore," she murmured. "I know I need time and I'm not sure about us."

She turned back to face him with unshed tears in her eyes.

"I think you need to handle this custody issue out of town and give me some space," she went on. "I need to focus on my family and what this new chapter will look like for us now that we're moving forward."

"Are you shutting me out?" he asked.

"I'm letting you go take care of you, and I need to take care of me," she amended. "There's no point in going over this again when I can't trust you right now."

She was letting him go. Fine. He could give her space, but he wasn't going anywhere. They were made for each other.

"I'm sorry, Jenn. I can't tell you how much, but I'll earn your trust back," he vowed. "I'm not giving up on us. You deserve someone who puts you first, who values you, and who won't leave you to do this life on your own."

A lone tear slid down her porcelain cheek and Luke didn't even try to resist anymore. He swiped the moisture with the pad of his thumb, then dropped his hand to his side.

"Thank you for keeping Paisley while I'm gone. No matter what is going on between us, she loves you."

And so do I.

The revelation hit him hard, but he shouldn't be surprised. Those feelings had been below the surface, but he hadn't faced them. He'd been too afraid to face them. But having Jenn stand before him in tears over his actions put everything into perspective.

"I'd do anything for that girl," Jenn whispered.

Then she turned and descended the steps. She stopped at the bottom and tossed a glance over her shoulder. "Make sure to text me her school schedule and anything else I need to know while you're away. I'll be praying for you."

And then she was gone, leaving him on the porch with his jumbled up feelings and his remorse. Yes, she was upset with him but still put his situation in her prayers.

Jenn Spencer was definitely a woman he wanted—no, *needed*—to have in his life. Just as soon as this custody hearing was over, he'd set out to prove he could be the man she needed.

JENN PULLED ON the reins to bring Starlight to a stop. Getting back on the old mare she'd ridden years ago felt like another piece falling right back into place.

And now, as she glanced up at the barn where she and Cole had lived during their short marriage, she waited on all the feelings to rush over her. Surprisingly, a sense of peace overcame her and she smiled up at the sunshine.

The warm sun seemed to beam right down on her. She'd taken the morning off, needing to gather her thoughts. She hadn't been on a horse in years and knew now was the time. She'd always been able to get a clearer head with fresh air and a ride through the property.

She'd needed to come here. To see the place she and Cole had made into a home. They'd only been married a few months before tragedy struck. They hadn't built their dream house on the land and they'd barely just started their lives together.

The level of peace that settled so deep within

her had to have come from God. Oh, sure therapy and a break from this place had all helped her heal emotionally, but that deeper level of healing only came from the One above. And nothing would erase that darkness in her life. No amount of prayer or counseling could take away what she'd experienced, but she could learn and grow. She *had* learned and grown, or she wouldn't be here. Coming back to Rosewood Valley at this precise time was exactly where she needed to be.

She just wished she could get a better bead on all of her emotions surrounding the sale and Luke's part in everything. Try as he might to explain his side of things, Jenn couldn't help but feel betrayed. Had he used her to get closer to the family? Yes, she fully believed he'd approached her parents before she came back into town, but hadn't she just made a convenient landing into his life? Could she trust her feelings right now? Between being back and facing her past, and feeling the first spark of a connection with a man for the first time since Cole, maybe she was in a vulnerable position and needed to slow down.

She'd always led with her heart, so she didn't really know another way.

"Morning."

Jenn startled as she glanced to the side of the barn where her sister stood. Rachel adjusted her hat against the morning sun, but remained by the entrance to the grain barn.

"Hey," Jenn greeted. "I just needed to ride and clear my head."

"About Luke?"

Jenn nodded. "And everything going on with us as a family."

"We're on the right track." Rachel slid her hands into the pockets of her jeans as she started toward Jenn. "Being trapped canning beets for hours will do that."

Jenn laughed and nodded in agreement. "I hate beets."

"None of us likes them." Rachel chuckled as she reached to stroke Starlight's nose. "But they'll be good to go for the farmers market next month and if we're going to move ahead with the farm-to-table idea you had, we'll use them. That was brilliant thinking, by the way."

That three-year-old wound on Jenn's heart started to mend. Simple words, well-meaning words, could provide a balm like nothing else.

"Thanks for your support," Jenn told her sister. "I really think this can be as big or as small as we want to make it. We can keep the events to a minimum or really grow it to be something weekly."

"Endless possibilities."

Starlight shifted and Jenn tightened her grip on the reins. "Just like our family now that I'm back… I hope."

"I'm glad you're back," Rachel told her, moving closer to her side and taking her hat off to meet her gaze. "I was angry for so long and felt you took the easy way out by running away, but I can see now that you handled the pain the only way you knew how. I don't want to be angry anymore."

Jenn gripped the horn of her saddle and swung a leg off to dismount. With a tight hand on the straps, she reached for her sister with the other. Rachel opened her arms and fully embraced her. The strength and love emanating from her filled Jenn with another layer of hope and joy.

"I love you," Rachel murmured before she eased back.

"Love you, too, sis."

Rachel adjusted her hat and took a step away. "I'm not sure what's going on with you and Luke, but I can tell you that from everything I know of him, he's a great guy. It's not his fault that our farm is in trouble and he happened to have a logical solution to fit his life and ours."

"No, it's not his fault," Jenn agreed. "But he kept that from me even when I poured my heart out to him, worried over how to help and even if you all would let me back in."

"I understand why you're confused and frustrated," Rachel told her. "And we both are well aware you're always fast to make decisions with your big heart and not your head sometimes."

"I feel like that's not a compliment."

Rachel smiled. "It's you, and we love you regardless. All I'm saying is that if you stop and think, especially from Luke's point of view, you might have a different outlook."

"So you're in his corner?" Jenn joked.

"I'm in the corner that brings you happiness and peace, and I think he could be good for you."

"I'm scared."

Admitting that out loud had to be a new level of recovery. She should be proud of herself, and she was, but she also still had a legitimate fear of giving her heart away again.

"It's okay to be scared," Rachel said. "It's when you let that fear hold you back and you look for reasons to run away from the fear that gets you in trouble. What if you ran toward the fear this time instead of away from it?"

Jenn pulled in a deep breath and glanced down to her old sneakers. So many worries and doubts had kept her from living her life these past few years. She had to start living and honoring her late husband instead of letting the pain and shame take over.

She couldn't be angry with Luke for trying to provide for his family, but that didn't soothe the bruise he'd left on her heart by omitting his intentions. Even with that harsh reality, she did understand he was in a tough spot. Luke didn't have a malicious bone in his body and Rachel might be onto something. If Jenn ran toward her fear, clinging to her faith with both hands, maybe something spectacular would happen. If she just let go and let God…

"Cole would want you to move on and be happy," Rachel added.

Jenn smiled as she met her sister's beautiful eyes once again. "He would."

"And I think Luke makes you happy."

Jenn nodded in agreement as a new outlook spread out before her. She didn't have to find a problem here and she had to give this second chance a second chance.

With a new vision for her future, but still one more thing left to do, Jenn mounted Starlight once again.

"Thanks for the chat." She glanced down to her sister and pulled back on the reins to get Starlight moving. "I need to head down to the main barn to see Dad."

"Maybe you can come to church with us on Sunday?" Rachel asked. "For Mother's Day?"

Jenn nodded. "I'll be there."

As she rode away, an overwhelming peace seemed to wrap its loving arms around her. Coping with all her unsettling emotions might be difficult, but she knew she had a whole host of people who loved her and cared for her, and she wouldn't have to take those next steps alone.

CHAPTER SIXTEEN

JENN FINISHED PUTTING the saddle and blanket back in the tack room, then wiped her hands on her jeans. When she turned, her father was standing in the doorway, leaning against the frame.

"Starlight has missed you."

Jenn nodded. "I missed her, too."

"Where'd you ride?"

"All around." Jenn lifted a hip on one of the tack boxes and relaxed. "Had to see where Cole and I lived. I hadn't been back there for so long. Had a nice talk with Rachel."

"Good." Will Spencer stepped into the room and took off his hat then hung it by the door. "You look good being back here, Jenn. I used to dream of you here. The dreams were so real that I'd wake and think I'd walk down and find you saddling up your horse."

Jenn eased farther onto the tack box, crossing her legs like she used to as a kid while her father talked. She missed these talks. Missed his wisdom and guidance. Missed just the sound of his voice.

But this talk would be the most important stepping stone to their fresh start. With no one around, they could get back to their basics.

"Your mother kept asking me to reach out to you," he went on, looping those thumbs in his suspenders as he rocked back in his worn boots. "I told her you had to mend in your own way and all we could do was pray you'd return. I knew you would, deep in my heart, I knew it. But I was starting to worry."

"I never meant to hurt anyone," she told him. "I know my actions proved otherwise, but I hope you can see that I do love you guys and I know I was wrong to just go like that."

"You weren't wrong to go," he countered. "Nobody can say what's right or wrong when it comes to grief. I certainly don't like how you shut us all out, and for so long, but you're back and I know you want to be here. You couldn't have come before."

"Shame kept me gone longer than necessary," she admitted, toying with the ties on her sneak-ers. "I would think about reaching out and then

I'd let so much time pass, I didn't know if I'd done too much damage."

"There's no such thing between a parent and a child." He took another step forward and took her hands in his rough, strong ones. "You could've come back in ten years, and I might still be bitter about you being gone, but I would've come around and welcomed you back just like I did this time. I had to push aside my pride and remember you're one of mine and no matter what happens, there's nothing that can break that bond."

She squeezed his hands, loving that familiar warm feel of the man who'd raised her. Those hands had done so much in over sixty years. They'd covered scrapes with bandages, they'd assisted in learning to ride bikes, they'd steered cattle from one pasture to the next, and every bit of those actions were done in love. While she hated that she'd been gone so long, she was here now and forever and that's what mattered.

"You know I love you and I really am sorry for blaming you." Jenn had said it before, but she couldn't stress enough her remorse. "I want you to know that I don't blame you. I never did, I just wanted to be angry with someone."

"I know, honey. And honestly, I blamed myself for a long time until we uncovered the truth."

Jenn wrapped her arms around her father, beyond thankful he'd welcomed her back home. When his arms banded around her in that bear hug she'd always sank into, she smiled against his shoulder.

"I have something for you." Her dad eased back, placing his hands on her shoulders. "Or I should say, I saved something for you."

Jenn wouldn't have a clue what he'd saved, but she waited and watched while he moved toward the storage cabinet in the corner. He opened the double doors and reached on the top shelf and pulled down boots.

No. Not just any boots. *Her* boots. The ones she'd left behind in this very room. She'd not put on a pair of cowgirl boots since leaving Rosewood Valley and never thought she would again. But this familiar pair in her father's hands brought tears to her eyes.

"I told you that I knew you'd be back." He set the boots on the tack box next to her. "No cowgirl can ride in sneakers."

He gestured toward her old shoes and laughed.

Jenn unfolded her legs and toed off her shoes, immediately reaching for her well-worn brown boots. Sliding back into them felt like just another hug from a familiar friend. She hopped off the box and stared down at her feet, loving how this looked exactly right.

"Much better," she agreed, glancing up to her father. "I can't believe you held on to these."

"What else would I do with them? You were going to need a pair when you returned and these are already broken in."

Jenn smiled as she stepped forward and wrapped her arms around his thick frame once again. She had years' worth of hugs to make up for.

Will Spencer enveloped her in his strong embrace. "We're going to be alright, Jenn. Nothing time and love can't fix."

She blinked away the tears and held on just a moment longer before she eased back.

"But we need to talk about this sale," he added. "I know you're not happy with it. None of you girls are thrilled. But your mother and I made the best decision for the family and honestly, for Luke and Paisley."

The logical side of her could see that point, but the emotional side still hurt over the secrets both men had kept from her.

"Luke is a great guy," her father went on. "I wouldn't have agreed to this otherwise. He values family just as much as we do and all he's doing is trying to get a firm foundation in place for his new life."

"I just wished he would've told me all those times I opened up to him," Jenn explained. She took a step away, leaned against the box once again and held her father's worried stare. "We were building something more than a friendship, but it's so new, I'm worried if I can truly trust my emotions. Rachel told me to run toward the fear instead of away from it."

"She's always been wise with her words."

"But still…"

"You're scared." Her father grunted. "If you let fear run your life and make all your decisions, you'll be miserable. I think it's time for you to be happy again, don't you?"

Her father's immediate response, so firm and so confident, had Jenn jerking back just a bit.

"Yeah, I do," she readily admitted.

There went those thumbs in the suspenders again as he sighed. "I know you, and I know that someone as kindhearted as Luke would scare you because you're afraid to trust your emotions. He's come into your life at a time when you need it most and you don't want to get hurt again."

Again.

The word hovered in the air between them. She knew he spoke the truth, but could she be strong enough to run toward this second chance without abandon?

"You can do what you want as far as your heart is concerned," her father continued. "But don't be upset with him because I asked him to keep the sale to himself. You wouldn't want to be with a man who couldn't keep his word, would you?"

That logical question had her mind racing. No, she wanted a man who kept his word, who could be trusted and was honorable. Luke possessed all of those qualities and more…which was why she knew she'd be welcoming him back into her life. She truly prayed this whole ordeal hadn't ruined something that could be beautiful.

It was time to fully come back, to embrace her family and her faith, and let the Lord guide her. She had to listen to Him.

"I've seen that look on your face," her father murmured. "You're working on a plan."

Jenn smiled. "Maybe I am. Maybe my eyes are opening to new possibilities for the first time in a long time."

"You deserve all the happiness, sweetheart. And Cole would want you to live your life."

Jenn nodded. "He would, I know."

"So you'll talk to Luke?"

Jenn nodded once again. But she was still anxious about what he'd be facing when he went to the custody hearing. She wished she could be there for him and offer all her support. Knowing he faced his worries and this unknown alone broke her heart. What would happen to him if Paisley was taken away? How would he recover from that? He'd upended his entire life to come here and had made so many plans to push into their new life together.

She leaned in for one last, tight hug before exiting the barn. She pulled her cell from her pocket and stared at the string of text messages. Her thumbs hovered over the keys and she ultimately knew she needed to reach out. She had to take this step and maybe this would help alleviate his stress even if just a little.

Praying for your hearing. Once you're home, we should talk.

She waited a moment, then added one more line.

You're forgiven and I understand your actions.

With a deep breath, she crossed the drive to her vehicle. Jenn could only pray for the future with her and Luke because from here on out, she was going to put her worries on God and focus on the happiness she could finally see and embrace.

LUKE'S NERVES ROLLED through his stomach. There was only one outcome where his world would be right. He adjusted his tie and came to his feet. He couldn't sit on that hard bench in the sterile hallway anymore. The judge was running late and each minute that ticked by only added to Luke's anxiety.

The text from Jenn gave him hope that once he got back, they were going to be on the right path. She'd reached out with her prayers and words of forgiveness and encouragement. As much as he wanted to dwell in that happy moment, he had to focus on today and his Sweet P.

"Shouldn't be too much longer," Autumn assured him just as he turned to pace. "Try to relax."

Luke shoved his hands into the pockets of his dress pants and tried to focus on her soothing tone and not the woman sitting just down the hall who was ready to take Paisley from him.

He hadn't even looked at Carol or her attorney since they'd arrived. Her husband must be the other guy, but Luke couldn't concentrate on that right now. He had nothing to say to them and was saving all his energy for the judge. He tapped the file of documents against his thigh, stared at the door to the judge's chamber and willed it to open.

"Excuse me."

Luke turned, shocked as Carol stood before him. She stared back at him with wide dark eyes. Her inky black hair framed her petite face.

"Would it be alright if we spoke alone before we go in?" she asked.

Luke glanced to his attorney, who had one brow lifted and eyes on Carol.

"I'm not sure that's best," Autumn stated.

Carol offered a smile that seemed genuine, but Luke didn't know this woman and could only trust his instincts.

"I promise, I'm not doing anything malicious," Carol assured them. "And he doesn't have to say anything. I just want to say something to him in private."

Autumn ultimately glanced to Luke and nodded. "It's your call."

"It's fine." Luke gestured for Carol to follow him toward the other end of the hallway.

Their shoes clicked on the marble floors of the courthouse, echoing throughout. He made his way to the narrow window and eased one hand in his pocket, while clutching his folder in the other.

"I'm sure this is difficult for you," Carol began immediately. "Talia and I weren't just cousins—we were best friends growing up. We lost touch somewhat when I left for the military. Long story short, when I returned home from my final deployment, I heard of her passing. I was devastated, as I'm sure you are. I'm sorry for your loss as well."

"Thank you."

Carol tucked her dark curls behind her ears and continued speaking. "Other than my husband, I've never been close to anyone like I was with Talia. So I wanted to know that I could still be part of her family, and she mine." Her eyes glistened for a moment. "Paisley is all I have left of my best friend."

Her voice caught on those final two words and Luke's heart ached for her. They were both mourning.

"And all I have of my brother," Luke retorted, needing her to also understand his point of view.

Carol offered that gentle smile again. "I know. I didn't think of the will or Paisley when I filed for custody. To be honest, my grief made me a little selfish."

Luke listened, taking in her point of view. He wasn't a heartless person and he understood her position, he just wished she could understand his.

"I know the will stated that Paisley should be with you," she went on. "Going against what Scott and Talia wanted isn't my intent. I want Paisley to be happy because at the end of the day, she's the only one that matters."

"I agree."

A new spark of joy surrounded him. He didn't want to jump to any conclusions, but he thought Carol might be pulling back from this fight.

"I don't want to fight with anyone," she told him. "I'm hoping you and I can maybe come to some agreement without getting the courts involved."

Frustration spiked in him. "And why didn't you call me before I traveled here if that's what you thought?" He shook his head and sighed.

"I apologize. I didn't mean for that to come out harsh. It's a stressful time for all of us."

"It is," she agreed. "I'm sure I didn't help your grieving process, and I could have called you. But I wanted to meet you in person and talk to you face-to-face."

"Understandable." He leaned against the windowsill and figured he could take a little bit of the control now. "So what are you thinking now?"

"I just want to be able to see her." Carol's eyes welled up again with unshed tears and she forced a smile. "I know she doesn't know me, but if I could meet her and maybe visit sometimes. I don't think that's too much to ask."

Visits? In lieu of having Paisley taken from him and moved to another state? No, this certainly wasn't too much to ask.

"Anyone who loves Paisley and is an extension of either of her parents would be beneficial to her upbringing," he replied. "I'm sure she'd love another female in her life, and visits would be a good thing."

"I would really love that. My husband told me that I should talk to you first before going in and that I should think of Paisley and that uprooting her from the life she's known probably wasn't the best, considering all she's been through."

"I couldn't agree with him more."

Carol dabbed at her damp eyes and turned toward the other end of the hallway. She waved her husband over and the tall, broad man joined them.

"Hi. I'm Dylan." Carol's husband extended his hand to Luke. "Nice to meet you."

"Luke." He shook the man's hand and nodded a greeting. "I think we've established a reasonable solution for now."

Carol slid her arm through her husband's and glanced up at Dylan. "I know that Paisley is best in the home she knows and with a school and friends she's familiar with. I've asked for visits, maybe we can even start with a phone call or video chat or something first."

"It's a good plan," Dylan agreed.

"Does she know anything about this?" Carol asked Luke.

He shook his head. "No. I wanted to see what happened today before I said anything to her."

"I'll give you my number and—"

The door opened down the hall, stopping Carol. An elderly lady stepped out and glanced to the few of them out here waiting.

"The judge is ready for you all."

Luke met Carol's eyes and she smiled before turning her attention back to the woman.

"I think we won't be coming in today."

Finally, this worry over losing Paisley was over. Now he could get back to Rosewood Valley and pick up that conversation Jenn wanted to have. For the first time in months, he didn't have the heavy burden of regret or guilt weighing on him. He could move on, with the two most important ladies in his life.

CHAPTER SEVENTEEN

"DID TOOT SAY why he'd be late?"

Jenn settled beneath the blanket fort—which was rather impressive, if she did say so herself—and plopped the big bowl of extra butter popcorn between them. Paisley had already stayed one night and Luke had texted and asked if Paisley could stay for the evening as he'd be later than he'd first thought. Maybe his flight was delayed or something, but she couldn't believe he'd said nothing about the custody arrangement. She wanted to ask, but the way they'd left things before he'd gone out of town didn't really give her that luxury.

"I'm not sure, honey."

Jenn grabbed the remote and pointed it toward the television. The fort was high and wide and open just on the side facing the TV. Paisley had been so impressed with how they'd set this up yesterday, Jenn had just left it. Good thing since Paisley had rode the bus here right after school and would be staying.

"Are you ready for another movie night?" Jenn asked, scrolling through the selection.

"And there's no school tomorrow," Paisley added. "I bet I can stay up late."

Jenn clicked on one of her favorites from her own childhood and eased back against the mound of pillows.

"I'm not making that call," Jenn told her. "I'm sure Luke will be back before bedtime and then he can say yes or no."

She hoped. Because if it was up to her, she'd pull an all-nighter, old-school slumber party and watch all the movies Paisley wanted. Of course the little one would likely fall asleep, but it would let her feel like a big kid. But Jenn wasn't her mother or even her guardian, so she wasn't going to decide.

"I really like staying here." Paisley grabbed a small handful of popcorn. "I don't know what we're going to do when we have to leave my house."

Jenn's ears perked up and she glanced to Paisley. "What do you mean?"

She had no clue what the little girl did or didn't know about the housing situation or the move to the farm or even the interim between leaving the rental and building on her family's property.

"I know that where we live now won't be ours forever," Paisley explained around a mouthful of popcorn. "I heard Toot and the landlord talking about how the end of the month is some date, but the guy told Toot he understood if we need a little longer."

Well, that was at least something. Jenn wasn't quite sure of his plan or vision. She'd been so upset, she hadn't allowed that part of his life to enter into hers. But now she wanted to know. She wanted to see the mental image he'd created and she wondered if there was room for one more.

As the movie played on, the chime from the back door echoed up the steps and into the loft apartment. Jenn eased her head from the blanket as footsteps grew louder up the staircase. The door swung open and Luke stood there filling the space. His eyes landed on hers and her heart kicked up. She wasn't sure what she was more nervous about, the talk she intended to have with him or how the custody hearing went.

No, that wasn't true. She was a nervous wreck about knowing the future for Paisley.

She couldn't imagine not having this darling girl in her life. She couldn't imagine either one of them not in her world.

"Who's hiding in that big fort?" Luke called out.

Jenn smiled as Paisley snickered. "No boys allowed."

He quirked a brow at Jenn and she merely shrugged. "It's true. We made a pact."

"Then I guess there's no surprises for anyone."

The blankets were immediately demolished as Paisley used her purple cast to thrust them aside and then ran toward Luke. His low laugh filled the space as Paisley grabbed hold of his arm with her uninjured one and started pulling.

"You're allowed," she said, "just give us the surprises."

This commotion pulled Cookie from her slumber on the ottoman, which they'd shoved over to the other side of the loft. The pup jumped down and did a series of stretches before making her way over to Luke.

He scratched the top of her head and leaned down to whisper something to Paisley. The secret seemed to last a while and Jenn had no clue what on earth he could be saying. But he finally straightened and smiled down at his niece at the same time she squealed and jumped up and down.

"What's your surprise?" Jenn asked as she came to her feet and stepped over the chaos.

Paisley turned to face her and shoved her staticky hair away from her face. "It's a surprise for you! Toot just needs my help."

Jenn glanced to Luke who had a smile on his face. "I had a great trip that turned out even better than I thought."

A wave of relief swept over her. "I can't wait to hear all about it. I'd actually like to talk to you privately if that's possible."

Luke's smile faltered, his brows drew in. "Am I going to like what you have to say?"

Jenn took a step forward and clasped her hands in front of her. She hadn't expected to get into this right here and now, but he seemed happy and she didn't like how they'd left things.

"I think you will," she told him.

"Then I think Paisley should stay, if you don't mind."

Jenn opened her mouth, but before she could say anything, Luke held up a hand.

"I think our talks might go together, but I'd really like to go first."

Because Jenn still had that sliver of fear from moving forward with her strong emotions for him, she gestured for him to go ahead.

"Absolutely."

He reached into his pocket and pulled something out, but kept it clutched in his hand.

Jenn eyed his fist, then brought her attention back to his. Was he about to propose? Was she ready for that big step? She'd already envisioned Luke and Paisley in her life and her future, but what exactly would that look like?

"I know there was a lot that went on without your knowledge," Luke started. "I hope you know that I can wait for you and whatever you need for me to do to show you that I'm here for the long haul. The more I think about our situations, which led us to this point, the more I think that it's been your default to run from what is hurting you. To shut it out. And I'm not saying you're wrong, but I am saying I don't want you to run anymore. If something is hurting you, I want to shoulder it. If your heart aches, I want to heal it. I want a chance to show you that I have fallen in love with you and that I want more. I want everything."

Jenn's breath caught in her throat. She

wasn't sure what to say, but she couldn't just remain silent.

"You're right," she murmured. "Our talks do go together."

His smile widened as he eased around Cookie to take a step toward Jenn. "Is that so?"

"I know you're an honorable man, one that's true to his word. I value that about you and I can see now that you were in a tough position. I don't think for one second that you used me and I'm sorry for saying that."

Luke shrugged. "People say things in the moment when their emotions get the best of them."

"You still deserve an apology. And you were right about another thing," she added. "I have been eager to run away when I'm hurting. I try to get far away, but that's not the answer. While you on the other hand, you run toward the heartache because you're ready to fix everything. I need to be more like that. I need to be more like you because you can bring out the best of me."

She held her breath while she waited for him to say something, but he turned his back to her and squatted down to Paisley. Then he passed her whatever had been in his hand, and Paisley took Cookie over to the corner. Jenn tried to see what was going on, but these two were being quite sneaky.

"What are you guys up to?" she asked.

Luke turned back to face her and had that wide, handsome smile she'd come to love.

Yes, she loved him. She couldn't deny her feelings another minute and she wanted him to know, but she had to see what on earth these two were planning.

"I know how important your family's land is to you," Luke started. "And I want you to know it's important to me, too. I see my future there with Paisley and my practice."

He took a step forward, reaching for her hands. Jenn's heart beat faster as she stared into those mesmerizing eyes. She could get lost in the gaze of this man who so clearly loved her, too.

"And I see a future there with you," he added.

Those strong hands holding on to her coupled with his bold statement sent a jolt of courage and hope through her. Like a switch had been turned on and for the first time in years, she had that light shining once again. Jenn knew Luke was the right one to make her live again, because he'd come into her life in a way that she hadn't expected and hadn't been looking for and he'd made her whole again.

"I love you." She blurted the words out with no lead-up or finesse, then laughed. "I guess I should have said something beautiful like you just did, but that's all I can think when you're holding me and looking at me."

"That's going to work out really well since I love you, too." He leaned in and pressed his lips to hers for the briefest of moments, so sweet and tender, then eased back. "Paisley has something to show you."

Jenn glanced at the little girl who'd come up beside them with Cookie. The dog wiggled her tail and panted with her mouth open, as if smiling herself.

"You know I kept telling you that Cookie needed a new collar?" Luke asked. "Paisley just put one on if you'd like to see it."

Paisley bounced on her tiptoes and squealed as Jenn bent down to check out the new accessory.

"Read it out loud," Paisley exclaimed.

Jenn moved the curly fur out of the way and gripped the gold circle charm.

"Will you marry us?"

Jenn straightened immediately and jerked her

attention to Luke. If possible, his smile had gotten wider and Paisley reached up to take his hand. Now Jenn had the duo staring at her, waiting on an answer.

"I know this is crazy," he started. "But when something is right, it's just right. And I'm not saying we have to marry next week. I'll wait for whenever you're ready."

"You're going to say yes, right, Jenn?" Paisley asked, her eyes wide and full of hope.

A swell of tears filled Jenn's eyes as she laughed. "Am I going to say yes? Of course I am. Who wouldn't want to spend a lifetime with the most perfect people?"

"She said yes, Toot! That means I'm going to have a mom and dad again and a dog. That's all I've ever wanted."

Paisley launched herself at Jenn, who burst into tears. "I'm so happy," she sniffed, holding the girl. "I don't know why I'm crying like a baby."

Jenn eased Paisley down and pushed hair from the child's face. "You're definitely not a baby and sometimes we have so much happiness inside, we can't hold it all in and it leaks out."

"I just really love you," Paisley added.

"Aw, sweet girl. I love you."

"Can we have more slumber parties and forts when you and Toot get married?"

Jenn tapped the tip of Paisley's nose. "Absolutely, but are we letting boys in?"

Paisley pursed her lips and glanced up to Luke.

He merely shrugged. "Don't let me infringe on girl time."

"Maybe sometimes," Paisley replied.

Jenn came back to her feet with her arm around Paisley. She wanted to hold this moment forever. She wanted to lock away these overwhelming precious emotions and always remember how it felt to fall in love for a second time. Another chance at the life she'd always dreamed of with a man who had a heart of gold.

"I know why I'm back at this moment," she told Luke. "To find you."

"I think we all found each other," he amended, then glanced down to Cookie. "I guess this means you're claiming the dog as yours, right?"

Jenn laughed and reached for him so they all embraced in a long overdue group hug. "I'm claiming all of you."

EPILOGUE

"ARE YOU READY for this?"

Jenn stared up at the white church nestled against the hillside. Instead of a feeling of dread or loss, she still had that hope that Luke had brought into her life.

She turned to him as she held his hand on one side and Paisley's on the other. With a smile and a burst of joy for this new, fresh start, she nodded.

"More than ready," she told him. "I need this."

Her first service back in over three years. The progress she'd made had her feeling like she could accomplish anything with her faith and this man by her side.

"Jenn?"

She released their hands and spun around at the sound of her mother's voice. There, walking toward her, was her entire family. Her parents, Rachel, Violet and Erin. All of them as one unit approaching her with smiles on their faces and love in their eyes.

"Oh, honey, I didn't know you were coming today," her mother cried as she drew closer. "And on Mother's Day. My heart is so full."

"It's time," Jenn replied. "Luke convinced me that our fresh start should be right here."

Her mother's focus shifted to Luke. "Then I have you to thank for giving my daughter that spark of light back."

"No thanks necessary." Luke grinned. "I'd do anything for her."

"I suppose since we're all here, I have some news to share." Jenn reached for Luke and Paisley's hands once again. "I'm getting married."

Her sisters squealed, her mother clasped her hands, and her father gave a nod of approval. Jenn expected nothing less from this crew she loved with her whole heart.

"Oh, darling." Her mother wrapped her arms around Jenn, then Luke, then Paisley. "This is absolutely the very best news."

"God has His hand on all of this and each of us," Jenn explained. "We don't have a date and we plan to build on the land that Luke is buying. For now I'll stay in the apartment and his landlord has agreed to extend the lease for as long as he needs while we build."

"There was always a plan," her father chimed in. "I couldn't be happier for you guys."

"Does this mean I get to swing on that tire swing all the time when we move there?" Paisley asked.

"Absolutely," Sarah stated. "You can come swing on it now all the time if you'd like. My house is your house now."

Paisley glanced up to Jenn and drew her brows in as if confused.

"What is it, honey?" Jenn asked.

"Will this make your mom and dad, like, my grandparents? Or what should I call them? I've never had this many people in my family."

Jenn's heart couldn't swell with love any more for this beautiful girl. "I bet you can call them anything you'd like," she replied.

"You bet," Will Spencer declared. "I've never had a granddaughter before, so what should we call you?"

Paisley smiled and shrugged. "I'm just Paisley, but you should be Gramps or something like that. You look like a Gramps."

Her father chuckled as people maneuvered around them to get into the church. Jenn didn't miss that mist in his eyes as he glanced away. The sun shone bright, as if beaming down from the heavens directly onto their family and casting that warmth only the Lord could provide.

"I'm almost afraid to ask what I look like," Jenn's mother replied with a grin.

"Hmm…" Paisley thought for a minute. "I think you look like a Nana. Is that okay?"

"Nana it is."

"We should get inside before we're late and have to sit in the back," her father chimed in.

"Because you know he hates sitting in the back," Rachel muttered, which had her sisters snickering.

"We're going to take up two pews," Violet stated as they all started up the steps.

"I hope as our family grows, we can take up even more," Sarah added.

Jenn hoped for that very same thing. Nothing was more important than family and she couldn't wait to start this next chapter of her life.

★ ★ ★ ★ ★